When You Look at Me

Me

Pepper Basham

When You Look at Me

Copyright © 2018 by Pepper D Basham

Published by

Woven Words

9 Cedar Trail, Asheville, NC

Cover image ©2018 by Roseanna White Designs & Pepper Basham
Cover art photos ©iStockphoto.com and Pixabay used by permission.

Published in the United States of America by Pepper Basham
www.pepperdbasham.com

Dedication

To Carrie and Beth, two of the sweetest and most encouraging introverts I know.
Your love for Jesus and stories brings such hope to others.

Chapter One

*J*ulia Jenkins was a glass-half-full person.

Well, most of the time.

Even with her sordid backstory.

So she'd spent massive amounts of energy over the past few hours trying to think of all of the positive aspects of her abdomen bulging overnight to show her full seven-months pregnancy. Stomach sleeping? Out. Reaching her feet without sandwiching an actual person in the middle? Impossible. Going *anywhere* without scouting out the restroom signs? Dangerous.

And now? Now the curious stares, unvoiced judgments, and annoying questions she'd kept to a minimum behind loose fitting clothes and an apron would increase with the obvious proof of her "sin"—though the truth stung with a much darker betrayal.

Plus, she really missed baths. Long, candlelit bubble baths, complete with acoustic guitar solos in the background.

She sighed as she parked her car in front of the bakery she ran with her parents. Just the thought of trying to climb out of a bathtub with all the grace of a beached whale left every aching muscle screaming a resounding 'no.' And who would rescue her, anyway? The two new guests who'd be staying in the apartment near hers were both men. *Englishmen.*

A shiver made its way down her spine at the possibility of one of them coming to her rescue. The thought resurrected unwanted memories, but she shoved them away and tried to replace them with something positive, just as her therapist had told her to do.

Usually she focused on Scripture. Sometimes she fixated on chocolate. Then there were those times she found herself re-watching sappy movies. Okay, she'd done that long before Peyton stole her innocence and left her pregnant. Still, the syrupy-sweet romcoms inspired all sorts of daydreams.

And music? Ah, music soothed away a few of the residual nightmares lingering from the assault.

Little One—her nickname for her growing son or daughter—took advantage of her lack of motion to make his presence known with a solid kick. The baby was probably a boy, or that's what she thought, anyway, and her sister Eisley had told her that moms had a sixth sense about such things.

Julia rubbed a palm against the upraised area where a foot or hand or...something pressed with impressive strength. "You can't have a cupcake yet, Little One, no matter how hard you kick."

With a shove of her car door, she drew in a deep breath and rocked her way out of the vehicle, envisioning bungie cords dropping from her apartment window above the shop and pulling her forward like a cow stuck in the mud.

The idea inspired a giggle. *No, no, no.* Two large sweet teas and a baby dancing on her bladder didn't equal a good outcome from a giggling fit. She shifted the two boxes of fairy princess cupcakes in her arms and waddled toward the shop front door, attempting to tame her skirt against the morning breeze.

Negative note to later-stage pregnancy: skirts are not only more balloon-like but shorter than expected.

Adding more humility to her life with a Marilyn Monroe-moment wasn't on her bucket list of pregnancy milestones, but embarrassment seemed to pursue her. She breathed out in resignation and let the fabric fall where it may. Shifting the boxes in her arms, she rested them on her bulging middle. Fairy princess cupcakes trumped a possible outfit mishap any day.

Positive note regarding later-stage pregnancy: Your stomach can double as a shelf.

The OPEN sign on the front door of the bakery alerted her that her mom was already inside, probably baking a batch of pastries for their early morning regulars. Oh, and hopefully a raspberry tart from their 'fruitful' shopping excursion the day before. She stifled a snicker at her pun, as the welcome scent of buttery croissants and fresh-baked muffins drifted toward her. A definite perk to the business.

Just as Julia reached for the door handle, a strong gust of wind blew down Main Street and, not only gave her skirt an unwelcome swell, but lifted the lid right off the top cupcake box. The box top spiraled in a funny dance down the street, mocking her for the many reasons she remained still. There was *no* way she was chasing it. Nope.

There were things passersby couldn't unsee.

And besides, she'd already spent enough time on the lips of the local gossipers.

As she turned away from the frolicking lid and reached again for the door, contorting her body to keep her skirt from flying up to reveal embarrassing pregnancy panties, a voice emerged from her right.

"Allow me to assist you."

The accent sounded different than the usual Appalachian twang. Classy, refined, and smooth. Tourists gave a little flair to the tiny town, especially the ones with accents.

While she paused to glance over her shoulder for the stranger, someone inside the bakery shoved the door open. The door hit the box in her hands with such force that the cupcakes sailed in all directions. In horrified silence, she clenched the remains of a cupcake box as a battalion of purple flew toward the stranger and...pummeled him in the face.

Well, some landed in his hair and on his shirt, but at least two made it onto his face. In fact, one still stuck there over his left eye like a purple eye patch. Oh, the shortening really worked wonders for stiffness in this batch.

Julia forced her stunned feet into motion and ran to his side, pulling an apron from her bag.

"Oh my goodness, I'm so sorry." She stood on unsteady tiptoes and plucked the cupcake from his eye, wincing as a giant blob of purple icing dripped down his cheek. His eye, a marbleized combination of green and gold rimmed with blue, blinked wide.

"It's homemade icing, just so you know. No preservatives." She smeared her apron over his face to clean some of the icing but only succeeded in pushing a little into his nose. Her pulse skipped into a staccato rhythm, washing her face with a sudden heat. "Purple is a great shade for you, though. It really brings out your eyes."

What? She cringed. Heavens, she said the stupidest things when she was nervous. Really stupid. Diagnosably stupid. And she couldn't seem to stop them from tumbling out in glorious absurdity like Granny O'Leary when she stayed up way past her bedtime.

The poor man stood in stunned silence.

"Gee, I'm real sorry, Julia. I didn't even see you there."

Julia turned to the assailant, old man Jacobs, and her frustration melted away. Widowed for a year and a regular morning visitor to the bakery, the kind man's eyesight was on the way out.

"It's alright, Tom. I'm sure our new visitor understands it was an accident." She swung her attention back to the stranger, whose expression hadn't changed.

Okay. Maybe not.

That wasn't good. Bad business—and an unpleasant experience voiced from a potential new customer who would certainly share how flying purple cupcakes landed on his person—traveled fast in a small town. She planned to have this bakery sold in three weeks, purple cupcake missiles or otherwise.

It was time for an intervention, and stat.

"Let me help you clean up your face, then we'll figure out what to do with the rest of you." Without thinking, she grabbed his hand and pulled him into the bakery, passing a small crew of shocked patrons to make it to the kitchen. She parked the man in front of the big-basined sink and gathered a handful of towels. "So, are you new to town? What a sweet introduction." She cringed at the pun and rolled her eyes heavenward. *Help me, Jesus.*

Those textured eyes studied her with an unnerving intensity, inspiring even more jitters in her stomach. Would he sue her? That was all she needed after just ending the rape case a few months ago. No more publicity. Ever.

"The icing has a lot of egg whites in it. I hear those are good for your skin."

His stoic expression slipped into a quivering smile above his strong, icing-covered chin. Heat zoomed afresh into her face. It didn't help that he smelled like vanilla.

Or was that the icing?

She ran another cloth over his face. "Not that your skin needs it or anything. I'm sure...I'm sure underneath all of this icing, your skin is already flawless."

She flinched at her own idiocy, but the man's crooked grin stilled on his face, then...he laughed. Deep and rich, it reverberated around her like the bass notes of a cello.

He seemed as surprised by his own reaction as she did, but when he tried to cover his mouth with his hand, he splatted another layer of icing directly into it. She tried to muffle her giggle, but it exploded in a ridiculous trill complete with a snort at the end.

"It tastes delicious."

His accent? She stopped on her way to the sink, washcloth frozen in midair. Good heavens, was this her sister's boyfriend's best friend? The musician? Was she hosting the guy she'd just decorated like a fairy princess cupcake? "You're English?"

His laughter ebbed, but the smile lingered, hesitant. "Yes."

She squeezed her eyes closed and sighed. She, Julia—a woman who'd been dodging single males like most kids avoided broccoli—had somehow managed to hold his hand, touch his face, and spend a full ten minutes alone with him without even knowing his name.

Her stomach twisted with a swirl of nausea that had nothing to do with Baby Jenkins's sleeping position. And *now* she was going to be his landlady! What had she done?

7

∞ ∞ ∞

Henry Wright stared in wide-eyed wonder at the petite woman. Yes, purple icing pasted to parts of his face. Yes, she'd pulled him into the strange kitchen of a bakery and he hadn't refused. Yes, she'd touched him more times in five minutes than he'd been touched in five years. His hands, his face, his hair.

And—most likely due to shock—he hadn't attempted to escape into a people-less room.

She'd apologized profusely and smeared more icing over his face while attempting to clear it, yammering in the most adorable way and oblivious to the glob of purple seated crookedly atop her golden head. And, most startling of all, she'd made him laugh! The entire scene created the strangest scenario—almost dream-like. He could practically hear the strains of Robert Schumann's whimsical tune *Fantasie* backdropping the situation.

The woman fluttered here and there like a beautiful butterfly, a *capriccioso* melody, attempting to reconcile the accident while navigating her extended abdomen and apparently his response about being English. And her eyes, a captivating twilight shade ringed with a lighter hue of blue, pleaded for his forgiveness while her gentleness and the need to assuage her guilt propelled him out of his introverted shell and directly into...talking. "It does taste delicious."

What? He was an utter buffoon. No wonder he kept his words few in the presence of most people.

"I can't believe I did this." She groaned then slammed her palm down onto top of her head only to have it land in the icing. A gasp released. She examined her hand then looked at him, her lips opened in an O. The most beautiful blush rose between the purple icing smears on her face. "Um...this isn't the introduction to the Jenkins family Eisley had in mind, just so you know."

Despite his internal reprimands, his grin slipped through his control. "I've heard introductions to the Jenkins family can be quite memorable."

Her lips twitched up on one side then laughter tumbled forth. The musical sound fit her perfectly, icing and all. He couldn't help but join in, his own bass blending into her lighter trill.

"Oh my goodness. I suppose it would be a disappointment to have anything less." She shook her head and wiped her hand on the cloth she held, her eyes brimming with barely controlled mirth. She held a lovely glow about her, very fairy-like to his mind.

Her gaze dropped to his lips.

A sudden awareness rushed into his face with unexpected heat, drying out his throat and stealing his smile. Why was she looking at his lips?

"Um...you have purple icing coming out of your nose."

His eyes shot wide. Of course she wasn't looking at his lips. *Idiot.*

She offered a helpless shrug and pushed a cloth toward him. "I...um...don't think we know each other well enough for me to intervene."

"I have no idea what I would have done if you'd tried." His lips perched into another grin as he took her offering.

"Right? I'm Julia Jenkins, by the way." She offered her hand but pulled it back when her purple-streaked fingers extended his way. Her nose scrunched in an apparent apology, and she quickly rubbed her fingers over her apron, highlighting the swell of her abdomen. "Eisley's sister."

What had Wes told him about this Jenkins sister? Was she married? He couldn't remember, but she was clearly expecting a child soon, so there had to be some significant other involved. The youngest? No, that didn't seem accurate.

"Henry Wright." He took her hand. "Wes's friend."

She slipped her fingers free after a light squeeze. "I'm sorry to tell you this, but I'm your landlady for the next two months. I can assure you, though, that cupcake explosions on guests are a rare occurrence. In fact, this is my first one." She gestured toward him. "So I wouldn't worry about dodging the bakery on your way up to your rooms—"

"There you are." Wes Harrison stepped through the door of the kitchen, followed by his girlfriend, Eisley Barrett, Julia's sister. "Oh dear."

Eisley's vibrant ginger hair always snagged Henry's attention. Of course, vibrant appeared to describe her entire personality from the first moment Wes had shown him a photo of his quite unexpected American sweetheart. Henry almost grinned. She and Wes suited one another but, in all honesty, Eisley's propensity for chatter and insistence on constant conversation terrified Henry to his core.

"Gracious sakes, Henry, what did Julia do to you? Slap you with icing?"

"Eisley!" Julia shot Henry another apologetic smile. "There was an accident at the door, and poor Henry became the victim of a cupcake disaster, but I think he's okay."

"Well, what can I say!" Eisley's laugh rushed forward. "We know how to make a memory." She linked her arm through Wes's. "Right, handsome?"

His best mate wore a look of utter adoration as he stared down at his ginger-headed girlfriend. "Undeniably, squishing grandpas and all."

Henry's smile eased. Who would have ever believed a movie actor and an Appalachian single mum would end up as a couple? Certainly not Henry, but his perception—based on his rather convoluted romantic history—left much to be desired.

9

"Okay, okay." Julia raised her palms to the group. "Let's get Henry to his room so he can clean up before the icing hardens in his hair." She stepped around him and a faint sweet scent—wisteria, perhaps? —followed her. The gentlest refrains of *Dance of the Sugarplum Fairy* tingled to life in his head. Yes, the golden-haired hostess reminded him of Christmas and sweet scents and a celesta welcoming a flurry of fairies.

He blinked away the distraction and shifted his attention back to his purple-tinted hands. What would her husband think of his wayward thoughts? Henry had learned his lesson about involvement with women who belonged to other men. He'd been too easily entangled—his heart a simple target, his will too frequently bombarded or manipulated. He was not bound to play the fool again.

"It's a good thing Dad just helped us bring in part of Wes and Henry's luggage." Eisley glanced back at him as they walked away from the kitchen, down a private hallway which seemed to parallel the dining area of the bakery. "I'm sure he doesn't want to come to the party dressed like that."

Party? Henry raised his brow to Wes for clarification.

"Dinner," Wes whispered as they stopped at the bottom of a narrow stairway. "Actually, it's a cookout, according to Nate. You remember, Eisley and Julia's father, the one I warned...told you about." Wes's grin tipped but Henry couldn't quite work up a smile.

Henry had done a few online searches to prepare himself for the cultural differences between Appalachia and England, but Wes' descriptions of the Jenkins' patriarch left him unsteady. The people, the culture—all of those brought the usual anxiety of the unexpected—well, except when it came to their music. Music he understood...breathed. People? Well, they'd never been his forte. His breaths scattered arrhythmically. He took a mental trip into a concert hall, performin *Blue Danube* to bypass his inner panic.

"At the end of that corridor is a sitting room you're welcome to enjoy when it's not in use." Julia gestured down a window-lit hallway to the right of the stairs which ended at an open door. Henry caught sight of something that looked like the edge of a baby grand piano. "Sometimes we'll have small parties back there."

"And then there's Julia's serenading." Eisley nudged her sister with her shoulder. They demonstrated a closeness he'd not witnessed in many siblings, much like Wes and his sister, Cate. Henry and his elder brother Matthew were close but not particularly affectionate. Their mother had always made certain to stifle such displays.

Julia rolled her gaze to the ceiling, a slight blush of pink highlighting her pale cheeks. "I suppose I should warn you. Some nights, after the bakery closes, you might hear me playing the piano. But I won't play too late into the evening." She smiled, her gaze focusing more on Wes than him. "It's my way of winding down after a busy day."

"Then you and Henry should get on well," Wes replied. "He's a composer, you know. He can play four or five different instruments and even brought his violin along, I believe."

Julia's attention flickered to him, interested, hopeful. "You compose?"

He opened his mouth to answer but, as was usually the case upon being asked a direct question, nothing emerged when he beckoned. He hoped she'd give him time. Conversations became easier for him upon further acquaintance, if the individual had the forbearance to make the extra effort.

And didn't mind a bit of silence now and again.

"Usually for movies," Wes intervened in his well-practiced way. "He's composed the music for the last two movies I've made and is composing for this new one we're filming near here." Wes placed a hand on Henry's shoulder. "So he came along to study the Appalachian culture and music and gather inspiration, right?"

The physical touch of encouragement and easy question loosened his tongue. "Yes. Wes told me the mountains inspire creativity, and I hope to glean from them." He gestured toward Julia, drawing in a deep breath for strength to forge ahead into the conversation. "I brought a large collection of new sheet music. Perhaps you'd enjoy seeing some of it?" Her eyes glowed with a welcome he felt all the way to his unsteady knees. "At your convenience, and if your husband wouldn't mind, of course."

The shimmer in her periwinkle gaze died. Her expression froze except for the shift in her bottom lip as Henry's dropped...along with the swell of success in his chest.

His attention swung to Wes for clarification, but his faithful friend looked as lost for words as Henry was. He turned to Eisley, whose crooked grin mismatched her crinkled brow. "That won't be a problem, I'm sure." She took Julia by the arm. "Julia, will you make sure their room is ready. I'll tell them about the communication board."

Julia blinked and looked over her shoulder in his direction, her eyes much waterier than they had been a few seconds before. His chest deflated. He'd hurt her. How had he managed that? His gaze followed her retreat up the stairs before landing on Eisley's face.

She looked to Wes, who stepped forward and cupped Henry's shoulder with his palm. "Remember the sister who'd been date raped that I told you about?"

Henry stared at Wes for a full three seconds then glanced back up the stairway. "But...but she's with child." Crickets sounded in his mind before the words clinked into understanding. *She was pregnant with the baby of the man who raped her?*

Henry bent forward as if he'd been punched. How could he ever rectify his blunder? Perhaps silence was his best option. "I'm an idiot."

Eisley's hand came to his other shoulder, and her smile drew him back to a full stand. "Listen, Julia knows you didn't understand. It's just that each time she has to repeat the news, it's...tough. Her life has been turned upside down over the past seven months. She's been broken, but she's strong."

"Wounds do not signify weakness," Henry whispered, a sickening knot developing in his stomach at his blunder. "My grandmother used to say that."

"Grannies sure do have a way with words." Eisley squeezed his shoulder. "And no, wounds don't, but many of them may still be tender enough to sting. Give her a few minutes then we'll join her. And I'm pretty sure you can plan on a sonata or some furious Bach tonight before bed. It's the way she copes, I think."

Henry's head came up. She used music to express emotion?

Oh yes, that was something Henry understood very well.

Chapter Two

*J*ulia pressed her back against the door at the top of the stairs and drew in a deep breath to wrestle back her tears. How many more times would she have to explain and watch brows crease in confusion or disappointment or, worst of all, eyes cloud with doubt? Weren't the residual nightmares enough— even if they'd grown less frequent? Or the reluctance of old "friends" to invite her out because she didn't fit into the single girls group anymore? Even from her church friends.

Life had shifted, shaken, and left her in an indefinable spot between two worlds. She couldn't fault Henry for asking his question. How was he to know that the baby growing in her belly wasn't the product of two people in love? The sting of his realization and the *new* expression of pity or discomfort certain to cross his face toward her would only remind her, once again, that she'd lost something...and there was no way of retrieval in sight.

The new life within her rumbled to alert at her stillness. She smoothed a palm over her stomach and sighed, using her other hand to swipe away the stray moisture from her eyes. "Neither of us chose this journey, did we?" Hard pressure moved against her hand and she smiled. "But we're not alone, Little One."

No, she'd not chosen this path. She'd never dreamed of single parenting or surviving an attack that left her shattered from the inside out. She'd never imagined having to crawl through the months of anxiety, anger, and mourning to find her footing again. But from the support group she'd attended over the past four months, she'd learned she wasn't alone.

The counselor who saw her, now biweekly, had affirmed her healing and growth.

Her grin crooked. And, of course, she had her family and her faith.

How would she have ever made it to this point without believing God took brokenness and transformed it into something beautiful? *Even this.*

She raised her head and turned toward the stairway door as voices carried up from the other side. She might as well get the conversation over with now given that their shared living quarters meant they wouldn't be able to avoid each other. With a shove to unstick the old door, she prepared herself for Henry's pity—or worse, his discomfort in the new knowledge of her predicament—but the door hit something, or someone, in the process.

A groan came from the other side.

Julia's stomach dropped to her shoes. Oh no! She cringed and jerked the door back toward herself. Which one of them had she hit? Please say, Eisley, and not the handsome British stranger she'd already pounded with cupcakes.

"Henry, are you okay?" Her sister's question reverberated through the hallway and under Julia's door with the concern she typically only used when one of her children was hurt.

Julia gasped, then much more carefully, pushed open the door to see Henry bent forward with his hand to his face.

"Oh my goodness!" Julia pressed her palm against her forehead. "Eisley, would you get some ice and a cloth from the kitchen?"

Her sister rushed into motion.

"Wes, if you would help Henry the rest of the way up the stairs, we'll bring him into the sitting room to assess the damages."

Wes guided Henry to one of the twin leather seats by a window that boasted a view of sprawling farmland framed by azure mountains in the distance.

"I'm so sorry, Henry." Julia lowered herself to the stool in front of him, trying to see around his hand for a wound...or a possible busted nose. She groaned. For a year she'd talked with her dad about switching which way that stairway door opened.

A head wound would certainly justify some quick results...hopefully. This time.

"I'm going to set my bags down," Wes said, looking from one door on one side of the large sitting room and back to the other.

Julia pointed to the left. "That's the larger apartment through there, the one you and Henry have. Breakfast is here, by that lovely window seat where the small table and chairs are."

"Thanks, Julia." He nodded toward Henry. "I'll grab your bags too, mate, and be back directly."

Henry grunted and lowered his hand to reveal a large red welt developing up the right side of his nose to his forehead. Julia winced and raised her hand, almost as if to touch him, but curled her fingers into her palm instead. She'd caused enough damage already. And what was she doing considering touching the face of a stranger? Hadn't she already looked like an idiot wiping cupcake icing up his nose?

"I'm so sorry."

The mutual declaration dispersed the awkwardness in less than one second. Her hand dropped to her lap. "Why are *you* sorry? I'm the one who tried to turn you into a pirate."

He stared at her for the longest time, one hand returning to cover his wounded eye, then his grin tipped again in that subtle way. Something inside her twittered alive.

"About my assumption earlier. I didn't know—"

"It's okay. You don't have to apologize."

"But I feel terrible." A grimace creased his brow, and his healthy eye searched her face. The immediate tenderness about him scattered her reserve just a little. "What a horrible way to make a first impression."

"In your defense, you didn't realize who I was. And I'm the one who clobbered you with cupcakes first."

"At least your introduction was... sweet?"

She grinned at his pun, and his smile, and the way his unusually-colored eyes hesitated to meet hers before holding her gaze with a curiosity she found almost mesmerizing. The quiver in her chest sprouted wings and took off like a scared hummingbird.

Attraction.

Everything within her froze with a fear her mind wrestled to control as her heart pushed the panic button. Memories crashed, one by one, unbidden and violent. A first-kiss-turned-possession. A painful grip. Her useless pleas. Helplessness. She hadn't felt attraction since Peyton, unless one counted the occasional swooning over romcom movie heroes.

Henry is not Peyton. She breathed in and out, mentally reciting the mantra, before she pushed up from the seat and backed away a few steps, cramming on a smile. "Well, with the near-concussion with the door, I'd add *bitter*sweet to the description. I'm so sorry."

His grin took a boyish turn. "I've always wanted to be a pirate, but I never had the..." His attention turned toward the window as he quieted in thought.

"Criminal record? Thirst for treasure?"

"Gusto."

His answer shook loose her laugh, and her unease. "Gusto?"

"Pirate music is always filled with such adventure and daring." He shook his head, one palm raising as if in surrender. "I suppose I'm more of a "Moonlight Sonata" or Chopin's *Raindrop* Prelude than a swashbuckling Badelt composition from—"

"*Pirates of the Caribbean.*" Their gazes locked as they spoke in unison and the connection between them nearly buckled her. The softest strains of *Someday My Prince Will Come* emerged unbidden to her mind...complete with a violin solo.

She'd *never* met another person who thought in music, and gave her head a little shake to dislodge the sudden fascination.

"Here's ice." Eisley topped the stairs with an ice-filled Ziploc in her hand, her auburn hair bouncing around her shoulders in rhythm with her steps.

Julia freed her clenched air as Henry's attention shifted away from her. What had just happened? Her insides beat a drumroll inconsistent with Little One's usual dance moves, which only left Henry as the culprit.

A stranger from England who was only in town for two months as a guest of her sister's boyfriend.

And she was a seven-months-pregnant woman who wasn't viable dating material for *any* man at the moment, even if she *were* interested. Which she wasn't. So maybe they could simply be friends? She nodded to herself. Friends.

Besides, no man would be romantically interested in a woman who was pregnant with another man's baby.

She was safe. Her breathing evened, and she ignored the contradictory disappointment. There was no doubt she needed to talk to her therapist about these yoyo emotions.

Eisley bent in front of Henry and offered him the ice. "Whew, Henry, you're gonna have a shiner."

His brows knitted together in confusion, and his gaze sought Julia's for clarification. Those gold-green-blue eyes of his brightened, highlighted by the deepening hue of purplish-green surrounding the wounded eye. Poor man. "She means a black eye."

"Come on, Henry, it's not *so* bad." Eisley grinned, standing back up and offering Julia a conspiratorial wink. "Besides, I think you can probably work up a good story about how you got it, to make things interesting."

"Pardon?"

Julia couldn't help but smile at the clueless man. He really didn't seem to have a sneaky thought in his head. She liked him even better. "Eisley, just because you're writing fiction doesn't mean the rest of us want to incorporate it into our lives." Julia hoped her expression showed Henry the apology she felt—for the black eye and her sister's lighthearted attempt to smooth things over. She'd probably reached some sort of world record for "apologies within the first half hour of meeting someone."

"Oh, where's the adventure in getting a black eye from a door? You should have a little fun with it. If you can't think of a good story, I bet Wes could help you create one."

"A good story for what?" Wes walked their way from his apartment as if striding along Hollywood Boulevard. No wonder he was an actor. The man wore handsome with the ease of his smile. Dark hair. Stormy blue eyes. Fatal grin. Julia's smile spread. That her sister had literally fallen into the man's life and eventually his heart made for its own amazing love story—an almost unbelievable one.

Unlike her unenviable crash, burn, and nightmare.

Julia's palm rested on her stomach, protecting the little life from those hurtful memories. They always lingered near the surface, but the sting had become less painful as months separated her from the event. And hadn't Eisley told her that God specialized in the impossible?

"Henry's black eye." Eisley gestured toward him. "Something to impress my dad and brothers, maybe?"

Wes looked from Henry to Julia, his eyes twinkling with a humor his lips hid. "Impress your dad and brothers? I'm not certain I have the skill set for such an endeavor, pet."

"Oh, Wes." Eisley linked her arm through his, their endearing romance tugging at a forgotten ache in Julia's chest. "If anyone can impress my dad, it's you."

Wes drew in a deep breath, shrugged, and turned back to Henry. "Black eye or not, this evening we're having dinner with the Jenkins family, and you'd best prepare yourself."

"Prepare myself?"

Henry? And her dad?

Oh dear. The poor guy looked utterly confused and a little concerned, which might have been an intelligent reaction. The same urge she felt to protect helpless animals surged to Henry's defense. If *she* found her family overwhelming sometimes, how would a reticent stranger endure?

Was Henry strong enough for such a shock? She examined his rounded eyes—well, eye—and sturdy shoulder. Maybe? Of course, after the cupcake collision and attempted decapitation, maybe she'd somewhat reinforced his constitution.

"It's going to be unreservedly...Appalachian." Wes slanted a smirk in Eisley and Julia's direction and left his friend in further bewilderment.

Eisley laughed.

Julia sighed. "Perhaps it won't be so bad." But if Henry were as shy and quiet as he appeared to be, how could it be anything else?

"What...What exactly does that mean?"

Wes looked to the ceiling as if contemplating his words then shrugged with a good-natured smile. "In all honesty, Henry, as much as I've tried to tell you, words truly fail to describe the experience. You'll just have to see for yourself."

Henry's textured gaze moved from Wes to Eisley and finally settled on Julia a lost look on his face. Perhaps he recognized an introvert-at-arms. Or maybe he, too, felt a connection he couldn't describe.

Oh dear Lord, help him.

Maybe, just maybe, her dad would be on his best behavior.

Of course, it was March Madness season...and madness carried a whole new connotation in her family.

Chapter Three

a cacophony of noise greeted Henry before he'd stepped onto the front stoop of Nate and Kay Jenkins's charming colonial home. The scurry of sounds crashed in contrast to the late spring symphony of birdsong and the hushed brush of the wind through the newly budding trees. He almost asked to linger outside in the spring-chilled air to enjoy the unfamiliar music of nature in the Blue Ridge Mountains instead of spending the next few hours navigating the unpredictable world of social interactions.

His mother berated him for his introversion, labeling him a people-hater, but it wasn't so. He enjoyed people, especially familiar people—watching them, learning from them, sometimes having a mental chuckle at their antics—but finding words to say, participating in small talk, attempting to appear smart and engaging... He swallowed through his tightening throat. He'd never managed those experiences well, especially in a new place.

Perhaps, Wes would ease the way with his natural friendliness and deflect a large portion of the attention, as he usually did. It proved beneficial during times like these to have an actor as one's best mate.

He squinted to clear the vision in his swollen eye as Eisley opened the front door of the house. A sudden burst of welcome pushed the volume in the room to a forte, and Henry's tension took an upsurge. His feet froze in place while he observed. Chaos of people and noise engulfed him in dissonance. He even took a step back in retreat, but Eisley grabbed his arm and pulled him through the doorway into the massive foray of people. Wes had told him of Eisley's large close-knit family, even shown him photos on Eisley's social media page, but words, and even those snaps, failed to give an adequate depiction.

Laughter surged forward in a rush of welcome, bringing with it an immediate sense of hospitality—boisterous hospitality. So many people spoke at once, all in this new Appalachian dialect, that he barely knew where to affix his attention.

Oh no, he'd never experienced anything like this.

"Wes, we're glad to have you back for another visit." A petite woman with blond and white shoulder-length hair emerged from the throng scattered throughout the vast living area and equally impressive kitchen. Her blue eyes held a striking resemblance to Julia's. Dark, rich—an unforgettable hue.

He gave the room a brief scan for the younger Jenkins. *Julia.* The name suited her. The blend of consonants and vowels a gentle melody of sound fitting for the ethereal-like beauty. What was it about her? Some balance of everything right merged in their interactions, even the awkward ones, leaving a strange pang in his chest. Like a battle of nerves, only less nauseating.

"This is my best friend, Henry, whom I've told you about. He's writing the musical score for the movie I'm here to film, and"—Wes shot Henry a grin, which provided a boost of reassurance—"I think he's hoping for a much-needed holiday from his busy schedule. Henry, this is Kay Jenkins."

The matriarch of the Jenkins family offered her hand, her smile as inviting as the salty aroma wafting from the kitchen. She certainly didn't look old enough to be the mother of children his age, let alone *seven* of them.

"It's real good to have you, Henry." Her words soaked in her accent with a calming effect. "Welcome to Pleasant Gap."

Henry swallowed through his dry throat and attempted to hone his focus on the woman. "A pleasure, Mrs. Jenkins. Thank you."

"Please, call me Kay." She offered a quiet smile, almost in apology. "And things are bound to get a little rowdy 'round here. We can't have a whole crew of people in one place like this without some noise."

As if in response to Kay's words, a squeal split through the conversations. "Oh my goodness!" A young woman with soft, honey-colored hair and wide eyes bounded toward him. "Another handsome Englishman!"

"That's Sophie. Brace yourself. She hugs," Wes warned right before the young woman took Wes into a hug, complete with another ear-piercing squeal.

"You smell just as a good as the first time we met." She sighed, lingering at Wes's shoulder before she turned her sparkling hazel eyes in his direction. "And *you* must be Henry."

The embrace transferred from Wes, and Henry steadied himself for the impact. "Mmm, you smell like vanilla." She closed her eyes, smile wide, and nose sniffing the air near his neck. He stiffened like the Venus de Milo. "That's such a delightful scent." Her eyes fairly twinkled. "Like a cupcake.

"Thank you?" Henry wasn't quite certain whether the unsettled twist in his stomach meant he needed a laugh or an escape plan.

"She's harmless, really," Eisley whispered on Henry's other side. "Every family needs a resident Disney princess, you know?"

And then other people came forward, each adding a new face and name. Henry turned from Eisley to Wes, attempting to interpret the scene but failing to find clarity before the conversation bled into another one. Or more than one. It was difficult to tell when there were four people speaking at the same time...on differing topics.

"I'm Rachel." A dark-haired woman offered her hand, then gestured with her chin. "Looks like Dad already got a hold of you. What happened to your eye?"

Comprehension stuttered. "Pardon?"

"Julia accidently hit him with the door at the bakery." Eisley offered an apologetic shrug and lopsided grin. "Henry's had quite the introduction to our family."

"And it's only just begun," Wes added, his smile giving Henry no comfort.

A burly man, his brown hair and matching moustache framing his stern face, walked forward while wiping his thick palms on his hips. Henry needed no introduction. Wes's description had been perfect, right down to the intimidating stare.

"Daddy, be nice to Henry, okay?" Sophie linked her arm through her father's and shot Henry a bedazzled grin. "Julia's already hit him once."

"Julia had to hit hi—" Nate Jenkins's dark brows shot into a furious V, and he targeted his narrowing gaze on Henry. "What did you do to my girl? You good for nothin' foreigner." He barreled forward, fists at his sides, and Henry stumbled a step back into the wall. "If you so much as—"

"Whoa, whoa, Dad." Julia stepped between them, seemingly out of nowhere, her palms on her father's chest. "You know the stairway door at the bakery? I opened it and Henry was coming up the stairs. The same thing happened to George Pinkerton last month when he stayed at the apartment, remember? The door hit him in the face...and you never came by to fix it."

"The—What?" His furious gaze darted from Julia's face to Henry's. "Door?"

The wall prevented Henry from fleeing the premises altogether. Perhaps accompanying Wes to Appalachia was a bad—possibly life-ending—idea.

"Really, Dad?" Eisley slapped her father on the shoulder. "Did you think we'd let a jerk hang out in the place Julia runs?"

"He's the best of men, I assure you. True as an arrow."

Wes placed his hand on Henry's shoulder, his lips upturned in good-humor, though Henry had difficulty understanding how anything good could come from seeing his life flash before his eyes.

"You...you didn't have to hit him?" Nate kept his focus on Henry, though his tone slightly softened.

"No, Dad, but maybe *now* you'll fix that door?" Julia glanced at Henry and mouthed *I'm sorry*. If he hadn't understood anything else from the twelve conversations occurring at once around him, those words would've been enough. "Like Wes said, Henry is the good sort."

Her comment pushed through the growing anxiety in his chest and dispersed a sliver of calm. Belonging. Like when they'd discussed music together.

The man's moustache twitched while he drew in a deep breath, measuring Henry from head to toe. As if he'd made up his mind, he sighed. "Well, I reckon we got more important things to do than to stand around and ogle over another sissy boy visitin' the family. We got supper and some serious basketball goin' on." He shot an eyeroll to the ceiling and murmured as he turned to walk away, "Smells like vanilla. Crazy women."

Conversations and teasing continued as the family gathered around the table. The liveliness and apparent genuine regard warmed every part of the room, wrapping around Henry and urging him to join the fun. He grinned at the colloquialisms and the welcome addition of the children to the conversations but remained quiet in his place. Abraham Lincoln's advice, once again, was thoroughly adequate for such situations. *Better to remain silent and be thought a fool than to speak and remove all doubt.*

Henry found it hard enough to speak when put on the spot, so silence remained his modus operandi. As far as the Jenkins family was concerned, their noises lulled into a contented hum around him. He was easily passed over in conversations given the number of people at the table, especially when three or more of them tried to talk at once. They ended up answering each other. It worked out quite well for him.

The only time the room had grown quiet was when Nate Jenkins had prayed over the meal—a poignant moment for Henry since he'd never held hands with anyone in prayer, except perhaps his paternal grandmother, let alone connected with over twenty people around a table. He'd attended dinners of more than twenty people, of course. His mother was the queen of dinner parties. But prayer? Not a word or action used in his home unless a death seemed imminent.

The act remained a very private part of his world, as intimate as music, but here the family shared without reserve or ridicule, somehow awakening a longing in him. The intimacy of holding hands in prayer gripped him with a connection to these strangers that he shouldn't feel. A mutual understanding of a greater plan, an expectation, a Father's love. This place, these people, stirred his senses—his heart—to life in a way words fell short.

And when words failed to comply, music swelled to the rescue.

The Jenkins family's interactions held the same warmth of affection as Wes's family's. Though the Jenkins's brand of warmth came with an increase in volume, chaos, and laughter, the mutual respect and kindness flowed without reserve.

Julia sat at the far end of the table, the quietest of the seven siblings. She'd twisted her golden hair up into some kind of knot on the back of her head, highlighting her slender neckline. Heat teased a shocking fire through Henry's middle at the awareness, so he flipped his attention toward Julia's twin brother, Greg, who was telling some story about rescuing a cow.

Henry fought the pull of his gaze toward Julia. He had come to Appalachia for the music, not a music-loving beauty.

Eisley's three children provided background noise for the adults' conversations. Wes had shown Henry photos of the kids, and Henry had even joined in a few video chats with them over the past two months, giving him more familiarity with the three. Two-year-old Emily's with her antics brought out protective instincts. He'd already rescued her twice from diving off a chair, and once from trying to scale the refrigerator. Talking with Pete gave Henry the urge to listen to the *Spiderman* soundtrack with a clever, web-wielding five-year-old in mind— complete with attached web-blaster. But it was Nathan who Henry understood best of all. The seven-year-old's quiet observation of the room, his quick mind, and readiness to exit the crowded room at the right moment mirrored Henry's childhood.

Yes, he understood that very well.

"Wes, you been studyin' your basketball the past few months since we saw you last?" Nate raised a brow to Wes in challenge.

"I've studied some of your favorite teams, Nate."

"Aha!" Nate smacked his hand against the table. "And which one are you rootin' for, boy?"

"The Tarheels, right, Wes?" Greg shouted from beside Henry, shocking him with the sudden explosion of sound. "The smartest folks know it's a wasted vote to pick any other North Carolina team."

"You'll be eatin' your words, Greg Jenkins. My Blue Devils are gonna make it to the final four, at least, and then you'll be the one payin' for my dinner at Lincoln's."

Henry looked to Wes for clarification, but Wes only shook his head with a chuckle.

"Lincoln's is Dad's favorite restaurant," Rachel whispered from across the table, clearly noticing his confusion. "Seafood and hushpuppies. The best."

Hushpuppies? Wasn't that a shoe store?

"The devil plays basketball?" Pete looked up from his plate, his furrowed brow demonstrating a bewilderment that matched Henry's. "I thought Papa said the devil played golf."

What on earth? Henry almost spat out his water.

"Why would anybody want to cheer for a blue devil?" Sophie crinkled her nose in disgust and waved her fingers in the air, showing off dark blue nails. "I'm rooting for the University of Connecticut this year."

Nate released a combination of a cough and growl. "I ain't raised you right, girl."

Julia's gaze found Henry's, and her lips tipped with humor...and another apology. He'd already memorized that look, but every time she sent it his way, he liked it more.

"Don't trust anything Sophie says about basketball, Henry." Greg rolled his eyes and raised a fork in Sophie's direction. "She picks teams based on the cutest mascot."

Rachel groaned. "Or worse, the cutest legs."

"It's a sin, really," Nate added, shaking his head as he shoveled in another bite of food.

"You make it sound like a bad idea, but if I'm going to sit through watching these displays of mass sweatiness, I'm at least going to find something fun to watch." She turned to Henry, her expression so animated she *did* resemble a Disney princess. "Did you know there are Fighting Irishmen too? I almost voted for them because I love *everything* from the UK."

Her nose crinkled with her grin, and Henry stiffened from whatever fascination sparkled in those eyes. Sophie's admiration combined with the constant pandemonium and the strange conversation about the devil playing golf clashed inside his head like a toddler let loose on a set of drums and cymbals.

"I think these may be the best mashed taters you've ever made, Mama."

"How can the devil hold a golf club *and* a pitch fork at the same time?" Pete's voice made a piccolo-appearance into the conversation.

"We need to have hotdogs tomorrow, Kay. It's one of the big games, and hot dogs just make it better."

Greg. Pete. Nate. Henry's mind swirled from the attempt to focus.

Julia stood from her place at the table and walked to Kay's side. Oh, no, no. She couldn't leave him alone with all these extroverts, surely.

"Why hotdogs?" Wes's question broke into Henry's fuzzy thinking.

Nate shrugged. "It always makes me feel like I'm at a baseball game, and I love baseball."

Henry attempted to sort out the logic but failed, and a sudden shot of pain snaked over his forehead. His people limit was approaching at lightning speed.

Perhaps logic had nothing to do with any of it.

"Henry, speakin' of food..." Kay's voice drew his attention like a lifeline. "Would you mind runnin' downstairs and collecting the cheesecake I've saved in the extra refrigerator?"

Henry's focus shifted from Kay to Julia, who sent a knowing smile over her shoulder as she disappeared into the kitchen.

"Pardon me?"

"As our guest, you can choose between the three kinds. The fridge is just at the bottom of the stairs on the right," Kay added, standing.

He followed suit and caught Julia watching from the kitchen doorway, brows raised in playful camaraderie. What was happening? And where were they sending him?

Once Henry rounded the corner of the room, Kay stopped and placed a hand on his arm. "We forget the whole world ain't like us sometimes. I suppose we can be a bit overwhelming for visitors. If Julia hadn't been paying attention, we'd have run you off for sure."

Julia? Attention? What was she talking about?

"She can see you need a little break because she's one to understand." Kay patted his arm and nodded to the stairs. "Take your time comin' back with dessert."

He raised a brow, comprehension dawning with his smile. They were giving him a people break, encouraged by mutual introvert Julia Jenkins. He smiled at Kay then glanced back over his shoulder, but she was nowhere to be seen. As if he needed any other reason, Julia had just become one of his favorite people.

Chapter Four

The delicious aroma of ham and sweet bread drew Henry from his room into the living area between the two apartments on the top floor of the bakery. As Julia had promised, the small table near the window stood laden with an abundant breakfast. Morning sunlight spilled in, displaying an amazing view of the azure-brushed horizon. Pleasant Gap crested a knoll overlooking the countryside, so even on Main Street the blue-tinted mountains framed the distance like stationary ocean waves.

Wes had mentioned the draw and beauty of those mountains particularly as they related to the historical movie he was filming about a WWI-era teacher's love for and impact on the community he moved to in deep Appalachia. Those mountains held an artistic appeal, a watercolor skyline of fog and ridges and morning sky.

What music did they make?

Henry checked his watch, then turned his gaze to the buffet before him. Steam rose from the pot in the center of the round table, bringing the familiar scent of tea. On the window seat nearby, a worn book lay open. He stepped closer and peered at the pages. A Bible opened to—he leaned closer—Isaiah 43?

"It's a good morning reminder."

Henry turned to see Julia at the top of the stairs with a plate of muffins in her hands. The vision of her with her hair in two braids, one falling over each shoulder caught him completely off guard. She was a chameleon of different forms of beauty. Today she wore country girl charm with a slight tint of embarrassment on her cheeks—from his discovery of her open Bible, he supposed.

His smile spread in welcome. He hadn't been able to keep her far from his thoughts since she'd rescued him from 'peopling' at her parents' home. He liked her—more than he should and certainly more than he'd admit.

He looked back at the Bible and skimmed the first few verses.

Fear not, for I have redeemed you; I have called you by name, you are mine...

"A very good reminder."

She walked past him and placed the muffins on the table. "It's one of my go-to chapters when I need to remember how to be brave."

His gaze lifted to hers, his brow rising in question.

"Or rather, a reminder of Who I need to rely on to find my courage."

He looked down at her abdomen then to her face. He couldn't imagine the weight of her wounds. "You are afraid?"

She placed one palm over her stomach and adjusted the napkins. "Sometimes."

"About the past?"

She kept her attention on the table as she set various plates into position. "Yes...and the future. I have a wonderful family, but the single parenting is rather daunting especially when the background story isn't the least bit sweet."

Henry contemplated her words—all authentic fears—and his gaze dropped back to the window seat. He tapped the Bible. "I heard a choral performance of these verses once. Excellent musical setting for such beautiful words." The sentence worked through his tightening throat, but there was nothing for it. He wanted to encourage her. "You are precious in his sight. And...and He is not prone to leave His children to face their fears alone, is He?"

She looked up at him, her hair a halo of gold in the morning light. "No, He isn't."

Henry usually looked away from a woman's direct regard, but the gentleness in her expression fascinated him, the gratitude. To him? For his words? The familiar swell of attraction held him in place but with an unfamiliar comfort. There was something new in this. Attraction could be acted on or not, encouraged or ignored, but this touch of sweetness brought something new and different. And the simple fact that his words had touched her, a woman who bore tragedy with such gentleness? Well, he felt almost heroic. *Almost.*

Could she use a makeshift hero?

He cleared his throat and looked away. *Idiot.* What was he thinking? Besides the fact he felt fairly incompetent at romantic relationships, Julia lived in America and he in England. If he could hardly converse with someone while standing across from them, how could he maintain a relationship across two continents? Another item on the look-but-don't-engage list: Julia's unwed-pregnancy status would mortify his aristocratic mother, in addition to the fact that Julia undoubtedly held reservations about entering *any* romantic relationship due to the assault.

He waved toward the table, avoiding her eyes, pushing the thoughts away. "Do you provide this type of breakfast every morning?"

"Heather, my cousin, will take my place tomorrow, so you can expect some sort of apple breakfast dish." Julia poured some tea into a cup. "She makes the most mouth-watering apple dishes known to mankind. I'll only be just over an hour away if you guys need me." She gestured toward the board by the stairs. "For the next month, I'll be cleaning out my great aunt's house. It's deep in the mountains, so cell reception is horrible, but I left her landline number on the board if you need anything. It should be in working order for a little while longer, until the sale goes through."

He must have shown his curiosity because she continued. "She passed away three months ago after a short illness, and with all the preparations I've been making for this little one"—she waved a free hand toward her stomach— "I haven't had time to go through her things. It's going to take a while. She was quite the eclectic collector."

Perhaps she could use your friendship? His spirit nudged the thought. Could she? The idea forced him into continuing the conversation. "Are you going alone...to her house?"

She offered him a hesitant smile, her gaze pausing on his before she answered. "I still have two months left before the baby comes, and Aunt Amelia's best friend lives nearby if I need anything. Besides, Dad's coming with me tomorrow to help move some old boxes, which are supposed to hold legal documents or something like that. I have no idea really. Her house is as mysterious as she was."

He nodded, enjoying the relative ease in this one-on-one interaction after the somewhat carnival-like exchanges at the Jenkins's house. He could do this sort, and the pleasantness in the partner eased the endeavor even more.

"Wes is still asleep?"

Henry blinked out of his stare. "He's speaking with his father. I thought he'd appreciate the privacy, and I was...um...wooed by the aroma."

His compliment tipped her grin. "Well, I'd start eating if I were you. It's always better when it's warm."

She turned to leave.

"Julia."

She paused at the stairs and turned her full attention on him, those violet eyes round and curious.

"Thank you for last evening. The...um...the dessert escape plan?"

Her full smile spread with understanding. "You're pretty quiet, aren't you?"

"Actually, my mother would be envious of how many conversations your family has thrust upon me."

Her laugh trilled across the distance and warmed him more than the blueberry muffin scent. What a lovely sound, like the joyful warble of a flute. "Terror is a great motivator to talk, huh?"

He chuckled out his agreement. "Indeed."

"But 'thrust upon you' is a perfect description. I'm glad there are so many extroverts in my family that I can disappear into the background."

Impossible. "I can't imagine you ever disappear into the background."

Her brows rose, and she placed her palm on the doorframe, as if for support.

What? His comment replayed with full mental clarity.

They both blinked.

He broke their connection first, his face flaming with a sudden heat. What had gotten in to him? He rarely spoke to women he'd known since childhood, yet he'd already had more conversations with this one over the past twenty-four hours than any other in his life. The circumstances appeared to force interactions with her—or distracted him enough to let down his guard.

And she made it easy. Her smile. Her eyes. The gentle way she urged him into talking without even trying.

"Good morning to the lot of you." Wes breezed into the room, his presence slicing through the awkward silence with the perfect timing of a planned movie scene.

Henry cleared his throat and turned toward his friend, whose healthy and happy transatlantic relationship proved Henry's internal argument false.

"Good morning," Julia offered first. "How's your family?"

"They're doing well. Father's keen to visit Pleasant Gap from all the stories I tell." Wes grinned at the bounty on the table. "This looks fantastic, Julia. Thank you."

"I'm excited to meet him someday and thank you." Julia braided her hands in front of her and stepped toward the door. "As I told Henry, my cousin Heather will take care of breakfast tomorrow morning while my *other* cousin Amy manages the bakery, but if you need anything, just place a note on the board over there and she'll get to it. Or when I return, I will."

"Actually, I could use your help." Wes took a seat and adjusted his napkin on his lap. "For a very special project."

"Project?" Julia stepped back toward the table. "What do you mean?"

"In fact, I'd like to enlist *both* of you." He looked up, his expression almost pleading. "And I can trust you to work it all out in secret."

Henry eased himself into the chair across from his friend, searching for clues to clarify the mystery. He had a guess. Wes's intentions hadn't gone unnoticed over the last month, but how did he and Julia fit into the plan?

"If I try to include your parents, Julia, there's a chance Eisley will find out. Plus, your bakery, away from the family home *and* Eisley, will be perfect."

"I...I'm not sure I under—"

"I plan to propose to Eisley."

Julia gasped and sank down on the window seat, her hand flying to her heart.

Henry relaxed back in the chair, basking in the contentment in his friend's smile. Wes had been through a great deal of heartache before finding such an excellent home for his heart with Eisley and her children.

"That's wonderful," Julia whispered. "She...she will be so surprised."

"I hope not too surprised. I've not hidden my intentions. She knows I'm playing for keeps, so why wait?" He took a sip of the tea and shrugged, his admiration beaming off his smile. "My filming plans are all happening in the US for the foreseeable future, which means I can be more of a fixture in the children's lives too. I don't care to take any more time away from us."

"No, I guess not." Julia's smile resurrected with an added sparkle in her eyes. "So what did you need us"—her gaze flipped from Henry to Wes— "to do?"

"I was hoping we could decorate your party room in a similar way to the first dance we ever had. White lights. Live music."

"Oh, at the gala in London, right?" Julia pressed her folded hands against her chest, obviously impressed with his friend's story.

Henry's grin surfaced at the memory of the moment Wes realized Eisley Barrett wasn't the fame-seeking, husband-hunting widow his past experiences told him to expect. She'd turned his friend's assumptions and heart inside out. Henry had never seen Wes so happy, and he had to admit, Eisley proved a perfect match for him. Why wait, indeed.

"Right." Wes squinted with his next request, and Henry's body took on some warning tension. "And I thought perhaps you and Henry could provide the live music? Jazz. Old standards."

"Oh." Julia's gaze hesitated in Henry's, but she held her smile. For Eisley's happily-ever-after. "I don't see why not. R...right, Henry?"

"Of course."

"And the food. I can—"

Wes raised a palm. "No, I'm already asking a lot of you at such a point in your pregnancy. I'll have it catered, if you'll recommend a place."

"O-of course." Her fingers went to her necklace. "How soon?"

He shrugged, his grin spreading like a boy with a secret he could barely contain. "In two weeks, if possible. I didn't want to get too close to your date of delivery."

"A Friday night? Saturday?"

"Friday, if it will work for your schedule, Julia. After closing?"

She nodded and glanced again at Henry. "If Henry's fine with all of that, I think we can make it work."

His own comfort wasn't his primary concern. "Will...you be fine?"

Her smile softened, and she lowered her hands to her lap, as if preparing for the challenge. "Yes." Her gaze swung back to Wes. "And my sister deserves the best happily-ever-after we can design."

"I'd like to give her one." Wes raised his teacup in salute.

Julia exchanged another look with Henry, and an unspoken pledge passed between them. Whether it was the unification of two introverts who found comradery in watching two people they loved find happiness, or something else that electrified the air, they'd make this arrangement work.

Chapter Five

*J*ulia shrugged off the memory of her conversation with Henry several times during the drive to her Aunt Millie's house, but he kept returning to her thoughts, revisiting with persistent timidity. In a world where most of the men in her life charged forward with boldness—wisely or foolishly—his uncertainty stirred a strange sort of comfort. He was a gentle fumbler. A quiet support.

A similar soul.

She'd not had a great deal of experience with men despite her current situation as an unwed mom, but most of the guys she'd known in high school and college were the usual suspects of exaggerated male bravado. Men who even remotely reminded her of the villain who'd taken advantage of her curled her stomach with nausea and left her searching for a place to hide. But Henry?

She grinned as she remembered the look of pure horror in his eyes when he'd complimented her about disappearing into the background. Her dad's truck appeared in the rearview mirror of her SUV, following her up the long gravel driveway to the house. She curbed her smile as if her dad could read her thoughts over the distance. Ridiculous.

Even thinking about a man's attention at this point should be wrong. Shouldn't it? She'd have to ask her therapist, Karen, about the idea. From all she'd read, Julia was supposed to remain distant and wounded for a long time before seeking romance again. She shook her head, attempting to dislodge the curiosity. Between Aunt Millie's house, the bakery, and Little One's arrival, the last thing she needed to add was mixed emotions over covert daydreams about some shy Englishman.

With pretty eyes.

And a gentle, cello-smooth voice.

Warmth poured down her neck and over her shoulders at the memory.

So much for wrestling those wayward thoughts into submission.

She growled and focused on the narrowing dirt road ahead.   Dreams had to defer to reality, but she'd been deferring to reality for the last seven months—taking a sabbatical from college, readjusting to a future with her business degree on hold indefinitely and *any* happily-ever-after notions nowhere near the horizon.

Her heart ached for possibilities.

The fishbowl-like town she lived in refused to release her from her past or even encourage those once-held dreams. Whether it was part of her imagination or reality, Julia couldn't shake how people seemed to view her in a different way now—as if the trust and innocence she'd held before had been shattered by someone else's heinous acts. Perhaps if she weren't pregnant people could've forgotten the court case and the small-town scandal—overlooked the wolves they couldn't see—but her growing abdomen gave a daily reminder of something forever changed, of a darkness lingering beneath the hearts of everyday people, and now the friends who'd once spent time with her were nowhere to be seen.

She released a shivering sigh. No wonder Aunt Millie had disappeared into the seclusion of the mountains after her unexpected pregnancy. Though Julia didn't have plans to resort to such an extreme, she couldn't deny the allure to leave it all behind.

She stalled her car in front of the grand Victorian and exited in the most graceful way she could with a stomach the size of a basketball hindering her progress. Tugging her overnight bag onto her shoulder, she removed the small cooler with a few easy snacks from the backseat of her car and nodded toward her dad, as he brought his truck to a stop beside hers.

Even three months after Millie's death Julia expected to hear the faint strains of the piano—a concerto, perhaps, or Tchaikovsky—as she climbed the white-washed steps to the front door in the center of the wrap-around porch. Or maybe smell the faint scent of the apple pie Sissy would have baked as a special treat for Julia's visit. Two misfit women huddled together along the backroads of Appalachia.

"You still plannin' on sellin' the place?"

Julia peered over her shoulder at her dad as she searched through her keys for the right fit to the colossal oak door. "As much as it breaks my heart, Dad, this place won't fit into my plans. You know how much I love the setting, but I don't want to be so far away from town." She fitted the key into the lock, the ache in her chest expanding. She loved this house. "And I can't even get Wi-Fi out here. What sort of bed-and-breakfast would I have without Wi-Fi for my guests?"

"One where people actually talk to each other instead of having their faces stuck all over Facebook or Trashchat," her dad mumbled, dropping his toolbox on the porch to push open the door for Julia.

"Snapchat, Dad."

"Ain't that what I said?" His dark moustache lifted at one corner. "I don't like people all over the world being able to get into my business, and I don't want to see all their business either. There are just some things you can't unsee."

Julia slipped through the door, reserving her chuckle in the quiet of the massive entry hall. So many memories tied her to her great aunt's country anomaly. The rooms smelled of sweet oil and hand lotion with the faintest hint of mountain cornflower—a fragrance as mysterious as her reclusive aunt.

The focal point of the entry—a grand mahogany staircase— rose front and center in the entry, splitting at the top landing for another small stairway to the left and right wings of the house, like something out of *Gone with the Wind*. Julia's breath halted in a quiet sob, the stillness a reminder of Amelia's absence.

Emptiness and quiet that highlighted the losses her aunt had lived with for years.

Loss of love.

Loss of a child.

There was an unfinished story here. Julia could almost feel it in whispers from the walls or the memories of her aunt's distance expression when she spoke of Lucas, but Julia would never uncover the truth now that Amelia was gone.

Oh, the loneliness of a life with an untold story.

Yet, Millie, as unusual and reticent as she was, had poured out her knowledge, affection, and finances on Julia, taking her on vacations she would never have experienced without her aunt's kindness. Traveling to countries an Appalachian girl rarely saw in a lifetime, let alone before the age of twenty-five.

They'd created an unlikely friendship, the two of them. A companionship. A woman who needed a friend and a young, quiet girl with a loud dream.

Aunt Millie had even encouraged Julia's hopes of owning her own bed-and-breakfast one day, saying, *God's view is limitless, vast and beautiful, even if pain stains our vision and fear falters our steps. He will be our strength. Our courage. Our guide.* And with a twinkle in her eyes, she'd add, *He can see in the dark, you know.*

But how could Julia trust her aunt's words? For all her talk of strength versus fear, when Amelia's dreams had been stripped away, she'd fled.

At least, that's the reason everyone gave for a world-renown pianist—a woman who'd even played before princes— to choose isolation in the vast quiet of Appalachia.

Julia understood life-seizing fear. Dreams of owning her own bed-and-breakfast seemed too far-fetched—crazy, even—for a soon-to-be single mom. How would she manage her time with a newborn? Selling Millie's house and the bakery would take care of finances, but what about energy? Smarts? The impact of a sullied reputation on business?

Courage had never been her forte, and whatever amount she'd once possessed had dwindled since the rape incident. But perhaps with the funds from the sale of Aunt Millie's house, Julia could save for the B&B she'd always dreamed of. When life slowed down. When courage resurfaced. The idea fueled her steps into her favorite spot: the music room.

"I reckon Aunt Millie had the right idea all along." Dad followed her, his voice echoing through the empty house. "Get away from people and just enjoy nature."

"Well then, maybe you should retire here in this big old house, Dad."

He squinted and leaned back in observation. "Too fancy a house for me. All the"—he waved toward the ornate molding— "frill."

She chuckled. "Well, someone will really love this frill, and I've already had two calls from interested parties. My favorite prospect so far is the headmistress of a school for girls. But a retired museum curator has made a competitive offer."

Her dad sniffed the air and nodded. "I can see that for sure. It's built real good but the place still needs some work before it goes to another owner." He whistled. "Lots of work, if you ask me. Millie was a packrat."

Julia paused in the doorway of the music room, trying to ignore her dad's gray-fringed realism. A granite fireplace graced the opposite wall, the rich-colored rugs her aunt likely purchased abroad covered the hardwood floor, and, of course, the elegant grand piano sat in the center of a crescent of floor-to-ceiling windows. Morning light bathed the instrument in such a mysterious glow that Julia could almost hear her aunt's ivory peal of Bach in the air.

Her chest compressed with the familiar pangs of loss. Julia twisted her simple silver chain necklace between her fingers and turned toward the doorway where her father stood, his broad shoulders taking up most of the space between the music room and the entry hall. "She provided funds for that, Dad, and I've already scheduled the workers." Julia grinned. "I can't think of a time she didn't prepare to perfection."

"Ain't that the truth. But...she was a weird one, holed up here in this house all by herself."

The scrutiny in her dad's voice echoed the rumors swirling outside these walls about Aunt Millie, but after spending years with the woman, Julia couldn't shake the idea of some horrible tragedy that propelled Millie into a self-imposed exile, of sorts. The far-off gazes seemed less of an aged mind and more of a longing heart, but no matter how hard Julia had tried to learn more about Millie's past, the woman kept her history of untold stories as silent as a grave.

Only a few times had Amelia slipped from her privacy into unveiling pieces of memories, and each time she'd spoken of two people. Rosalyn and Lucas.

Julia's gaze fixed to a gilt-framed portrait of a little girl with caramel-colored curls dancing around her cherub face. Rosalyn. Amelia's daughter who'd died much too soon.

"I wonder what these walls would tell us if they could speak, Daddy."

He grunted as he toted his toolbox down the long hallway toward the kitchen. "They'd say they was bored from not havin' enough to see." His low whistle echoed off the tall ceiling, oak floors, and empty space. "I hope you get a good price on this place. I ain't a fan of fancy houses, but it sure does have some excellent woodworking. It'd be a shame to sell it to someone who wouldn't appreciate the craftmanship."

"Millie spared no expense. These *frills* show it. Clearly, she had money from somewhere." She followed her dad, lingering at each doorway to peek inside. Despite the general bossiness, a healthy dose of protectiveness and love bounced off his grimace. "And you'll be glad to know that neither potential buyer balked at my offer. I did my research."

Her dad crinkled up his face. "What?" He shook his head and sat his toolbox on one of the long counters lining the massive kitchen, a work-worn hand braced on one hip of his dusty jeans. "Well, don't let him steal this place from you, girl. You're soft when it comes to a sob story or two."

She stared down her dad and rested her crossed arms on her extended abdomen. "I've run a successful bakery for three years while attending community college, Daddy. I can bring on the thick skin when I need to."

Though he'd turned away from Julia as she made her claim, his snort still reached her ears. "Just because your cupcakes have won over the whole town and you've aced me as a rifleman, doesn't mean you're thick skinned." He grinned at her over his shoulder with equal shares of mischief and pride crinkling the corners of his eyes.

Her smile replied, and she nodded toward the sink. "I'll leave you to fix that leak, and I'll go..." She hesitated to say she would investigate the one room she probably needed to explore the most. "... I'll start in Aunt Millie's office. Sissy told me she left some papers for me on the desk."

"Well, if anybody knew Millie, it was Sissy. The woman had been with her for ages, far as I know."

"Then I'll come back downstairs and use my shrewd judgment on the furnishings in the music room. I hope to have the house empty before this baby comes, and Mr. Greer says he and his moving crew have some days set aside for me in a few weeks."

"You only got a month?" Dad wiped his brow with the back of his hand and opened the cabinet door beneath the sink. "Then what you doin' jawin' with me instead of workin', girl?" He dismissed her with a wave of his thick hands. "Git on with it."

She shook her head with a laugh and took the stairs. She could count on one hand the times she'd stepped inside the sanctuary of her aunt's office. It wasn't so much that Aunt Millie forbade the entrance, but there was something private about the elegant woman's equally elegant space that kept Julia from entering.

Dust swirled in the air at Julia's entry, waking the sleeping room.

The cornflower scent gave off a stronger aroma here, almost as if it permeated the azure-and-white floral wallpaper. It was a French-styled room, with ornate white crown molding, rounded-top windows, and a patterned ceiling with almost a renaissance-look.

A grand oak desk embossed with faint hints of gold as trim stood against the far wall, framed in by windows.

Papers and photographs Julia didn't remember seeing before littered the desk in a haphazard manner.

Had Aunt Millie been sitting in this room the night before she died? Looking through these papers? Preparing for the end?

Julia tugged her sweater closer around her shoulders at the slight chill wafting over her arms. Millie had died in her sleep of a heart attack, according to her doctor. There had been barely a hint of any developing weakness, but Julia had noted a marked change in her aunt's behavior in the weeks leading up to her death: A distance. A quiet. Longer daydreams. The housekeeper, Aunt Millie's faithful companion for over thirty-five years, had found Millie upon arriving for her morning duties. Gone as quietly as she'd lived.

Julia fingered a golden-framed photo—one of her aunt, much younger, sitting in front of a grand piano on stage, fingers pressed against the keys and eyes closed. Was this particular one from her time as the world-renowned pianist Amelia Dawn Rippey? Julia had seen a few other photos of her aunt during that era, but only briefly and without much commentary from the subject.

Next to that photo waited a sweet picture of a young Amelia with a beautiful little girl. The brush-painted color of the era highlighted their shared wealth of dark hair and unusual gray-green eyes.

Rosalyn. Probably not too long before her death.

Julia's palm swept over her stomach in a protective way.

At the desk's center stood the most curious of all photos. Aunt Millie, quite young and dressed in an elegant evening gown, stood beside a dashing man whose arm was wrapped around her waist in affectionate familiarity. He had a tousle of wavy brown hair and a crooked smile that almost lit up his eyes with some inner beam. Her grin tipped in response. Was this a photo of the mysterious Lucas? The name her aunt had mentioned in quiet reverence. The man she'd loved who no one in the family knew anything about?

A recent, more colorful photo diverted Julia's attention to the corner of the desk and encouraged a sting of tears. It had been taken last summer as Julia and her aunt sat in their favorite spot: the grand gazebo at the top of the mountain behind Millie's house that overlooked a view of the Blue Ridge and the Cascades. A place Julia had no intention of selling.

The house and the three acres surrounding it, yes. But the additional twenty acres spanning the mountainside? The place with a tiny cottage where she and her mother and sisters went every year for a girls' weekend? No. She'd hold to that keepsake while funds allowed.

Her aunt's face had aged over the span of these photographs, and the light in her eyes dimmed with the passing of each one. She'd told Julia once that her heart belonged more in heaven than on earth now, since the two people she'd loved the most in the world waited to meet her there. Julia pulled her gaze away from the faces in the photos, lingering another second on Lucas's face. Just out of the periphery of the frame, an envelope with her name on the front paused Julia's breath.

She set down the photo and with careful fingers peeled back the envelope's opening. A small key slipped out followed by a single page written in her aunt's beautiful hand—a letter.

My dearest Julia...

Chapter Six

The mountains carried their own song. A melody beginning with soft brass, perhaps a stray violin solo or—even more accurate to the history of these hills— an Irish flute, grew in his thoughts to a full orchestral explosion as vast as the blue horizon. Henry could feel the music stirring to existence with every new discovery of this Appalachian world. Each view, each conversation with a native, every hint of the raw talent in the mountain musicians tempted the tune in his head closer to becoming a reality on his fingertips.

Wes had brought Henry to a historical frontier reenactment site near the filming area, and some local musicians played the blue grass Henry had been studying for the past few weeks. Just what he needed to further his exploration of Appalachia's musical culture.

Its sound carried a similar genre to the tunes of his Irish kin—a mixture of lively and melancholy. A local luthier allowed Henry to examine some of his handcrafted instruments: a violin—referred to as a fiddle in Appalachia—a guitar with lower tones, a mandolin with higher-pitched tension, a bass, and a beautifully crafted stringed instrument that looked something like a lyre, but the luthier called a dulcimer. Henry proceeded to purchase one straight away then watched the instrumentalists play through four or five pieces, fixing the technique to memory before Wes pulled him back into the car to make their appointment with the producer and filming crew on the movie set.

After Henry had a long talk with one of the Appalachian historians followed by several other conversations related to the expectations of the movie, he'd reached his peopling limit. The quiet called to his weariness, and the forest promised an answer.

A lonely trail split between heavy trees and drew him up the hillside and into the wealth of wooded shadows. The scent of pine engulfed his senses as birdsong serenaded the pine-needled path. Voices in conversation and the tick, tick of a hammer on set-design faded behind him as tall oaks, pines, and maples—woods used to create those homespun instruments—drew him deeper into their home. The path rose gradually before him, almost like an earth-woven carpet of anticipation for what lay ahead. He turned his headset to the bluegrass soundtrack the producer had recommended—a unique mingling of string instruments and tight harmonies as earthy and lush as the spring world blooming around him. The cool air against his face filled his lungs with a promise of discovery.

He took the challenge.

On he climbed, adjusting his pace to the rhythm of the music, allowing the melodies and ballads to pour through the creative recesses of his mind. He'd been with Wes during the creation of the script—a story of clashing cultures and the hardships of a life etched in this wilderness. Yet two similar hearts found commonalities in their faith, love of stories, and mutual compassion. It was a tale of two worlds and a common theme.

Love made the impossible...possible.

The music he composed for this movie had to convey the many-layered story as well as celebrate the culture and history of a rustically beautiful landscape. He continued farther up the trail, waking the forest with his footsteps, and grinned as a couple of squirrels at his feet scattered beneath an unusual bush with rubbery-like dark green leaves hanging low.

The clean smell of earth and the rush of a good walk held similarities to his excursions in Derbyshire, but something different stirred the air of these mountains—an untouched, almost mysterious, sense of anticipation as elusive as the sweet yet unknown scent surrounding him. He took a deep breath but couldn't regain the aroma. Perhaps it was a fragrance only found in Appalachia that rewarded travelers along the way.

He adjusted his pace to the incline as the path steepened. Traces of an azure-hued view played peekaboo with him through the healthy growth of spring forest, promising a reward if he persevered to the top of the hill.

The mandolin and violin in his ears tinged in surging duet toward the pinnacle of Henry's walk. He pushed through a cave of bush and brambles onto a rocky ledge as the music reached its climax and the earth fell away into an endless vista of sky and mountains.

This moment could only be defined by music.

His knees weakened at the expansive panorama that spread before him in rolling layers of every shade of blue, from cobalt fading to a smoky-periwinkle just above the ridgelines. He lowered to his knees, breathing in the sight, the scents, the music, until every other thought disappeared from his being. Only then, with the story replaying in his head, could he find the melody for this soundtrack—this new challenge of unfamiliar music and culture.

His heart wrung with a sense of wonder, a need to praise. What a majestic masterpiece from the Supreme Artist!

He waited for the initial strains of a tune to emerge in his mind, tentative and quiet, before he finally took his leave.

Silence remained predominant during the drive back to the apartment. After years of friendship, Wes recognized Henry's need for quiet to piece together his research and experience with music—composing then obliterating then recomposing—and finally ending in a breakthrough fitting for the project. He needed to capture the infant melody on a piece of sheet music and the strings of his violin before the sounds of the world returned to steal this fresh inspiration.

"Eisley should be here soon to take me putt-putting with the children." Wes kept his voice low as they approached the back entry to the bakery.

Henry's brow furrowed, emerging from his creative fog in an attempt to decipher Wes's words.

His friend must have noted Henry's confusion.

"It's miniature golf, but they refer to it as putt-putting."

Henry nodded, a hint of a smile crinkling through his concentration at the joy in Wes's expression.

"I don't suppose you'll join me?"

Henry almost grinned at the slight humor in his friend's voice. "Not today, thank you." His fingers tingled with anticipation, almost making out the position of some of the notes he knew fit into this melody.

"The composer at work." Wes took the steps onto the porch, but as he opened the door, an unexpected piano melody crashed in against the budding composition in Henry's mind.

He put one hand to his head, attempting to make sense of the collision of sound and expectation.

"It seems someone else has music on their mind today too." Wes grinned and gestured toward the beautiful strains spreading from the hallway to meet them. "It may be a good time to talk to her about the engagement party music, seeing as she's already at the piano."

Henry's feet froze to the ground, the clash of two desires keeping him in place. "I...can't. I must get this melody down."

Wes shrugged a shoulder and took the stairs. "Then perhaps once you've done so?"

Henry forced his steps away from the music room and followed Wes. "Today?"

His best mate's smile held no mercy whatsoever. "As good a time as any, isn't it? I'm rather keen to make Miss Barrett my bride, and you have less than two weeks now."

Henry shot a grimace to Wes then glanced toward the hallway before completing his walk up the stairs as one of Brahms's piano concertos pursued him. He'd barely made it over the threshold of the apartment door, when the piano music shifted. What was it? The harmonic structure certainly wasn't classical.

Wes disappeared into his room, most likely to freshen up to meet Eisley, and Henry placed his things on the desk by the door, still trying to decipher the tune Julia was playing. His grin spread as melody met recognition and his feet moved of their own volition, pulling him toward the unique and complex melody.

She was playing a complex improvisation of the jazz standard *Stardust*. A violin accompaniment soared to life in his head, blending with the beauty of the piece. Her notes continually shifted in unexpected directions, keeping his attention and feeding his love for intelligent chord progressions.

Oh, she was very good. Excellent, even.

He halted in the doorway of the music room, hesitant to interrupt yet unable to turn back. Julia sat at the piano, eyes closed, fingers moving over the keys like a caress. Her golden hair hung low down her back with a few threads spilling across her shoulders. A glow of sunlight escaped the curtain's barrier and fell like a halo over her head, almost as if she were a God-sent vision for his eyes alone. Henry stilled, entranced. The melody outside of him dampened beneath the surging symphony within.

She'd become the music.

Her eyes opened to reveal layers of cobalt blue blended with sapphire and brightened by the joy of music. He couldn't move, could barely breathe, and for a moment it appeared she hadn't fully registered his presence.

Yes, she'd become lost in the melody too. He knew that otherworldly draw, the magic.

She took her fingers from the keys, ending the music—well, the audible music, at any rate—and stared at him almost as if she too were unsure of what to do next.

Despite the usual compulsion to retreat during uncomfortable situations, the music between them somehow acted as a bridge, coaxing him into conversation. He cleared his throat and stepped into the room, gesturing toward the piano. "I see you're back from your aunt's house."

He pinched his eyes closed and nearly groaned. Idiot. Was that the best he could do after her immaculate performance? *You played exquisitely. Your technique is impeccable. Where did you learn to improvise with such delicate and effective style?* But no. *I see you're back?* Brilliant, old chap. Positively brilliant.

Her lips shifted almost imperceptibly, as if she'd read his floundering thoughts but didn't want him to notice her doing so. She turned her attention back to the piano. "I only returned about an hour ago. Millie's house encourages the...need for music." She looked up, the smile falling from her eyes. "Did my playing bother you?"

"No, no. Of course not." He shook his head. *It was perfect. I want to spend the rest of my life listening to you.* He cleared his throat again. "I... It was only that I thought we could discuss music for"—he looked behind him and lowered his voice—"the engagement party."

Her eyes widened, and she stood, the oak-finished grand remaining between them.

He stalled his approach, but she rounded the edge of the instrument, her palm resting against it, almost as a support.

"Oh yes, that's an excellent idea." Her attention slid back to him. "It's so important to make a beautiful memory for the two of them, and I can only imagine how special Wes will want to make it. After all, it's a lifetime declaration of true love." Her voice shook with the slightest vibrato. "No pressure there, right?"

"No, not at all." His slight laugh caught them both off-guard. "Only forever ingrained in their minds."

Her smile tightened into an expression of mock terror. "Piece of cake." She redirected her focus from him and reached for the chain around her neck, waving toward a bookshelf nearby. "I...I've considered a few pieces. But is there something in particular you'd suggest?"

He advanced a few more steps, planning through the next conversational turn. "I know one song Wes has requested. A jazz piece entitled 'That's All.'"

Her brows crinkled, and she tightened her hold on the chain around her neck, a signature movement of hers that he was beginning to recognize as one that mirrored her doubt or nervousness. He hoped, in this case, it meant the former rather than the latter.

"I can't recall that one."

"Um..." He gestured toward the piano. "May I..."

She blinked and followed his movements, then looked back to him, her smile blooming in welcome. "Oh. Oh yes. Of course. Please."

She stepped forward at the same time he did, nearly colliding with him. His hand came out to steady her. Her arm shot forward to balance herself, and the subtle scent of wisteria washed over his senses.

"Oh, I'm sorry." She pushed back away from him with a little stumble.

"P...pardon me." His fingers tingled from the trace of her skin, her unexpected closeness. "Are you alright?"

"Yes, just clumsy." She slid passed him, leaving the way to the piano bench open and a whimsical fragrance in the air.

He slid onto the bench, his head down, and as soon as his fingers touched the keys, his body relaxed. Comfort. Confidence. Without another look to the beauty watching him, he began the intricate chords, adding some of his own improvisation to the music. *This* was the world he knew. Nat King Cole's voice crooned the words to the melody in Henry's mind.

I can only give you love that lasts forever
And a promise to be near each time you call.
And the only heart I own for you and you alone,
That's all, that's all…

He couldn't help the smile those words inspired. The author said things much better than Henry ever could. This song spoke of Wes's heart, his love for Eisley, a fitting tribute.

Henry had seen Wes come to life in an entirely new way since meeting Eisley and her family. Her love for him and her family's ready yet somewhat unconventional acceptance of him kindled an almost-enviable joy and belonging in his friend. Love fit the chords of life together perfectly, each beat blending two hearts into a single song.

Henry's unfortunate romantic disasters, paired with his mother's domineering personality, had deterred thoughts of a romantic future. She never failed to remind him of his inability to master the social dance and the long-term impact of his poor choices on his family's social standing.

Not to mention the continual reminder that relationships required well-honed conversational skills, initiation, and at least a tiny bit of charm. Who would have the patience for him in his bumbling, reticent state?

He looked up at the woman standing near the end of the piano, her expression filled with such gentle welcome that fairytales almost seemed possible. Fairytales and happily-ever-afters, even for introverted, awkward, and observant men who knew the right notes but had difficulty turning the melody into a duet.

∞ ∞ ∞

Julia stared at the man playing the piano. As soon as his fingers pressed the keys, the quiet, hesitant Henry Wright gave way to a confident, almost passionate counterpart. His stature broadened, his face relaxed into an expression of coming home, and his previous reticence bent beneath a boldness that held her captive.

Could music make a man more handsome? Or…braver?

She stepped closer, resting her hand against the top of the piano, examining his fingers as they fitted into chord positions or danced along the ivories with fun skips of their own. As he played, the melody became more and more familiar, but he added his own special touches —a bit playfully, even, teasing her senses to life with curiosity and... something else. She recognized this pleasure, this passion, the complete abandon of losing oneself in the music, but sharing that same magic with another person? Someone else who understood?

As if remembering her presence, he brought the song to a close, keeping his focus on the keys as the last strains lingered in the room.

Her breath had grown shallow, her face warm. The power in the moment compelled her to speak. "That...that was beautiful."

His swift gaze came up to meet hers before returning to the piano. "It's what I know."

She didn't believe for a minute that was *all* he knew, not with the way he watched people around him, but maybe *he* believed it was true. A false truth contorted the way a person viewed the world. She'd learned that through months of therapy.

Quiet fell upon their conversation in the wake of the piano music. Henry glanced up at her, tentative, the reluctant hero returning to the scene. His reticence calmed her and somehow inspired a gentle need to... rescue him. "Music has always been a part of me—a piece of who I am."

His attention shot back to her. "The same with me." He shrugged a shoulder, his smile crooked. "I've never been the outgoing sort. Always bumbling. Never sure of what to say in most company. It was only when I could create music that I felt as if I'd found a part of myself. A way to express what I struggled to say."

Her thoughts turned to how piano playing had been therapeutic for her after the rape, her rage too large for words, her wounds too scathing for description. Hammering her fury on the keys gave her a power and means of expression her words had failed to achieve.

Yes, she understood.

"Music has a way of giving deep emotions a voice, I think."

"Exactly." His whispered response mirrored the softness in his eyes.

They were such a curious feature, his eyes. Changing—gray? Green? Somewhere in between? And his hair kept an approachable unkempt look, like a disorganized professor's. She tempered her rising smile at the thought and tapped the piano. "I think I've heard that song before. Maybe we could attempt a practice now? Just to get it beneath our fingers?"

"I don't have the sheet music, but we could search for it online."

"That's all right." She rounded the piano, closer to him. "The chord structure is fairly simple, and it's a slower tempo, which will be forgiving. I think I can figure it out as we go."

His smile spread full to the other side, tempting hers to respond. "I'll fetch my violin. We can see how the song works as a duet."

A duet? Why did that usher a strange shiver through her? Was it fear? No, not exactly. "Sure. We might as well practice while we can, right?"

He dipped his head in acknowledgement, pushed up from the piano bench, and slipped from the room, leaving the scent of amber and...something else. Her face turned to identify the other smell. Something creamy and warm, like hot chocolate. It *was* vanilla, like the first time they'd met.

She balanced herself with a palm to the piano and settled down on the bench. Voices on both sides of her situation warred to be heard. The wounds from having her heart and humanity plundered beat against the truth that she was still whole and loved—and worthy of a good man's care. She forced that knowledge to a more prominent podium in her head. The right man would take her and her child as she was—would see beyond the circumstances of her life—but was she ready to find out if Henry was a man like that? Was it wrong to even imagine?

Every fear rose and screamed *too soon*, or *he isn't to be trusted*, but beneath the roar, a still, small voice whispered.

Fear not. I am with you. I have called you by name. You are mine.

Was she brave enough to listen to the right voice?

Chapter Seven

*E*isley Barrett took the back steps of the bakery to the suite of her favorite Brit. Having him this close after six weeks of separation felt a little like a daydream, and she wanted to make that daydream a regular occurrence. Who would have imagined after their somewhat unfriendly first meeting during her research trip to Derbyshire that they'd be an "item", as her mom said? The little girl in her offered an internal squeal of delight. She was an item with actor Christopher Wesley Harrison. The man *had* to be crazy. But she was okay with that.

Yep. Woohoo! Bring on the fairytale.

Before she could knock on the suite door, Henry Wright rushed out with violin case in hand and almost bowled her over. "Pardon me, Eisley."

"Whoa, Henry." Her palms came up with her laugh. "Where's the fire?"

His brow pinched with a quizzical expression then cleared. "Oh, yes." He grinned. "I'm off to..." His eyes widened in another of his awkward pauses. "Well, you see." He cleared his throat. "Your sister was playing the piano, and I thought I'd join her."

Odd behavior, even for people-make-me-nervous Henry. "That sounds...*nice*." Jazz chords proceeded from downstairs corroborating his plan. Jazz? *Really* nice.

"It was at her suggestion, of course," he offered.

Eisley blinked Henry back into view as if he'd spoken in Swahili. "She *asked* to play with you?"

"Yes, we were discussing..." Henry looked away again, rubbing his palm against the side of his leg. "Jazz music and...and things progressed, you see."

Oh, she was beginning to see for sure.

"Well." Eisley took a slight turn away from him, trying to piece together this interesting development. Julia? In a room alone with a man she barely knew?

Eisley swung her attention back to the quiet man, examining him with fresh eyes. He was handsome, but that wouldn't surmount Julia's caution—in fact, it would probably deter her even more. Peyton had been a stunner. Henry didn't talk enough to draw a lot of attention to himself, so that seemed an unlikely reason.

Her gaze dropped to the violin in his hand and realization pierced the fog.

Music, of course! He *was* a composer, after all, and Julia loved music. Gentle? Yes. Enough to put her sister at ease?

"I guess you'd better get on down to her then, huh?" Eisley waved toward the stairs. "It's a big compliment to you, Henry, that she's so...comfortable with you."

His smile took on a boyish charm as he left her. It was one of the sweetest sights she'd seen.

"Good morning." The bass tones of her charming Brit warmed her skin with a happily-ever-after flush.

Talk about sweet sights...She grinned over her shoulder at the dashing man, and his dimpled smile almost distracted her from her musings about Henry Wright and her sister.

To make her mental focus worse, Wes slipped an arm around her waist and placed a chaste kiss on her cheek. "My day just improved exponentially." The kiss took a slightly less G-rated turn toward her ear. "How are you this morning, pet?"

The glorious haze of romance started its decent over her thought processes. "You really are the best distraction in the whole world. Do you know that?" She touched her lips to his, and in the stillness of their mingled breaths, the strains of a violin joined the piano.

She jerked back and grabbed the lapel of Wes's jacket. "Do you hear that?"

His stormy, blue-gray eyes narrowed as he inclined his head. "Music?"

"Yes. Music." She seized his hand and pulled him down the hallway, her volume on stealth-mode. "But not just any music."

"Eisley, what is going on?"

"Shhh." She turned with a finger to her lips and continued her march down the steps. "Something is...I don't know. They seem strange."

Her handsome hero gave her a look as if the musical pair on the first floor weren't the only ones. She sighed. He'd fallen in love with her as the crazy woman she was, so he shouldn't be surprised, really.

"They?"

"Julia and Henry. Something is...different."

"Different." He repeated the word like a befuddled parrot.

A swoony, cleft-in-his-chin befuddled parrot. She slipped on a step, but he was quick to steady her against his spicy-leather-scented sweater. Mama mia, what a man!

She stopped at the bottom of the stairs to reward his chivalry with a smooch—or two—before she tugging him to the doorway of the music room. Like the amateur sleuth she wished she were, she peeked around the opening.

Julia sat at the piano, looking up at Henry with something like wonder on her face as he played his violin to... Ugh, Eisley couldn't recall the name of the song, but at least she remembered she liked it, whatever it was. Ever since the horrid rape, her sister had kept more to herself than ever before. Quieter. Retreating to her music and baking. But in this one scene, a glimpse of the former Julia—smiling and confident—resurfaced. For Henry?

Oh. My. Goodness!

"Look at that."

Wes's lips took a crooked this-woman-is-crazy turn, and he examined the couple again before returning his attention to her. "And?"

"Do you see what I see?"

His smile slipped into an adorably confused pucker, and if she'd not been so curious about the couple in the next room, she'd have been tempted to kiss the look right off his handsome face. How was he clueless?

"You are a *romance* actor for goodness sake and one of the swooniest men on the planet! Julia and Henry. There." She gestured with both her hands in karate-chop form, lowering her volume before she got too carried away. "Fine, happy, *talking*."

Wes shrugged. "Doesn't it make sense that two kind-hearted, reserved, musically gifted people would end up getting along?" His gaze flipped to Eisley, eyes widening. "Together!"

She nodded like a caffeinated chipmunk, her grin widening so far that her face hurt. "Together"—she snickered— "in perfect harmony, even."

He rolled his eyes at her pun then examined the pair again. "They play as if they—"

"Were made for each other." Her voice squeezed the words into a higher pitch.

"I was going to say as if they'd played together before, but your theory is an interesting one." Wes studied his friend. "I've never seen Henry like this with a woman. He's so nervous and reserved around them, even those he's dated in the past. Always has been. Most likely because of that terrifying mother of his and all the expectations to please her, but this? Over music? This is new."

"And it gives me a *great* idea."

"Oh dear." He slipped his palm back around her waist and she snuggled in close. What a keeper!

"Sometimes two people are too fearful to see when they're a perfect match."

"Yes?" He squinted, almost as if he were suspicious of her. Hmm...Perhaps he knew her just a bit too well.

"We had some loving matchmakers help us find our way to each other."

"Eisley..."

"And since the two of them are so reserved and quiet, they could probably use the help."

He raised a brow in challenge, and she tugged on his jacket. "Don't you remember how people—like Lizzie and your Dad and even my mom, once she got over the shock—loved us so much that they knew we'd make a great match?" She sighed and patted his chest. "Which is still kind of hard to believe from this country girl's standpoint, but you're not allowed to change your mind. My whole heart, all three of my kids, and even my dad are invested now."

He kissed her forehead. "I'm not going anywhere, pet."

She searched his face, then flashed him a renewed smile. "Perfect! Then let's figure out how we can pair one introverted, music-loving girl with one introverted, music-loving guy. Imagine what their happily-ever-after could *sound* like."

"You really are incorrigible." His chuckled and kissed her head.

"I'm so glad incorrigible works for you."

∞ ∞ ∞

Evening darkened into early morning before Julia finally crawled into bed. Her head and heart spun from the past two days inventorying furniture in Aunt Millie's house and working with a home inspector as well as finalizing paperwork for the sale of the bakery, but her body, though weary, refused to settle down for the night. It didn't really matter. She wouldn't sleep long anyhow. Within a few hours, she'd be up to go to the bathroom or uncomfortable from her sleeping position *or* Little One would wake up and play the mamba on her ribcage.

Later pregnancy note: naps may save your life.... or the lives of other. Take them.

She rubbed a palm against a little heel or elbow, that was distorting her abdomen in a way that freaked out her nephews. The one time they'd seen the strange occurrence, eight-year-old Nathan's eyes had widened behind his glasses and, with brilliance only a child could claim, he'd exclaimed, "It looks like you have an alien in there!"

Six-year-old Pete had scrunched his nose in confusion...or concern? Julia still wasn't sure. He followed his brother's statement with, "I think you better let your baby out, Aunt Julia, because if he breaks your tummy open it's going to be really messy. You had oatmeal for breakfast."

Julia leaned against the pillows with a resigned smile, the reality of her situation settling deeper and deeper with each passing week. She was a mother. The thought pricked a memory, and she reached to the bedside table to retrieve her aunt's letter.

Seeing Millie's familiar handwriting brought another squeeze of pain through her chest. Aunt Millie had been ready to leave this world—in fact, she'd carried an otherworldly look in her eyes as long as Julia had known her—but the loss of her still stung.

Julia carefully peeled open the letter and reread its words.

Dearest Julia,

If you are reading this, I have quit my long life here on Earth for a more heavenly one. I knew it would be soon. I hoped it would be soon.

Do not mourn me. My heart has longed to take its leave from this world for many years—especially since the loss of my dear Rosalyn. But God did not leave me comfortless with her death. In my sorrow He sent you, drawing me back into the land of the living, and I am daily grateful for your dear friendship to a woman nearly three times your age.

As you peel apart the life I packed away within my house, you will uncover a different woman from the one you've always known.

Julia paused each time she'd read that sentence. What had Aunt Millie meant? So far, all Julia had found were a few piano books, exquisite artwork, and an excellent collection of moth balls.

Much like you, I was the benefactress of a wealthy family member— something unique for a young Appalachian girl of the time. He changed the trajectory of my life, spurring me into a direction very few ever live, or survive. He saw giftedness and interest in me at an early age and funded my education in Europe. Whatever you discover about me, my dear, especially the surprises, do with them whatever you like. Hide them. Research them. Use them to benefit yourself, but, for my sake, keep them. The memories held within these walls need not go erased by time or unused by those who see them as dated. In hindsight, perhaps I should have told my story, but I'd protected it for so long, I wasn't certain how to share it. Even with you.

I pray that even in my absence my patchwork history will somehow encourage your heart to be braver than I was.

I'm writing in riddles, aren't I? Mysteries are hidden everywhere. In closet floorboards or hinged within secret nooks. You may even locate my dear Lucas's love letters. Oh, what a find! All of them tell a remarkable story that I was privileged to live yet unable to finish.

The best way for you to know him is through his letters. If you could have known him, you would have loved him. A quiet man, he felt emotions so deeply, with such a passion, that even now as I think of him I can feel the presence of his love as if decades were but days.

And Rosalyn? Her laughter rang out more beautifully than any sonata. I feel certain that, when I join my beloved ones again, I shall find the end of the unfinished melody in my heart that has lingered over seventy years.

Julia wiped at a stray tear and looked out the window into the night. What a love! A quiet, gentle man with a fiercely loyal heart. She imagined her parents knew such devotion— even if her dad's display of affection came on more like a bear attack than a prince charming.

Did Julia have a chance to find such a love too? Had this tragedy stolen not just her innocence but also her future?

The paper pinched in her hands, drawing her attention back to the words even as the ache in her heart stung with a deeper longing. But her aunt spoke to that ache.

May what you uncover, my dear Julia, bring you hope in the middle of your pain—hope for a steadfast love, no matter how brief or unexpected. Pain, loss, and grief are all dreadfully commonplace in our world. But love? It is rare enough that those from the wealthiest of kings to the poorest of paupers spend lifetimes in search of it.

As I write this, I pray you will do more with your pain than I did. You will rise above it and truly live your life. Love gives us courage to be brave. It is the spine beneath our faltering to keep us from falling despite the circumstances.

May God bring you a man of such steadfast, tender, and furious love, and may you live long with him, far beyond what I had with Lucas.

And do not be afraid to capture the dreams God has placed within you, dear Julia.

With Him, be brave and finish your story well.

Amelia

Dream? Be brave? She folded the letter and closed her eyes against the tears threatening to fall. Brave was the last thing she felt. Each night she checked three times that the doors were locked, just to be sure. Nightmares woke her in a cold sweat— not as much as they used to, but enough that she could hardly claim her past didn't come back to haunt her. The most unexpected paranoias would surface out of nowhere, and she'd have to convince herself Peyton wasn't following her or waiting in the shadows.

Brave? Not a chance.

She placed the letter on her nightstand and turned off the lamp, rolling onto her side as she stuffed her body pillow into position around her bountiful baby curves.

Bravery is stepping into your fears and finding the strength to keep walking. Her granny's words whispered through her mind like a reminder from God.

A vision of playing music with Henry vied to contradict her inner statement. Could that simple moment be an act of bravery?

She rubbed her cheek into her pillow and stared out the window, its frame haloed with pale street lamps. Taking on the sale of her great-aunt's house on her own? Was that brave?

Having papers drawn up to sell the bakery to her cousin Amy?

Keeping this baby? She sighed. The biggest fear of them all, but a decision forged within her very being.

Maybe...maybe she *did* have some courage. A little.

She summoned the courage to step into her reconstructed life—and her reassembled dreams—with an even stronger hope. She'd hidden in the kitchen of the bakery for months, stayed shrouded by her family at church without getting involved in the group she once knew, and walked through Pleasant Gap's streets with her head down, all while carrying shame she hadn't earned.

She fisted the pillow against her chest.

"Lord, help me be brave."

Chapter Eight

"Are we going to eat lunch with the Jenkins family *every* Sunday?" The twinge of a whining timbre in Henry's voice belied the force he'd applied to curb his slight annoyance.

Wes's laugh did nothing to alleviate Henry's agitation. "You'd best be glad I dissuaded them from us joining for Friday Burger Night as well." His friend's gaze remained on the narrow road ahead as they weaved up a hillside to the Jenkinses's home. Barely budding trees, in white, lined the drive, welcoming them toward the house of chaos like a contradiction. "As I understand it, they engage in family games such as American football."

Henry cringed.

"Wii bowling."

Who were these people?

"And even Twister."

Henry pinched his eyes closed. The idea of participating in such activities with strangers—even if he had become slightly more familiar with them over the past week— nearly had him crawling out of his skin. Good heavens, the Jenkins family was unlike any he'd met in all his life. "I suppose I should thank you for only Sundays."

"I know they're a polar opposite to *your* family, and somewhat different from mine, but if you spend enough time with them, you'll realize the same qualities you love about my family can be found in the Jenkinses, only a little less..."

"Refined?"

"Exactly."

"And they're incredibly demonstrative."

"Some of them." Wes chuckled. "Though Julia is more like you, I think."

Henry looked back out the window, the tall colonial coming into view, a spray of mountains outlined over the tree line in the distance. "She is the quietest of the bunch, isn't she?"

"And she is fond of music."

Henry focused on Eisley's three children, who were running about in the front garden, but his thoughts strayed to the piano duet he'd played with the beautiful blonde a few nights before. Another tangible connection. How could he feel as though he knew Julia so well already? "Yes."

The car came to a stop, and Eisley's brood ran toward them, screaming Wes's name like the fans from his latest hit movie. Henry couldn't stop his chuckle. Perhaps there were benefits to bombastic affection. Henry had always been fond of kid-hugs, as Eisley called them.

"And," Wes added as he exited the car, "she's entirely single."

The inuendo jabbed Henry in the chest like a sudden forte to his ears. Was Wes mad? How on earth could he even suggest such a thing? It was nonsensical. Impossible.

Besides, Henry had made a mess of his romantic life and shamed his family enough.

He ran a hand through his hair, watching through the car window as Wes greeted the children.

How could Henry have gotten involved with a married woman? How hadn't he known she was married? Or fallen for a woman whose heart quickly transferred to his younger brother? An event put on public display because of her high-profile life. The heat of both scandals still stung his face with a fresh coat of shame. He'd allowed his natural compassion for a woman in need to turn into a trap on both accounts. Women saw him as an easy target, his mother said. Easily manipulated.

He released a sigh and opened the car door. All he wanted was someone genuine—authentically his. Someone who cared for *him*, not his family's position or the financial stability he could provide.

But he was a miserable judge when it came to damsels in distress, and how could he trust his own choices with such a track record? He raised his eyes to the sky as he exited the car. *Lead me not into temptation...unless it's not temptation at all but the right choice. Help me have clear vision.*

Within five minutes Eisley's children and their cousin, Clay, had pulled Henry into a game of tag— a great diversion from the house full of adults. Children were easy conversationalists. They enjoyed talking, which suited Henry just fine. He preferred listening.

Emily wound her way into Henry's heart within seconds. She was the underdog, of course, being the youngest, so he had to take her side. Her tiny stature ensured almost no chance against the competition, so Henry swept her onto his back, and they played as a team.

"I thought for sure Emily bein' on your back would slow you down," Nathan said, frozen in position from a tag. "But I think you're faster than Uncle Greg. Where'd you get your reason for speed?"

Henry grinned at the little boy, whose circle-shaped spectacles gave him a bookish-charm and adjusted a giggling Emily on his back. "Reason for speed?"

"Mama says most folks who run really fast have had practice runnin' from or to something." Nathan grinned and pushed his glasses up the bridge of his nose. "She says Uncle Greg got his speed runnin' after girls."

Henry's brows shot high and a burst of laughter erupted from deep inside him. "Perhaps mine was running *from* them."

Nathan nodded and crossed his arms. "They're awful scary, if you ask me."

Henry's grin faded as he assessed a little truth behind his admission. He ran from failure, from conflict, from repeating a disaster.

A movement on the porch drew his attention. Julia stood there, one hand shading her eyes from the sun, lavender dress blowing in the gentle breeze. Wes's comment lit within him.

Weaving in between his fear and his anxiety came the softest strains of Bach's *Cello Suite No. 1*, building hope from a single instrument of what *could* be...perhaps. He shook his head. No—romance was probably the last thing she wanted after her ordeal.

But what if you're wrong? What if you are what she needs? The questions came out of nowhere. The possibility.

He jerked his attention back to the boys as if they'd said something. Emily squeezed her hands around his neck and snuggled close.

"I have been frozen for...eee...vver." Ginger-headed Pete's volume increased as he squirmed in place. "If you don't unfreeze me, I'll never get to eat Aunt Julia's banana pudding. Eee...ver. And then it will all be gone, and I'll have to settle for crackers—or worse, green beans."

Nathan leaned in, his eyes twinkling with enough mischief to resurface Henry's grin. "Pete really thinks he's frozen."

Henry gestured with his chin toward the younger boy. "Then the right sort of chap would immediately go and unfreeze your brother to end his torment."

Nathan hesitated, as if weighing Henry's words, and then sighed. "Yeah, I reckon so."

"Supper's ready, y'all." Kay joined Julia on the front porch, mimicking her daughter's contented pose, bent at the waist—or as far as Julia could go with her extended abdomen—and arms relaxed on the porch railing.

"And *now* would be the opportune time, mate."

Nathan nodded and gave Henry a long look. "Wes calls me 'mate' sometimes. I like it."

Henry warmed all the way down to his toes. "It's a good word...mate."

Nathan smiled and ran off to free his brother, and Emily wiggled so far up Henry's back that she nearly sat on his head. The giggle she released while he spun her around into his arms brought a wonderful staccato pulse to his heart. Laughter, freedom, conversation... Kids were so much easier than adults.

"I think I should call you a monkey."

Emily's wide blue eyes grew wider. "I not a montey. I Mimily."

"Well, Mimily, we'd best get inside before your mother thinks you've been frozen too."

The boys joined Henry on a march across the lawn. The silence of the spring day disappeared before they even crossed the threshold of the house. Even after a week to prepare himself, he still hadn't built up enough stamina to make it through the Jenkins family's boisterous conversations and ready physical contact without feeling a little terrified and somewhat exhausted.

"You've got such a way with the kids, Henry." Eisley walked over to him and snatched a reluctant Emily.

He crossed his arms over his chest at the loss of his child-barrier and shrugged. "I always volunteered to take the children during family gatherings."

"Ah, an escape plan." Eisley winked. "Well, I'm grateful for any time you want to take my wild ones outside. Disappear from the crowd all you like. If they stay inside for too long, they become much less angelic in their behavior."

Henry followed Eisley to the crowded table, taking a spot between Greg and....Eisley. An escape plan, indeed.

"Time for grace." Nate's deep voice roared over the throng of voices, and within a second, silence fell over the entire crowd. Even the children stopped wriggling in their seats—almost like magic.

Another anomaly Henry puzzled over. Faith flowed naturally, as much a part of this family as Southern cooking and colorful narratives.

"Have you had much of a chance to explore Pleasant Gap, Henry?"

Henry looked up from examining the contents of his plate post-prayer to meet Kay's smile. A white concoction of chicken and bread waited for his taste buds' discovery, but after trying the goulash from last week, he entered this meal-adventure with more trepidation. "The movie site allows for a great deal of opportunity to walk the countryside. It's truly beautiful."

Kay nodded her appreciation, the warm glow of welcome in her blue eyes so similar to Julia's that Henry glanced in her direction. Julia's gaze locked with his as she took a drink of her iced tea.

Surely Wes couldn't be serious in his implication.

"No better place than here in our mountains." Nate pushed a bowl of something that resembled dark green leaves toward him, the man's attention flipping from Henry to his daughter then back again. "Here, try ya some collards."

Collards? "Thank you." He forced the reply and spared Wes a look, but his best mate apparently couldn't hide his enjoyment at Henry's discomfort over this new food. Ah...he was enjoying a scene he most likely experienced himself only a few months before.

"You'll want to douse them in vinegar, Henry." Greg pointed with his fork at the bowl of damp-looking leafy greens. "Ain't no better way to eat creasies than with a good dose of vinegar."

Wes's brow raised to new heights, and Henry's stomach dropped to the depths. Adventurous in his imagination? Certainly. In his eating? Not so much.

"Be kind to the poor guy, boys." Eisley tugged the bowl away from Henry. "You've already given him enough chicken and dumplings to last three days. One introduction to Southern cooking at a time."

"There ain't nothin' wrong with southern cooking." Nate seared Henry with a glance— at least it felt like a searing glance, though there might have been a twinkle involved. "Best kind there is. It'll put hair on your chest, boy."

Henry's face blanched cold. "P-pardon?"

"Daddy!" Sophie shook her head and took a bite of potatoes.

Greg laughed and nodded in vigorous agreement. Wes's brow crooked. Kay pinched her eyes closed. And finally, Henry's attention fastened on Julia, who stared wide-eyed at her father.

"What? Ain't nothin' wrong with a man bein' proud of how he's made and the good food that gets him there." Nate peered around the table as if everyone else had said something amiss then shoveled another bite of food into his mouth.

"Daddy, I am certain English cooking did a fine job in forming Henry. It...it probably added a sufficient amount of chest hair."

All eyes turned to Julia, and the shock within him from seconds before pretzeled into an untamable grin. She was bumbling through a defense for him. He knew the cost of that.

Her gaze met his at about the time she seemed to realize what she'd said aloud to everyone in room. "Um... I mean..."

"Ain't no reason he couldn't add more," Nate responded, completely unaware of the redness rushing into Julia's cheeks. He sat up straighter. "Good taters, hon."

Greg chuckled, and Eisley's eyes glittered with some unvoiced humor she seemed to share with Wes.

"I'm...I'm here for research, Nate," Henry offered, tugging the bowl of creasies toward his own plate and making sure to draw as much attention away from the pink-cheeked blonde as he could. Julia's defense would not go in vain. "May as well go all in, don't you think?"

"Now there's the idea, boy." Nate gave the table an approving tap. "You're here to research mountain folks. Well, you can write a whole lot better stories if you know what you're talking about."

Henry paused his movements and scanned between Nate and Wes for clarification.

"Henry doesn't write stories, Nate. He writes the music for the movies."

"Say what?"

"You know, Dad." Eisley leaned forward, the glimmer in her eyes matching her energetic tone. "Like the themes for the *Indiana Jones* or *Star Wars* series. Henry adds the music behind the acting and scenes."

The man's dark eyebrows shot high. "You wrote the music for *Indiana Jones?*"

"No." Henry choked on his water and laughed through the awkward silence. "I'm not as advanced as the composer who wrote those themes, but I have composed...do compose...for movies."

"Did you write the music for *Spiderman?*" Pete's voice rose above the throng, his bright blue eyes wide.

The tension in Henry's shoulders deflated a little. "No, Pete, but I'm certain I could create a Spiderman-like theme just for you."

Pete gasped. "My own Spiderman music?"

"You realize you have a friend for life now, right?" Eisley beamed and turned to wipe Emily's mouth. "And he'll ask you about that theme until you create one, so you'd better prepare yourself."

"A composer, eh?" Nate took a swig of his tea and nodded, studying Henry for a few seconds, his stormy brow furrowed tightly against his tanned skin. Seconds that could have been minutes ticked by as Nate continued to examine him. What was he thinking?

As if he'd finally accepted Henry's involvement in some sort of musical career, Nate sighed into his chair and loaded his fork with dumplings. "Hmm...Well, what else do you do?"

A dumpling lump lodged in Henry's throat. "Pardon?"

"You can't make a living out of writing music. Do you sing too? I reckon them people who're up on stage dancin' around in their shiny clothes makes all sorts of money." He sniffed and raised another brow. "Though you don't seem the fancy sort."

"There's quite a business for composing, Nate," Wes intervened, clearly struggling with his smile. Surely Wes could tell Henry was quite out of his element in this conversation. And what did *fancy sort* even mean? "Henry's made a name for himself in England, and it's only a matter of time before his talent is recognized by larger studios. He's very good at what he does."

"It's pretty neat meeting a *living* composer." Greg poked a knife in the air toward his father. Did every Jenkins use their utensils as conversational props? "Most of the ones we learned about in school were foreign and dead."

"What do you think of the creasies, Henry?" The unexpected question came from Nathan, his hazel eyes blinking behind his glasses.

"I...I've not tried them yet."

"I don't like them at all." The boy's nose crinkled in a frown. "But I like the vinegar."

"Julia enjoys those dead composers, don't you, sugar?" The question brought the focus of the conversation back to the Jenkins patriarch, which was probably good because Henry's forehead had started to ache from the tension of trying to keep up with the conversation...or conversation*s*, as it were. Though, he'd made it further into dinner than last time before the warning signs began.

Julia slouched forward, almost in resignation, then held his gaze, as if in apology, before turning to answer her father. "And a few living ones. Gifted composers have a real job, Dad. It's not just a hobby like my love for music."

Nate rested his elbow on the table and turned his body toward Henry. "Here's what we're gonna do, boy. I got a *real* job in Julia's shop that needs doin'—laying a new floor. Greg's off to some critter conference and Fancy Pants can't help me 'cause of this acting stuff he's doing." He gestured toward Wes with his chin, shook his head as if his daughter's soon-to-be fiancé's excuse wasn't satisfactory, and returned his eyes to Henry. "You don't even have to talk in the movie. You need *something* to do."

Panic rushed to the defense. "I can assure you, Nate, I am sufficiently engaged in learning the music of this culture and researching how to—"

"Didn't you say you had some free time in the morning, though, Henry?" Greg's eyes danced with childlike mischief.

Henry's heart rate shot to a higher speed, pulsing in his ears. He didn't know anything about flooring—and spending time alone with Nate Jenkins produced the most discordant internal reaction. Would laying flooring with Nate mean he'd see Julia more often? Warmth spread up his skin beneath his polo. Did he want that? Would *she* want that?

"See? You've got all the time in the world." Nate stabbed Henry with a look of unadulterated challenge that Henry felt to his toes. "A bit of hard work won't hurt your fiddle pickin' fingers a'tall."

"Unless he hits one with your hammer," Sophie called from the end of the table. "Wes lost his fingernail from the smash your hammer gave him when he helped you work last time."

Nate's laugh rumbled through the room. "That's right, ain't it, Wes? And you passed the cussin' test despite it all."

Henry's eyes enlarged so much he could have sworn they reached his eyebrows. He knew that story. Remembered Wes telling him about Nate's interrogation about Wes's intentions toward Eisley. But why on earth would the man feel the need to interrogate *him*? It wasn't as though he had intentions toward...

"See there, Henry. Wes ain't no worse for the wear. And it's a good skill to learn. Just think—you can go back home to your fancy house and put down your own floors. Fiddlin' and floor installin'. That sounds like music to my ears." Nate laughed at his pun and almost pulled Henry from his fight-or-flight response.

Could he possibly make it through a morning alone with Nate Jenkins?

"I'm off to finish making the banana pudding." Julia rose from the table, her lips in a tight smile and her attention zeroed in on him. "I wonder, Henry"—her gaze flitted to his— "would you mind giving me a hand? I see you've finished your meal."

Her raised brow and subtle gesture with her chin encouraged his immediate cooperation. He pushed back from the table with a grin, pretty sure he'd never seen anything as beautiful as Julia Jenkins to the rescue.

∞ ∞ ∞

Heat rose into Julia's cheeks as she waited for Henry to stand. Everyone in the family would make assumptions about her feelings for Henry, but she had to do *something*. The longer her father had kept talking, the wider Henry's eyes had became, the farther she'd pushed back from the table in anticipation of an intervention. She couldn't let him sit there without some assistance.

He'd hardly eaten anything, but at her not-so-subtle suggestion, he popped up with plate in hand and started toward the kitchen. "I'd be happy to help."

Poor guy! She knew that look of desperation all too well—and no one instilled it with such unintentional—or sometimes intentional—accuracy as her dad.

"Julia knows when an introvert needs saving from her brute of a dad." Her mother chuckled and grazed Henry with a tender look. "He'll grow on you, Henry. There's a lot of fluff beneath the growl."

Dad's brows dipped, and he patted his belly. "Hey now, don't talk about my fluff."

Henry's smile wobbled to life, and he slowed his pace as he disappeared through the kitchen door.

Julia patted her dad's shoulder as she passed him, but he caught her wrist before she could escape, looking as confused as a man could be. "I wasn't mean a'tall. Ain't nothin' wrong with asking a boy to help do some real work now and again."

Julia squeezed her eyes closed, refraining from groaning once more at another of her father's brusque remarks. Her mom's chuckle grew into a laugh along with Eisley's and Sophie's.

He really didn't have bad intentions. "Music is real work, Dad. I know it's hard to believe that a piano or a violin or a cello could actually be a workman's tool like a hammer or saw but they can."

He rolled his eyes. "You ain't gonna see nobody building a house with a violin."

"No." She sighed, her gaze flipping to the kitchen door. "But they can build a world or mend a heart."

"Oh, how beautiful," Sophie called from the other side of the room. "That sounds dreamy."

"A bunch of malarkey is what it sounds like." The teasing glint in her dad's eyes belied the gruffness in his voice. He loved music. Not her tastes, so much, but give him a bluegrass band and he'd clap with more delight than Pete with a Spiderman goo web blaster. He pointed his finger up to her. "You just be careful, you hear. You and this introverted foreigner who builds worlds with music." He rolled his eyes. "I'm keeping my eye on him."

"Yep, Henry is a scary one." Eisley raised her glass with a shake of her head. "What gave it away, Dad? That he wants to create a Spiderman theme for Pete or that he was gentleman enough not to pull up his shirt to prove his chest-hair status?"

Dad pointed his fork at Wes, his moustache twitching. "That English gentleman thing is what got you going googly-eyed over Mr. Fancy Pants."

Eisley leaned her head on Wes's shoulder and exaggerated her sigh. "Indeed, it did."

Of course, Wes's grin grew three sizes...and so did Julia's gratitude. God had sent her sister more than any of them could have imagined when he brought Wes into Eisley's life. Julia placed her hand on her dad's shoulder. "Dad, you're like Mom's chocolate chip torte."

He nodded, his chin lifted to accept the compliment. "Sweet, smooth, and rich taste."

Julia laughed. "And most people can only handle a few small bites at a time." She gave his shoulder a squeeze. "Be easy on Henry. He could use the grace." Her grin tilted. "And you could use the practice."

Chapter Nine

"Thanks for giving me a ride into town to pick up my car, Julia." Sophie tugged her long honey-colored hair into a flawless side-braid as they rode along. Paired with her fitted cold-shoulder top, skinny jeans, and flats, her little sister defined a cute classy-country mix that matched her natural charm. In fact, it seemed that all the Jenkins charm and looks had landed on her youngest sibling.

Sophie bubbled with enough charisma and energy to light an entire stage. "I'm so excited to have bought my own car—and without Dad at my side during the test rides and negotiations. Landon at the garage said it checked out well, so I can now prove to Dad that I'm not car-stupid." Her index finger rose in defense. "I did my research and held my ground." She bounced in her seat, her fingers tapping against the dark blue fabric of her jeans, then she released an ear-splitting squeal. "And it's teal." She blinked her hazel eyes, all hint of the maturity accrued within her twenty-three years erased her excitement. "Teal is so beautiful."

"I can't wait to see it."

She sighed back into the seat. "It's four doors, so I can be an awesome aunt and tote baby Jenkins around whenever you want me to." Her attention flipped to Julia's abdomen, and she unleashed her wrinkled-nose grin. "In style."

Julia chuckled. "I can't imagine you doing anything that wasn't *in style*." She tried to imitate her sister's toss of her hair, and Sophie's laughter bubbled through the space.

"Well, I have to find some way to stand out from the crowd. After all, I am the youngest in the Jenkins herd."

Julia shook her head, her smile growing. "Sophie, you've never had difficulty standing out in a crowd. Besides, I was driving this way for one of my meetings with Karen, so it all worked out anyway."

"Oh yeah? How are the counseling sessions going? You're down to twice a month now, right?"

Julia stared ahead, clinging to the renewed strength her previous few sessions had brought about. Dr. Karen Owensby had been pleased with Julia's healing process, attributing much of it to the strength of her faith when going into the ordeal and the support her family continued to provide her afterward. Yes, she'd struggled with nightmares and phobias and some avoidance of unfamiliar males for a while, but distance from the assault as well as the sweetness her family shrouded her in buoyed her to near-normalcy. "We both agreed to keep them at twice a month until the baby is born. After that, she thinks I can reduce to one session per month."

"That's great, Julia. Maybe then you can start hanging out with your friends, too." Sophie gestured toward the green, white, and red striped awning of Jay's Pizza and Subs. "You know, you used to meet up with your college friends at Jay's every Tuesday. Maybe they'll be there tonight."

The familiar void swelled into Julia's throat, and she shifted her attention away from the restaurant windows. The court case and Julia's college sabbatical had created a rift among her small group of friends. Penelope had been the only one of the four who'd kept in touch with Julia over the past four months, and the last time she'd called Erica, the energetic blonde had told Julia the girls weren't getting together much anymore. Things had changed.

Oh, things had most certainly changed.

"You know, Sophie, I've always preferred a small circle of people in my life. Those friends are still great to have, but my family, including a few girls from church, is enough for me. I'm not like you, with your love for the social scene."

Sophie blew out a noisy stream of air between her pursed lips. "Well, you can't marry someone in your family, Julia, so eventually you're going to have to find friends outside of us."

The knot solidified in her throat. "I'm not really looking for marriage right now, Soph. Having a newborn is going to be plenty, especially with all the other changes going on in my life."

Elation from hidden knowledge only sisters and best friends could guess glimmered in her sister's eyes. "Oh yes, yes!" She patted her hands together like a five-year-old with a birthday cake. "Dreams-coming-true time. Your own inn? You'll be so great at it, Julia! You were called for hospitality. It just flows from you like the music you play. You've wanted to run your own inn ever since you were in Mrs. Smith's home economics class in middle school. Would you look for a place away from Pleasant Gap? Maybe somewhere closer to the city? Or what about the beach?"

"Whatever I choose, I'm going to take my time and make sure it's what's best for me and this little one." She rubbed one palm over her belly and allowed hope to pearl warmth within her. The bud of a dream shook away a few more cobweb-y doubts. "But...well...I think I'd like to see what's out there. Maybe. The possibilities."

"Yes!" Sophie's fists shot into the air before she collapsed against the car's seat. "Oh Jules, traveling with Aunt Amelia had to have inspired you to dream big and reach wide." Her eyes grew as round as cupcakes. "What about France? Or Italy? Or England? Oh! England would be nice."

England? Where on earth had Sophie pulled that thought from? Surely her sister hadn't discovered Julia's teenage journal. Her shoulders fell. Knowing Sophie and her penchant for snooping, she could have discovered her journal, teen-crush posters, *and* the boyfriend-girlfriend letter she never sent to Bobby Thompson in ninth grade. It was an excellent letter though, so someone needed to appreciate it.

"Whoa there, day dreamer. I don't think I'm ready for an adventure quite that grand."

"Oh, I don't know." Sophie's raised brow contradicted her nonchalant shrug. "You've always had something about you that set a room at ease, that...well...that created a sense of welcome. God has something amazing planned for you and your gifts, and I'm excited to witness the plan unfold."

Julia quelled a shudder at the faith Sophie's words held. Amazing? God certainly wasn't taking the shortcut for her to get there. "With a newborn on my hip and a bruised reputation, I don't think you should hold your breath for anything too amazing from me, Soph."

As usual, Julia's sensical words bounced off her sister's daydreams like rain on a tin roof. Sophie brushed her braid off her shoulder and nailed Julia with a look too mature for her usual disposition. "It's the ones with the bruises and scars that have the most amazing potential for greatness. God wouldn't use them as examples throughout history if it weren't true." She sighed back into her seat again. "Hey! If you built a B&B in England, you could visit Eisley when she marries Wes. And now you have a new friend in Henry."

Henry's name snagged her pulse for only a second, but it was enough that she wished she'd ignored the minute shift, especially with Sophie watching. "Acquaintance, perhaps. I don't think we know each other well enough to say we're friends."

Sophie waved away her words. "Well, I've decided our new *acquaintance* isn't the right man for me after all."

"Oh really?" Julia's laugh burst out of her with abandon. "And how did you come to this certain conclusion?"

"Don't get me wrong." Her palm shot up. "He's a nice guy, he's English, and he smells good enough to eat, but the poor man hardly says a word and he rarely shows real emotion, besides shock. How can that possibly lead to any romance?"

Julia tapped the steering wheel as she formulated her defense. "He talks when he has something to say." Like he had with her on several occasions. They'd conversed about the virtues of Bach and Beethoven while serving the banana pudding after lunch, after all. "And he seems very sweet."

Yes, she could see him as a friend. But she'd keep that to herself for now.

"And he plays the piano more expressively than some people ever talk."

"He does? Sounds like you sometimes."

She blinked away the softening of her thoughts and attempted to keep her expression as neutral as possible. Sophie didn't need ammunition for romantic notions. They practically oozed from her pores as it was. Besides, this was no time to even consider falling for a guy, especially one who lived halfway around the world. She had a child on the way and the wounds of an assault to work through, not to mention a house and business to sell—though, both of those tasks were almost finished.

"I...I'm not really on the market right now anyway." Had she voiced those thoughts out loud? "I mean, it's not like I'm dating anybody, of course, but not many guys are going to want to date a pregnant introvert with a messy backstory. And...and I...I'm not looking."

Sophie's brows rose with her widening eyes. "Um...I never said anything about *you* and romance and Henry. I was talking about *me*." Her pink lips spread with Cheshire Cat cunning. "But I don't see why, if God sends the right guy, it wouldn't fit perfectly into His plan, messy or not. Circumstances don't really bother Him."

Julia's face heated to baking hot. "It's just not right, after...everything."

"Not right? To want romance after having some jerk attack you? Hope is what you need, Julia, and it just so happens I'm your girl." Sophie nodded. "I'm the most hope-full romantic you'll ever meet, and I've read all of the right books to prove it."

Julia's tight lips relaxed into another grin. "I appreciate your optimism, Soph, but—"

"I think you need to talk to Dr. Karen about this thing with Henry."

"There is no 'thing'."

Channeling her inner *Wheel of Fortune* persona, Sophie raised her palms rose in the air like she'd just guessed the winning phrase. "Oh! You and Henry are actually so perfect for each other." She blinked. "How did I not see it before? It's brilliant. Both sweet, quiet, love music, love England." Her volume increased with each addition to her list. "Is he a Christian? Does he watch rom com?"

How did the latter two follow each other in any way? Julia raised a palm to her sister. "Sophie, don't get carried away."

"And of course, you have every right to a happily ever after, just like everybody else. All the best romance stories start with a heroine who has a tragedy to overcome, and you've already had yours, so all that's left is the handsome prince and the magical future."

"I don't wish for my type of tragedy on anybody's happily ever after, Sophie."

Though God had more than brought her through the pain. He'd shrouded her with such support, and even now, the financial means to actually *see* the future she'd thought the pregnancy may have altered—or even ended altogether. Oh, He *loved* her so well.

"Of course you don't." Her sister sobered, a calm quiet filling the car for the first time during their ride, until her face brightened in the burst of sunlight shining through the passenger-side window. "But Henry?" She looked up, smile growing. "I can see him as a prince, you know? The quiet sort of hero with a deep-held passion that only surfaces when he meets the woman of his—"

"Sophie, don't. Okay?" Julia raised her palm to quell the verbal fairytale onslaught. "Can you imagine how horrified poor Henry would be if he even imagined us planning out his life? Oh, and did I mention that I'm *not* on the market right now. I may never be."

"Our nevers are just one of God's ways of making miracles."

"Sophie!"

Sophie huffed but her eyes still glimmered with her residual smile. "I still think you should talk to Karen about it."

Julia brought the car to a stop in front of the dealership and turned to her sister. "How about we focus on that cute teal car of yours and allow me to focus on this little person getting ready to join our family, okay?"

Sophie pinched her lips. "Okay. For now. But Julia, sometimes God uses what we least expect to bring us what we need the most."

Chapter Ten

*H*enry sat by the breakfast nook window, violin nestled in his hand and chin resting in place as his fingers searched for the notes playing in his mind. The mountains in the distance danced with the golden colors of the sunset, casting amber hues against everything within his view. A valley of molten sunlight.

The crunch of gravel followed by the snap of a closing car door drew him from the phantom melody in his head. As he slowly resurfaced into the present, he glanced down from his perch to see Julia struggling with what looked to be too many bags.

Without further hesitation, he laid his violin on the table and ran down the stairs, rushing toward her with the speed of a soccer player...but none of the grace. He tumbled over a random boot by the back door but recovered his footing before coming face-to-face with her. "Allow me to assist you with those."

Julia peeked at him as she negotiated an armful of sugar, flour, and other baking items, weariness in those large eyes pulling his steps forward even faster.

Henry gently tugged a few bags from her, his gaze searching hers for answers. "I think you're carrying quite enough already."

Her body relaxed against the side of her car. "I'd appreciate the help. I didn't mean to get so much at the store, but then I..." She held her silence for a moment until rallying with a confident tone. "How about I pay for your kindness in cookies?"

Her pale face belied the steadiness in her voice. Were those tears on her lashes? His heart stuttered through a helpless pang, but he pushed on a smile. "I...I like your cookies, but my kindness is always free." He collected almost all of the bags, and she reached in for the last one before leading the way into the house.

"Don't deny me the pleasure of watching you eat some of my famous dark-chocolate pecan-cluster cookies." The faintest light emerged in her watery eyes. "I love baking, but I like watching other people enjoy what I create even more."

He caught the door with his foot, holding it ajar until she stepped through.

"Thank you." Her gaze flickered to his as she moved past him, a single strand of golden hair slipping loose from her clips and falling across her face.

"My pleasure." He whispered the words but let his eyes freely roam hers for some hint to her sadness.

He followed her and her wisteria scent down the hallway to the kitchen and placed the bags on the counters, handing her items to put away. The silence groaned between them. How could he attempt to comfort her? What could he say? *Something. Anything.*

"I...I enjoy watching people respond to what I create too."

Her fingers stilled on the bag in her hand, and she quirked her lips into a half grin. "Our secret way of making an impact on others without having to be seen, eh?"

He chuckled. How could he bring out more of her smile? Or lessen the sadness in her eyes? Would she open up to him? He cleared his throat. Probably not but...but perhaps he could try. "It's a harrowing business, isn't it? I stand in awe of people like Wes, Eisley, your sister Sophie, my brother Elliott. They jump into those situations with such relative ease, even"—he shuddered— "pleasure."

Her shoulders gave the slightest shake from her quiet laugh. "It is a marvel. Sophie drinks it in like chocolate." She slipped off the lid of a white jar and turned to him, cookie in hand. "Speaking of chocolate."

He accepted the proffered cookie with a nod and bit into the moist dough, its sweet taste pooling over his tongue in soft, rich harmony.

"You know, as strange as it sounds"—her voice drew him closer, her profile thoughtful as she continued putting away groceries— "this bakery was my first step toward my real aspiration. My...heart dream... as Mama calls it."

"Your heart dream?"

She nodded and turned to face him. "I've always wanted to own my own inn or bed-and-breakfast. I love the idea of creating a getaway, a different world." She lowered her gaze to the counter, a flush darkening her cheeks. "Sophie says I'd be a fairy godmother to my guests—pop into people's lives to give them something special, watch them delight in it, and leave them with good memories." She shrugged a shoulder as she placed milk and eggs in the refrigerator. "That probably sounds silly."

"Not at all." He waved the uneaten half of his cookie at her. "You have a gift for it. Besides, I understand the pleasure of creating something beautiful, so others can revel in its purpose, absorb its being. Offer something unique and move them without words."

Their gazes locked. "Music," she whispered.

"Yes." He watched the sadness wane a little in her expression. "There's a sense of being a part of those people without the—"

"Pressure of *really* being a part of them."

"Exactly."

Her smile resurfaced. "And then there's knowing that you've used your talents to bring joy to others. That you've opened their eyes or hearts in ways they wouldn't have discovered on their own because they've been so busy engaging—"

"Instead of just observing and listening and—"

"Being." Her gaze flickered back to his. "Yes."

Quiet swelled around them as his face heated with thoughts of his own unvoiced "heart dream". For some reason—whether his own assumptions or ideals ingrained from his mother—he had the sense the simplicity of his dream proved too sentimental to ever voice aloud: the desire for a family of his own, one filled with tenderness and laughter and kindness rather than harsh demands and unattainable expectations. One with music and friendship.

But men didn't speak of such things freely, did they?

Perhaps not, but that didn't stop his prayers for the real thing.

"I think you'd make an excellent hostess for an inn." He raised the last bite of his cookie in the air. "And the guests would certainly benefit from your baking. These are delicious. I can only imagine the ease with which you make friends with this excellent fare."

Her eyes widened, and she shook her head, turning her face from him. "I... I..."

He rushed forward, almost placing his palm on her shoulder, but catching himself. Could his compliment have offended her? "Forgive me. What did I say?"

"It's...it's not you." She shook her head again, her glistening gaze flickering to his. "It's just that I...saw... I thought..."

His body and thoughts froze in concern at her trembling bottom lip. *Think, Henry!* "Julia, what is it? What do you need?"

She blinked up at him, a few tears spilling from her eyes. "Excuse me." She pushed past him and ran from the room, catching a sob as she exited.

He stood cemented to the spot, staring at the way she'd gone. What...what had happened? His shoulders sagged forward, and he leaned his palms against the counter, offering up a prayer for understanding. What had he done wrong?

Silence reigned in the room as he considered his potential errors until, with an echo loud enough to send his heart from Appalachia to England, music began.

The clash of piano chords shook him upright. Furious strains of Chopin's *Revolutionary Étude* blasted from down the hallway, almost loud enough to reverberate in his chest. No hesitancy in her skill nor reluctance in her abilities. Only...*fury.*

He slipped down the hall and peered into the room, palm paused on the doorframe. Julia sat with her head bent toward the keyboard, attention focused on her fingers' tempestuous assault on the keys and cheeks wet with tears.

Now he understood even better. She wasn't only sad but outraged and pouring her anger into Chopin's turbulent piece. Henry stared, transfixed as the melody climbed to another pinnacle over the left hand's storm and wrath. Should he leave? Stay?

Just as she reached the middle of the piece, a sob wracked her body and her fingers faltered over the notes. She smashed her hands down in a clash so crushing it seized his breath. Oh, the pain! It reverberated through him from the notes still lingering in the air to the thrumming of his pulse.

Let me help you, Julia.

She buried her face into her palms, releasing another pitiful cry, a sign she wanted privacy. He took a step back to the threshold, but another sob stalled his retreat. Perhaps...perhaps she needed a...friend.

"I thought I saw Peyton at the grocery store." Her muffled admission came from behind her palms. She sniffled and lowered her hands to her lap. "I...I haven't seen him since the courtroom, and I never want to see him again, but when I turned into a different aisle at the store, I thought he stood at the other end. And I froze."

Her watery gaze found his, so pained, so wounded. This time he stepped closer to her. Peyton. The cad who'd attacked Julia, no doubt. Henry's fist tightened at his side. "He's not in prison?"

She shook her head and wiped a hand beneath her eyes, her smile too hesitant to be sincere. "The court found him not guilty because of a lack of evidence..." A flush crawled up her cheeks, and she pushed the short pieces of blond hair that had fallen away from her braid behind her ears. "That it wasn't consensual." Her gaze shot to his. "It *wasn't* consensual. He drugged me, but by the time I reported what had happened, the police couldn't find a trace of whatever it was in my system, and then..."

"Scoundrel." Henry's word choice was an unsatisfactory slur, not strong enough to describe the unconscionable deed done to this gentle and beautiful woman. His chest squeezed with the effort to maintain his composure. What he really wanted to do was punch something, particularly the villain who'd attacked her.

Julia's expression softened at his response. "Everyone in the court room knew the truth, but no one could prove it beyond doubt. Thankfully, the outcry from the community did what the court couldn't. He'd gained such a reputation that he moved away, but his family all still live here, and then...in that moment, in the store, I thought it was him." Her bottom lip quivered again. "And I didn't know what to do. How...how to fight."

He desperately wanted to hold her, to comfort her, but they weren't well enough acquainted for such a gesture. But how could he show her he treasured the fact that she'd entrusted him with her wounds? Offer her some solace? "I am so sorry, Julia."

His words appeared to unlock some barrier. Tears rushed down her reddened cheeks while her fingers reached for the chain around her neck. "Everything in my life has changed because of that one night. New fears. Horrible nightmares. I've postponed my senior year of college so that I can be available for the baby." She sniffled, placing her hand on her protruding abdomen. "I'm thankful for him. Of course, he's not to blame. But everyone outside my family...well...they see me as broken in some way now. Even though it wasn't my fault. It's impossible to go back to the way things were. To who I was." Her palm rose. "Tonight, I went to the pizza place my friends and I used to go to every Tuesday evening during the semester. They'd told me they weren't meeting anymore."

His stomach dropped at the intimation. *No.*

"But there they were."

He closed his eyes, the ache for her loss and frustration over her "friends" shallowness branching through him.

Her joyless laugh sliced into the silence. "I should have known, you know? Almost all of them stopped calling months ago and came up with the most ridiculous excuses not to see me when I'd try to get together." She wiped another hand beneath her eyes. "And...and it takes a lot of courage to try." A deep breath sighed out of her, the weight of her sorrows drifting toward him like the echoes of Chopin's étude. "I'm still *me*, you know? It's a new me in some ways, but I'm still here and want to be seen...to feel I matter."

I see you. You matter. He fumbled for his back jeans pocket, tugged out his handkerchief, and handed it to her.

"Thank you." She smiled and took the offering. "You know, Eisley talked about Wes having a handkerchief at the ready, but I didn't actually believe how...how valiant it would feel to have a man offer you one when you're sobbing like a baby."

"You have every right to cry, to grieve."

She wiped at her face again, sniffling and shaking her head. "I'm sorry to dump all this on you, Henry. You're so kind to listen, but here I've been pouring out my horrible story—"

"No, please don't apologize. I count it an honor you feel safe sharing your thoughts with me..." He raised a brow. "As a *true* friend..."

Her attention flickered between his face and the floor as if she were uncertain whether or not to trust his words. On the last rise upward, her gaze held his, she lowered the handkerchief, and a small smile crossed her face. "Thank you."

"I hope you never see the cad who hurt you ever again, but if you do, I'm certain you're strong enough to face him." His jaw clenched before his last words forced their way out. "And I'll stand with you, ready to dispose of the body, should you need me to."

She blinked at him, and then seemed to catch on to his semi-teasing, because her smile widened a little more, inspiring his confidence to continue talking—even for an idea to take shape. "The best of friends, I see."

"Of course." He sobered. "And, I'm sorry to say, those friends of yours aren't friends at all if this is how they behave." Heat swirled from his chest into his face as he stepped out on a hunch. "In fact, I'm furious for you and think the only proper thing to do is..." He searched the room, hoping to lighten the mood again. "Have you a four-hands piece—perhaps a Chopin polonaise or one of Liszt's Hungarian rhapsodies?"

"Or the four-hands *Pirates of the Caribbean* main theme?" The beautiful twinkle in her eyes doused some of the sadness that had lingered there only moments before.

His smile joined hers. He'd guessed right. "An excellent choice."

"Played with a great deal of fury?" She pulled a book from the nearby shelf and placed it onto the piano, her brow raised in challenge.

He slid beside her onto the bench, cracking his knuckles in a dramatic flourish. "With all the fury this piano can stand." He tilted his chin in her direction. "Saavy?"

Her shoulder touched his, and her sweet smile somehow made him feel like the hero he'd always wanted to be. "Saavy."

Chapter Eleven

*S*awdust covered the ground between dozens of tents and vendors at the base of a towering mountainside, as music flooded in from every direction. The strum of guitar. The ting of the mandolin. A run of a banjo or two. And then there was the raw, authentic beauty of the native voices.

Eisley had encouraged Henry to visit the annual bluegrass festival in the nearby town of Orchard Falls, and he was grateful she'd thrust him out of his comfort zone. The scene brought the benefit of excellent research and the engaging musical talent of the native musicians, but Henry's focus kept wandering back to last evening's time with Julia.

She'd left him with a smile after they'd played through three more four-hands piano pieces, ending with a classic that wasn't quite as furious as the previous ones. Sitting beside her somehow fit his world in a way nothing else every had. There was understanding and...fun, and despite his fumbling, he knew his presence had mattered to her, that he'd done something to touch her heart, and all he wanted to do next was to see how he could make it happen again.

And again.

Would God use Henry to help Julia heal?

God, I am willing. Would you help me...help her?

He sat in front of a large outdoor stage, listening to a vast array of music the natives labeled as "old timey", and enjoying the variety, ingenuity, and talent swarming all over these hills. The entire morning had unfolded with inspiration, from jigs and English-sounding reels to heart wrenching ballads. Some left a lonely, unsettled ache behind. Some even called upon his heart to pray. The culture and history pulsed through the music like no other genre he'd studied.

The announcer introduced the final act before the lunch break. Three people—an older gentleman, fiddle in hand, a young woman with a long dark braid down her back, and a man holding...a homemade flute? The two men dressed in typical clothes of the other men around Henry. Jeans, t-shirt, and a large flannel-type button-up hanging open. But the woman wore a dress of vibrant colors, rainbow-like, perhaps a nod back to their Celtic ancestry?

The crowd's applause drifted into silence, and, after an almost reverent hesitation, the man brought the bow to the strings. A lonely solo with a melody as haunting and fascinating as any from the Irish coast swelled to life from the fiddler, a caress on the breeze, a haunting whisper.

Henry's breath caught.

The tone rose into the quiet—a tune faintly familiar from his childhood, yet new. What was it? *The Ballad of Captain Kidd?* He'd never heard it played like this— with unique embellishments to give the song an even greater peculiarity. A deeper sense of yearning.

Henry closed his eyes, allowing the melody to seep through him and settle deep as the first verse finished. The flute joined on the second, a hollowed-out sound at one with the wind through the trees, their duet rising and leading to the next verse when.... the woman joined, with a voice unlike those he'd heard within studios or concert halls—a native one raw with emotion and natural talent.

What wondrous love is this, oh my soul, oh my soul!
What wondrous love is this, oh my soul!
What wondrous love is this that caused the Lord of bliss
To bear the sinful curse for my soul, for my soul,
To bear the sinful curse for my soul.

Henry leaned closer, the perfect combination of words and tune captivating him. They'd take an old English tune and transformed it to their culture, blending two worlds. This was the theme of Wes's movie. This melody needed to weave its way through the corridors of the scenes and story, displaying the constancy of faith and the faithfulness of love.

As was so often the case with perfect word-melody pairing, the tune brought out the message of the song with more clarity than either could do alone. God's love displayed how? By Christ stepping into a curse to save souls. The truest act of love and courage.

The woman's fresh cadence continued.

When I was sinking down, sinking down, sinking down,
Christ laid aside his crown for my soul.
Another telltale sign to the depth of love.
To God and to the Lamb, I will sing, I will sing.
While millions join the theme, I will sing.

Her voice lingered in the air with the strains of the fiddle and flute and the soul-stirring message. Unashamed. Bold. Beautiful.

Henry's eyes burned.

The same passion and boldness for faith, the same love he'd witnessed in the Jenkinses reverberated in this straightforward text. Oh, to have the gift of words—so simple yet profound. The melody braided in his mind with the endless horizon and the recent tenderness of the time he'd spent with Julia. He'd found his focus for this soundtrack. Now, to braid the music and message into something of his own.

Wes picked him up from festival shortly after the fiddler and singer finished their piece, keeping the conversation to a minimum on the late drive back to the apartment. Wes disappeared upstairs as soon as they entered the bakery, but Henry paused at the bottom of the stairs.

Put the melody to string first or find Julia?

He liked her more than he ought to, especially for a man who lived in a different country and a woman who probably had no intention of seeking a romantic relationship for a long time.

But he couldn't help it. She was genuinely kind. A lover of music—and not just that, but an *understand-er* of music.

His feet turned toward the music room, but it was empty except for the baby grand standing sentry by the window. He paused, took in a breath, and kept walking, bypassing the dining area and peeking around the back doorway into the kitchen. She stood at the counter, working some dough with her hands, a lump of white—he supposed was bread—sat in a pan to one side of her and a long tray with smaller dots of dough waited on the other. Her blond hair sat on top of her head in some sort of messy bun, a style that drew his attention to the elegance in her profile. Warmth rushed to his face, and he looked away, only to have his attention fall on a familiar piece of paper pinned to the board above her work station.

The paper he'd left on the communication board for her. What had she thought of his note? Had it been too much? Too sentimental?

He started to turn away, but she caught sight of him first, her surprised smile holding him captive in an endless *fermata*. She gestured with her chin toward the paper. "Where words fail, music speaks."

"Hans Christian Anderson."

Her attention turned back to the note. "But music shared with a friend is even sweeter." She met his gaze. "Thank you for last night."

His shoulders relaxed at the acceptance, the welcome in her voice. "I was happy to be there and...helpful." He cleared his throat—attempting to navigate this shift in their relationship without blundering too much— and gestured toward the counter. "I don't wish to distract you from your work."

"I'm only preparing some pastries for tomorrow." She raised a brow and a white glob of dough. "Want to help?"

∞ ∞ ∞

Want to help? Had she said that out loud? What on earth was she doing? A few amazing piano duets and a good cry, and she was inviting him to bake with her?

And yet, Henry Wright brought calm and gentleness with him that set her tremulous heart at ease in the most surprising of ways. A steadiness. Whether from their mutual introversion or a little divine intervention, she felt as though she knew him. She understood him. And if she were completely honest with herself, she wanted to know more.

He blinked at her offer then shifted his feet as if uncertain how to respond. Her grin resurfaced. He was so likeable and wonderfully easy to rescue.

"I... I would be happy to help but I'm no baker."

"Only if you're not willing to learn."

That subtle smile of his tipped slightly, sending her heart into an *andantino* tempo. He took a hesitant step forward into the kitchen. "I'm willing, if you're sure?"

"I'm sure." She slid to the side and made room for him at her counter. "Actually, I'm making a few things you might enjoy." She gestured toward two poms of dough in front of her. "Blueberry scones and caramel toffee scones, in yours and Wes's honor."

He moved beside her. "I do have a fondness for scones. Even more now."

"Perfect, then." She shifted a bit awkwardly to reach the plastic wrap on the counter in front of him, catching the faint hint of his vanilla and amber scent. Oh, she remembered that from last night. The wonderful aroma awakened a craving for some vanilla butter cookies with a dash of cinnamon.

"How are you today? Better?"

His question probed much deeper than obligatory, pulling upon their last conversation. She placed the wrap around the first pom of dough. "Better than I was."

"I'm glad."

"How about you wrap this one?" She slid the other dough toward him, attempting to take the focus off her. "We'll put the dough in the refrigerator for about a half hour while we make some dark chocolate cupcakes."

He stared at her, those myriad-hued eyes wide. "The refrigerator?"

"The dough is easier to cut when it's cold." She pushed the plastic wrap his way.

He followed her example with painstaking precision, reminding her of when Eisley's son Nathan had helped her make chocolate chip cookies for the first time. Careful to please.

"This way?"

She nodded and carried the dough to the large, double-door refrigerator, taking advantage of the distance and silence to gather her thoughts. He deserved a more thorough answer, and after last night, she wanted to give him one. "I've healed a lot over the past seven-and-a-half months. It's just that sometimes, like yesterday, things hit at once, and all those months shrink away."

"I can't imagine the pain you must carry."

She pushed an errant strand of hair off her cheek with the back of her arm and began pouring the ingredients into her mixing bowl. "I keep reminding myself that God brings the most beautiful things out of the most difficult situations. I've *seen* it happen. I know it happens"—she tapped her head with the back of her hand— "but it's easy to forget here." She pressed the back of her hand to the center of her chest, where the ache of yesterday gave a weak pang. Yes, God was healing her, through time and family and... She grinned at Henry. And new friends. "Would you pass me the sugar and cocoa?"

It took him a moment to register her words, but he turned to the containers on his left, examining them with the same intensity with which he'd listened to her until he made the proper choices and pushed the bags her way. "I learned an Appalachian song today that reminded me of your circumstances." He cleared his throat and looked away. "I mean not your...circumstances...but how you've endured. I wonder if you might have heard it. 'What Wondrous Love is This?'"

"Oh, that's a wonderful song. Would you hand me that measuring cup?"

His eyes sparkled as he followed her request. "The melody and words are perfect together, and I thought about you...and...your family. The love you have." He hesitated. "The love and courage Christ has given you."

Her hand paused on the measuring cup. "You...you think I have courage?"

His gaze softened into hers, the strange awareness that he somehow *saw* her and found her fascinating shifted from his eyes into her heart. The last thing she felt most days was fascinating—especially since she was starting to wear the same four outfits over and over for sheer comfort. Between swelling ankles and an occasionally puffy nose, the only time she garnered attention was when inadvertently wearing cooking ingredients or...battling unseemly mishaps with skirts and a strong breeze.

He stared at her in silence, his brow puckered. "Of course you have courage. A tremendous amount of it. Look how far you've come after what happened to you. You're facing your future with hope even though your life has been altered, and yet, you still dream. What is courage, if not, in part, continuing to dream even when there are nightmares?"

Her eyes stung. He *did* see. "You saw that in me through a song?"

"Indeed. Your family is much more open about faith than I've ever known." He smiled with a shrug. "We Brits aren't usually as demonstrative about personal things unless they involve sports...or sometimes politics, and perhaps the theatre."

She chuckled.

"But the song references what Christ had to endure to show His love to His children. He went to the cross, but not only that, He had to face the fear of separation from His Father, all because of this...this immense love. The same courage and love that live in *you* because...because you belong to Him."

His face blurred in her vision, and she shoved the measuring cup into the sugar. If the same bravery that kept Christ on the road to the cross lived in her then she had all the courage she ever needed and then some. "I...I hadn't thought about it that way."

She sniffled as she poured the sugar into her mixing bowl followed by the cocoa, her voice too uncertain to respond.

"If I may say so, your child is fortunate to have such a mother."

She offered a weak laugh and dropped her palm to her burgeoning middle. "I think he will definitely be that something beautiful out of a horrible situation."

"He?"

"Well, I don't really know for certain, but I just feel like the baby is a boy." A sudden kick seemed to confirm her words. Or negate them. She wasn't sure. "A very busy little boy." She pushed the mixing bowl toward Henry. "Will you stir that while I get the eggs and mixer?"

The slow scrape of metal against metal followed her to the fridge and back, but his words lingered, soaking into her thoughts.

"You know, I've always been fascinated with baking. Or at least learning about it."

She came back to his side. "Oh goodness, don't let my dad hear you say that. It'll knock your manly points down a few notches."

Without warning, his chuckle swelled into a laugh, with which she couldn't help but join in. The sound sparked some sort of inner glow through her chest, and the fact she'd inspired it...well, that was even better. She snatched the egg carton to her left and placed it between them. "Here, you crack half of the eggs, and I'll crack the other half."

He looked from the carton back to her face, his eyebrows almost at his hairline. "Are you sure?"

"No way to learn except by practicing, right?"

He quieted, focusing on his task until every egg was cracked without issue.

"See, look at you." She placed the mixer in the bowl and turned it on low. "You're a natural."

"You're very kind." But he did look a bit proud of himself—and the expression didn't hurt his handsomeness one bit. "As far as your father's manliness rating of me is concerned, I feel confident I'm so far in the negative numbers that there's no way out. I'm a musician"—he ticked the word off on his finger— "an introvert, I wear button-up shirts, and I talk funny."

Julia laughed so hard she had to turn off the mixer for fear of losing her grip and smattering Henry with another dose of batter. Her eyes watered for a whole new reason, and the grin he bestowed on her communicated that he understood the significance of the apparently insignificant action.

He'd inspired her laughter. And if the pitter-patter of her heart meant anything, he might have encouraged something more. Her gaze softened in his. The world around them paused in recognition of the sweetness.

Oh dear, she *liked* him.

"There you are, Twinkle Toes."

Nate Jenkins himself burst into the kitchen and clashed against the contented quiet with his usual boldness, dissipating the warm fuzzies.

Julia shuffled back a step, reorienting herself, her thoughts.

Henry took a step back too and almost lost his balance, which tickled her funny bone to life again. He gave a helpless shrug and pushed the mixing bowl between them as if a physical object might provide an ample barrier between them to keep her daddy's unwelcome comments at bay.

"Twinkle Toes?" Julia squinted toward her bear of a daddy. "Henry is a *composer.*"

He frowned through an indifferent shrug. "Same difference. He does something fancy with music."

Julia squeezed her eyes closed and pushed her fingers into her forehead. "Dad, his name is Henry. Would you please use it?" Julia shot Henry an exaggerated grin, fake to the core, to which Henry responded with a one-shoulder shrug in apparent acceptance of her daddy's unique brand of nicknames.

"Now, why would I do that? I already have a good name for Wes." Her daddy's smile turned ruthless, and he thumbed over his shoulder just as Wes entered the kitchen. "But Fancy Pants can't help me tomorrow morning."

"As I told you, Nate, I need to work in Summit and Maple Springs." Wes cast Julia and Henry a knowing look. "Making a movie and all that."

Her daddy's grimace deepened, and he waved away Wes's comment. He was the embodiment of incorrigible.

"I wouldn't call movie-makin' work a'tall, boy." The wicked glint in her daddy's eyes would have been comical if Julia didn't dread where the conversation was going. "I'd call that playin' dress up."

Wes didn't even flinch at the direct jab, which proved he knew Nate Jenkins well. All talk and tease, not a whole lot of meanness—though his brazen thoughts-to-words tendency didn't always rub people the right way. Especially new folks.

Wes flourished a dramatic bow. "If playing dress up pays the bills, how can you argue, good man?"

Her daddy exaggerated his groan, but the glimmer of fun still lit his expression as he leveled his full attention on Henry. Julia wanted to jump between the two men to protection her soft-hearted friend, but that would only further stir her daddy's teasing. "You got some dress up to play tomorrow too?" He examined the batter, looked at Julia, and focused again on Henry. "Well, clearly he ain't got enough work to do if you're teachin' him how to bake."

Past conversations indicated this could produce a panic moment for Henry, but quite to the contrary, his smile quirked. And Julia's heartbeat picked up. Oh dear. Was he beginning to understand her father a little?

She rushed to the defense of her profession and creative men in general. "Dad! Some of the best chefs in the world are men."

Her daddy placed his palms on his hips as if examining the hopeless situation. "Now's the time to lay them floors, boy."

Wes frantically shook his head in Henry's direction.

"Actually, Nate," Henry started, "I think that—"

"Don't you pay no mind to Fancy Pants behind me, boy." He placed a massive palm on Henry's shoulder. "I reckon since you like spending so much time in the kitchen, then I'll give you something to do besides lollygagging." Dad slid a look to Julia before gesturing to the storage room behind them. "Julia had a leak a month back, and I'm just now gettin' to fixin' it, and you're my lucky volunteer. Besides, we're expanding the kitchen, and now's as good a time as any."

Henry's face paled.

"Dad, Henry has other things to—"

"Come on, now. He can get right back to writin' his fancy music after he learns how to lay a floor. Life skills." He tapped his forehead. "Never know when it will come in handy." He slapped Henry on the back, nearly toppling him.

Julia cringed. "Dad."

"Don't worry one bit, boy. I'll go easy on ya. We'll make those pretty fingers of yours a little sore, but we won't break 'em." He leaned close and winked. "Unless my nail gun don't like you." Her dad released a loud laugh.

Wes's palms rose helplessly.

"Dad, I think—"

"It's alright, Julia. Truly." Henry released a sigh of...resignation? Frustration? No, his expression boasted a teensy bit of humor, if she knew her new friend at all. Henry Wright might not need as much protection as she thought.

"In fact,"—he turned to her daddy— "Julia and I were just discussing how to be brave, Nate, and I feel fairly certain time with you is a sure way of improving my courage."

Her dad, brow furrowed, stared at Henry for a full five seconds as if digesting his words and "funny talk." A laugh burst out. "Ain't that the truth. If there's anything I'm good at, it's improving a city boy's courage."

Chapter Twelve

*E*isley weaved through the dining room of Julia's bakery. Destination: kitchen and a bacon-and-egg breakfast sandwich. Nathan followed behind, a book clutched by his side as usual. She tossed a wave to her cousin, Amy, who stood at the register, her walnut-colored curls back in a ponytail. "Good morning."

"Back atcha." She pointed her pen toward the kitchen doors, her periwinkle eyes narrowing in warning. "Your take-out's in the back, Eis, but watch out for the noise."

"Noise?"

"Your dad's laying the new floor for the kitchen expansion, and he's pulled Henry in on the work. I don't think I've heard Henry say a word since they started, but Uncle Nate's filled the silence without any trouble."

"I have no doubt." Eisley groaned and slowed her pace. "And exactly *when* did they start?"

"They were already back there when I arrived."

Eisley winced. Amy usually pulled in about five thirty in the morning. Why, oh why, did her dad feel the need to do the dominant 'rooster' action with any guy who acted like he was from a city?

Julia stepped out of the pantry just as Eisley and Nathan entered the kitchen. Her dark blue eyes, so much like their mama's, glimmered above a genuine smile that, after months of hiding behind the pain of her attack, was beginning to appear more often. "Stopping by at nine o'clock on a Friday morning, Eisley? Aren't you supposed to be at work?"

"I had to take Nathan to the eye doctor to fix his glasses." She tousled her eldest's sandy hair. "We've stopped in to grab a quick breakfast treat before I drop him off at school then head to work."

Julia stepped to the counter and opened one of the compartments. "Hey, Nathan, I have a couple of those chocolate croissants you like."

"Yep, let's sugar him up right before social studies class." Eisley caught the two croissants in transit and passed one to her frowning seven-year-old. "How about a cup of Greek yogurt with that, sis? Or a piece of bacon? Or something to counterbalance the sweets?"

"I tried, buddy." Julia grinned at Nathan and passed along a yogurt from the fridge.

Aunts and grandparents. They could get away with *anything.*

"At least I got out of school for the morning." Nathan's smirk curled his adorable little nose. "I missed the entire P.E. class."

"You go, man." Julia raised a palm for a high-five.

"You really shouldn't encourage him in his truancy, Julia." Eisley barely held her grin in check. "It's not very auntly of you."

"We introverts have to take care of each other...in a nonintrusive, low stress kind of way." She shot Nathan a wink.

Eisley's laugh burst free. "Right."

"And it's P.E." She shuddered, passing Nathan a plastic spoon for his yogurt. "I don't want to ever relive *those* memories. They're almost as fun as pep rallies."

"What's a pep rally?"

"I'll warn you long before you need to know, buddy." Julia leaned close. "Just remember, there's no shame in hiding in the bathroom."

His hazel eyes grew wide. "Are they as bad as spelling bees?"

Julia gasped and her palm flew to her chest. "No way. Nothing is as bad as spelling bees—even when you know all the words, like a smart kid like you. On a stage!"

He shuddered. "And all the people watching!"

"I loved spelling bees. *And* pep rallies." Eisley's statement, punctuated with her hands on her hips and a quirked eyebrow, meant nothing to her sister and son based on the knowing look they exchanged.

Introverts. Seriously? Pep rallies were awesome! One of the highlights of her high school experience had been when she volunteered to dress up as the mascot for one of them. A pirate, complete with the giant, suffocating head. *Good times.* "I thought you were going off to Aunt Millie's today. You don't have much more time to clear out the house, right? Doesn't the moving truck come in two weeks or something like that?"

"I know." Julia shot a look to the back room. "But I couldn't leave Henry *alone* with Dad. Can you imagine? I mean, it's not like Henry can't take care of himself, but it's...*Dad.*"

"Good gravy, Julia. It's not like you're a walking time bomb yet, but you are cutting it close." Eisley scanned her sister's protruding abdomen, a little envious that the baby bump looked considerably smaller than anything she remembered carrying. "We need to figure out a way to rescue Henry *and* get you to Aunt Millie's, despite Dad's 'toughen up the city boys' routine."

"Well, I have to admit, Henry's handled him well." Her sister's gaze drifted to the back room, a gentle smile softening her entire expression. Something was...different. No worried crinkles in Julia's brow. No twisting of the necklace until it looked like she might choke.

Julia *liked* Henry.

Eisley's lips slid into a slow, wonderfully match-make-y smile. Oh, yes, there was definitely something there that wasn't there before! The matchmaker melody from *Fiddler on the Roof* resounded in her head in full chorus to such a degree that Eisley almost started swaying to the imaginary beat. She blinked out of her daydream, and a sudden idea formed into a plan of yenta proportions. "I think I can fix this."

Julia froze in her walk back across the kitchen and turned. "Fix?"

She raised a finger to her sister to "hold on" and then marched through the kitchen. "Just leave this to me."

Eisley followed the hammering sound and found her dad on his knees, nail gun in hand, with a gloved Henry holding a glossy wood floor plank. His hair stood in erratic confusion—she hoped more sweat-induced than getting toggled around by a gruffy mountain man.

"I see you've roped poor Henry in as your wingman today, Dad?"

Her dad's head came up from his work. "He needed something worthwhile to do." Dad nodded toward his unlikely cohort. "And he's been a good help. Smart one, there. Too quiet for anybody's peace of mind, but we've gotten along alright, ain't we, Twinkle Toes?"

Twinkle Toes? Eisley looked at Julia, who rolled her eyes heavenward.

"I'm grateful for the opportunity to learn, actually." Henry grinned and shifted his position to get a better grip on the flooring. "And Nate says we've made great time."

"Should be done in 'bout an hour, I reckon."

Eisley examined the work. They *were* making good progress, in more ways than just the floor. Perhaps her plan would work better than she'd hoped. "Hey, Dad, Julia and I were just talking, and she's heading to Aunt Millie's today. You know how much work she still has to do with sorting and all?"

"A whole house full of crazy stuff." Her dad shot another couple of nails.

"Well, she feels a little uncomfortable traveling all that way out there alone since she's so close to delivery."

"Eisley, I never said—"

Eisley ignored her sister's harsh whisper. "Any ideas who could ride up there with her for the day and maybe help her move some of those boxes?"

"Did you check with your mama?"

"She's tending to Emily, remember?"

"That's right." Dad rocked back on his heels and looked at the ceiling. "Did you check with Greg?"

Eisley bit her bottom lip. If her dad kept going with his list of names, she'd never get Julia alone with Henry. "You know how he is. Off on some veterinarian adventure somewhere. I doubt he'd be available."

"Rick's gone to pick up computer parts in Mt. Airy, or she could ask him." Nate narrowed his eyes and studied Julia. "I reckon she ought not to be moving any of them big boxes in the shape she's in. Don't want baby Jenkins comin' before his time."

"Definitely." Eisley shrugged. "I'd help but I have to get to work. And you've got to finish that porch on the back of Creed Spencer's house while the sun's shinin', right?"

He rubbed his jaw and scanned the room. Eisley nearly squeezed her hands together waiting for the realization to happen.

Dad slapped his knee. "Well, why don't she take Henry with her! He ain't got nothing better to do."

Eureka!

The exchange between Julia and Henry confirmed Eisley's matchmaking joy. Their gazes locked with shock first then melted into a sort of shy curiosity. "Dad, that's a great idea! As long as Henry doesn't mind."

"I...I'm sure Henry has work to do." Julia's voice edged up half an octave. "And...and I wouldn't want to inconvenience him."

"It's no inconvenience." Henry's quiet response, paired with the look he gave her sister, confirmed all the fairy dust twinkling to life in Eisley's head. "I'd be happy to help."

"And if you're worried about getting through Aunt Millie's papers, I'll pop by this afternoon before my date with Wes and help you sort them."

Julia's eyes widened, and she looked to Henry, who shared the same shocked expression as her sister. He stood from his place on the floor, his mouth opening to speak but releasing nothing. What was going on?

"No, no." Julia's palm came out as if to console. "I really appreciate your willingness to help, but there's no need to come to the apartment this evening. Just...enjoy your night with Wes."

"Right. And...and if she needs extra help with...papers, I can offer my services," Henry added, a little rushed.

Eisley narrowed her eyes, attempting to peel away what little secret these two held.

"Exactly," Julia agreed. "I'm sure Henry is a great...paper sorter."

Her sister cringed, apparently realizing she'd agreed with Henry's offer a little too quickly, and his smile stretched so far it completely distracted Eisley from her suspicions. They were perfect for each other—and completely horrible at hiding anything.

"What's going on?"

Julia backed toward the door. "Taking your advice, of course, as younger sisters should."

Eisley rolled her eyes. Her sisters hardly ever took her advice.

"Y'all are about to drive me crazy, that's what going on. Ain't you got places you need to be?" Her dad pushed himself up from the floor and began pointing his nail gun as he talked, starting with Eisley. "You need to get that grandson of mine to school." He shifted the nail gun toward Henry and Julia. "And y'all don't seem to be in too much of a hurry to get to Aunt Millie's house for sortin' whatever it is you're gonna sort. I've a mind to put Henry back to work, is what I think."

"No, no." Julia's cheeks reddened while she fidgeted with her apron strings. "We'll be on our way now, right, Henry?"

"Indeed." He nodded toward her dad and stepped up to the door. "If you're certain I can't help you further, Nate."

"Right now, the best thing y'all can do for me is give me some peace and quiet to get some work done," he grumbled then winked at Nathan.

Eisley sent Julia and Henry a wave as they ran from the room, and then took a long-awaited bite into the chocolate croissant she still held in her hand. "Something's going on around here, Dad. I sense it."

"Well, why don't you sense your way right over there to the wood by your foot and hand it over so I can finish this job." His sentence pulled her from staring at the doorway through which Julia and Henry had disappeared.

She sighed and reached for the wood. "Oh Dad, what am I going to do with you?"

∞ ∞ ∞

"Do you think she suspects anything?" Henry slid into the passenger seat and closed the door, the sparkle of mischief in his eyes unfurling the laugh Julia had stuffed underneath the need to get out of the kitchen before she spilled Wes's engagement party secret.

"I think we're pretty horrible secret-keepers, Henry." She started the car and reversed out of the space, casting him a look as she did so.

He chuckled and turned her way, buckling his seatbelt. "I'm brilliant at keeping secrets if no one asks me questions about them, but once pinpointed?"

"Guilty as charged." She shook her head and put the car into drive. "Maybe it's a good thing we're going to be out of the way for most of the day. We'll be less likely to blow the entire surprise."

"And once we return, I can help with decorations."

"That would be amazing." She shot him a look from her periphery. "But, I'm sorry you got roped into going with me in the first place. Don't you have an appointment with one of the luthiers today?"

"I phoned him this morning and rescheduled." His gaze met hers. "We agreed on this plan with Wes together. We should finish it together, don't you think?"

She shoved her hair behind her ears and faced him head-on, biting back a sliver of worry. The thought of spending time with him inspired her pulse into an *accelerando* with contradictory undertones of panic and hope. "Thank you."

Quiet followed for a few minutes as Julia adjusted to his presence beside her and navigated the transition from town to the increasingly unpredictable backroad toward her aunt's house. Though the silence carried a little awkwardness, something about Henry's natural gentle demeanor tamped down the tension in her shoulders.

She trusted him. And that hadn't happened with a man in a long time.

"Hey, Henry." She waited for him to look at her before she continued, acknowledging the breaking of the silence and giving him time to focus on her words rather than the passing woods he watched through the window. "We're going to be heading way back into the mountains to get to Aunt Millie's house, so the road may be a little bumpy."

"I've enjoyed what I've seen of your mountains so far." His finger slid over his phone without making any contact with buttons. A nervous action, perhaps? He had long slender fingers—she'd noticed them when he played the piano. Elegant. Strong.

"I...I hope my presence doesn't cause you to be uncomfortable, though."

His gentle response pulled another glance from her periphery. She drew in a deep breath and returned her attention to the road, sifting through her pretzel-like emotions for a solid answer. "I...I'm not uncomfortable with you."

His fingers paused in their movements. "I thought...perhaps..."

"Me too." Her lips tipped up on one side. "I think...I think it may be partially because I know you're as nervous as I am. A kind of kinship."

"I suppose we must stick together."

"Especially in the face of challenging personalities like my dad's."

The awkwardness unwound a little more with his chuckle. "I believe he meant to frighten the introversion out of me."

Her laugh tumbled out. "And he only gets louder the quieter you are."

His palms rose. "In my defense, I did try to talk once the shock had worn down. I'm much better one-on-one."

"Me too."

She nestled into the comfortable silence among...friends. Her smile spread despite her best attempts. A vanilla-smelling, British-speaking, tenderhearted friend. *That* sounded a whole lot like a cupcake with all the extras.

And she loved cupcakes.

The road narrowed a little more, losing some of its refined pavement to partial gravel.

"We *are* going into the country." He gripped the door handle.

She tightened her hold on the steering wheel, tossing him a grin. "I'm scaring you, huh?"

"I may or may not have the theme from *Psycho* playing in my head right now."

Her laugh erupted again. "It *does* seem to be the quiet ones you have to look out for, remember."

His chuckle tingled a welcome hum over her skin, and even Little One joined the fun with a kick or two. What was happening here? Could she truly feel safe enough to *care* about this man? Heat returned to her cheeks. She really needed to talk to her counselor.

"Actually, Henry, you might find Aunt Millie's story interesting."

He sat up straighter and focused on her, his rapt attention encouraging her to continue.

"She was a world-renowned pianist during the 1940s."

"Your Aunt Millie—who lived out here, in the middle of nowhere—was a world renown pianist?"

"I know. It's as much a mystery to me, and I probably knew her better than anyone except her housekeeper, Sissy. But Millie never talked much about her past... After her death, she left me a strange letter. Something about how I would discover who she really was as I went through her things."

"And have you found anything?"

"Nothing, really, but I've mostly been marking furniture instead of going through drawers and boxes. It's something I hope to start today." She gestured with her chin to his phone. "You should look her up."

His phone lit to life at his touch.

"Her name was Amelia Dawn Rippey," Julia continued. "But most of the time she went by Amelia Dawn on stage."

The car became quiet as he read through the information Google pulled on her aunt. Stuff she knew because she'd researched it too.

"She toured for a couple of years on her own, then joined a cellist." The old photograph of her aunt on stage in front of a piano filtered through Julia's mind as she recalled her aunt's history. What story was left to uncover?

"Lucas Randolph."

"Exactly. And from the snippets I've been able to piece together from things Aunt Millie said, the two of them became romantically involved."

"And a heartbreak pushed her from the spotlight?"

She rewarded his question with a grin. He was actually interested in this quirky little mystery of hers. Her twin brother, Greg, had yawned through her explanations, her dad only took in so much before he needed a change of topic, and her mom listened sweetly but didn't ask many questions...and definitely didn't make conjectures.

He gestured toward his phone's screen. "That's the abrupt ending of her career? Or as is reported here, 'After her performance on March 7, 1944, Amelia Dawn disappeared from the musical world.'"

"She became pregnant."

"Ah!"

"Right." Julia's kinship to her aunt deepened even more as she spoke. "So she came here, built an extravagant house in the middle of nowhere, and gave birth to a daughter."

His raised brow asked the question Julia had known would be next.

"Her daughter, Roslyn, died when she was a child."

"And so your aunt remained hidden from the world? Nursing her grief, I would suspect."

Julia nodded, turning on to the crooked mountain road that lead into Shadow Gap. "She became the ultimate recluse yet kept her panache. Her house is immaculate, almost as if she were waiting for a very special guest to arrive at any moment."

"Her lover, perhaps? Come to find her after all the years?"

"Oooh." A chill ran over her arms at his suggestion. "Nice! Brainstorming with you is about as exciting as brainstorming with Sophie."

His chuckle brewed across the space between them. "I can't imagine anything competing with Sophie's overall enthusiasm."

"Oh goodness, no! You should see her after a candy run." She waved a hand toward his phone. "You may as well put your phone away now, Henry. It's going to become useless once we pass that red barn over there.

"What do you mean?"

"The mountains block any cell phone service from this point on."

His brows crinkled into a V. "But when I purchased the phone for this trip, I was informed it should have excellent reception."

"And it probably does...anywhere else except this part of the Blue Ridge Mountains. There are places around here that are notorious for cloaking reception or completely annihilating it."

"Which does give an added mystery to your aunt's story."

Julia flipped her gaze back to his. "What do you mean?"

"Well, if she was determined to disappear or not have the world find her, she chose the perfect place."

Chapter Thirteen

The house stood frozen in time.

Henry had helped Julia tag a few furniture items in the parlor and the music room, labeling them *storage*, *bakery*, or *sell*, and a few special things, *cabin*. Each item, though decades old, remained in pristine condition, very much like the overall look of the house.

Amelia Dawn Rippey had not only been wealthy but sophisticated, carrying the refined taste of an artist. Her house could have been one of the celebrated homes of Derbyshire in style and furnishing—perhaps a bit smaller, but not a great deal.

After the first hour downstairs, he and Julia entered Amelia's office where most of the furniture sat tagged for distribution. Their conversation had turned from one topic to another: favorite movies, previous schooling, childhood. Julia's had been much more joyful and loving than his—though the memory of his grandparents softened the edges of his mother's affectionless expectations.

"I haven't been through the wardrobe there." Julia nodded toward its glossy edifice of dark maple with ivy wood carvings framing its doors.

Henry half wanted to open it to see if Narnia waited on the other side. "It's beautiful."

She grinned. "Yeah. It's going into my 'someday bedroom.' It won't fit into the apartment, but once I figure out where I'm going to establish my B&B, it's following me for sure. It just looks magical."

"Quite Narnian."

Her eyes lit with agreement, and he became caught in her gaze for the umpteenth time that morning. She made conversations so easy. If he'd known someone like her waited on the other side of the world, that a friendship with a woman could be so effortless and genuine, he'd never have fallen for counterfeits.

"If the grand piano downstairs goes with you, what do you plan to do with this upright?" He walked over to the beautiful old instrument and examined its structure. His brows rose. "A Steinway, no less."

She walked to his side, arms crossed as she studied the piano. She'd worn her hair in a braid that fell over one shoulder, and his fingers twitched to give it a little tug. Would she grin? Be annoyed? And where did that desire come from, anyway?

"I'm donating it to the School of the Arts in town where I taught piano lessons for two years. I love the owners' vision to offer affordable quality instruction, especially for kids whose families don't always have money for those kinds of extracurriculars."

"You do realize how much this piano is worth?"

"Yes." She smiled at him. "But teaching a child the beauty of music...well, that's priceless."

"You know you're rather extraordinary, don't you?"

Her smile faded, and her large, dark eyes broadened as a rush of pink highlighted her cheeks in the most beautiful way. She looked ahead and cleared her throat. "I'm extraordinarily behind in getting this house cleared out is what I am." She turned and approached the wardrobe, leaving him to curse himself for another unintended compliment-turned-mistake.

"I...I didn't mean—"

She raised a palm to stop him but didn't turn her attention his way. "It's not you." She pulled the door open to the wardrobe without another word on his error. "Are those...ballgowns?"

He approached, still attempting to decipher her reaction. Not him? Then what had gone wrong?

"These must have been some of the gowns she wore when she performed." Julia's fingers smoothed the fabric of one after another. "They're amazing and in excellent condition."

"Unbelievable."

She glanced over at him, her gaze holding his before turning back. "Aren't they? I never knew she still had these." She reached for a dark blue gown. "This must be where she found the dress she gave me to wear for prom one year. I thought she'd bought it at some consignment store or even ordered it from a company online that sold retro gowns, but now I wonder if it hadn't been hers all along. I've always preferred vintage styles."

A suitable choice for her, he'd say. "I suppose they'd be worth a hefty amount if they're vintage."

Julia rested her palms on her hips, highlighting her protruding abdomen. Oh yes, she was a mother! A sobering reminder of the differences between his interests and hers, no doubt. How did he keep forgetting that truth when lost in her conversations and kindness?

She had to have much more on her mind than an impossible romance with him.

"I'll keep my favorites, I guess, but there's no reason to keep them all." She raised a brow and scrunched up her shoulders in a little apology-shrug. "Would you mind carrying them down to the car? I can sort through them at the apartment."

"Of course."

As Julia explored the drawers of the massive gold-trimmed desk, Henry took garments, and any other items Julia added, to the car until he'd reached the back of the wardrobe. But the final piece wasn't a gown. Behind all the vintage glitz waited a garment bag with a men's suit on display through the partially unzipped bag.

"Curious.

"What is it?"

He drew out the bag, the light showing the fabric's charcoal gray color. "A three-piece men's suit. Posh, from the looks of it."

Julia reached over him to unzip the bag the rest of the way. "Why would she have a man's suit in her wardrobe?"

"And only one."

Julia's posture straightened. "Wait. I've seen this one before." She rushed to the desk and picked up a framed photo, then returned. "Yes. It looks the same."

She turned so he could see the photo of a handsome man, probably in his late twenties or early thirties at the time, with a beautiful woman at his side. Henry had seen the woman's face in other photos they'd packed. Julia's Aunt Millie.

"Doesn't that suit look the same?"

Henry examined the suit in the photo then looked back at the one in his hands. "It does, though with the age of the photos it's difficult to be sure." He slid a hand over the lapel. "In the photo, that was your aunt's lover? Lucas Randolph?"

"That's my guess."

The cloth beneath Henry's fingers hardened, and he pushed back the jacket. "I think there's something in the pocket here." Careful to cause the least movement to the antique suit, Henry reached into the pocket and brought out a strange blue booklet similar in appearance to a passport.

Julia peered over his arm, her shoulder brushing his in a snug, cozy sort of way.

Cozy worked for him.

"What is it?"

95

In answer, he draped the suit over his arm and opened the booklet. A photo of Lucas Randolph lay pasted on the first page with the name Jack Milton printed beneath it

"I wonder why he had a different name on this paper."

"I don't know..." Henry flipped the booklet over, but the back revealed no answers. "Do you suppose he went by another name? Or the man in the photos was someone else?"

"No, it has to be Lucas from the way she talked about him and his love for her. Why would she have a different man's photo on her desk? But...but do you think this"—she gestured toward the book— "was an alias or something. Maybe a joke?"

"You think he may have had a false identity?"

"Maybe... But why would he need one? It doesn't make any sense."

Curiouser and curiouser. He tapped the booklet. "Unless he was a spy."

Their gazes locked, and he could see Julia's mind working through his suggestion with a subtle following nod. "That would make sense, wouldn't it? World War Two."

"Your aunt's seclusion."

Julia gasped. "Do you think she was in danger and hid here?" Her brow crinkled. "But the danger couldn't have come from Lucas. She spoke so fondly of him. I'm certain they were on good terms."

"Is there any documentation that would show us more information about the two of them from this time period? In her desk, perhaps?"

"I haven't finished going through it yet." She peered into the wardrobe. "But there's one more box in the wardrobe. Maybe it'll provide some more clues?"

"Of course." Henry handed Julia the paper and garment bag, then reached for the box. Just as he pulled the container into the light of the room, a small, furry creature skittered out of the box and over his fingers.

"Ahh!" He stumbled backward and tossed the box into the air, the contents and papers, shredded and whole, flying in all directions while his furry assailant disappeared from the scene of the crime.

An ottoman behind him tripped his stumbling feet, and he landed on his backside, the remaining papers and paraphernalia raining down on him and the surrounding floor. The entire scene, complete with a soundtrack from Tom and Jerry, played behind his eyes as he imagined it from Julia's perspective. Oh yes, he was most certainly the dashing hero she'd longed for her entire life.

"Henry." Julia was at his side, her hands on his arms. "Are you all right?"

Heat bathed his face, and he refused to look at her as he pushed himself to a sitting position, dusting off his shirt as he righted. "I'm fine."

"What on earth happened?"

His gaze lifted to hers with the hesitancy of a primary school student playing alone their first solo on stage. He ground out the insidious words. "A mouse."

Playing brave music was much easier than living brave.

∞ ∞ ∞

Julia stared at him and replayed his words as flashbacks of Henry stepping back, screaming out, tripping over the ottoman, and being doused in papers flashed through her mind. And all because of a *mouse?*

She bit her teeth together to hold in the tickle. He was fine. Well, bits of shredded paper decorated his hair and shirt, but otherwise he looked as handsome as he had before the mouse attack.

A snort of laughter shot out between her closed lips.

He turned a very deliberate gaze on her, tilting his head and examining her through narrowed eyes. Oh, he *knew* it was funny.

She covered her mouth just as another burst rushed out.

His lips twitched and she lost all control. Her laugh shook her with such force she had to sit down, right there on the floor beside him, and pray her bladder held.

"Ah, you laugh. And here I thought your compassion was boundless."

His reaction encouraged another bout of wild giggles. Oh, how long had it been since she laughed this hard? Even the baby didn't know what to do with her response. He kicked away, probably wondering what on earth had gotten into his mother. She rubbed at her stomach, then bit her lip to quell the chuckles. "My granny says you can tell a lot about a man when he's scared or embarrassed...a lot about his character."

He tilted his head, still examining her, and tossed an arm over his knee, the glint in his eyes highlighting more humor than his grimace declared. "What did you learn? That I'm cowardly? Or that I have the scream pitch of an adolescent girl?"

"No." Her laugh flung loose again, and she swiped at her eyes. "Fear and embarrassment are two ways to bring out a person's unchecked emotions, especially if they're trying to hide anger or pride." She reached over and dusted loose strips of paper from his shoulder. "I think you passed the test."

He chuckled and stood, then offered his hands to help her off of the floor. "Well, it's nice to know that some good can come out of my terror."

"And don't worry. I'm a country girl. I can protect you from mice."

He shot her a mock glare, but the playful twinkle in his eyes shifted a shaft of warmth through her heart—a gleam of something sweet she'd thought her past had distorted, but here it was, real and authentic.

He still held her hands with a gentle touch...and she still let him. Tingles spread from their entwined fingers, through her palms, and into her forearms before shocking her heart with reality. *What are you doing, Julia?* With the sudden awareness of his warm fingers around hers, the little voice in her head screamed *halt*. She didn't catch her nervous chuckle in time and slid her hands from his, pushing back a stray hair from her face as she scanned the papers on the floor.

He followed her lead without a word, examining the paper explosion on the floor.

"They're...what? Playbills?" Henry knelt to the floor and gathered some of the papers. "No, wait. They're pamphlets of your aunt's performances. Look!"

He raised a few to Julia. Vintage flyers, some featuring pictures of Aunt Millie in various elegant gowns by the piano, and others with Aunt Millie and Lucas poised by a piano, lay in his hands, waiting for her perusal. The oldest, from 1940, told of Aunt Millie's first acclaimed concert when she'd been only eighteen. New York, Chicago, London, Paris, Venice... Later performances from when she'd stayed in England, most likely due to the strains of war, finished the pile.

"Here's a concert she performed for the troops." Henry offered another flyer featuring an almost cartoon-style Millie in a less elaborate gown, surrounded by applauding troops.

"I never realized how extensively she'd traveled."

"It's rather remarkable and...intriguing."

Julia brought one of the flyers closer to examine Lucas's face. Who had he been? Why had he left her to raise a baby on her own? Had he died? "And this proves that the false identity does belong to Lucas, because his name is all over these pamphlets with his photo, even if he looks a little different in the passport."

"Julia, you must see this." Henry stood, a tattered envelope in his hands, his gaze finding hers. "Quite the name for a child."

She took the paper from him and drew three items from the envelope. The first piece was a birth certificate for Rosalyn Brigitta Rippey Sweitzer.

"Sweitzer?" She looked over at Henry, who'd resumed picking up the scattered papers. "But Lucas's last name was Randolph."

He gestured toward the envelope in her hands. "Keep looking."

A card came next.

Congratulations on the birth of your daughter. I hope to see her very soon. Your contribution to our world will be greatly missed, but I feel certain you will find the joy of motherhood an equal challenge to your many talents. Keep heart, brave one.

Sincerely,

Mrs. Emmeline Sterling

Julia rubbed her thumb across the final phrase, almost as if this mysterious Emmeline reached from the past and spoke to her. An unexpected pregnancy. A shift in plans. The last thing she felt was brave.

A short letter came next in the envelope. The handwriting turned sharply, giving the letters distinct peaks and valleys.

My dearest Amelia,

I am in awe of the photo you sent me of little Rose. She is beautiful, just like her mother. Forgive my absence as you start this journey as a single parent. I will come to you when I can—and when it is safe—but know my love is already with you, no matter what oceans separate us or time parts us. You are as close to me as memory.

Keep safe, my darling.

Lucas

Julia reached behind her for the desk chair, slowly sitting, her thoughts grasping for out-of-reach connections. "It doesn't make sense. If the baby's last name is Sweitzer, do you think Millie became pregnant from a different man before meeting Lucas?"

"I suppose it's possible. The life of a celebrity is fraught with temptation." He kept his attention on the papers in his hands, but a small frown puckered his brow. "Just ask Wes."

Julia knew her sister's famous boyfriend suffered from a profligate past, but she'd never imagined the same for devout Aunt Millie. Of course, Wes was a different man than he used to be too, so perhaps Aunt Millie had also had a life-changing experience that led to her faith. Maybe her pregnancy was the catalyst?

"Do you think Lucas fell in love with her even though she carried this"—she looked once more at the letter then back to Henry—"Sweitzer's baby? He certainly seems to have cared about both of them, even if he was a spy."

Henry paused, his gaze boring deep as he gave silence a part in the conversation. "I should think the right sort of man could love like that."

Her gaze flickered to his. Or the Wright sort?

Her heart leapt at his words, at the confidence in his voice. But...but could it be true? Could Henry Wright be as sincere and almost yesteryear in his tenderness as he seemed? "Then that would mean Aunt Millie became pregnant by this Sweitzer fellow, fell in love with Lucas, and yet kept the Sweitzer last name? Why does that feel wrong?"

"There was a war going on, yes? Perhaps Sweitzer died in combat and Lucas was his best mate who felt compassion for your aunt that then turned to love?"

"Clever speculation, Mr. Wright." Julia couldn't tame her grin. "I think you're a romantic."

He chuckled and shook his head. "I believe it's a byproduct of being a musician."

"Or"—she raised a teasing brow to challenge him— "visa versa."

He lowered his gaze, a slight blush of red darkening his cheeks. Poor man. Better change the subject. "So then, who is this Emmeline Sterling, I wonder?"

"I'm not certain but her name is at the top of the sheet music." He brought the paper close and proceeded to read in his beautiful English accent. "'Music for the illustrious Emmeline Sterling of Chelsea, London.' But...something isn't quite right about the score."

She leaned in, a lovely whiff of his vanilla scent wafting over her. "What do you mean?"

"It's clear this music was handwritten, not printed, of course." He gestured toward the note markings with their inconsistent shapes and sometimes uneven lines.

"Are you saying Millie or Lucas was composing this piece? They *were* musicians. Why would that be so unexpected?"

He brought out both pages of sheet music. "If it's a composition, it's not a very good one." She stepped closer and examined the page as he continued. "The first page is a replication of one of Brahms's piano sonatas, but the second..." He brought the other page up for her better view. "As you can see, the line of melody is consistent and playable, but the chord structures beneath? They...they wouldn't sound..."

"They'd sound awful."

"Exactly." He walked to the upright piano. "Listen." A discordant progression of mismanaged chords with an occasional tingle of the sonata's melody rising above the dissenting notes sounded throughout the room.

She cringed at the horrible misuse of notes and melodies. "Why would she save something like that? Or even have it?"

He studied the music, leaning close and taking on a very Clark Kent-ish intensity. Yes, he did remind her a little of the humble alias for The Man of Steel—in the best possible ways. Unassuming, a little fumbling, gentle. Her lips slipped into a smile. And with the heart of a hero?

Her throat dried out at the sudden thought and she looked away. Her emotions kept bungee jumping between embracing this unexpected interest in Henry Wright and running from the possibilities. Why couldn't she give herself permission to feel this attraction to him? Her head screamed *no* but her heart...well, he had something she craved.

She really needed an additional appointment with her counselor...and a whole lot of prayer.

"I don't know." He stood from the piano bench and took the sheet music back in hand as he crossed the room. "But it's safe to say your great aunt left you something of an intriguing mystery to uncover."

She took the sheet music he offered, studying it, trying to fill in the missing gaps of information, but coming up empty. "It certainly seems so, but I don't know if I have time for a mystery with a house to empty."

He put his hands in his pockets and nodded, examining the room as if trying to use x-ray vision to unearth more secrets. To compliment her mental digression, a brown wave rebelled against the flow of his hair and dipped down over his forehead. She grinned. Very Clark-Kent-ish indeed.

"We need to get back to the bakery to prepare for the party tonight, but I'll be here on Tuesday." Her breath strained for release, but she forced her thoughts into words. "Would you like to...come with me?"

His gaze shot to hers, searching, before he finally seemed to work out an answer. "Yes. Yes, I would be glad to."

Her smile trembled into place. "Good." She gathered the rest of the papers and moved toward the doorway, Henry not far behind, carrying the box of papers. What a wonderful strangeness to find comfort in both conversations and silence with him. To feel...safe.

She locked up the house and approached the car, Henry by her side, his smile a ready encouragement whenever she glanced his way.

No, he was nothing like Peyton. With each additional minute she spent with him, the truth sank deeper, more certain.

"Henry." She rounded the car and stopped just before getting into the driver's seat.

He paused as he placed the box into the backseat, his eyes visible over the top of the car. "Yes?"

"Earlier, when you said I was extraordinary..." She swallowed through the unexpected emotions rising in her throat. "Thank you."

Chapter Fourteen

here was no mistakin' it, and the very idea made Nate Jenkins almost sick to his stomach.

Another highfalutin city boy from across the world had made his way into their family.

As the last guests arrived for Wes and Eisley's party, each finding a place to hide in the shadows of the room, Nate couldn't ignore the way his wounded girl, Julia, bloomed around Henry Wright. He hadn't heard her laugh so much in almost a year. And her smile when she looked at the good-for-nothin' foreigner? It brightened up the whole room. What was a daddy to do about that?

And Henry? Well, that boy didn't hide his interest a'tall. He waited on her like she was the princess Nate had always told her she was. Daggone it! He should have called her somethin' else, because Henry was tryin' real hard to meet the expectation.

There was somethin' unnerving about a boy who talked so little, spent so much time with an instrument, and wore his skittishness like a bowtie. Nate shook his head. And if it didn't beat all, Henry Wright had shown up wearing a bowtie for church last Sunday. What sort of boy wore bowties?

God sure did have a sense of humor, and He was most likely havin' a good ol' laugh about this Jenkins situation right now. Nate shot a look to the ceiling, highly suspicious.

Was some twinkle toes really what his girl needed most? A pang shot through his chest at the thought. If Eisley married Wes, which sure seemed in the future, there might come a time when they'd move plumb across the world and then...what would happen to that part of a daddy's heart?

And what if Julia and Henry were next? He pressed his palm against his chest to massage away the deepening pain. Sure, young'uns were supposed to grow up and all, but how was a daddy supposed to let them fly all the way to England? Was his heart strong enough for that?

"They make a good pair, you know?"

Nate looked to his right where Lizzie Worthing had sneaked up beside him, securing his ungracious thoughts about the British at the moment. Even if Lizzie left England to elope with Uncle Joe, which somehow made the man all smiles and giddy and energetic like he was half his age, Nate wasn't inclined to be generous toward any possible traitors who might steal his young'uns away. Good for Uncle Joe, though. And Lizzie wasn't half-bad, though Nate kept the compliment tight-lipped.

"He's too quiet. Makes you think he's hiding something."

Lizzie brushed back a strand of her silver-lined golden hair and exaggerated an eye roll—just for his benefit, if Nate knew the woman at all. "Oh, pishposh. I've known Henry since he was six years old, and there's no man sincerer in all of Derbyshire."

"Yeah? But sincere about what? 'Cause I don't like the way he's lookin' at my girl." Even if Henry's actions had been perfectly fine and his expression kind, Nate knew exactly what was going through Henry Wright's head and, well, it wasn't right. No sirree. "Besides, we ain't in Derbyshire right now, are we?"

She waved away his words, her attention following the crowd in the room and not him. Some people just couldn't handle good sense. Nate copied her movement, settling his sights on another woman whose golden hair was softening with age, but who still held on to her youth *and* his heart without reserve. Kay bustled here and there, arranging plates at a two-seater café table in the center of the room—the "special couple's" table, decorated with a bouquet of wildflowers and "romantic" flickering lights of an old-fashioned oil lamp, to use Sophie's words.

That girl probably bled fairy dust.

"They both like music," Lizzie added.

"And me and the town drunk both like Marilee's chocolate pie. Don't mean we're made for a lifetime commitment."

"You're pigheaded, you know?"

"And you're a busybody."

The glint in her eyes hinted she liked the banter. Silly woman. How on earth did Joe put up with her?

And yet, Joe had never looked better.

God sure had some crazy notions sometimes. Neither Julia nor Henry knew either sparked the other, which was just fine with Nate because they hadn't known each other long enough to think about sparks.

His grimace deepened. Though, that hadn't stopped Eisley from sparkin' like the Fourth of July over her fancy pants British actor. Nate gazed at the ceiling and raised his hands into praying position. Maybe if he stared long enough, God might send some clarity on the influx of British boys into the Jenkins family—or at least the punch-line to the joke. "Just one good country boy, Lord? Just one?"

"You're impossible, Nate Jenkins." Lizzie nudged his shoulder with her finger. "Country boy or city boy, the heart is what matters, and you know that's true, as well as I, despite all your protests."

"I wouldn't mind a good-hearted country boy who didn't speak all hoity-toity. Is that so much to ask?"

She shook her head, but her grin remained wide. "You're hopeless. Positively hopeless."

"I'm startin' to feel a little hopeless about finding any country boy for my remaining girls. I only got two left if Twinkle Toes gets serious."

"Country boy, is it? I'd take whatever sort as long as they loved my child." Her blond brow skyrocketed in a needling way that made him like her argument less—even if he agreed with her. "You know, Henry helped Wes through his difficulties. He stood by him, quiet but true. He may be more reserved than you expect, but he takes excellent care of the people he loves." Lizzie nodded toward Henry, who was carrying a punch bowl to another table as Julia followed behind with the ginger ale and juice. "And I should think that notion trumps many differences."

Nate's stomach pinched. Why did Lizzie have to mention the L word? Love brought marriage, and marriage to a man who lived across the ocean brought... Well, not what he wanted.

But the boy was so careful and...kind. Gentle. Nate's lip snarled. Too gentle, if he had anything to say about it. His gaze fastened on Julia, and the memory of those first few months after her attack surfaced. He'd been so helpless—and angry enough to want to pound the good-for-nothin' boy who'd hurt her into the dirt. The very idea of his rough hands leaving the bruises he'd seen on Julia's arms, of the liberties he'd taken, of the wounds in her eyes when she'd finally become aware of all that had happened...

He looked again at timid, citified Henry.

Maybe gentle was what she needed most of all.

And Nate *wanted* what Julia needed most. Even if it hurt him to the marrow of his country-boy bones.

He nearly growled. *Lord, help him.* His family was turning into a bunch of British fancy boys, and there was nothing he could do to stop it.

His gaze landed on Sophie, who teetered on a step-ladder while stringing the last bunch of fairy lights across a window, her eyes sparkling with who knew what sort of fairytale notions. He wasn't even going to try to imagine what boy would catch her. *Oh Lord, please don't let him dress in pink.*

That only left Rachel. He zeroed in on his raven-haired tough girl and nodded. Yeah, maybe she'd be the one to bring home the football-playin', nail-drivin', Chevy-sportin' son-in-law.

"They're here." Nathan ran into the room, hands flying as he darted around the tables, his warning sending the room into instant chaos. "I just saw Wes's car stop outside. They're here."

Everyone darted in different directions to find their hiding spots.

"What if she said no?" An uncomfortable silence fell with Greg's question. His son shrugged his shoulders from his hiding spot in the nearest corner of the room. "You think this celebration might be a little awkward if she turned Wes down?"

"There's no way she'll say no, Greg," Sophie barked, one hand on her hip, as she halted her descent down the ladder. Rick rushed to her side as she wobbled, and gave her a hand.

See, he'd raised his boys to be gentlemen too.

"This is her fairytale dream." Sophie sighed. "A girl doesn't turn down an offer like that, ever."

"Get the lights! Get the lights!" Nate's little wifey crossed the room to his side, her pale eyes sparkling with an excitement she often kept hidden behind her soft smile. He knew Kay trusted their kids' futures to God, even if it meant another place became home. He grimaced. Or another country. Somehow, she'd come to peace with it and helped the idea grow on him too.

He rubbed his chest again. The thought still hurt though.

The lights flickered off except for the lantern-lit tables peppered in various spots around the room, and then the faint sound of a closing door followed by laughter echoed down the hallway.

"What on earth are you doing, handsome?" Eisley's voice carried into the room. "Julia's bakery is the last place I thought we'd come to share our big news."

Well, that was a pretty good sign of what his oldest daughter's answer had been.

"I told you, I have an extra special celebration planned," Wes replied.

"The ring on my finger proves it's already been an extra special evening."

"Well, how about one more thing." The door opened and Eisley stepped over the threshold, her eyes squinting against the bright flashing lights that sparked to life at her entrance.

A rousing surprise sounded from all around. The glow on his girl's face. The bright smile. And Wes grinning at her like a fool in love. Eisley's young'uns ran up to them, hugging Wes as much as their mama, and Nate nodded, allowing the sweet warmth to press in beside the pain.

They were good together. A family.

Laughter ushered them deeper into the room as Sophie bounded forward like a kangaroo, leading them to their special table. This was right. Good.

Music pulled Nate's attention toward the piano. Julia played while Henry stood next to her, his fiddle propped on the inside of his left arm, a bow rising and falling against its strings. Maybe...maybe they did share something special.

The same sweetness and ache swelled in Nate's chest all over again. *Oh Lord, help me.*

The hardest part of being a parent was letting go.

∞ ∞ ∞

Last night had been a beautiful success.

Julia grinned as she stopped by the communication board on her way up the stairs to gather linens for cleaning. Her body ached from her work the previous day at Aunt Millie's followed by Eisley's engagement party, but so many exciting things were happening.

Things she wouldn't have imagined eight months ago.

Eisley getting married again. Julia selling the bakery—in fact, she'd closed on the sale with Amy on Monday. Aunt Millie's amazing inheritance left behind so Julia could finally fulfill those dreams she'd tucked away for another day. She'd even emailed her professors that morning to ask about resuming her final semester of classes in the fall and contacted the registrar office to get the ball rolling.

If money remained a non-issue, Little One and school could be her focus, and by December, she'd have her degree in business with an emphasis in hospitality management.

And *then?* She rubbed her belly. She'd make her dreams come true, even with a little person in tow. Others had done it before. So could she.

A note with her name on it waited on the communication board. She knew that handwriting.

Henry.

Heat rose up her neck chasing a few happy tingles. She shot a look over her shoulder, to check for onlookers, and then tugged the folded paper from its pinned place. He'd been finishing up the back room of the kitchen with her dad all morning, and from the sound of it, Henry had *volunteered* to help.

Beneath her dad's overall rough and sometimes shocking personality, beat a tender heart that most people noticed if they looked hard enough. As observant as Henry was, she'd guess he'd somehow figured it out. Besides, from bits and pieces he'd mentioned about his own family, he missed having his dad and grandfather as older male influences. Even though her dad certainly wasn't a refined British businessman, he gave off solid mentor vibes.

Well, to those brave enough to stick around.

Julia unfolded the paper with its short note inside.

It takes faith to see beyond the storm.

It takes courage to continue smiling in its midst.

Thank you for allowing me the opportunity to learn from your courage yesterday.

Henry

Her courage? She reread the note. How had he seen courage in her? If anything, he was the brave one for working with her dad then going with her to a house in the middle of nowhere to label furniture and undergo a mouse attack.

She chuckled, pressing the note to her chest, and her gaze fell to her faded gray slip-on shoes. She sighed. Despite the fact that breathing had become a little easier over the last few days, she desperately missed wearing her cute shoes. Sure, her feet slid into personality-less slip-on shoes easier than lace-up boots, and trying to navigate heels at this state was...humorous, at best, but a pair of cute shoes could make a girl feel braver. Seize-the-day brave.

Shoes had that kind of power—at least, that's what Sophie said.

Julia placed the folded note into her pocket and waddled up the stairs, a laundry basket positioned against her hip. She gathered a few towels from her bedroom, then walked through the sitting room to the other apartment. The OUT sign hung from the doorknob, but Julia knocked just in case. Some things you couldn't un-see.

No answer. *Great.*

She used her master key to unlock the door, and with a gentle push, entered the large apartment. The usual scent of honey and peaches from the cleaning supplies she and Amy used mingled with two more scents: the spicy-leather cologne Wes wore and the softer hints of Henry's vanilla.

She drew in a deep breath and scanned the room with fresh eyes. As of Monday, these rooms, this bakery, had become Amy's. Paired with Aunt Millie's inheritance, Julia finally had the freedom, both financially and time-wise, to pursue her long-held dream. And now, after months of healing and fighting for hope, she believed she could.

She stepped across the richly colored Persian rug in the living area of the apartment and headed straight for the small closet just outside the shared bathroom, where guests left their soiled linens for pick up.

Oh goodie, only a few towels. She already had enough additional weight—and pregnancy clumsiness—on her to keep her duly humble in navigating stairs with anything over twenty pounds. She took the soiled load, adjusted her basket on her hip, and stepped lightly—well, as lightly as a massively pregnant woman could—through the quiet sitting room.

Pregnancy note: hide-and-seek gets pretty tricky in the third trimester of pregnancy.

Just as she made it halfway across the room, the bathroom door swung open, revealing Henry...wearing only a towel. Julia jolted to a stop. Henry did the same.

Her mouth dropped open, her throat went dry, and, despite her best efforts, her gaze took in every available piece of skin on his body. His shoulders looked broader in full exposure, and he had the defined abs of a man who probably worked on them. At least a little.

The basket slipped from her hand and dropped with a slight thud onto the carpet, the sound shocking her into motion. "I...I thought you were downstairs helping Dad."

Blinking was his only response.

She pointed back toward the door, working up her defense. "I...I knocked first."

His frozen stance began to thaw, drawing her gaze to the muscles flexing in his chest. She swallowed the lump in her throat and then turned her gaze toward the floor, after taking inventory of his very fine self one more time.

Get a hold of yourself, girl!

Oh have mercy! She'd not allowed her mind to think of Henry in...*this* kind of romantic way. But a towel scene definitely sent her thoughts zip-lining across friendship valley to the possibilities on the other side.

He folded his arms across his chest—there went those butterflies again—but then must have thought better of letting go of the towel because he gripped the knotted front at his waist and cleared his throat.

Nope. There was nothing at all wrong with Henry's physique. His British food worked just fine, chest hair or otherwise.

"I didn't hear." He tugged at the earbud cord she hadn't noticed because of...well...distractions and gestured toward his chin. "Shaving."

"Right." Her gaze dropped to his newly-smooth chin, still a little damp from his efforts. How had she never noticed his excellent chin? She took a step back and held in a whimper as heat climbed up her body and landed with fever-like potency on her face. "The...the OUT sign. It was still up on the door."

"I...I forgot it was hanging up. After finishing with your father, I came straight to shower." He ran his free hand through his damp hair, upsetting his waves and releasing that Clark Kent curl over his forehead again. The poor man seemed almost as discombobulated as she was.

Julia couldn't collect her thoughts at all while Henry's free hand continued its agitated wandering. She just kept staring—and unintentionally appreciating—his...self.

His roaming hand ended up on his hip as if he were going for a nonchalant look. Oh heavens, there was nothing nonchalant about this situation. Heat rose so hot into Julia's face that sweat began to bead on her forehead.

Move, feet. Look away, eyes.

Neither moved. Henry looked at her, his brow furrowed over the questions in his eyes. Had he said something to her?

Shower. Half-clad man. The sign on the door! Oh yes! He'd forgotten. "Of course." Julia cleared her throat and bent to snatch the basket she'd dropped in her half-naked-man wonderment. "I came to collect your used towels." Her gaze dropped to the one around his waist. "Um...not *that* towel, of course, but...um...the other ones."

"Allow me."

Words—grateful, protesting, or otherwise—refused to leave her dry throat as he approached. He kept a firm hold on the towel around his waist while bending at the knees to grab her basket and hand it to her. Then, avoiding eye contact, he moved the spilled soiled towels from the floor and placed them in the basket in her arms, his nearness flooding all her hyperactive senses in freshly clean vanilla-spice.

And everything nice.

Heaven help her! She'd never see Henry Wright, towels, or vanilla the same way again.

Every inch of skin on her body lit with awareness, but he didn't stay close for long, backing away as quickly as he'd come, his attention riveted on the towels in her arms. That was a good thing because, maybe, if he kept his focus on the dirty laundry he wouldn't notice how much she fought to look everywhere except his very manly chest.

Oh, oh, oh! Superman lived under his Clark Kent persona.

She shook her head to clear the thought and continued moving toward the door. "Th-thank you."

Good grief! It wasn't like she'd never seen a shirtless man before.

Just not so close. And somehow the fact it was Henry made it even more...something, but she wasn't sure quite what. Good...ish? Her gaze fell back to his skin. Yep, definitely good. She shook away the thought and took a step back. "So...um...I'll just go."

And with that she took a quick turn...and collided with the *closed* door.

She rolled her eyes heavenward and tossed a shaky grin over her shoulder. "The door's closed." She groaned and almost pressed her forehead against it in surrender. Obvious much?

"Bye," she murmured as she flung open the door and rushed from the room.

She didn't stop until she made it into the privacy of the stairwell, and then the entire scene replayed in her head in full cheek-burning delight. Her burgeoning grin turned into a full laugh she hoped Henry didn't hear, but then again, maybe he was laughing a little too.

Chapter Fifteen

"All right, I ain't shootin' with British boys no more."

Nate Jenkins sat at the head of the table for Sunday lunch, his moustache a bit crinkled from his grimace. Henry almost grinned. The man sounded a great deal of thunder without the storm. Though somewhat less refined, Nate reminded Henry of his grandfather, whose boorish personality had concealed a warm heart. Julia's father still kept Henry a little on edge, but he'd seen beneath the exterior and found an unlikely...friend. Or at least a friendly acquaintance with potential.

Speaking of seeing beneath the exterior...

Henry's attention slipped to Julia in her usual place at the massive table—across from him and a few seats down. Something had shifted between them since yesterday's towel fiasco, and he didn't like it. Throughout the Sunday church service, she'd barely made eye contact, let alone spoken to him, but her almost ethereal look in her pale blue dress had succeeded in distracting him more than once from the pastor's sermon. It fluttered around her like the airy whimsical tone of Bach's *Brandenburg Concerto No. 4*, adding to her fairy-like aura. The blend of memory and music produced a warm cadence of rightness in his chest.

And she'd agreed to be his friend. Yes, he'd nurture that friendship and hold out a hope for more. He shot a look heavenward. He'd not offer one complaint if God gave him more.

"So, Henry outshot you just like Wes did when he visited the first time." Greg chuckled at Henry's side, but Nate fired a dangerous look, complete with furrowed brow.

"As I recall"—the patriarch pointed his fork— "me and Fancy Pants *tied* at our shooting competition."

"Which means it hurts all the more that Henry actually beat you." Eisley nudged Henry's shoulder and tagged on a wink, inspiring a full-on smile from Henry as he added some salad to his plate.

"Now, now," Nate offered in a consolatory tone. "Henry took my best gun."

Eisley laughed. "Are you serious, Dad? Your best gun?"

"Dad"—Greg's eyebrow raised to his hairline— "that's stretchin' it even for you."

"Not making excuses now, are we, Old Bean," Wes added through a chuckle.

Despite his growling retort to his future son-in-law, Nate's grin slipped into view beneath his dark moustache, and he waved his fork in Henry's direction. "Those quiet ones. They're usually hidin' somethin'."

"Like excellent aim?"

Nate glared at Rachel and sniffed, then reached for another piece of grilled chicken from the dish in the middle of the table. "Henry's got some top-notch skills hidin' underneath all that hoity-toity talk and pretty clothes."

"Yep, enough skills *and* muscle to take you on, Dad." Eisley laughed again and turned to give Emily another helping of potatoes.

"Good shootin' don't mean good muscles." The undeniable twinkle took some of the potency out of the glare Nate sent Henry.

A sudden cough erupted from across the table. Henry looked up and met Julia's wide-eyed gaze. With her pinched-lipped expression in the forefront of his mind, he replayed the turn of the conversation.

His smile tipped. He was pretty sure he knew where her thoughts dove.

His throat tickled with a sudden urge to laugh even as heat crawled into his cheeks. He well-remembered yesterday, and though awkwardness had lathered the entire scene, a surprising realization had occurred—Julia *liked* what she'd seen in him. He'd never been the sort to seek attention, but as her gaze had taken him in, something inside of him gave way to believe in the impossible. For the first time in his memory, he'd felt very heroic indeed.

He *wanted* her to know him, to see him for who he was, and...maybe...

"I feel certain Henry will only keep surprising you, Nate." Wes gave him an encouraging nod.

Henry gave his friend a nod in gratitude for the encouragement and then slid his gaze back to Julia. She'd raised a napkin to her mouth, and from the mirth dancing in her eyes, she was likely trying to hide a grin of her own behind the fabric.

"I'll get you on a roof, Twinkle Toes," Nate went on. "Then we'll see how much your manliness shows."

The cough exploded again, and this time Julia's struggling smile burst wide before she covered it with her napkin.

"I reckon your manliness has Julia all choked up, Henry." Greg nudged his shoulder. "Next thing you know, Dad'll start pushin' chest-hair-growin' food on you again."

Julia's eyes widened and her cough took a strangled turn as she stood from the table. "Dessert anyone?"

She rushed toward the kitchen, and Henry cleared his throat to appease the growing laughter, shrugging a shoulder at Eisley as she silently questioned him with her raised eyebrow.

"You sure Julia can manage those pies on her own, Daddy?" Julia's older sister kept her focus on Henry, the glimmer in her hazel eyes dancing with enough mischief to hint at her intentions.

Pixies ran wild in this family.

Nate looked up and his brow crinkled as he took in what she said. "Naw, she don't need to tote around all those pies by herself." His gaze narrowed on Henry, then he waved his fork as he spoke. "Go help her, Twinkle Toes. Y'all can talk music or something' fancy like that."

"Of course." Henry tried not to get up from the table with too much enthusiasm, catching Wes's snicker as he passed by him.

Julia stood by the counter in the middle of the kitchen, leaning forward, her gentle chuckle shaking her shoulders as her hair fell down her back in a rain of gold. His fingers tingled with a desire to run his hands through those silky strands, but he shook them out at his sides and stepped forward.

"I've been sent to help with the pies."

She spun around so fast that she wavered in her balance, leaning to her left as the weight from her belly threatened to pull her horizontal. He jumped to the rescue, steadying her with a hand to her arm. A tear that escaped during her chuckling fit trailed down her cheek, her smile fading from every part of her face except her eyes. "I'm pregnant, not helpless."

"I would never accuse you of being helpless, but I must remain on your good side."

Her brow rose like a question mark.

"You're the only person here who has offered to protect me from rebel mice."

Her smile spread wide with another laugh. "Well, I suppose I should allow you to help me then, if it's in payment for possible services rendered."

"Our secret, of course." He released his hold on her arm and lowered his voice. "I'd never want your father to find out *that* particular weakness of mine. I have a feeling it could be detrimental to my current manliness status."

Her laugh burst out again, a sound inspiring his own, until she finally sighed. "Oh Henry, I'm so sorry about yesterday."

He pushed his hands in his pockets, studying her through narrowed eyes. "Is that why you've been avoiding me?"

Her nose crinkled with an adorable grimace. Yes, he was a lost cause. Utterly and completely. And he'd never been happier. Now, how did one go about telling a woman he'd just met that he was beginning to see her in his future? And long-term at that.

She placed her face in her hands. "It was so embarrassing to see you like that." Her fingers curled to almost touch her chin, revealing wide-eyes peeking up at him. "Not that there was anything wrong with what I saw. It was nice." She cringed then closed her eyes, waving one hand in the air as if she might make the words disappear, before returning her face to her hands. "Um...never mind."

He stood even taller and gently touched her arm, drawing her gaze from behind her hands. Her cheeks glowed with a beautiful rose color. "It was an honest mistake, Julia. No harm done."

"I'm glad. I'd hate to cause any awkwardness between us when we've just started becoming friends." She shrugged. "Well, okay, it *was* already awkward."

"Manageably so."

She studied him and lowered her hands to the counter. "Good, then. That's good."

He hoped his smile softened the awkwardness lingering around them. "And we still have a date for Tuesday?"

"A...a date?"

He replayed his words. Date! He stifled a growl. So much for decreasing the awkwardness levels...and right after he'd felt so heroic too. "Um, I meant plans... plans to return to your aunt's house."

Her laugh tumbled out on a musical lilt. "Oh, yes. If you're still interested."

There was something so endearing about her nervous embarrassment, her ready kindness, tugging his future ever closer to her hold. Only God knew how long it would take her heart to heal after her past. Only God knew how they'd manage a long-distance relationship across an ocean.

But Henry knew one thing most assuredly: winning Julia Jenkins's heart was worth the wait. "Of course I'm interested."

Their gazes held for one second longer than necessary, offering him another taste of hope before animated voices from the other room broke their connection. "Great." She gestured toward the pies, her cheeks still a ruddy hue, but his doubts gratefully dispelled. "Sounds like the natives need pie."

"Hungry natives." He took a pie in each hand. "The scariest kind."

"I think we can handle them together, don't you?"

"Most certainly."

∞ ∞ ∞

"How did the closing on the bakery go this week?" Dr. Karen Owensby came from around her desk and sat on one of the plush red chairs next to Julia. "Amy must have been excited to finally make it her own."

Julia's nerves eased at the calm in her therapist's voice. Amy's complete exhilaration, along with a very unexpected squeal when Julia officially handed over the keys, had solidified Julia's choice. Good timing. "She was ecstatic, to say the least, and since we already hired three new employees together over the past few months together, she has incredible support as I step back."

Karen raised her ebony brow and gestured toward Julia's stomach with the teacup she offered. "Cutting it close, I'd say, but I'm glad it all went well."

Julia ran a palm over her abdomen. "I have to stay busy in some way. Just sitting and *waiting* for the days to pass until this little one arrives?" She shook her head and took the tea with a smile. "I can't imagine how slow the hours would go."

"So you're still going to work some at the bakery?"

"Yes, but I'll focus on the guests who stay in the apartments—that's a more flexible arrangement with a baby around. And occasionally bake, of course."

Karen's caramel eyes lit. "That's right. You have guests now. And congratulations are in order for Eisley, I hear."

Julia's smile pinched into her cheeks. Every time she thought about her oldest sister's fairytale-come-true she couldn't help but celebrate from the inside out. Eisley's situation offered a real-life example to hold onto hope, even for Julia's circumstances. It wasn't that she doubted God's ability to turn every situation—even the most horrible ones —into something good, but God didn't stop there.

He brought the standing ovation...and then some—like a wealthy movie star.

"After all both of them have been through, it's amazing to see how perfect they are for each other."

"A good reminder of what happens when God writes the story of our lives, isn't it?" Karen's smile flickered wide. "He sees the grand landscape while we're often stuck on one chapter."

"Or one sentence."

Karen nodded, tagging on a chuckle. "True. And sometimes a particularly difficult one."

"Filled with confusing prepositional phrases and unnecessary adverbs."

Karen's chuckle bubbled into a laugh. "And we may keep reading the same rotten sentence to ourselves instead of moving forward to see what happens next."

Julia paused her lips on her cup, her therapist's words striking at her reason for scheduling the meeting to begin with. Moving on to the next sentence of her life? Chapter? Was she ready? Could she trust her heart to do that?

A voice within her smoothed over her doubts. *You can trust Me.*

Her mouth went dry. Bravery seemed so much harder than it used to be. Believing in her own choices felt like a leap in the dark. But God? Before the assault, she'd trusted him almost effortlessly, but after, everything tinged with doubt...or fear.

Her throat closed around the memory. Her vulnerability. Her helplessness. Broken people tended to break others. She'd become one of the broken ones, but God, in his mercy, had begun to heal the shattered pieces of her heart. Was she strong enough to believe in this possibility? In something so sweet and improbable?

"What happens next..." Julia's soft words faded into the gentle clatter of the spoon against her cup as she swirled her tea.

"Closing on your aunt's house, I believe."

Karen's answer pulled Julia back to the conversation. "Yes, that's the plan. Then I should have about three weeks left to get ready for the newest addition to the Jenkins family." Julia took a sip of her hot berry-flavored tea. "Closing is in a week, and Henry and I are going to try to finish some packing tomorrow."

Karen's head tilted, brow shifting upward. "Henry? You mentioned him last session, I believe. Wes's friend, right? A composer?"

Julia nodded and set down her cup, returning her hands to her lap and trying not to divert her gaze too much. The woman had amazing perception—almost superpower-like. "Yes, he's writing the music for the movie Wes is filming in Summit."

"I suppose the two of you have music in common, at least."

Her voice edged with the hidden knowledge Julia had come to expect in Karen's excellent skillset. "He's a brilliant musician. He's mastered at least three instruments, probably more."

Karen's gaze peeled back information Julia hadn't even voiced yet, maybe even thought.

"And you're comfortable enough with him to have him join you at your aunt's? Alone?"

Julia released a long sigh, her sagging shoulders mirroring her defeat in fighting the obvious. "I know it's strange and probably wrong. I've only known him a little over two weeks, and he's from *England*."

"Which makes him suspect, of course," Karen added, deadpan.

"Ha. Ha" Julia placed her cup down and sighed. "But the thing is, he'll end up going *back* to England."

"What makes that so wrong?"

Julia stared at Karen as if she hadn't quite heard her. "What's *not* wrong about it?" She waved at her stomach. "I was attacked eight months ago. I'm having a baby by another man. I'm an American who wants to finish college."

"So, what's the conflict? If these things are wrong, then Henry shouldn't be a problem at all, right?"

"Right?" Julia groaned and ran a hand down her braid. "No." She pinched her eyes closed and relaxed into the chair. "There's this connection to him that I...I can't explain. He's such a kind person, one of the gentlest men I've ever met." The memory of him and the mouse brought a chuckle out from her hesitation. "And funny. We have these conversations I've never had with any other man. Honest and interesting and...sweet."

"Sounds pretty nice to me."

"It's wonderful." She bit her bottom lip, wincing through narrowed eyes. "And confusing. I mean...I don't know how to fix it."

Karen's head tipped as she examined Julia with those x-ray eyes. "Does it need to be fixed?"

Argh. Therapists and their rhetorical questions. "Of course it does. I'm not supposed to be interested in a romantic relationship right now."

Karen's lips twisted into a humored slant. "You're not?"

Julia's hands went to her forehead, fingers massaging the skin above her eyebrows until the pulsing beneath stopped. She returned her gaze to her therapist and stiffened her shoulders. "You're the therapist. You're supposed to tell me that I've survived a trauma and my heart isn't ready to engage in romance—at least, not for a very long time. And that I'm supposed to focus on this baby and my healing. And that the idea of being romantic with any man should terrify me and have me running in the opposite direction."

"Sounds like you have my job figured out for me."

A squeak came from Julia's open mouth then she rallied. "Aren't I right?"

Karen placed her tea on the table, folded her hands, and leaned forward, eyes focused on Julia without one hit of concern. "Julia, have we been praying and working on your healing for the past seven months?"

"Yes."

"Did we ask God to bring into your life a comforting awareness of His love for you?"

"Of course we did, but—"

"And you've made *such* excellent progress that we're only meeting once or twice a month for support as the time for your delivery approaches, right?"

A giant *but* hung in the air, waiting to knock down Julia's well-honed objections. She ground out her reply. "Right."

"And does feeling this attraction—"

"I didn't say attraction."

"Okay." Karen pressed her lips tight as if holding back a laugh. "Does feeling a *connection* to a man in your life mean you're not focusing on becoming a mom?"

"No." At her too-quick answer, Karen raised her eyebrows. Julia sighed. "Does it? Because this sweet baby hasn't done anything wrong. He deserves a dedicated mama."

"There's no reason why you can't juggle both, *if* a relationship were to come along. I've known you a long time, Julia. You love family, and you have the strength to manage being a parent and"—her brows rose once more along with a crooked grin— "a girlfriend."

Julia's throat clogged with all sorts of arguments. Even the word 'girlfriend' straightened her spine in objection. "But...but that's assuming I should even think about those sorts of things. I mean, shouldn't I wait a few years before even contemplating dating or spending time in a guy's company just to hear him play his amazing music...or to listen to his beautiful accent?" Julia fisted her hand and pressed her knuckles into her lips, holding in her words until they all but burst out of her. "Conversations with him are...easy, and conversations with men have *never* been easy for me."

Karen's smile loosed. "Okay, I know that in many cases of this kind of trauma, women don't engage in any romantic relationships for a long time, but that's not true for *every* woman. Each situation, each person, must be viewed independently. You are surrounded by an amazing support system. You also have a very good head on your shoulders and a mature strength in your spirit, a solid perspective. And, may I remind you, you believe in a God who can do remarkable things even in the most unexpected ways out of the most horrible circumstances."

"No pain is wasted." Repeating the mantra from an earlier therapy session didn't remove the trauma of her assault, but Julia's heart calmed in the slightest way with the purpose filtering through them. What Peyton did to her was heinous...but not beyond God's ability to form the brokenness into a new kind of wholeness. Miracles. Julia grinned down into her tea. "And Sophie reminded me that our nevers are just God's opportunities for miracles."

"I like that. There's no one-size-fits-all to how God will craft the story He's writing for your life, in your heart."

Julia breathed in the information. Could it be true? "Are you saying that it's okay for me to be attracted...to feel a connection to Henry?"

Karen sat back and regained her tea. "I'm saying that if you do, and you feel safe with him then it's a clear sign God is healing your heart, which is exactly what we've been praying for. And don't forget, God *created* relationship. It's one of His favorite things."

Julia's breath slowed, her thoughts patching together this new idea. Instead of tossing away the notion as if it were a horrible prospect, she listened to the truth she'd ignored the past few days. Every conversation with Henry, every moment of laughter and gentleness, every encouraging word or thoughtful response. She *wanted* him to be the right man and this to be the right time.

"Wouldn't it make sense that God would use love to help heal your heart, as a beautiful example of His ultimate healing of your soul? There is no greater medicine for brokenness than love."

Could Karen be right? The niggling of doubt that had resided in her stomach for so long lessened slightly. "Do you mean, as impossible as a relationship with him might be, and as unconventional an interest, it's not wrong?"

"You must seek God's way in this, but there's nothing wrong with pursuing a relationship with a godly man who God's placed in your path."

Julia sighed back into the chair, her breath pulsing with a sudden sense of...relief? She could *care* about Henry? Like *that?*

"But you need to remember something, Julia." Karen raised an index finger, almost in warning. "*If* you begin a relationship with him, or any guy, there's a chance you may experience some anxiety as the intimacy between you grows."

Julia nodded, an earlier conversation about the topic returning from her memory. "Like a panic attack?"

"Or a bout of unexplained anxiety at the most inconvenient times, I'd imagine—with a touch or a kiss. They could be mild or severe."

Julia's hand went to her lips. She hadn't thought about kisses in a long time.

"But it's part of the healing process, and the right man will work through those episodes with you as long as you communicate what's going on. Communication, trust, and patience are the keys."

"That seems like a lot for Henry to handle along with a pregnant woman." Julia shook her head, the tiny spiral of hope in her chest deflating with each acknowledgment of the surmounting issues.

"Not for the right man. The right one will see your worth because he has godly vision. He'll have patience because he cares about you." Karen took Julia's hand and squeezed it. "You get to choose, Julia. You can choose to allow the fears from the past to blind you to a present possibility, or you can push through your fears and allow God to use the kindness, friendship, and possible love of a good man to help your heart heal. The right man comes on *God's* timetable, not *ours.*"

Julia stared at Karen, allowing the truth to soak through her trembling heart, to pour over memories stained with wounds. A beautiful peace pierced like a shaft of light into the doubt. The knotted-up fear over her attraction to him, her desire to be with him, began to unwind. She ran her hands down her face, her smile bulging against its borders. She was free to care about Henry. She caught some sound between a sob and a laugh in her palm and offered Karen a helpless shrug. "Would it be ironic if I told you Henry's last name is Wright?"

Karen nearly spit out her tea with her laugh. She wiped her lips with her napkin and shook her head. "Nope, I'd say that's God showing off His sense of humor."

Chapter Sixteen

"Becoming a regular handyman, are we?"

Henry looked up from the half-finished sheet music to see Wes leaning against the doorframe of his bedroom, a cup in hand. "Am I?"

"Nate said you're going to help him add a storage closet at the bakery on Thursday."

Henry pressed back in the office desk chair, stretching out his fingers from a solid hour of writing out his composition. "He needed help, and I'm not due to the meeting with the Appalachian musicians until that afternoon. Besides, who knows how useful the knowledge may be for me in the future."

Wes raised his drink to his lips, eyes almost twinkling. For an actor, he concealed very little in his expressions in private. "Why the sudden interest in becoming a handyman?"

Henry returned his attention to his music, ignoring the nudge of curiosity in Wes's implication. "I'm always interested in learning, and I feel certain Nate's skills will benefit me as I purchase my own home."

"Mm-hmm. And *I* have a feeling a certain lovely blonde may have...um...encouraged this educational endeavor."

Henry spun around in his chair, his palms out in surrender. "The idea of being with her is implausible. Two different worlds. Her wounded past. My....my fumbling about and rather dismal track record with women." He shrugged and ran a hand through his hair, his growing interest steamrolling over every doubt. "But she's so kind and smart and talented. I've never connected with any woman the way I have with her. I never believed in love at first sight or a *perfect* match before, but now?" He leaned forward, braiding his fingers and staring up at his friend. "I...I think I could be of some good to her heart, and I feel certain she could be good for mine."

"I like your plan." Wes slid from the doorway and took a seat across from Henry. "Pursuit is certainly a new strategy for you— Usually the women are chasing you down."

Henry's shoulders bent beneath the weight of his foolishness. "Or managing to mislead me into relationships of the worst sort."

"You've learned a great deal over the past four years, Henry. As I recall, a very good friend of mine told me something when I believed my past choices irrevocably destroyed my future."

Henry's brow rose.

"Don't allow your past to steal something God has clearly brought into your present."

A chuckle released as the compassion in his friend's words washed over Henry's internal self-flailing. "I said something that profound?"

"You did. You may speak more easily through music, but when pressed, your words are well intact." Wes gave Henry a measured look while he sipped from his cup. "Seeing you and Julia together...Henry, I don't think I could have ever matched you so well, and Julia isn't the tricky sort." He smirked. "Well, no more so than the natural mystery of every woman."

"A daunting task for us blokes."

"Without a doubt."

They stared at each other, the comradery and care from years of friendship confirming Henry's tremulous desire to overcome his history of poor choices. To discover the same belonging Wes had found within Eisley. Somehow, like the perfect placement of chords for the right music—and despite how outlandish it seemed—he knew he belonged with Julia Jenkins.

"Slow down there, mate. I can already see your mind working on happily ever after."

Henry closed his eyes. Was there any way to keep Wes from prying into his thoughts? Probably not with the years of practice he'd had attempting to pull thoughts from Henry.

"You've always been an 'all-in' sort of person, which I value about you, but her past is a painful one, and neither of you is the bold sort. Patience is what's needed, I think."

Henry shot him a mock glare. "This from the man who got engaged after knowing his girlfriend for"—Henry counted out loud the months on his fingers— "three months, is it?"

Wes stood, his sheepish expression in full bloom. "Do as I say and not as I do?"

"Very funny, old friend."

"Fine. When you know it's the right choice, why wait? But Julia's different from Eisley."

The gravity of her situation stilled Henry's smile. "I know."

Wes paused at the door. "I have an idea. Would you and Julia care to join Eisley and me for lunch on Friday? Eisley's taken the day off, and as soon as the kids get out of school, we're leaving for a weekend trip together to celebrate our engagement, since it's the last chance we'll have before filming takes a more intense turn. It may be nice to spend time together. To visit. Encourage Julia along, you know?"

"What was all that 'patience is what's needed' talk?"

"Right. About that..." Wes stepped out the door, then turned back. "But it will give me more time with her, so I can see if she's good enough for my best mate. Not just anyone will do, you know?"

∞ ∞ ∞

"We've made such great progress." Julia stretched out her back as she stood from the chair she'd spent the last half hour in while sorting through various boxes from the larger of her aunt's two bedroom closets. "I can't thank you enough for coming along."

Henry ceased whistling in the soft way he'd done on and off throughout the morning and looked up, his grin at the ready. Karen's encouragement filtered through Julia once more, and she allowed herself the freedom to view him as a...what? Possible romantic partner? Boyfriend?

Maybe.

His lips crooked.

Definitely.

"I'm glad I came along." He certainly appeared to be, having helped her with the most mundane of tasks as they moved from one room to the next, categorizing, talking, and sharing more and more little parts of themselves through conversations.

"I think we should head home after we finish with these last boxes, then we can return on Friday for the last bit." She cringed at her assumption, and she peeked at him from the corner of her eyes. "I mean, if you'd like to come back then."

"I think it's safe for you to assume, Julia."

The sweet warmth that accompanied each time he said her name spread through her chest and into her cheeks. She drew her gaze from his and scanned the room, her attention pulled toward the massive walk-in closet on the far side of the room near the gold-embossed white four-poster bed. When she'd opened the closet a few days after her aunt's death, the scent of mountain cornflower had unraveled her grief into sobs. She'd avoided the space for months after that heart-wrenching scene, but Friday...Friday she'd shore up the courage to go through the most intimate of her aunt's possessions.

"Julia, I think I've found something."

Henry's voice pulled her back to the present, and she joined him outside the smaller closet. He tugged a crate from the closet and placed it on the white table in the corner of the room to give her easier access.

"There's more sheet music—and Emmeline's name is at the top again." He opened a folder for her, the first handwritten composition entitled *Untouched Fields* laying fragile beneath the cover.

Julia took the folder from him and fingered the pages of the thin yellowed sheets. "The music stops this piece stops on page three with someone scribbling out the last line of notes."

"A poor copy, I'd wager. Most likely the composer had to start over again."

She cringed at the thought of re-forming all those notes on a page. It would take hours. "Is that what you do when you're composing?"

"Sometimes I still compose by hand, but my iPad makes mistakes easier to correct." He winked. "Much less crying that way."

"I do hate seeing grown men cry...unless it's during Hallmark movies."

He lowered his voice and swapped his grin for a stoic expression, though his eyes still sparkled with his subtle humor. "At the risk of losing your friendship forever, I must admit that I cannot bear those sorts of movies. The music is much too repetitive and simple."

She released an exaggerated gasp before grinning.

"However," he continued, "I have been known to shed a tear or two at the end of *The Lord of the Rings*, *Lawrence of Arabia*, and, at one time, *Star Wars*."

Her snicker turned into a full-blown laugh. "*Star Wars?*"

"The music." His palm rose to his chest. "The brass sections. They're perfect."

"Okay, so we may not agree on Hallmark movies, but I can totally agree with the other choices. Maybe even *The Last of the Mohicans?*" She narrowed a look from her periphery.

"Excellent. Or anything by the legendary John Williams. I've been a fan of his since I was eight and watched *Jaws* for the first time."

Her hands stilled on the next piece of paper in the box. "You saw *Jaws* when you were eight? And you slept at night?"

He raised a finger. "Slept, yes, but avoided water for a week. I must say, my mother was quite put out at my lack of bathing. Even the toilet was suspect."

Julia's laugh burst out with such force she pressed a hand to her stomach while the baby wriggled to life beneath her palm. Henry sat so close to her she could make out a faint line of gray crowning his chameleon-like eyes. Subtle and unique, like him. Their gazes held. She swayed toward him, her body taking the lead and then...a sudden panic exploded through her, crashing into the attraction, stealing her breath.

No! She shifted away ever so slightly. Why should she be afraid of Henry? He'd proven himself to be as kind, gentle, and considerate each time they were together. Yet despite the acknowledgement of his gentlemanly behavior in every way, she couldn't stop the two opposing forces battling in her chest. Her head and her heart warred with her emotions, and the fear won.

Her breathing congealed into a knot, and she turned away, tears threatening to spill while she focused on inhaling and exhaling. A strangled sort of feeling rose in her throat. What was wrong with her?

"Are these as unplayable as the ones we found last week?" She forced the question out as a distraction, a way to turn his attention away.

He leaned close enough for her to catch his scent, enticing both emotions to the forefront again. "They do. The first page is perfectly composed, but the following pages aren't real music."

"Why would Aunt Millie *keep* music she couldn't play? It doesn't make sense at all."

He sat back, taking some of the uneasiness with him. "Sentimental reasons? To show how she grew as a composer?"

She clung to the banter, to the sweetness, pushing back the unnamed fear and, praying it away. She *wanted* him close, but...but her body didn't. "Highly unlikely. You can do better than that."

His brow raised at her challenge. "Ah, better." He looked up to the ceiling, eyes narrowed as he deliberated. "These were the last pieces her lover composed, though poorly, and she couldn't part with them despite the fact she cringed as she played through them."

His humor worked like magic to disperse even more of the anxiety. *Oh Lord, help me.* Julia shook her head and looked down at the paper in her hands. Could this reaction be what Karen had talked about? An unexpected response to the trauma she'd experienced? Panic mingled with interest? No, no, please. Not with Henry. He didn't deserve her fear.

"A little better but still not believable."

"Well, perhaps this other box will provide a more suitable explanation for you." Henry pushed aside an elegant scarf and a pair of vintage heels to display an ornate wooden box with an envelope taped to the top. "It looks rather special and similar to the one we found last time."

"It's the same. Wooden, with a golden clasp." She looked over at Henry before gently peeling the paper from the box and opening the envelope graced with *Amelia Dawn* in beautiful script across its front. A simple note, written in the same hand as the previous one, contained a few lines:

'These two are not two; love has made them one...and by its mystery each is not less but more.' I read this from Benjamin Britten and felt it applied beautifully and succinctly to us, my darling. Despite the dangers and uncertainties of our lives, thank you for agreeing to be my wife.

Yours forever,

Lucas

"They...they were married," Julia whispered. "Lucas and Amelia." She turned the letter so Henry could read its words.

"Benjamin Britten?" Henry sat back and ran a hand through his already tousled hair. "Do you suppose it's the real Benjamin Britten?"

Julia blinked from her thoughts back to him. "Who?"

"Benjamin Britten was a famous composer and conductor of the era. A renowned pianist too."

"It would make sense that they ran in the same circles, wouldn't it?"

"How remarkable." He stared at the page a moment longer, and then went back to his work on the crate, his soft whistle taking on a happy tune and easing over her fringed emotions. Communication. Patience.

As the top of the box cracked open, Julia's breath seized.

Letters. Dozens of them. Each with the same handwriting as in the letter she held in her hand except for a larger envelope mixed among the letters. A card fell out of that envelope after Julia slit its top.

Congratulations on your marriage. You are one of the most well-suited couples I've ever known, and I'm glad to hear you'll still be working together to bring me the beautiful music you've always provided. Your gifts never go unappreciated.

Affectionately,

Emmeline

Julia looked from the card to the sheets of music in Henry's hands. Surely Emmeline wasn't referring to *that* music, with its mismatched chords and unusual patterns. Perhaps these were Millie and Lucas's drafts. But why keep them?

Julia placed the card back in the box. She would read some of the other letters in the privacy of her apartment once her mind had taken time to digest this latest mystery in Aunt Millie's past. As she grasped a random bundle of the letters her fingers found another envelope. Larger, once again. And hidden at the very bottom.

Cardboard on either side protected the paper, which slid from the envelope as if accustomed to leaving its place. Inside was a certificate of marriage for Amelia Dawn Rippey and Lucas Randolph Sweitzer.

"He...he was the father," she whispered, piecing the names together.

Henry's whistling came to a stop. "Pardon?"

"Lucas was Rosalyn's father. Look." She handed him the paper. "And he was German."

Henry examined the certificate. "But for which side, do you think?"

Julia sat back with a sigh, blinking down at the box of letters. "Why would she go into hiding if he was for the Allies? It would only make sense that she'd disappear out of disgrace or to protect herself and Rosalyn." She placed the box onto the table and stood, pacing the room, the story taking a much darker turn than she'd wanted. "This is the perfect place to hide from anyone looking for her. And this Emmeline Sterling"—Julia waved toward the box— "she must have had some hand in all of this."

"It's an intriguing theory."

Julia stopped and turned to him. "Do you think Aunt Millie was involved? Could she have been helping the Nazis because of her love for her husband?" A chill trembled up her spine and she started walking again, at a faster pace than before, as if to outrun the possibility. "Oh no, I can't even allow my brain to go there. Surely she'd never help a cause that murdered millions of people."

"Slow down." His calm voice slowing her pace. "These are all conjectures. Just because the man had a German name doesn't mean he or your aunt were Nazis."

She walked forward, finger pointing at him. "But he had an alias, remember? Regular people do not have aliases."

"True, but I'd rather we not forge ahead into the worst." He gestured toward the box. "Perhaps the letters will give some insight, and we still have a few more shelves and closets to explore before we're left to create our own ending to her story. Don't lose heart. I feel there's still more to discover."

Chapter Seventeen

A phone call to Karen before the drive to Aunt Millie's the next day gave Julia a little ammunition for the possible anxiety that lay ahead. Her therapist had reiterated that communication was key to any relationship—but especially when working through trauma—and that the feelings Julia had experienced when Henry drew intimately close to her were unsurprising...and healable.

What a difference it made to know something troubling had an ending.

She and Henry drove in companionable silence to Aunt Millie's house with welcome intermittent conversations about music and faith charming her anxiety further away. She'd thought Henry might not wish to speak of his faith—it seemed a close-mouthed choice for the English people she'd met—but he'd surprised her. Again.

He talked about some of his favorite theological reads and books of the Bible, and despite being from two different countries, they both enjoyed some of the same podcasts from certain international pastors. She couldn't think of one man from her small group at church or college classes who was anything like him. Most of the guys she'd known growing up were tough extroverted country boys, more likely to have a tug-of-war than a heartfelt discussion. Well, except her brother Rick, or Caleb Larson, a quiet cousin who lived down the road from her parents. They broke the usual mold. She didn't begrudge the extroverted sporty guys or think less of them—it's who they were and how her culture raised men. Strength meant physical ability. Virtue showed in hard work and providing for your family. Romance involved snatching a woman and kissing her until her lips went numb—at least that's how it seemed with her daddy.

She grinned at the comparison. Loud, direct, take-charge versus gentle, careful, empathic?

But Henry had stepped right in to help her father and somehow fit in with all the crazy, in his own quiet way.

"I keep studying on this entire situation with your aunt and her husband." Henry's voice broke into the engine's rumble as they drove down the dirt road toward Millie's house. "You know the feelings you have about Emmeline Sterling?"

"Yes?"

"All of the music has her name at the top. Was she Lucas's agent, perhaps? A contact?" He grimaced. "It would have been highly unlikely since most agents I know rarely review the music as much as set up the schedules and venues and such."

"But if she wasn't an agent, what else could she have been?"

"A benefactress who gave some sort of financial support for their music?"

She caught his gaze in her periphery.

"Did your aunt ever mention her?"

"Not that I recall, and I only read through a few of the letters last night. There were one or two references to meeting with Emmeline, particularly when Millie and Lucas were apart, but otherwise nothing to shed any light on her role."

Henry looked back out the window, his brows pinched together, and she could almost see him working through the clues, as though seeking resolution to a dissonant chord. She'd never engaged in much sleuthing before, but his interest, and companionship, certainly kept her hoping for a little more time.

"A little off-topic, but what's your home like? I've never been to England." Though, she'd always wanted to see it, especially since Eisley had returned from her trip with such amazing photos and stories. The quaint towns. The beautiful countryside. Something about that world tugged on her curiosity like few other places. "Eisley said England has a lot of similarities to Appalachia, especially the countryside. Is that the same for your home?"

He turned in his seat to answer, giving her a little better view of his face. "I only live a few miles from Wes's family's cottage in Derbyshire, called Rose Hill. And though I still have a room in Wright Hall, I've been renting a flat in Matlock while I look to purchase my own house. The rolling hills are similar, except you have mountains, as whereas we have cliffs."

Something tickled against Julia's leg as Henry described the town of Matlock with its cobblestone streets, old buildings, and landscape of emerald. She gave a passing glance to her pantleg but pushed aside the need to investigate. The cloth of her slacks must have shifted against her skin.

"What sort of house are you looking for?"

"Well, something with character, perhaps a bit historical, and close to town."

The tickle happened again. She shook her leg while Henry continued to talk, but the tickle sensation moved up to her knee. What? She glanced down, and her breath congealed into an unlocked scream in her throat.

On her knee, looking around as if it were the most normal thing to do, sat a tiny brown field mouse.

"I've always loved the rock homes, or even barns people have refurbished to maintain the general appeal of Derbyshire's countryside and architecture."

The mouse twitched its nose up in the air in Henry's direction. Oh no! Henry! Her stomach coiled into a knot. She had to keep Henry from realizing a mouse was in the car with them. After all, she'd promised to protect him. She focused her gaze forward and pushed words from her throat. "Rock houses? And...um...what exactly are those?"

He hesitated, examining her for a moment. Had her voice shaken? Was her face pale? After a hitch in the silence while she forced a smile his way, he began explaining the beauty of the gray fieldstone homes sprinkled through the lush green hillsides. The mouse skittered an inch or two up her thigh. Her body stiffened, and she held in a squeak but couldn't keep her leg from jerking. With ninja-move stealth, the mouse leapt from her knee, to the door handle and then paused on the edge of the dashboard nearest her window, his little chest pulsing with breaths about the same speed as hers.

And there it sat, staring at her with its round, black eyes, its whiskers twitching as if it knew exactly who to visit next. Her stomach tensed. Her body froze. How could something so small be so unnerving?

Henry continued to talk, oblivious to the entire situation, but Julia quickly took inventory of the road ahead while keeping the mouse in her periphery in case it decided to pull another ninja move. One the right, the road dipped into a deep ditch. On the left, oncoming traffic blocked a possible pit stop.

Three cars. *Three* cars.

When had there ever been so much traffic on this isolated country road?

She gritted her teeth together.

When there was a mouse loose in her car and a mouse-phobic hero trapped inside, that's when.

She examined the passing landscape. They weren't going fast, so maybe if she rolled down her window, she could just flick the mouse out.

The soft cadence of Henry's accent stopped. She hadn't heard a single word, but she conjured up another question as distraction—one she hoped he hadn't already answered already.

"How soon do you hope to buy a house of your own?"

His eyes narrowed, one brow taking a northerly turn. "Like I said, as soon as possible. I've been saving a long time and had some solid success with my last few projects."

"Oh, how wonderful. Which movies have been your favorite to write the music for?"

Silence followed her question, so she glanced his way.

"Are you all right?"

She nodded like the energizer bunny. "Mmmhmmm."

After another pause, his voice filled the space again, becoming the background music for the battle between pregnant woman and her furry, brown nemesis. With almost imperceptible movement, she stretched her fingers to the window button. Only an inch at first. The mouse didn't move, just kept plotting. *Just a little more...*

His whiskers twitched.

Another car passed them on the left.

Another inch. Julia released her hold on the window button and began a stealthy ascent toward the furry rodent, ready to bump him right out the window, but at the touch of the wind on his fur, he took off...across the dashboard, stopping directly in front of Henry.

"There's something about creating the unexpected and having others appreciate it that's reward—"

Yep. Henry saw the mouse. Man and beast stared each other down. Well, as much as a grown man and a pint-sized rodent could have a stare down. Could a little field mouse be referred to as a beast? From the expression on Henry's face, maybe.

Julia tried to keep her gaze forward and somehow prepare to vault in front of Henry should the mouse decide to leap. Her abdomen tensed in protest. "In thirty seconds, I can pull over."

"It's staring at me." He rasped in a pitch much too high for his usual cello-sounding voice.

"I've never heard of anyone dying from a mouse attack. I promise. Twenty seconds and we'll pull over."

He'd gripped the armrests so hard that his knuckles turned white. "I may have a heart attack in ten because my pulse is playing a hard and fast drumroll in my ears."

Julia accelerated. "Ten seconds."

"Do you think it's rabid? Is this typical mouse behavior?"

The mouse shifted its feet, and Henry pressed back as far into the seat as he could. At his movement, the mouse skidded off the dashboard and disappeared...somewhere...onto the floorboard.

"Ahh!" Henry's feet slid up onto the seat. How on earth could an adult male manage to squeeze himself onto the small space?

The sudden need to laugh—or cry—at the entire situation nearly brought Julia to tears. Her body began shaking all over—little tremors from her clenched muscles screaming for relief.

"Where is it?" Henry's gaze roved the floor in a frantic search.

"I don't know." Julia pressed the button to roll down all the windows and pulled over on the side of the road.

Before the car stopped, Henry vaulted from the vehicle. Julia's vault resembled more of a wounded elephant's attempted leap. She'd barely cleared the car door before she lost her balance. In a vain attempt to keep from falling, she flailed one arm to catch the open door but missed and stumbled head-first toward the ground.

Before she made contact with dirt and gravel, strong arms wrapped around her, tugging her into vanilla-scented cotton and strength. She pressed into him, trying to collect her thoughts, but the unexpected embrace distracted her from the next step of her mouse-eradication plan. He steadied her and she looked up, mere inches between their faces.

A fission of anxiety forked through her chest and into her throat, but the sweetness of his presence battled against her fear with an almost impenetrable force. His palms slid over her shoulders to her arms, comforting, and his gaze searched hers.

Then came the anxiety, swooping in with unwelcome claws to steal her momentary calm. Oh, she wanted to hold on to the warmth.

He smiled, a teasing glimmer lighting his eyes. "You promised to protect me from mice."

The unexpected humor put a hitch in her rising fear and she laughed. "In my defense, I've never had one crawl up my leg while driving my car before."

His bottom lip dropped. "The mouse did what?" His gaze dropped to her legs. "Thank heavens you were wearing trousers."

A sudden cold splashed through her chest. The thought hadn't occurred to her. What if she'd been wearing one of her usual dresses. A tremor started at the base of her spine and moved up to shake her shoulders. "Thanks for that. I'm sure to dream about it tonight."

He grimaced. "Sorry." They both turned to look at Julia's car sitting on the side of the road, all its doors open.

"What do we do now? Do you think it will just leave on its own?"

She almost whimpered, knowing her next course of action. "We'll probably have to encourage it."

"How?"

She stared at the car for a second. They'd have to scare it out, but how?

With a deep breath, Julia marched toward the open door, a madwoman laugh in the back of her throat waiting for release. This had to be the most bizarre moment she'd experienced in her adult life. A Braxton Hicks contraction slowed her steps, but she reached inside the car and snatched her purse. Those practice contractions had really increased their intensity over the past few weeks.

Her bright pink purse sitting by the front seat caught her attention, and she took mental inventory of its contents. Yep, it would be a good weight, and the strap was long enough.

Why not end this three-stooges scene with a classic purse-whompin'?

Without giving Henry warning of her upcoming antics, she grabbed the purse and began beating any visible space inside her car. Every seat. The floormats. Dust flew. Papers crunched. Protesting contractions continued, as she took out her frustration on the car until the little critter finally leapt from the car and into the nearby field, running as if it knew exactly what would happen if it made contact with her swing.

"There it went." She sighed, and with a little swagger in her spin—or as much swagger as massively pregnant woman could possess—turned back toward Henry, who stared wide-eyed, his mouth open.

"What?"

He cleared his throat, his expression softening. "I actually feel sorry for the mouse now. You and your purse are terrifying."

Julia stared at him for a moment then all the tension she'd held since the mouse first greeted her from her kneecap released into a torrent of laughter. She laughed until tears streaked her cheeks and her stomach hardened into another Braxton Hicks. She'd had more in the past five minutes than she'd had in the last month. When she finally found her breath again, she placed a hand on her hip and sent him a challenging look. "Told you I'd protect you from mice."

He stepped closer, his grin emerging with a playful tilt. "My hero...ine."

∞ ∞ ∞

Wednesday hadn't been as productive in giving clues to Aunt Millie's mysterious past as Tuesday had been, but Henry couldn't fault the day at all. He'd spent the morning in Julia's company—even if their time involved a mouse fiasco rather than, say, a preferred four-hands duet. She was simply perfect. In his past he'd never been comfortable having deep conversations with women, and though his humor usually emerged after a somewhat brief acquaintance, Julia had brought him out as no woman ever had. Perhaps it was her genuine sweetness mixed with her humor, but he knew, regardless of the obstacles ahead, he'd make any effort to see a future with her.

He certainly hadn't planned on an instant family, and his mother would be appalled at the idea, but he'd tasted this authentic mutual partnership, this genuine comradery, and he wouldn't return to the pretense of what he'd known before. Not when Julia lived in his world.

He'd spent the afternoon with prominent luthier Lark Spencer, learning how bluegrass instruments were created. Afterward, Lark invited Henry to his home for dinner and an evening jam session during which Lark's family had played and sung bluegrass together until late. Their music held a magical, almost mesmerizing quality Henry had never heard before. Their tight harmonies, unique to the blends of family voices, paired with their music to capture what Henry had come to love most about the Jenkins family: a beautiful melding not just of hearts but of personalities and history. Of hardships and celebrations. Of longing and loving. The music visited all those poignant emotions, instrumentally and vocally, pulsing deeper into Henry and creating its own melody.

Another theme for the movie and for whatever else God ushered him to in the future.

The song of Appalachia would stay with him.

He'd barely sat down in his driver's seat before he pulled out his phone and violin to record a simple melody for remembrance until his fingers and heart could fill out the tune later. The orchestral score resounded in his mind behind the fragile melody of his violin. He could hear it, growing wide as the mountain vista, plunging the depths of fog-covered valleys and swooping over the timbered peaks like a golden-feathered hawk on the hunt.

With a month left in the Blue Ridge Mountains, he'd found all the melodies he needed to bring to life the music of Wes's movie. The surge of his calling, this music-making, coursed through his fingers onto his violin with a force beyond his understanding—a deep certainty of God's pleasure.

As his creator fashioned the world with words, on a much lesser level, Henry shaped music into a story. Over the past few years, his composing had fallen prey to consumerism and the pressure to develop something quick and easy, and the inauthentic pressure dulled the sheen from the purpose of his gifts. But God had brought him here to renew that passion, that beauty.

He'd rediscovered the love of the music for the sake of the music.

And, perhaps, found the love of his life too.

He slipped through the back door of the bakery and tiptoed into the kitchen, following the call of his growling stomach. The clock over the stove read 12:50am. He cringed, slowing his pace to ensure his stealth. Music, Appalachian history, and intricate harmonies rang through his mind but perhaps a spot of tea, and a biscuit or two, might appease the creativity monster until morning. After a few minutes of scouring the cabinets, he located a teapot and filled it with water, but just as he reached to turn on the stovetop, a movement to his left froze his steps.

Julia stood in the doorway, her mass of golden hair spilling over the shoulders of her pale blue robe, her saucer-sized eyes staring back at him in the pale light of the room...and in her hands, raised for the attack, a music stand.

Henry's body thawed enough to place the teapot onto the counter before it slipped from his hands. The faint strains of *When You Wish Upon a Star* flitted through his mind as he contemplated her resemblance to the Blue Fairy. Of course, the Blue Fairy didn't arrive with a homicidal look in her eyes or a music stand in her hands, so perhaps Henry's mental orchestra needed adjusting.

She'd frozen too, staring at him as if trying to remember who he was.

"Henry?" She blinked and looked around the kitchen. "What...what are you doing here?"

"Making tea?" He gestured toward the teapot as evidence. "What are you doing with a music stand raised as a weapon?"

"It's one o'clock in the morning and you're making tea?"

"It's quieter than making music right now." He walked over to her, palms raised, and gently helped her lower the music stand to the floor, her fragrance wrapping around him like an aphrodisiac. "I've seen your skills with a purse and have no desire to see how you wield a music stand."

She exaggerated her eye roll and almost smiled. Good progress. "I don't usually have people other than myself in my—Amy's kitchen in the middle of the night."

"Point made." He searched her upturned face, her hair in unruly gold waves over her shoulders. "And why a music stand?"

She released a sigh and let go of her hold on the would-be weapon. "I heard someone downstairs, so I picked it up from the music room as I passed in case I needed to defend myself." She narrowed her eyes at him. "On a high note for you, the piano was too heavy for me to utilize in this particular situation."

"A high note?" He grinned with unabashed pleasure. "I don't mean to *harp* on the music-stand idea, but did you plan to *beat* me to death with it or did that idea fall *flat* once you saw I wasn't a vagrant?"

She tilted her head, examining him as if he'd gone mad, and then a smile tipped in response to the challenge. "Well, using a purse is more my *forte*, but this was all I had available, so I thought it would have to *measure* up."

"You're brilliant," he whispered, basking in her adorableness. "But truly, tonight is more of a *minor* offense than the *major* mouse catastrophe."

"That one was bad."

He shrugged a shoulder. "I'll *scale* back on the puns, if you will."

"Good idea." She walked to the counter and tossed a smile over her shoulder. "We should give it a *rest*."

He snickered. "Excellent. You have a great gift for puns."

"Yes, yes." She reached for a bottle from her spice rack and shook it at him. "Some of the time."

And...simply put, he loved her.

She peeked into his teapot then transferred it to the stovetop. "Why are you coming in so late? Everything alright?"

He pushed the music stand against the wall, farther from her grip. "I spent an amazing evening with the Spencer family and their music. It was remarkable. I felt it here." He pressed his palm against his chest. "*Found* it here."

She sent him a knowing look before reaching for a cannister on the shelf, then a mixing bowl in the cabinet nearby. "They're fantastic." She began placing ingredients into the bowl. "One of the best around here."

Henry moved closer to her side, glancing from her actions to her face. "What are you doing?"

She shrugged a shoulder. "I'm awake. Baking makes me sleepy."

"Baking makes you sleepy?"

"I enjoy reading too, but this way I'm productive. Besides, I'm already down here."

His chest deflated. Not only had he frightened her, but he'd stolen some much-needed sleep? "I'm sorry I interrupted your sleep."

She reached out and touched his arm. "I wasn't asleep anyway, Henry. At this stage in my pregnancy, getting comfortable is a challenge at best."

He looked down at where her hand lay. What would it feel like to take her fingers into his? Soft? Most certainly.

Pink flushed her cheeks as their eyes met, and she slipped her hand away, leaving flour-fingerprints on his navy shirt.

"Oh goodness." She dusted at the marks. "I'm sorry about that."

"It's nothing, Julia."

Her gaze flickered to his and away. She retreated to the refrigerator and brought back butter. "Sometimes I even play the piano to help with sleep."

"The right music works wonders."

"Exactly." The sweet scent of sugar filled the space as she readied more ingredients for what looked like a cookie concoction.

He leaned against the counter and folded his arms across his chest, trying not to stare at the way the lowlight fingered bright and dim gold over her hair. "Have you ever wished to play professionally?"

She took the teapot from the stove and added bags to steep. "I'm not a performer. Music is my...comfort, I guess. Not something I *have* to do for a paycheck, but something I *want* to do as a joy." Her eyes widened and she shook her head. "Obviously you love your job, so you get the best of both worlds."

"For someone who uses music as a hobby, your talent is extraordinary."

"Thank you. It's been fun playing with a fellow musician recently. I'd forgotten the pleasure of sharing music with someone who...understands."

"Me too."

The corner of her smile tipped and he took another step closer, now at the corner of the counter where she worked. She turned off the mixer, drew the bowl out, and took two spoons from a nearby drawer. After swirling them in the taupe-colored batter dotted with chocolate chips, she offered him a loaded spoon.

"Isn't this cookie dough?"

She pushed the spoon closer. "You know your dough."

"But...but are you supposed to eat dough uncooked?"

Her eyes glittered like two sapphires, golden brow raised in defense. "I didn't add the eggs yet, just so we can taste test. It's *always* important to taste the dough, Henry. Sometimes it's even a good idea to only eat the dough."

Her playfulness caught and held. He paused, studying her face, her eyes, a soft cello solo melding through his thoughts in the quiet of the moment. "I see." He took the spoon and placed it into his mouth. "This is delicious."

She paused the spoon on its way to her lips. "You've never eaten raw cookie dough before?"

"No, never. I don't think I've been in the kitchen at my home more than a handful of times."

"Well, then, this dough will definitely not be cooked tonight." She scooped out a large dollop of dough and placed it into a small bowl then repeated. "One for you and one for me. A perfect addition to midnight tea, don't you think?"

And excellent company only made it even better. "Perfect, indeed."

Chapter Eighteen

"You've mentioned your family a few times, but not enough to give a clear picture. I get the sense you're not close to your mom and younger brother?"

Julia studied him from her place across the table. Would he open up to her as he'd allowed her to do? A gentle encouragement to deepen this unexpected friendship? The bits of information he'd shared painted a lonely childhood with little glimmers of sweetness from his grandmother and father, but nothing like hers.

"Elliott is roughly five years younger than me and eight years younger than Matthew. Mother miscarried a baby girl between Elliott and me, so she took special care of him when he arrived."

"Reading between the lines, you mean spoiled rotten?"

His grin hitched up on one side. "Most certainly. And Mother always kept him close, so we never spent much time together, as your family has done."

"I can't imagine not having a positive relationship with my family."

"It's why I've sought it elsewhere." He took a sip of tea, his expression pensive.

"With Wes's family."

"I believe that's where I first started understanding how beautiful family could truly be...why it was so sought after."

"And your mother?" Her own mother came to mind. Strong of mind and heart, but a peacemaker above all. "Did she realize the brokenness inside your family?"

"Oh no." He ran a finger around the rim of his cup as a frown pulled at the corners of his mouth. "She's always been the controlling sort, liking things just so and such, but when father died, the buffer between her and my brother and me disappeared. It was almost as if she took out her grief on us by attempting to mold every facet of our lives."

Poor Henry. So much loss and sadness. Julia leaned closer, her hands wrapped around her warm cup. "How long ago did your father die?"

"Ten years now. I was nigh on twenty, Matthew was twenty-three and engaged, and Elliott had just turned fifteen. For Matthew and me, losing Father was like losing one of our closest friends because he understood us."

"I'm so sorry, Henry. I can't imagine what that must have been like."

A hint of pain flashed in his eyes before he dropped his gaze back to his tea, brow crunched into a V. "I was like a boat without an anchor, drifting from one wave to the next in search of something to direct me, to steady me." He stirred the tea then placed the spoon down without taking a sip. "I met Stephie Lukes during one of my first considerable composing jobs, only weeks after Father died."

"Stephie Lukes? The actress Stephie Lukes?"

He rolled a one-shoulder shrug. "I'm not the limelight sort, but I was more so back then than I am now. We began seeing one another and, like the young fool I was, I imagined it was true love."

"Oh no, Henry."

"It wasn't until we'd been together for two years that I learned she'd been secretly seeing my younger brother as well, and when I confronted her, she told me in no uncertain terms that her affections had long since been attached to him, but she didn't want to hurt my fragile heart with the truth. Then the disaster erupted before the whole world because of her fame."

"How horrible." Just having people in her town know what happened to her, to know they made their own judgements about her situation, was hard enough. But to have your broken heart displayed in the media? She slid her hand across the table and covered his. "I'm sorry. Betrayed by both of them."

He stared down at her hand covering his, unmoving. Had she made a wrong move? Just as she started to pull away, he brought his other hand up, warming hers in between both of his. "Yes, especially my brother. But I should have known, you see. The signs were all there in hindsight. And Elliott had always been the competitive, jealous sort. I should have seen it."

"I think we have that in common. We take people at face value then are surprised when they're not as forthright."

His gaze locked with hers, offering something like a caress over her features. What was he thinking?

"Yes, exactly. I wish I'd learned my lesson then, but my muddled-up mind didn't."

Julia braced herself.

"In true form, I retreated into my music, occasionally venturing out to join local orchestras but keeping a low profile with various projects. I was making a name for myself...then I met Beatrice."

His fingers rubbed against hers, sending warmth gliding from her hand up her arm.

"We met in the local orchestra. She was a cellist and had an Eastman. Beautiful instrument."

Her smile softened at his mental derailment, and she involuntarily squeezed his fingers. Brokenness reflected in his expression. "After six months of seeing one another, my mother confronted me about the relationship. Beatrice was, apparently, married to the pastor of a nearby rectory."

Julia gasped and covered her mouth with her free hand. "No!"

"Indeed." His words edged with regret. "I had no idea. Of course, we never saw one another on a Sunday, but I assumed it was due to her spending time with her family." He ran a hand through his hair. "I was right."

"What happened?"

"It became the talk of the town. My mother was horrified. I was labeled a homewrecker."

"And you retreated back into yourself."

His thumb traced a circle over her knuckles, almost as if the repetitive motion soothed him. "I would have, had Wes not been there. You see, even before he knew Christ, he was the best mate a man could have. He wouldn't allow me to beat myself up too much. Drew me back, reminded me of my music. And his parents reminded me of my faith. I began attending church with the Harrisons and staying more at Rose Hill than home. When Wes fell into similar heartbreak, I was ready to return the favor, because by then, I'd healed. With their help and the Lord's, I'd healed."

She'd only heard bits and pieces of Wes's heartbreaking story, all caught in the limelight during the pinnacle of his acting career, but the weight of Henry's confession proved the gravity of the wounds. A sweet compassion swelled through her for this tenderhearted, wounded man and for the scars he bore with such gentleness. "How long ago?"

"Since Beatrice? Four years."

Four years. "And have you been with anyone since?"

His gaze locked with hers, holding her captive with its intensity. "I prayed the next choice would be the forever choice or not at all. So no, I haven't dated anyone since then—except Stella, my violin, but I'm hopeful she won't be the only woman in my life."

She couldn't pull her gaze from the wordless message in his eyes. Her breaths pulsed shallow, uneven, and her mouth seemed to take on a will of its own. "And have you met that forever choice, you think?"

Was that her breathless voice?

His stare beckoned her, held her in place in anticipation of an answer. How could she have been so bold as to ask? They were still new friends, yet, not so new. He didn't respond, and the old insecurities resurrected with a vengeance. A forever choice? What had she been thinking?

"I think so."

His whispered words pushed through the dizzying insecurity-fest going on in her head right into her pulse. "What did you say?"

"I have no expectations at this point, Julia. I know you're still healing, and your life is on the brink of a transition."

She gripped the edge of the table with her free hand. He was saying what she thought he was saying—what she'd hoped he'd say.

"But I've never met anyone like you, so kind and genuine." He shifted his fingers to take her hand in a more secure hold, searching her eyes. "I have no immediate expectations and would never pressure for anything you're not ready to give. But I want you to know that I am ready when you are...if you want to try."

Her smile resurrected, pushing away the niggling fears from only seconds ago. "I'm not sure when I'll be ready...but...I know that when I am, I want it to be with you."

∞　∞　∞

"Henry, this work is amazing." Wes entered Henry's room shaking his phone in Henry's direction, earbud cord swinging from his neck. "I think it's your best ever."

Henry twisted around in his desk chair, a rush of pride in his new creation straightening his spine. "Imagine what it will sound like in full orchestration, then."

"I know I've told you this before, mate, but you have a remarkable gift. I'm happy the world is beginning to recognize it."

The compliment offered by someone he respected so much nestled deep, buoying his spirit with another burst of confidence. He'd not slept since returning to his room last night after his conversation with Julia, and the long day of research had started to take its toll as evening fell, but hope lingered around him—hope for something better than the counterfeit relationships he'd known before. And yes, music permeated most of his working hours, but a new, more precious understanding kindled in his wounded heart.

To have someone like Julia in this journey of life? The thought humbled him. It felt almost too wonderful to believe. Too massive a blessing for words...and maybe even for music. Somehow the idea swelled into an all-encompassing silence of pure gratitude. Could it be true? For him?

"Are you going back to Millie's house tomorrow?"

"Saturday. Julia has some meetings today with the movers as well as a visit to her college for reenrollment, I believe."

Wes's brow rose, and he crossed his arms. "Well, well. It seems as though things are moving along."

"Better than I'd imagined, especially with the start we had." Henry pressed his palms down his thighs, stretched out his back, and attempted to hide the starry-eyed look he felt sure he displayed for the whole world to see. Perhaps he could excuse it by saying he needed sleep. "So much so that if I didn't have another project to return home for and the job interview, I'd try to stay on another month."

Wes groaned, slacking against the frame. "The distance is not pleasant."

"I should say not."

"But you can make it work, if she's the right one."

Henry's gaze shot to his friend's. "She's the right one."

Wes's brows made an almost imperceptible shift. "You'll make my fiancé the happiest woman in the world if that's true. Not only will she think she instigated it all, but she'll know her sister's heart will be well taken care of."

"I would do my best."

Wes drew one of the nearby straight back chairs closer and took a seat. "And you'd be an instant father, you know."

Another thought that had kept him awake throughout the night. "I know."

"It's an adjustment, Henry, but Eisley's children have taken hold of my heart as if they'd always lived there. It's remarkable how God not only fit Eisley into my life but her children too."

"I'm not in a hurry. I made it clear to her that I would be ready when she was—*if* she was."

Wes leaned forward, staring up at his friend. "You're a good chap, Henry. You deserve a woman who will recognize that."

As Wes stood, his hand hit the desk, and a few of Millie's pieces of sheet music scattered to the floor.

Wes chuckled and bent, with Henry, to collect the pages. "Why are you keeping these? Aren't they rubbish musically?"

"They are." Henry took the sheets and glanced over the notations. "But I feel there's something special about them. Why would Amelia have kept them all these years if they weren't important?"

"Have you seen the shows on the telly about hoarders? I don't think there has to be a reason, just an...obsession." Wes shuddered and reached down to pick up another stray piece of sheet music that had floated farthest away. "And I'm no musician, but putting notes and letters together is confusing enough without adding patterns you cannot play. It's almost as horrid as the idea of combining letters and numbers in math. Heresy."

Henry grinned and snatched the final sheet from his hands. "Standing before millions to act out imaginary lives is much more boggling to the mind, in my opinion."

Wes's laugh trailed behind him on his way to the door. "I have an early start in the morning, so I'm off to bed. Good luck with your research."

"Goodnight." Henry turned back to the scattered sheets lying on the desk in front of him, and something in Wes's words clicked into place. *Notes, letters, patterns...*

He bent over the desk and studied the closest piece of music, lightly penciling in the letters of the melody under each note. Nothing unique there. The notes created a simple melody without any clues to subterfuge.

He dropped to the chords beneath with a few single notes interspersed, marking each chord, then the single notes. No matter how hard he studied, they didn't make any secret sense. He sighed and dropped back into his seat, staring at the stubborn paper. What did he expect to find? Some hidden message?

He groaned and glared at the pages.

Sitting in his relaxed position gave him a distorted view of the pages, where the chord names from the bottom line mingled in with the top-line melody names. He titled his head in examination. Combined, they created...words. Nonsensical and disjointed words on their own, but what if each chord beneath represented a letter not available in the musical octave? He sat up, returning to the pages.

What words could he decipher with letters A through G?

Dead, café...

But wait, if Lucas designed this and he was a German, perhaps he'd distinguish between B-flat and B-natural in his native way? Which would mean...which one was which? Oh yes. B-natural would denote the letter H!

He took that knowledge and applied it to the pattern. New words emerged. *Beach, dead, café, had, head...*

His breath held, and he shifted the desk lamp closer to the papers, pencil at the ready. Perhaps the G-minor chord represented a...He studied the letters in the melody above. An S? Maybe for Gestapo? No, that didn't seem right. He pressed his fingers into his forehead and growled.

This was ridiculous. A secret code? *Really, Henry?*

But his gaze fell back to the chords. What if G-minor represented R?

G-E-R.

And A-major stood for M.

G-E-R-M-A...

And the last chord, G-minor with an added seventh, was N.

He immediately jotted these letters beneath their chords as they appeared, unearthing more words. *Real* words. He blinked and made more conjectures based on some trial and error. The musical rests were punctuation, and it appeared that E-major with its added seventh equaled the letter—he counted seven letters from E in the alphabet—L. He grinned and imputed a few more deductions, plus a history guess at O based on context and reread the message.

GERMANS ARR_ _E AT OMAHA BEACH _N T_ _ _EE_S. F _ _ R DEAD AT CAFÉ MEET_NG _ LACE. AGENTS A_A_T_NG...

"The same chord near N-G every time has to be I." He input the changes.

GERMANS ARRI_E OMAHA BEACH IN T _ _ _ EE_S.

Arrive. A-major with an added seventh represented V.

GERMANS ARRIVE AT OMAHA BEACH...

His throat tightened.

FO _ R DEAD AT CAFÉ MEETING PLACE.

He matched the chord and letter sequence to finish out the message, his fingers clenching the page. This was unbelievable.

GERMANS ARRIVE AT OMAHA BEACH IN TWO WEEKS. FOUR DEAD AT CAFÉ MEETING PLACE. AGENTS AWAITING INSTRUCTIONS IN PARIS AT THE BLUE HAVEN HOTEL.

Henry sat back and stared at his work, running his hands through his hair as he reworked the code on the page in his mind. The sheet music wasn't playable because it was never meant to be played.

It was meant to save the Allies.

Chapter Nineteen

*J*ulia had just finished putting on her pajamas and unraveling the braid she'd had in her hair when a knock sounded at her apartment door. She snatched her robe from her bedpost, wrapping it around herself, as she made her way through her living area to the door. The clock on the side table read eleven fifteen. Who would come calling this time of night?

Henry's face appeared in the small crack in the door. She couldn't hold her smile. She hadn't seen him all day, but he'd left another note on the communication board this morning.

Courage is not the absence of fear but rather the assessment that something else is more important than fear. – Franklin D Roosevelt.

Thank you for making my sanity more important than your fear today as you defended me from the ferocious three-inch vermin while also trying to navigate a motor vehicle. I am amazed by your everyday courage.

Everyday courage?

Courageous was the last thing she felt most days, but somehow Henry seemed to disprove many of her self-doubts. Lack of courage being one. Lack of beauty being another, especially after looking in the mirror while wearing her polka-dotted maternity pajamas.

A blonde, purple-polka-dotted whale.

"You're still awake." He whispered the words while searching her makeup-free face without one grimace.

"Did you need something?"

He pinched a roll of papers in his hands. "Actually, I think I've discovered something of interest to you."

Oh, she just loved the way he spoke. She tightened the belt of her robe—or tried to—and opened the door wider. "Let's go to the kitchen. I have some leftover brioche that needs to be eaten."

He stepped back for her to exit her room and patted his flat stomach, his smile growing into a laugh. "I have a feeling I need to get back into running if I'm to continue an acquaintance with you, dove."

The endearment appeared to surprise him as much as her. It pooled over her like cream cheese icing over a cinnamon roll.

He cleared his throat and diverted his attention, pointing the papers toward the stairs. "Kitchen?"

Julia bit her bottom lip to steady her grin. "Kitchen."

Once she'd retrieved two raspberry cream brioches and started steeping some tea, they sat at the small table in the back of the kitchen. Henry spread some of Aunt Millie's sheet music in front of them, his eyes lit with an excitement much too energetic for eleven fifteen at night. He gave off mad professor vibes complete with erratically spiked hair.

"I think I know why your aunt kept these seemingly unimportant sheets." He tapped the nearest one.

Julia picked up a piece of the brioche and popped it into her mouth. "I'm all ears."

"Right." His eyes took on a little-boy-at-Christmas glow. "What if there's much more here than meets the eye?"

"What do you mean?"

"The chords *and* the melody work together to create a pattern of letters. The melody keeps to the basic A through G letters, except for a little German note-lettering trick, and then the chords create the rest of the alphabet to..." He drew in a deep breath, building anticipation. "To create a secret message."

She stopped chewing and lowered her brioche. Perhaps sweet Henry had been working with movies too long. "A secret message?"

"See here, I've written out beneath each chord the letter it represents." He slid closer to her to share the paper, his vanilla scent mingling with the brioche for a heavenly combination. What would vanilla cream taste like on a brioche?

"The letters make out a message, but only if you look at both the melody and chord lines together."

She pulled her thoughts from imagining how vanilla might taste in just about everything—hot chocolate, strawberry muffins, spinach quiche—and focused on the words on the page.

GERMANS ARRIVE AT OMAHA BEACH IN TWO WEEKS. FOUR DEAD AT CAFÉ MEETING PLACE. AGENTS AWAITING INSTRUCTIONS IN PARIS AT THE BLUE HAVEN INN.

Her brioche nearly stuck in her throat. "This...this is—"

"A coded message. Yes. A logical find, since we've surmised that Lucas was a spy."

"But...this is a secret message." She blinked from the page to him.

His grin spread from one cheek to the other, like he wanted to laugh. "Yes. It is."

"And this is how he sent his messages," Julia whispered, rereading the note. "But...but this note is against the Germans, which would mean Lucas was a spy for the Allies."

"Yes."

She relaxed back into her chair. *Oh, praise God!* "He wasn't a traitor after all."

"Exactly." With a gentle touch he handed her more sheets, his voice nearly shaking with excitement. "Here are a few of the others I've decoded."

PILOTS DOWNED NEAR BORDEAUX. GERMAN BATTALION NORTH OF CITY. TOOK FIRE. PILOTS RESCUED. BATTALION MOVED NORTHEAST TO SURPRISE ATTACK FRENCH.

"Oh my goodness."

"It's remarkable," Henry said, almost breathless, eyes glowing. "Here's another."

U-BOATS PATROLLING BY SOUTHERN COAST. ENEMY NOTED ON SHORE. DO NOT TRUST LAWRENCE MADDEN. HE HAS TURNED.

Julia looked through them, one message after another proving Lucas's allegiance to the Allies. She breathed out a sigh at her aunt's connection to this man. He hadn't been a rogue at all. He'd been a hero.

"But why keep these if they were meant for British Intelligence?"

"It's my guess these were unfinished copies. The smallest mistake could have given the wrong message. Your aunt kept the drafts, so to speak—whether as a memento to her husband, a safety precaution, or something else, we cannot know."

Julia looked from one sheet to the next, Emmeline Sterling's name appearing at the top of many of them. An idea emerged through the fog of this discovery.

"Could Emmeline Sterling have been Lucas's contact? Maybe the person who reported their notes to Intelligence to be decoded?"

Henry reexamined the papers, his chestnut hair falling over his brow as he nodded. "That makes sense, doesn't it? Lucas must have been an excellent spy to obtain so much information over"— he examined the papers— "a year? Maybe two."

"And Aunt Millie knew about it all." Julia brought the tea kettle to the table and filled their cups, stifling a yawn as she did. What an untold story. "What must it have felt like to hide such a secret?"

He met her gaze. "Weighty enough to go into hiding?"

"In a remote part of Appalachia where no one would find her."

"To protect their child."

Julia pressed her hand against her stomach and sank back into her chair. "Because if someone found out Lucas was a spy and connected Aunt Millie to him, then she and the baby would be in danger."

"Exactly. So the only way to ensure their safety was to disappear."

"And be separated from her husband forever." The aching realization of the depths of her aunt's loss weighed heavy in Julia's heart. All those years, longing for a love she'd never see again. All that time, lost. Julia rubbed at her burning eyes and leaned her chin on her braided hands, searching Henry's face. "But what happened to Lucas?"

Henry scanned the papers. "I don't know. The last note I've found is from June 1945. Nothing after."

"Rosalyn was born in September 1944. Do you think...do you think Lucas ever saw his daughter?" The idea hollowed out her chest. To have and love a child you never met?

Henry paused sifting through the papers and finally took a sip of his tea, the compassion in his eyes nearly bringing tears to hers. Why was she suddenly so emotional?

"I think we've had enough adventure for tonight. What do you say?"

"But we haven't finished our tea." She caught another yawn in her palm.

"We'll make up another pot tomorrow." He helped her up, keeping his hands on her arms even after she stood. "For now, I believe you and your little one need rest."

He was so close, his touch sending wonderful awareness up her arms and across her shoulders to her neck. Her body gravitated toward him. His palm slipped to her cheek, but when his gaze dropped to her lips, the welcome warmth of his touch took a sinister turn, curling into a panic.

Her breath stalled...and she couldn't catch it. She pressed a palm to her chest, willing air into her lungs. Her stomach roiled with a surprising bout of nausea as she backed away from him. She turned away from him, her eyes stinging, and pressed her hands against the nearby counter.

"I...I'm sorry, Julia. You had a piece of cream on your chin, is all."

Oh, sweet Henry. He had no idea.

She raised a palm to stop his words, wrestling the panic into submission. *One breath in, one breath out.* She wiped a tear from her cheek with a trembling hand

and turned back to face Henry. His wounded expression tore at her heart. How could she fix this?

Communicate. Yes. The awareness gave her strength to meet the powerful emotions head-on. To try.

"I'm sorry, Henry." She wiped away another tear. "I...I felt a sudden rush of panic at your touch that...that I can't really explain."

He took a step back.

"No, please, it's not you. My counselor told me there might be times where a touch or situation might trigger an unsavory memory or unexpected fear."

"Because of what happened to you?"

She nodded, searching for words to explain. "For...for me, it seems to be more of a feeling of terror than a memory, but I don't want you to ever think it's you." She slid a step closer to him, trying to regain the sweet connection they'd enjoyed only seconds before. "It's a sudden fear that seems to have no rhyme or reason." *In and out, in and out.* She controlled the movement and shifted another step. "Dr. Owensby said that time, communication, and"—she searched his face, beckoning him to hear her— "patience would help these episodes disappear. They...they shouldn't last forever."

He slid another step back. "I don't want to hurt you."

"I know, and I don't want to hurt *you*, either." She held his gaze, stepping forward, holding the internal trembling at bay. "And I don't want you to stop...to stop trying. If you're willing to...to be patient with me."

He tilted his head, watching her, weighing whether his next movement would send her away again, she guessed. "You know I'm willing."

Her breath escaped on a little sob of relief. "I know this isn't typical, and it's not going to be easy, but..." With a tremulous breath, she stepped within his circle of touch, fighting against the claws gnawing in her chest for her retreat. "I...care about you."

A loose strand of hair fell from its spot and blocked part of her vision. Henry raised his hand, almost as if to brush it away, but then let his arm drop back to his side.

No, she could meet him halfway. She was prepared now. Without breaking eye contact, she took his hand and slowly brought it to her face, her breath still shallow but her heart determined. He froze, gaze taking in her face, gauging her status as if she might break. Her pulse slowed, resting in his gentleness, his patience. She offered him a reassuring smile, her eyelids dropping closed, as she adjusted to—even appreciated his touch.

There is no fear in love, but perfect love casts out fear.

Her thoughts paused on the revelation. Could Henry love her, his tenderness piercing through her fear? Was that even possible in such a short period of time?

She opened her eyes, tears blurring her vision, and reached up to cover his hand on her cheek, holding his warmth there.

"I know fear," he whispered. "My whole life has been a study of anxiety, it seems, but I've become braver since knowing you."

She braided her fingers over his. "Braver? How do you mean?"

"Seeing you face your circumstances with such...courage and hope," He looked away, his brow crinkled as a small hint of red rose into his cheeks. "It makes me want to become a man worthy of you."

Her breath caught for a whole new reason. Love? A tear slipped free and warmed a trail down her cheek, but his thumb slipped over to catch it, cradling her face with such care. Almost hesitantly, he released his hold of her and stepped back. "I'll wash up."

His words shook her from the daze. "What?"

He collected the cups on the table. "I'll wash up. You go rest."

"Oh goodness, Henry, that's very sweet of you" She tugged at a cup in his hands, but he refused to budge. Her eyes narrowed. "But I am quite capable of cleaning up"

"I have no doubt, but it's my turn."

The cup kept a tug-of-war between them. "You really don't—"

"Julia." Her name rasped low, weighed with tenderness, stopped her argument. He slipped her fingers free from the cup. "It's all right to allow someone to take care of you. In fact, it may even be a distinct...pleasure for some."

Tears gathered in her throat. He *wanted* to serve her? *Care* for her? She had no words.

Without thinking, she rocked up on tiptoe and pressed a kiss to his cheek, allowing the warmth in his scent, the strength in his kindness, to combat the fear resurfacing through her chest. "Thank you, Henry." She slipped from his side to the door but turned just before leaving.

He stood in the middle of the kitchen, a teacup in both hands and a look of sweet surprise on his face. She'd kissed him. True, it was only on the cheek, but that simple breach somehow gave her courage for the next time. And she wanted there to be a next time. "Thank you."

Chapter Twenty

*J*ulia was going to England in June.

She couldn't tame her grin as she went through another of box of Aunt Millie's things, which she'd brought back with her to her apartment. Cute shoes. And vintage clothes. Even more reasons to giggle like a school girl.

During her and Henry's lunch date with Eisley and Wes, the happily engaged couple shared the news of a ritzy engagement party at Wes's family's estate house in Derbyshire so the Harrison's friends and family could celebrate with the couple. And...they'd invited anyone from the Jenkins family who could make the trip.

In June! Julia gave a little squeal.

Surely she could travel with a two-month old, right? And she'd get the chance to meet Wes's family who Eisley claimed were fabulous. And, possibly best of all, she'd get to see Henry's world. His home. His beloved Matlock and Derbyshire. Take the opportunity to discover how this whole relationship might work from England to Pleasant Gap.

She'd have given a little excited jump if she weren't afraid of pulling a muscle in her extended abdomen.

Was it ridiculous for a pregnant woman to feel like a lovestruck school girl? Maybe it was because she'd been so wounded, so...alone, that Henry's gentleness and care offered a hope she'd not expected coming her way for a very long time.

And how could his tenderness *not* draw her to him? Maybe even make her a little braver than she'd be on her own?

It wasn't until after the bakery had closed that she heard the faint strains of piano music floating up the stairway, begging her to investigate. He must have returned from his visit with Lark Spencer after his day at the movie site.

She slipped down the steps, her palm resting on her stomach—a new habit she'd taken on over the past few weeks. The little one seemed to sense her anticipation, rolling against her palm, encouraging her forward.

The song Henry played reverberated through the rooms, a melody mixing anticipation and mystery, but also something else—a vast sort of sound, as if she stood on a precipice and looked out onto a forever horizon.

She peeked around the doorframe into the music room to find him exactly where she thought he'd be, but his appearance inspired her grin. The endearing mad professor look was back—hair sticking up in all directions, a somewhat crinkled, open-collar shirt, and an intense expression. His less groomed appearance teased her thoughts in unexpected directions, and the music only seemed to encourage them.

Drawing her to him.

The music rumbled into an approaching storm of chords and glissandos—building, battling, bringing thunder, taking her through the tempest—but just as quickly treble birdsong broke through the storm and the melody gentled to a calm after the storm. His skillful playing wove a spell over her, reaching into her spirit and transporting her to a place she couldn't quite define. She closed her eyes and leaned her head against the doorframe, allowing chords and strains to weave a magical setting of beauty and...peace. Almost like a prayer.

As the hum of the melody settled into a sweet silence, she opened her eyes to find Henry watching her, his smile soft as if he knew his playing left a lingering redolence.

"Did you write that?"

"Yes."

She stepped into the room. "For Wes's movie?"

"I believe it's going to be a particularly important scene of spiritual understanding for the hero, on a rock outcropping overlooking a view of your mountains."

She pressed a palm to her chest. "I could feel it. It's beautiful."

"I've enjoyed creating it." He gathered his sheet music and stood. "Would you care to play? I was finishing up here."

"Actually, I could listen to you all night." She rubbed her stomach. "And so could Little One. As soon as he heard you playing, dancing ensued."

A look of unhindered fascination brought Henry closer. "Really?"

"It certainly felt that way." The baby kicked, then did some sort of roll. "Oh, see, right here."

Without thinking, she grabbed Henry's hand and placed it on her stomach just as the baby performed something akin to a somersault.

His eyes widened and he alternated his attention between her stomach and her face. "I felt it." Air burst from him like a laugh. "What about that!"

The baby proceeded to show off, pressing a pointier body part against her belly so that her skin protruded. Henry's changing expressions of fascination kept her doing crazy things like allowing him to move his palms over her extended belly without one thought to the oddness of it all.

"Does it hurt?"

She rubbed her fingers against the side of her stomach where the tension pressed with added force. "Not usually, but sometimes the baby can get into a position that's really uncomfortable for me."

Another kick hit Henry directly in the palm. He laughed. "That was hard."

"I think he wants out."

"Are you ready to meet the world, little one?" He bent forward ever so slightly, gaze on her stomach, voice soft. "We'll play more music for you, duck."

We? Duck? The gentle curl of his words, the endearment, spoken in his beautiful accent to her baby, nearly melted her to the rug. She stared at the top of his head of erratic hair, a rush of tenderness sweeping over her. Could God...would God do something this...beautiful for her?

"You just called my baby a duck."

He looked up at her, one brow rising to her challenge. "In my culture, that's a term of sweetest affection."

"And what about the term *dove*?" No, she hadn't forgotten him calling her that.

He stood, his eyes searching hers, his face growing ever closer. "It's not quite as common for babies, I don't think."

Her breath grew faint, and she waited for him to bridge the gap between them, half hopeful, half...uncertain. "And who would you commonly call *dove* as a term of endearment?"

He hesitated, then inched closer. "The woman who holds my heart." His voice, cello-soft, swooped low and took her breath with it. She placed a palm to his chest, her pulse thrumming in her ears, and held his gaze. She hadn't kissed anyone since—

Every thought faded to black and her insides began a fight-or-flight ascension. *Please, oh please, no.* His hands slipped from her stomach to encircle her waist, warm against the small of her back, but when his gaze dropped to her lips, the panic rose like claws closing around her throat. *No, no. Lord, help me.*

His arms transformed into shackles, his closeness trapping her escape. She fisted her hand at his chest, battling the inner monster. Her mind knew the truth, *saw* the tenderness in his expression, but her heart pulsed a frantic retreat. She pushed against his chest, tears flooding her vision. With a wounded whimper, she broke free from his hold. "I'm...I'm sorry. I...I can't. I'm so sorry."

His own breaths rushed out in spurts, then he studied her with an unreadable expression, his eyes voicing the questions he restrained. Silence pierced a distance between them that her heart didn't want but her body needed.

155

With nothing but a nod in her direction, he turned and left the room.

She blinked at the sting in the suddenly empty room, the silence moving through her to leave an emptier pit in her stomach. After the sweet moment they'd shared over the baby, her stupid anxiety ruined everything. Tears invaded every corner of her sight, and her breath became uneven for a new reason.

Why *wouldn't* he leave? What man wanted a woman who sent mixed signals like this? Her hand gripped the edge of the piano, and she sank onto the bench. Oh, how she wanted to be held by him. Why couldn't her body follow along with her heart?

She buried her face into her hands, allowing the grief for yet another lost thing in her life to pour out into quiet sobs and empty space.

"I've found that when words are not enough to calm my spirit, music can."

Julia looked up at the sound of Henry's voice, his words an *adagio* tempo through her heartache to comprehension. "What?"

"There are wounds within you that words cannot touch." He drew close, papers in hand, his gaze continuing its search. "So perhaps we can find some other way to reach them."

She wiped a hand over her eyes. "I don't understand."

With a careful approach, he placed pages on the piano rack then gestured toward them. "Perhaps you could try this?"

She blinked back her tears and looked at the title of the music: *Broken & Brave.*

Her gaze shifted back to his. What did it mean?

"I wrote it so you could choose to play it on your own, here." He pointed to the top two piano staves, then cleared his throat and gestured to the two staves beneath them. "But I also wrote it as a duet, so if you didn't wish to play alone"— his gaze found hers— "you wouldn't have to."

She looked from the music to him, tears closing around any response. How would she ever fathom his thoughtfulness? She caught another sob, and he stepped back, as if he were the reason for her reaction.

Well, technically he was, but in a good way. Before he could retreat, she grabbed his hand. "I'd rather we play it together. If...if you're willing."

His smile softened. "Of course, I am."

She scooted over on the bench toward the treble keys, and he sat beside her, awaiting her initiation. Her fingers trembled as she placed them on the ivories, but after a cursory study of the music, she drew in a deep breath and began. Henry followed her lead.

Her fingers started off uncertain, quivering slightly as they kept their distance from his. The music complied to her intention, allowing her to move up the treble scale, away from his lower notes. He was there, though, his subtle scent of spice and vanilla teasing her to release her fears to the music...and to him.

As the *legato* melody of halts and trills wound into a faster *staccato* rhythm in time with her pulse, their fingers moved closer, shoulders brushing. Vanilla stamped the melody with Henry's presence as much as the notes on the pages. Music grew in volume and intensity until it surrounded them. Synchrony, harmony, and delicious rightness crashed with cymbal-strength inside of her as his fingers swooped beneath hers to play notes between her hands. Her breath pulsed with the notes, her fingers dancing around his, with his.

The music took them on separate sides of the piano and brought them back together, through her insecurities, directly into Henry's waiting melody. He'd written this for *her*. For *them*. To show her his intentions captured much more than words, even more than her fear. Words couldn't reach to the soul-level that his actions, his music, awakened within her. Despite her fear, he'd found a way to bring her courage.

It was the most beautiful, intimate experience she'd ever known.

The music rose on a crescendo, their hands overlapping, their shoulders pressed together. His breath warmed her cheek, taunting her to breach every hurdle to stay near him. To trust her heart, her fears, with him.

As the music slowed, returning to its original *legato*, she kept close to him. She drew in a shaky breath as the last reverberation of notes faded into silence. The air zinged with words unvoiced and music spoken.

Julia slipped her fingers from the keys and into her lap, capturing courage from the melody-infused air.

Henry shifted beside her and...she turned toward him, raising her gaze to his. Her pulsing breaths caught. The tenderness in his eyes held her locked in place. His chest pumped with the same rush as hers had a few moments ago. His face flushed with a rosy glow.

How...how could she love a man she'd only known for a month? A man she hadn't even kissed? But she did. His kindness, his...care. How could she respond in any other way but love?

He brushed a strand of hair from her cheek, his smile bidding a benediction to the powerful performance. Love looked like this. Gentle, passionate, sacrificial...beautiful.

Without a word, he bowed his head, stood, and walked from the room.

Her emotions hung on a thread—a fraying thread. He didn't take a kiss from her, though he must have known he could have, and yet, instead of releasing her, his choice bound her stomach in knots.

The intimacy of the music had calmed her anxiety, or at least distracted her from it long enough for it to dissipate. Perhaps, if she played this song in her head, the music, paired with Henry's affection, would finally build the bridge her heart needed to bring about a kiss or two.

She turned to the empty room, a resolution pooling against the uncertainty. Music spoke when words failed but—she had a feeling—so did kisses.

$$\infty \quad \infty \quad \infty$$

Julia sat in her aunt's massive bedroom siphoning another box from the final closet in the room. One box revealed old photos including some she thought her mom would enjoy seeing from her grandmother's younger years. The contents of another box brought tears to Julia's eyes.

Baby clothes.

Dozens of delicate and beautiful outfits that Rosalyn must have worn.

Julia had Henry take it to the car immediately for safe keeping. Even if she wasn't having a girl, there was something incredibly precious about owning those beautiful keepsakes. And who knew? Maybe one day, if God gave her the opportunity, she'd have the chance for another baby.

Her gaze drifted to the closet, where Henry tugged out two more boxes. His hair curled from perspiration, but his outlook remained evergreen. He'd been extra cautious around her, not getting too close—a choice she didn't like at all. She *wanted* him nearby. In fact, if she could learn how to manage this anxiety, she'd probably end up doing something crazy like taking charge and pulling *him* into a kiss.

He caught her watching him and raised a brow, as if asking her what was taking so long. Well, she was working on it.

"I'm really glad you got to come along with me one last time. It wouldn't be the same, trying to unearth Aunt Millie's mysterious past without you."

His gaze took on that sweet, tender look she found almost too powerful and raw to maintain, tugging at her heart.

"I'm happy to have been your sleuthing partner. It isn't every day one discovers a true story so compelling as this." He lifted one of the boxes and sat it in the chair in front of her. "And perhaps there are a few secrets yet to uncover. We have these two boxes left."

"Well, we've pretty much gone through everything in this house, so if there's nothing in these boxes or a magical secret compartment somewhere, I guess the rest of our questions about Aunt Millie will have to remain unanswered."

"A magical secret compartment?" The humor in his voice dripped with playful sarcasm.

She offered him a mock glare. "It happened with Wes and Eisley."

"And they were in a centuries-old tower in England. I'm not certain pseudo-Victorian homes in American carry the same"—his brows gave a playful wiggle— "magic?"

Oh, give her enough time and it sure could. Lip to lip.

She waved one of the newly discovered music sheets in front of her warm cheeks. "I don't know about that, Mr. Realist."

His smile bloomed into a grin accompanied by an eye-twinkle. "Ah, that would be the eldest Wright brother, Matthew. Not me."

"Oh really? And who would you be?"

"I'm the romantic." He winked and her face flushed with the welcome warmth of a shared attraction.

Oh yes, kissing sounded better and better all the time. "You're trying to distract me from my valid magical argument."

"Only confirming that I am keen on believing in magic, dove."

Her teeth skimmed over her lower lip as her smile spread at his endearment. The piano duet had somehow bound her heart to his in an even deeper way. He'd moved beyond the friendship zone and planted himself firmly in her future.

He disappeared once again into the closet, and she stared at the empty closet doorway for a few seconds, releasing a very daydreamy sigh. Sure, he may not be the best fit for Disney-princess Sophie, but he fit the desires of Julia's heart like a missing puzzle piece or a perfectly tuned third in a chord.

She adjusted in the chair to ease the tightness in her lower back, but comfort hadn't been her friend all day. Her mom and Eisley had told her the last month of pregnancy proved the longest and most uncomfortable, but she'd barely begun her ninth month and already drooped from a sudden weightiness—although it did make breathing easier.

A very unladylike groan slipped out. To think she had *three* more weeks left of this?

In an attempt to distract herself from the discomfort, she explored the new boxes, one revealing carefully wrapped trinkets of various shapes and sizes. The next container held two vintage hats. A beige cloche with a matching flower on the side, and a navy fascinator that looked like something the Duchess of Cambridge might wear as a throwback to classic forties. Julia slid her fingers over the delicate design, both hats in pristine condition after all these years.

"Julia." Henry emerged from the closet, his brow pinched into such tight wrinkles she shot—or rather rocked—to her feet. "I think there's something else back here."

She braced her palm on her back and stretched a little from the ache in her lower abdomen at her sudden movement. "What did you find?"

"I'm not certain, but would you shine the torch this way?"

The torch? She searched the room then looked back at the closet where he'd disappeared. *Torch?*

"Flashlight," his muffled voice called.

Ah. She took the flashlight from the desk and met him at the closet door.

"Here. Shine on the far back wall, if you will."

He was so polite. She loved British-speak. "What is it?" Why did she feel the need to whisper?

He turned, brow raised. "Um...I think it may be a magical secret door."

She gave his shoulder a light slap as she moved to his side, all whisper-tendencies evaporating. "Are you kidding me?"

"Actually, no. Look." He took the light and guided the beam toward the back of the closet, where it hit a small, square-framed door halfway up, about the size of a large shoebox.

"What is it?"

"Clearly, you have no faith in your own magical secret door theory."

She rolled her gaze to the ceiling but shifted closer to him as he moved toward the compartment in the long, narrow space. It must have stretched half the length of the bedroom. The further in they stepped, the darker the shadows and stronger the 'old' smell became. Somewhere along the way, she grabbed his arm. The strength in his presence grew bigger than the anxiety in her chest, giving her a little more freedom to stay near, to accept this sweet attraction without fear. Perhaps, the more she pushed through her fear, the more courage overcame it.

And he certainly was a nice person to be close to. All vanilla-scented and cuddly.

"I do like this particular position, I think." He shot her a crooked smile from his periphery, as if reading her thoughts. "I'm feeling heroic...as long as no mice appear."

She snickered and squeezed closer. "I don't measure heroism in mouse-size."

"Excellent for me, then." He shifted and placed the flashlight in her hand. "Here. Hold the torch, and I'll see if the door is locked."

She kept one arm around his and leveled the light on the small compartment, shifting with him like static cling as he edged closer to the door.

"Exactly how do you measure heroism, then," he whispered, his focus forward.

She thought a moment and couldn't stop her grin at her own brilliance. "Heart-size."

He wrestled his smile and tugged at the handle. After a jerk or two, the small door creaked in protest but opened to reveal one *unmagical* item.

A black metal box with an old-fashioned padlock on the front.

"Another box?" She relaxed against him with a pout. "Haven't we seen plenty of those already?"

"This is our first locked one. Must be something very special," Henry pulled the box from its place in the wall. "Have you any idea where we may find a key?"

"I have a few from her desk we could try, but almost all of them have been door keys."

Julia backed out of the closet, but then halted in the doorway. "Wait, Henry. There was one key, a small one." She examined the keyhole to the box. "Small enough for that, I think. It was in an envelope that Aunt Millie left on her desk for me." Her gaze came up to meet his, the sudden realization resurrecting her pout. "But it's back at the apartment."

"Prolonging the anticipation of something magical, then?"

His voice, so close and rasped, poured like warm oil down her neck and over her shoulders. She had a funny feeling he wasn't referring to the box anymore. Her attention dropped to his lips for a split second as she struggled for her voice. Oh heavens, the man made her knees weak with just a look. "I think it will be."

"I have no doubt."

Chapter Twenty-One

*H*enry came upstairs for the last boxes to load into the car as Julia gave the house a final walk-through. It stood as a shell of its former self, with marked furniture waiting in barren-walled rooms, but Henry couldn't help but smile nonetheless. He wasn't the same person who'd entered Pleasant Gap over a month ago. His perspective had grown into something much fuller than he could have imagined discovering when he'd ventured with Wes to Appalachia.

He'd observed another healthy family besides Wes's and found himself accepted as he was. Included, even by the patriarch, Nate Jenkins. He'd reignited his passion for creativity through music. But more than any of those, he'd found a kindred soul.

"Well, I think we're done here until the movers show up on Monday to take the furniture and then the cleaners arrive." Julia leaned against the office doorframe, her palm rubbing her abdomen, a grimace pulling at her lips. "I can't believe we finished."

He dusted his palms against his slacks and lifted the locked box into his arms, the last piece to include in the overpacked car. "I'm certain you have mixed feelings."

She nodded, her other hand going to her lower back—a gesture she'd done a lot lately. Was that a habit or gesture that accompanied pregnancy?

"I think Aunt Millie knew leaving me this place would change my future for the better, so even though there are a lot of memories within these walls, I also like to think that a few of her dreams might become reality through me."

He propped the box against his side as he met her in the doorway. "I feel certain you have the strength to accomplish whatever you set your mind to. Look at how far you've come. It's remarkable."

The rose-color in her cheeks deepened with her smile and she slid into the hallway, waiting for him to join her. "Thank you, Henry."

There was a distinct pleasure in knowing he held the power to bring her smile to life, to somehow hold a clearer mirror up to her so she could see the truth of who she was—an activity he hoped to replicate for a long time. Till-death-do-us-part kind of long.

Her comment about hero-measures reflected him in the same way. Could it be possible that the best relationships in life did that very thing? Portrayed God's truth back to the person through love?

She slipped her arm through his as they walked down the long hallway toward the winding staircase leading to the first floor, taking their time. A good-bye walk.

The hallway was a magnificent work of architecture because floor-to-ceiling windows on both sides welcomed a wide-angle view of the surrounding countryside, while in the back revealed a partial prospect of the layered-mountains vista. "No wonder she built her house here."

Julia followed his gaze. "That *is* a fine view." She sent him a grin, raising a mischievous brow. "But I can show you an even better one, if you want."

"Is it far?" His gaze skimmed her body. "I wouldn't want to overtax you."

She waved away his concern. "I'm Nate Jenkins daughter. I won't let a little thing like pregnancy stop me from taking a short walk up the hillside. Besides, you can't leave this place without seeing my aunt's favorite spot."

They continued their way through the empty house to the driveway, and he placed the lock box in the car, then met her in the garden. Walking a well-worn path up a hillside, they weaved between large rocks and aged trees that touched overhead. Julia kept the pace slow, occasionally stopping for breath, but even at Henry's insistence to turn back, she continued.

"We're almost there." She gestured ahead as she pushed back a damp swath of hair from her face and continued up the incline. "Wait for it."

With a final burst of energy, she completed the steps to the top of the hill and up to a leveled grassy area.

Henry had expected the mountains but not the massive waterfall...or a molten sunset. Below them to the left, the water tumbled at least a hundred feet into a river, and in the distance, the orange-hued mountains gave backdrop. A rush of cool air brushed his face, carrying the scent of the mountains and water combined. Amazing.

He drew out his mobile to take a few snaps, including Julia's profile in one or two for good measure, which she caught him doing.

"If you're going to take a photo, you might as well get in it too, Henry."

He slipped his arm around her waist, and fumbled through trying to snap their photo, but she quickly took the phone and completed the task with much more selfie-expertise.

"Do you see down there?" She pointed to a roofline through the forest to the right.

A small cabin emerged from the forest-growth across the ravine, its porch facing the waterfall.

"That's mine now. I'm keeping it for vacations and...well, times to get away, you know?"

Henry could only imagine what a getaway that would be. Remote. Quiet—except for the sounds of nature and the welcome consistency of the waterfall. "It's lovely."

She opened her mouth to respond but then grimaced, her palms going back to her stomach, as they had done several times throughout the walk.

"I think we should start back, Julia. I've allowed you to walk too far."

"Nonsense. I chose this walk and I'm fine." She waved again, starting the descent down the hill. "My body doesn't know what to do, probably. It's been a little while since I've taken a walk like this."

He offered her his arm, and she slid her hand through, leaning in close to him—whether from fatigue or nearness, he didn't care. He liked the fit.

They'd made it halfway down the hillside, Henry helping her over various unsteady spots along the way, when she stopped, wide eyed and clutching his arm. A whimper escaped her lips and she looked down.

What a curious reaction. Henry followed her gaze to her feet. A sudden shock of cold traveled from his head to his toes. Liquid pooled at Julia's feet and her increasingly pale face did nothing to soothe his sudden sense of dread.

He took her by the shoulders. "Please tell me you're hiding a bottle of water somewhere on your person and it just ruptured."

A squeak like the sound of a wounded animal came from her mouth as she shook her head.

That narrowed it down to two possibilities, and Henry had a sinking feeling he knew which option this was.

"I...I think my..."

"Yes, I think so too."

"I...I'm not due for three more weeks." She blinked up at him, searching his face as if he had some sort of solution to the dilemma.

"Does the baby know that?" He winced at the question and placed his palm on her back for support. "Should we..."

"Yes." She made a stiff turn back toward the trail. "I think we need to get to the—"

"Most certainly."

Her first few steps came slowly before she stopped altogether to hold her stomach.

"How can I help? What do you need?"

How fast did babies come? Would he be required to...help? He shook the thought from his head and prayed for heavenly intervention. From his limited knowledge of the process, that required him to...And how did one prepare to...

His thoughts couldn't even form full sentences at the idea.

Her gaze came up to meet his. "Henry, we're well over an hour away from the nearest hospital, and I've already disconnected the phone service for Millie's house."

"That means we can't phone for help."

Her bottom lip began to quiver as she slowly nodded her head.

At the vulnerable look on her face, strength surged into his body, and without a word, he slipped Julia into his arms and started down the hill as fast as his feet would go.

"Henry?" She gasped, sliding her arms around his neck. "What are you doing?"

"Sweeping you off your feet, dove." His bit of humor lit her gaze before she grimaced from another pain. "Hold on, Julia." He forced confidence into his voice he didn't feel. In fact, his pulse hammered retreat drums in his ears. "You and this baby are going to be all right. I'll make certain of it."

∞ ∞ ∞

This was not happening.

Henry had cut a twenty-minute drive down to fifteen, and phone reception was mere minutes away. He needed directions to the nearest hospital, and fast, because Julia's discomfort grew by the second.

Her contractions had increased to nearly nonstop in the past few minutes, pacing themselves at...two minutes apart. What did that mean? Was that a good thing?

Not for him, if Julia's chattering on proved true. She was talking as if...they wouldn't make it to the hospital. Heaven help him! He clung to the soothing sounds of Beethoven gentling from the car speakers. He'd chosen it to help keep Julia calm, but he felt fairly certain he needed the music just as much.

"You know, my mom says that nature takes over and things happen naturally." Julia's words spilled out in a nervous outburst. If Henry weren't already driving much faster down the gravel road than he should have been, he'd have taken her hand to reassure her. He'd tried once, and she'd nearly squeezed his fingers off when another contraction erupted.

He checked his mobile again. Still no bars. But they had to be close to reception now.

"Though I had hoped for some medication to help with the pa—"

Her words disappeared into another bout of breathing exercises. With a look and a few vigorous nods, she encouraged him to join in. He'd always wondered what the breathing exercises did in the birthing process when he'd seen them in movies. After a few minutes of pacing his breaths to Beethoven he felt slightly light-headed, but the exercises seemed to help Julia get through the pain. Were they just a distraction from what was to come? Or truly relaxing? Because they weren't working, if that were the case. His body tensed at her every whimper, and there was nothing he could do to help her.

"There's the pole. We should have reception." Julia pointed to the right side of the front windshield and pulled out her mobile.

"Yes, excellent. Directions to the nearest hospital, then?"

She sent him a look from her periphery. "Or directions for how to deliver a baby."

Henry nearly stopped the car. "Pardon?"

"I've taken all the birthing classes. Any time contractions get to three minutes or below"—she held up the number of fingers— "all the medical advice is to go directly to the hospital. I'm at two."

He squeezed words through his dry throat. "I'll drive faster."

"We have to prepare." She froze. "Here comes another one." She reclined the seat and began her rhythmic breathing again.

Henry tugged out his mobile and spoke into it for the nearest hospital.

"They're getting much more painful." Her words came soft and weak through her pain.

He chanced a look at her. Her hair flowed loose and wild around her face and her eyes shone large and dark in the fading daylight. He pushed a strand of hair from her face. "What can I do?"

She relaxed back into the seat, her breathing slowing despite his accelerated driving pace. "Listen to me, okay? I don't know exactly what's happening with my body, but things are moving fast."

He glanced down at his phone as it searched for an answer, the screen emerging with text and a map, and the lovely little red symbol of a cross noting the hospital. Perfect. Destination.

"Okay, what do we do?" Julia read the information displayed on her slightly larger phone screen. "This post says to make the mother as comfortable as possible in a reclined position."

"The hospital is only fifty minutes from us." His suggestion released in a *staccato* rhythm that matched his heartbeat. "That isn't *too* far."

"As contractions increase in intensity and become closer together, the mother's hips will need to be elevated."

The voice inside his head was screaming at *fortissimo*, but by some divine intervention the tone escaping his mouth remained calm. "What is the emergency number in America? Nine-one-one?"

She nodded and breathed through another contraction. Halfway through, her breath turned into a whimpering cry. Henry's foot pressed down with more pressure. *Oh Lord, help us.*

"Turn off the music, Henry."

"Pardon?" Surely she couldn't be serious?

"I...I can't concentrate. It's getting too difficult to concentrate."

He stared at her a moment and then switched off Beethoven but held on to the final strains internally. Yes. He needed some calm. Focus.

"Allow the mother to be as close to the floor as possible if there is no bed"—she squeezed out the words— "because the baby will be slippery when he arrives."

With those words, the music in his head came to a jolting halt. "Julia, you can't have this baby in a car, can you, dove?" He cleared his throat of the frog obstructing his deeper tone.

She rolled her eyes and glared at him in an un-Julia-like way. "Do you think I want to have this baby in a car, Henry?"

He cringed. "Stupid question."

She began a strained reading again. "Ensure that your hands are clean before you begin examining the mother."

A small bottle of hand sanitizer hit him in the chest. The fortissimo scream in his mind returned with a vengeance. No music. Only screams. And panic.

"I think we should stop the car."

He pressed down a little harder on the accelerator.

Another contraction hit her as he dialed nine-one-one.

"Nine-one-one, what's your emergency?" the female voice responded through the speakers as he focused on keeping the car on the road.

"Yes, thank you." He breathed out the words as relief poured over his shoulders. Help. Clarity. "My...my..."—he looked over at Julia— "girlfriend."

Her attention shot to him, and her bottom lip dropped. Well, at least he'd distracted her. He offered an apologetic shrug and hopefully a smile, but he wasn't certain. His mouth was so dry he could hardly feel his lips.

"She's in labor, and we are still some distance from the nearest hospital."

"And we don't think we'll make it," Julia whispered through her pain, but the force of her waving for him to repeat her message to the operator belied the softness of her words.

His throat seized at the possibility. "And we don't think we'll make it to the hospital, if you know what I mean."

Dead air hovered over the line as Henry waited for the operator to respond. Five seconds. Ten. His grip on the steering wheel tightened.

"What is your current location?"

Henry repeated Julia's rasped directions to the operator before the contraction sent her writhing against the seat. His breath constricted in his throat. He had to do something, *anything*. "Please, we need help. She's in a great deal of pain."

"That's usually part of the process, sir. How close are her contractions? Every three minutes? Five minutes?"

"Oh no, much less. She's having at least one every minute."

Another ten-second pause. "Sir, you need to pull over on the side of the road and prepare to deliver a baby. An ambulance has been dispatched to your location. Remain on the phone with me, and I'll talk you through it."

An explosive drum rhythm beat in his mind, blocking out everything except that he, Henry Wright, was about to deliver a baby. *Lord help us all.*

"Henry." Julia's hand covered his, grasping, squeezing, pleading through her touch. "This...this baby...I...I need to push."

Julia's desperation sent him into motion. He met her watery gaze, and the same force of purpose infused him as it had on the hillside looking over the waterfall view. She *needed* him to be strong. He steered the car to the side of the road and jumped from the driver's seat to round to the other side, calling out to the operator as he opened Julia's door. "All right, we've stopped. What...what now?"

"Is there a place in the car she can lie back, to get as comfortable as possible?"

He glanced into the box-filled backseat and hatch of the car, then to the front of the vehicle. If he pillowed her back and head, she could relax against the armrests at least. He dug through the boxes in the trunk for one of the quilts they'd found at Millie's as well as a massive fur coat.

Julia examined the miscellany as he drew the items around to the front. "A fur coat?"

"You need something soft to recline on for comfort." He fumbled with the cloth in his arms. "I'll wrap the quilt around it, see? To protect it."

She looked up, her eyes weary and sweat beaded on her brow, but her smile quivered into place. "I'm so sorry to put you through this."

"Shh." He stuffed the fur into the blanket and reached around her to place the massive pillow-like shape. "I'd rather you have a hospital, but I'm happy to be with you right now."

Her eyes widened again as another contraction swelled her into pain he couldn't control or take away. One breath. Two breaths. A truck pulled up behind them as Julia released her third exhale, and a middle-aged woman with a long, dark braid ran from the vehicle, her white uniform labeling her as an emergency service provider.

"Hey, I heard about your situation on the radio as I was driving home from my shift"—she thumbed back toward her truck—"and knew you'd be on my way. I'm Sue."

A swell of relief nearly brought tears to Henry's eyes. "Henry. Thank you."

She offered a crooked grin. "No father ever wants to start his child's life this way, and I can assure you, no mother does." She pushed past Henry and assessed the situation. "Do you think we can get her to the truck, in the back? At least then she can lie back a little more."

Julia shook her head as another cry escaped her lips. "I can't. I need...I need to push."

Sue pulled a pair of surgical gloves from her pocket and put them on. "I'll examine her first, then see if we have time to move her." She gestured toward Julia with her chin but kept her eyes on Henry. "What's her name?"

"Her name?"

The paramedic gave him a long-suffering look. "The woman having the baby? Your girlfriend?"

He blinked. "Yes, right. Julia Jenkins."

As Sue knelt before Julia, Henry turned his back to the scene, his face aflame with the awkwardness of it all. He might have affirmed to Sue and the operator that Julia was his girlfriend, but would she ever consent to actually becoming so after he'd put her in this situation?

"Well, honey, there's no time to spare." Sue's voice held a hint of surprise. "Your baby's crowning, which mean it's going to be here any minute."

Henry felt a slap to his arm and turned ever so slightly to see Sue's incredulous face staring him down. "Do you have something to wrap the baby in?"

"Pardon me?"

"A blanket? Cloth of some sort? Anything? I need something warm to wrap the baby in when it comes. And that's now."

The vintage gowns in the back of the car came to mind and he grimaced.

"A shirt or jacket will do." Her voice tensed.

Henry's fingers rushed to the buttons of his outer shirt, quickly jerking it off and handing it over.

"Okay, Julia. I want you to give me one good push."

Julia's cry followed. "Fantastic." Sue's voice smoothed out the words, calm and steady. Henry couldn't thank God enough that a competent individual had shown up like an angel of mercy to relieve both him and Julia of such a task for each other.

"The head is out. Rest a second. Breathe in and out. Good. Now, I need you to push again so we can get out the shoulders."

Henry stood behind Sue, his face turned away from the car, but every sound, every breath kept him on alert. He crossed his arms, rubbing the bare skin exposed by his sleeveless undershirt. He wasn't cold, but he needed to do something. He raised his face to the sky and started another prayer as he waited through a painful cry from the woman he loved. There was nothing he could do. Nothing to be said. No music. He was helpless to her.

A siren sounded in the distance, piercing through the growing evening noises.

"Looks like your ride to the hospital is here just in time," Sue said. "But Julia, I need one more good push then you'll get to meet your baby."

"I can't. I don't think I can."

The anguish in her voice broke him, and he turned, training his focus on her face. "You can. I know you can." Sue's body blocked his view of Julia's lower half, but Henry only sought out Julia's eyes, attempting to transfer whatever strength he had to her. "You're one of the strongest and bravest people I know, remember? Once more, Julia."

Her gaze locked with his, binding them somehow in this instant of uncertainty and pain and fear.

And courage. "You can, Julia."

With a deep breath, she pinched her eyes closed to focus on the task at hand.

He turned back around, aching through the sound of her cry that only moments later was replaced by the sound of a very different one. A baby's cry. He caught his relieved breath in his hand as the wobbling tone built in volume and filled him from the outside in.

"Henry, here." Sue's voice pulled him from his reverie, and he turned long enough to find her handing him a wriggling bundle wrapped in his shirt. "Hold your daughter."

"Daughter..." Henry stared in awe at the red face scrunched in a cry. "You're a girl." He pulled the bundle closer, and the baby calmed against his warmth.

"A girl?" Julia's voice peeled into the sound of the approaching ambulance.

"We need to finish up here, Julia. One more push should do it, then we can move you and your little girl into the ambulance, all right?"

The baby stared up at him, apparently oblivious to anything else but his face. He ran a finger down her cheek and gave away his heart for the second time in as many weeks. *His* daughter?

"She can't be a girl," Julia cried through another push.

Sue's rich laugh bubbled out. "And why not?"

"I don't have any clothes for a little girl."

"Well, that can be remedied easily enough. I bet your handsome prince here can go off and purchase something for your little one, can't you, Henry?"

Henry pulled his attention from the curious baby in his arms and met Sue's expectant expression. "What? Yes, of course. I'd be happy to."

"I think your boyfriend is as smitten with this baby as you're gonna be, Julia." Sue reached out her hands for Henry's bundle, and with a slight reluctance, he gave the baby over to the paramedic, who then settled the newborn on Julia's chest.

Julia's entire expression transformed as she stared down at her daughter. "She's...she's beautiful."

"Like her mother." Henry flushed at his too-quick answer yet refused to take back the sentiment—out loud or to himself.

Sue grinned. "And that is the right answer."

The ambulance pulled up in front of their parked cars, and two men emerged from the white vehicle. Henry stepped back, separation from a scene in which he'd been much more than a spectator gripping his heart? But what was he? Boyfriend? No, she'd given him no indication of that for certain.

A friend?

Yes, that was all for now, despite the whirring of his heart that insisted otherwise. The paramedics assisted Julia from the car and moved her onto a stretcher and toward the ambulance.

"I'll phone your mother to bring your things to the hospital?"

Julia looked up from her daughter. "Yes, please."

He nodded, thrusting his empty hands into his pockets. "And bring the car to your apartment?"

"Yes."

He kept his gaze on her as the paramedics placed Julia and the baby into the ambulance. Why did he feel like he *should* be there? As if they were...*his* family?

"Henry," Julia's voice reached him before one of the paramedics closed the doors.

He surged forward a few steps. "Yes?"

She held his gaze, her hair a wild mass of curls around her face, and then she sent him one of the most beautiful smiles he'd ever seen. "Thank you."

His palm rested against his chest as the doors closed and blocked her from his sight.

Even as the ambulance pulled away, he stood staring, praying, holding to the connection he'd experienced with Julia and the baby.

"There's nothing like the love of family, is there, Henry?" Sue walked over to her truck and opened the door, measuring him with her eyes. "Those ladies are lucky to have someone who cares about them like you do." She nodded before stepping up in her truck and driving away.

The night sounds emerged around him. Crickets. Perhaps a frog? A wisp of breeze through the nearby forest.

He leaned against the car, his knees weak with the miracle he'd witnessed. In the distance, the outline of the mountains stood watch around the vast landscape and led up to a fantastic starry sky in bloom. Henry's smile grew, spreading full as the certainty pulsing through his tired body.

Dear God, thank you for introducing me to my family.

Chapter Twenty-Two

*J*ulia ran a finger down the side of her baby's face, the tiny eyelashes brushing against those round cheeks as her darling daughter slept. *Daughter.* The thought settled into her heart with sweet power, pressing in with a tenderness that stole her breath. Her parents had met her at the hospital, armed with her bags and a determination to keep every family member at bay until Julia could get a little rest.

The doctor later told her he'd never had twenty people come for a visit at once.

Clearly, he was new to Appalachia—and more importantly, to the Jenkins family.

They'd filled the small room with their love, laughter, and loud voices, until a nurse urged them out for the day and Julia finally attempted to take in this new part she had to play in her own story. *Mother.*

She'd slept on and off throughout the night, eaten the hospital breakfast as if it were the best meal she'd had in her life, and then nestled into the momentary quiet of mother-and-baby.

What a strange, beautiful, and scary place.

Was she strong enough for a responsibility like this? Was she the best mother for this little girl?

Julia looked over at her bag on the counter in the maternity room—a bag that held an adorable blue teddy bear outfit and a train gown with the colorful words *bouncing baby boy* emblazoned across the front.

If she couldn't even get the baby clothes right, then what about big decisions like preschools, friendships, college...marriage?

Her throat constricted with each new possibility for an epic fail. She tugged the little body deeper into her embrace as if a hug might be enough to beat bad thoughts away.

Hugs were powerful things.

And then a whisper of a voice melded through the uncertainty in her spirit.
I'm holding you. Do not be afraid.

She stilled, closing her eyes, listening. God held her even more securely than she could ever hold her baby girl. More than that, God held her daughter, too.

You are a part of My love song.

A verse from Zephaniah flowed over her with an overwhelming peace.

The LORD your God is in your midst, a mighty one who will save;
He will rejoice over you with gladness;
He will quiet you by his love;
He will exult over you with loud singing.

Loud singing? She grinned. Nope, God didn't love small and quiet. He loved big and loud. And the knowledge of such a love calmed her soul and wrapped her future in hope—no matter the verse or movement in the symphony of her life.

Tears pierced her vision. Everything fit, woven into a beautiful duet of His love for her. She squeezed her eyes closed and let the tears slide down her cheeks. God even braided the painful pieces together into a glorious *Hallelujah Chorus* ending.

She wiped away a tear, her smile pinching into her cheeks. What love!

She pressed a kiss to her daughter's soft head and thanked God for the hundredth time, her lungs filling with the desire to sing much too loudly for a sleeping baby's peace of mind. But she did hum a newly loved tune a certain Brit had written for her.

"Oh my goodness! Oh my goodness! I can't believe I missed all the excitement." Eisley burst into the room, her auburn hair flying around her with the same enthusiasm that spread her smile from ear to ear. She ground to a halt and quieted her entry when she saw the sleeping baby. "Sophie texted me as soon as Mom called, and Wes and I loaded up the kids to head back home from our trip." She rushed to Julia's side and placed a kiss on her sister's forehead, leaning close to get a better view of the newest Jenkins. "Oh, Julia. She's beautiful."

Julia chuckled at her sister's exuberance. Not quite as brilliant as Sophie's but definitely on the vivid side of normal. "Would you like to hold her?"

Eisley's shoulders scrunched in an internal squeal, and both palms came forward in answer. "Of course I do!" She winked. "What took you so long?"

Julia shifted the tiny bundle into her sister's arms, careful to press the blankets around her daughter's little body. "Mom's supposed to bring over a few different outfits for her today, so for now she's just hanging out in her diaper."

"Aren't the diapers so tiny?" Eisley pressed her face near the baby's. "Oh man, I love clean baby smell. Isn't it the best?"

"It definitely beats dirty baby smell." Julia wrinkled her nose at the memory of sticky milk and dirty diapers.

"Whoa, yes. She must be healthy, though, to already have shown off her stinky stuff. It took Pete four days to finally—"

"I remember." Julia raised a palm to pause the story. "It was the first time I'd ever prayed for anyone to poop."

"Right?" She took the baby's fingers into her hands and cooed a few minutes longer over how lovely she was. "Did you decide on a name yet? Mom said you didn't have any girl's names picked out by the time she and Dad left last night."

Julia drew in a breath. She hadn't voiced her choice yet, but the idea had come to her early in the morning. A nod of gratitude to the lady who'd made Julia and the baby's future much easier than it would have been without her generosity.

"Yes, she has a name."

What a responsibility! A name. A legacy.

Eisley peaked an auburn brow. "Are you ready to share?"

"Rosalyn Elizabeth Jenkins, and I plan to call her Rose, for short."

"Rosalyn," Eisley whispered down to the sleeping bundle. "It's perfect. Hello, little Rose. Welcome to our family."

Family. A pulse so strong it resounded through every part of Julia. And now, somehow, she and Rose had become their own little family of two within the larger Jenkins family. Well, a family of three since God was holding onto them both. She cradled the thought close.

"It's a remarkable feeling, isn't it?" Eisley grinned as if reading Julia's thoughts. "This powerful, overwhelming love for a person you only just met?"

Julia touched the little head of her Rose. "It is."

"Oh, wait. I forgot." She straightened and tucked Rose into the crook of her elbow like the experienced mom she was and leaned down to gather a brilliant-purple bag on the floor. "Henry sent this along with me."

"Henry?"

"Yeah, he came by the house with Wes this morning to check on you and asked me to deliver this." Her brows wiggled and she handed the bag over. "No pun intended."

Julia stared at Eisley and then opened the bag with care. Out of the purple paper she pulled a tiny purple onesie with white words emblazoned on the front: *If you think I'm cute, you should see my mom.*

Complete with matching socks.

And a hair bow.

Julia couldn't get her voice to work. She stared at her sister, who looked up from cooing over Rose to see the gift.

"Oh, come on! How sweet is that?" Her gaze zeroed in on Julia's. "Julia, you need to keep him."

"Keep him? I don't know if he'll ever want to see me again after what he's witnessed."

"What on earth are you talking about?" Eisley waved toward the gift as if she were karate chopping it. "This clearly shows he's in for the long haul."

"It shows that he's sensitive and kind and thoughtful." The vision of him as the ambulance doors closed last night brought another foggy sheen to Julia's view. "And strong in a way I've never measured strength before. But...but *if* there was anything between us, which I never said there was, it's over now."

Eisley's face crinkled with confusion. "Why is that?"

"Because of yesterday and the car and Sue and me." Julia covered her face with her palms and cringed at the very thought of him experiencing her unconventional birthing session. "I'm sure he feels like he's *seen* a'plenty."

"Are you crazy? So, clearly you're the only one not seeing right now?" Eisley gestured toward the gift. "Sweet baby gift. Sweet man. Loves music. Stares at you like you're the most beautiful woman in the whole world."

"He does." Julia almost lowered her hands from her face, then remembered her valid argument and hid again behind her palms. "No, no, you don't understand. He was there for *the delivery*." She cringed and peeked through her fingers to look at her sister. "What guy would ever be able to look at me the same way again, especially a man I'm not even married to?" She shuddered all over again at the vivid memories.

Eisley watched her in silence for so long that Julia shifted in the hospital bed. Her crazy sister then placed Rose into her arms and pointed at the still-sleeping baby. "She's going to poop on you, spit up on you, maybe even throw things at you and tell you she never wants to see you again. She may even do worse. Will you still love her?"

Julia looked at her sweet baby then back at her sister. "Of...of course."

"Exactly. Because love sees behind all the"—she waved a hand in the air then rested her palm on Rose— "stuff to what really matters. Love bears all things, believes all things, hopes all things, endures all things. It never fails. If Henry Wright is the *right* man for you, which only *you* can decide..." She rolled her gaze to the ceiling, a look of pure innocence on her face as she whispered beneath her breath. "Although I think you two are pretty amazing together." She tugged on Julia's braid. "Then whatever happened yesterday isn't going to deter him. In fact, I wonder if it hasn't already made the two of you closer—even if neither of you has realized it yet."

Julia stifled a mock laugh. "Closer?" Could it be? The memory of the look he gave her at the end of her delivery as he encouraged her to be strong surfaced to mind. Yes, his presence with her yesterday had certainly solidified the beautiful bond their piano duet began.

"But...but how can anything between us work out, Eisley? He's from England. I live here." She touched Rose's cheek. "We're here."

Eisley nodded. "That's a real dilemma. I've thought about it myself."

"But Wes has agreed to stay here in the States with you and the kids."

"For now, but that might not be forever." Eisley took Julia's hand in hers. "Listen to me. Wes and Henry present a unique case in that they live in another country, so if you care about a future with Henry"—she searched Julia's face, a gentle smile softening her lips—"and I can tell that you do, you have to go in with your eyes open to all sorts of possibilities. Wes and I are getting married, which means he's going to be a priority in my life, and for now, we've decided that living in the States is the right answer, but I know that might not always be the case. If his parents need us, I have to be willing to move."

"All the way to England?"

"All the way to England." Eisley stood and placed a palm on Julia's shoulder. "We have a great family with a whole lot of love. They've taught us to be strong and compassionate and...even brave enough to go where no Jenkins has gone before."

Julia grinned and shook her head at the *Star Trek* reference.

"But I'm choosing Wes and whatever future that means for me and the kids because I love him. And I'd rather have a future with him and all its unpredictable possibilities than one without him and whatever false safety I think I'll find in staying." She hitched one shoulder. "We have no control over a lot of the circumstances that come our way." She waved toward Julia. "But we can choose who will surround us when those circumstances come, and I choose Wes, wherever that may be." One eyebrow rose and her eyes took on a pixie twinkle. "He's also a great kisser. Never underestimate the importance of a great kisser. I feel pretty certain kingdoms rise and fall over the kissing level of some marriages." She raised a finger to match her pointed brow. "Bonus points when he has a dark-chocolatey sweet voice, excellent cuddling skills, and is amazing with kids."

Julia shook her head, heat rising into her face. "Well, Henry and I haven't...you know."

Eisley's grin took an impish turn. "Oh, I don't think it's going to be too long before you find out."

"I'm not moving to England, Eisley. I have Rose to think of."

"Rose will be as happy as her mama is." Eisley tossed her purse strap over her shoulder and winked. "And remember: kisses, an English accent, and the right guy are pretty powerful steps toward happiness."

∞ ∞ ∞

Henry had waited until after lunch to visit the hospital, at Eisley's encouragement. He wasn't certain if Julia would even wish to see him after all that transpired with the delivery, but he couldn't get her or the baby from his thoughts.

Not even composing distracted him.

He pinched the bouquet in his hand as he peered into the open hospital room. Most of the room was blocked by a curve in the wall—well-designed for privacy, no doubt— but the very end of a bed jutted from behind the wall along with the partial view of a window, allowing some light into the room. He gave the door a gentle knock.

"Come in."

No turning back now.

He stepped into view and found Julia sitting in a chair and dressed in a t-shirt and sweats. Her blond hair lay in a braid over her shoulder, and the baby cuddled in her arms.

"Oh, Henry."

He shifted a step back at her look of surprise. "I can go, if you'd like."

"No, stay." She hesitated, her gaze shifting from his face to the baby. "I...I mean, if you want to stay."

He looked back toward the door, then to the wriggling infant, then to Julia. "Do...do you..." He cleared his throat. "Do you *want* me to stay?"

Her smile unfurled. "Yes."

The tension peeled off his shoulders, and he walked a few steps closer to her. Weariness shone in her eyes—which was expected—but otherwise she looked as perfect as she had when standing on the mountainside, gazing at the waterfall. "I...I brought these for you. It's been my experience that mothers don't usually receive the gifts even though they're the ones who did most of the work."

"Except for generous men who either carried them to the car or encouraged them to be strong. Those are some pretty important roles too."

"I was happy to fulfill them."

She took his proffered bouquet, a beautiful blush of pink highlighting her cheeks. "Thank you, Henry."

"She looks content." His gaze pulled toward the tiny person cradled in her arms, his hands opening and closing at his sides to keep from reaching out and touching either the baby or her mother.

"Would you like to hold her?"

His gaze shot to Julia's. "Really? May I?"

"It will give me a chance to do something with these lovely flowers you've brought." She gestured toward the chair near hers. Once he lowered himself into the seat, she placed the baby into his arms. "Thank you, by the way. For the flowers."

He pulled his gaze from the little one to Julia. "I wasn't certain of your favorite type, but when Eisley told me the baby name you chose, I thought roses would be welcome."

"And they're beautiful pink roses, too." Julia emptied a large plastic cup of its contents by the sink in the room and filled it with water. "I *am* fond of roses, but my favorite flowers are dahlias."

"Dahlias?" He barely heard Julia, his attention fixed on the little bundle in his arms. A faint hint of purple shone from beneath the blanket, and he couldn't stop his smile at the sight. She was wearing the outfit he'd bought for her. Purple proved an excellent color for those wide, blue eyes staring back at him.

"I wanted to thank you again for yesterday. I don't know what I...what *we* would have done without you, Henry."

He looked up from his trance and became lost in another set of blue eyes, only these had become increasingly more familiar and dear over the past month. "I was happy to be of service to you and little Rose here."

"Happy to be of service?" She set the bouquet on the table beside her and returned to her chair, shaking her head at him. "How can you do that? I'm going off about four hours of sleep without a thread of makeup, and you spent yesterday seeing me at my worst, yet even now, you...you make me feel like those things didn't change how you see me."

What was she talking about? Despite the weariness in her eyes, she looked as beautiful as always. "I...I don't think I understand. Why would my view of you change because of what happened yesterday?"

She closed her eyes and sighed. "It's not a common occurrence for a woman to give birth in front of a guy who she"—a grimace lined her face— "hasn't known a long time." Her eyes opened, pleading with him to understand. "And if that weren't enough, you have a ruined shirt now too."

He looked down at Rose, her little finger wrapped around his. "My shirt has never known a worthier cause." His gaze came up to hold Julia's. "And I hope for a *much* longer acquaintance."

Her teeth skimmed her bottom lip as she gave him a reluctant smile—the kind he was learning meant he'd given her particular pleasure. He attempted to quell the sudden acceleration of his pulse, calm the anticipation. Twice he'd come close to kissing her, and both times she'd recoiled from him, trembling. His gaze dropped to that lip tucked beneath her teeth. He'd have to wait.

He cleared his throat and returned his attention to Rose. "Besides, she seems no worse for wear from her delivery adventure."

"She's been so observant and quiet. I hope it's a precursor of things to come." Her nose wrinkled in a grimace. "Although, I've heard horror stories. Mostly from Eisley."

He chuckled. "You don't think Eisley tends toward embellishment, do you?"

Julia's smile spread into a laugh. "A little, but I remember Pete's first few months. Heaven and earth, the boy's colic had her living through the 'nights of the living dead'." Julia gestured with her chin toward the bundle in his arms. "She's studying you awfully hard. Maybe she remembers you."

Rose's blue gaze fastened on his face, her brow puckered in concentration. *He* remembered. She'd stilled and watched him, as if she knew he belonged with her and her mother. As he ran a finger down her cheek, the pucker smoothed.

We only need convince your mother, duck. That's all.

"You seem comfortable holding her."

"I helped my brother Matthew and his wife with their two when they were born." He looked over at Julia, shrugging a shoulder. "I've always felt more comfortable with babies and children. It's the grown-ups that cause all the trouble." Rose squeezed his finger, and he grinned at her. "Children take you as you are."

"Well, this grown-up thinks you're...pretty amazing."

"Then you're the best sort of grown-up for me, Julia Jenkins."

Her teeth skimmed her bottom lip again. Yes, she'd understood him perfectly.

Rose's stare brought his attention back to her cherub face. "She's beautiful, isn't she? Rather perfect."

Julia leaned in, resting her palm on her daughter's head, the full scent of her hair wafting around him, their foreheads almost touching as they watched Rose.

He swallowed through his tightening throat and looked back at little Rose, her big blue eyes shifting slowly between the two adoring adults above her. "She has your eyes, that dark, piercing blue."

"Well, that may change with time, but I hope not."

"And I think she has your mouth too. Perfect lips, like yours."

Julia's gaze shot to his, their faces mere inches apart.

Heat swarmed into his cheeks at the unintended innuendo in his words, but he refused to move his focus from her face. "Not that I...I've been *solely* looking at your mouth." Which is exactly what he proceeded to do, against his will. *Somewhat* against his will.

"Um...but other parts of you are beautiful too, of course."

Those attractive lips tipped into a tremulous smile.

"Nice goin', Romeo." Nate Jenkins burst into the room from the open door, shaking his head in a slow, exaggerated fashion.

Henry straightened, distancing himself from the proximity he'd enjoyed to Julia. He nodded his welcome. "Nate."

Nate's thick hand landed on Henry's shoulder, giving a hefty rub as he leaned in. "We're gonna have to work on those romantic lines of yours, Twinkle Toes. You say 'em like you're not sure about 'em. Gotta be strong. Confident." He winked then stepped around the pair and kissed Julia on the head. "How's my girl today?"

Julia shook her head and offered Henry an apologetic smile. "Enjoying my time with the man who was strong enough to help deliver your grandbaby yesterday *and* confident enough to come back to the hospital today despite the...unusual circumstances."

Nate leaned over and peeked at his new granddaughter, his expression softening around his hazel eyes. "Well, I reckon that's worth somethin'."

Henry couldn't tame the smile her defense inspired. Things had changed and grown between them over the course of twenty-four hours, and even though neither had voiced it, he knew whatever barrier had separated them before had somehow disappeared.

She wasn't afraid anymore.

Chapter Twenty-Three

*J*ulia pulled into her parking spot at the bakery and gave a grateful sigh. She'd needed to move back to her apartment.

After spending over a week at her parents' house as they helped her adjust to motherhood, her independent streak had started screaming for her own schedule. Her books. Her favorite comfy chair and her mismatched vintage furniture.

Her privacy.

If bleary eyes and foggy brains were her new status quo, then at least she wanted to have them in her own place.

And...she missed Henry.

He'd sent her a few texts and photos over the past week and half. Some amazing sunset pictures from a hike. A clip of his newest composition. A question that turned into a conversation then...an expectation.

Of his words. His humor. His presence. *Every day.*

After some coaxing, he'd even sent her a selfie taken in front of a beautiful horizon, his smile uncertain, his hair endearingly disheveled, and a little bit of thumb over the screen. His messages and phone calls had become a regular fixture over the past five days. A morning greeting and a final goodnight. A few conversations in between.

A simple act that somehow carried the weight of a promise.

The way he took care of her and Rose, the tenderness in his touch and expression, stripped away any doubt in her heart as to pursuing a future with this impossibility. After all, if Wes could make the choice to stay in America with Eisley, couldn't Henry do the same?

They'd seen each other at Sunday lunch a few days before, but with all the excitement over the newest Jenkins baby and with the usual crowd in attendance, they'd had little time to talk.

She shook her head and pushed open the back door of the bakery, holding the door ajar as she tugged the infant carrier through on one arm and three bags of groceries on the other. Okay, this was doable.

After some special contortions only a mother—or gymnast—could appreciate, she made it up the narrow stairway to her room with Rose happily sleeping in her carrier.

Praise God for small favors.

New mother tip: Carriers and wraps are heaven-sent.

The scent of peaches and mangos, remnants of her favorite shampoo and lotions, greeted her as she entered her apartment. She appreciated her parents' love and support more than ever as she adjusted to these new demands in her life, but she needed to succeed on her own—even if the idea generated a great deal of healthy fear. It also propelled her into her new future—one that included motherhood, a degree, a bed and breakfast, and, hopefully, a certain composer.

She checked on Rose, smiling down at her sleeping little one with a sense of success at their first solo endeavor.

New mother tip: Celebrate small victories because, in the grand scheme of things, they're huge.

After unpacking her clothes and the new clothes she'd bought for her daughter, she walked back into her cozy sitting room and sat down, mentally prepping herself to catch up on emails. The comfortable tug of her large armchair tempted her from her good intentions, but just as the tiredness began to overtake her, a box on her desk caught her attention. What on earth...

The locked box from Aunt Millie's!

Julia stumbled over to her desk, almost knocking over the office chair, and opened the drawer where she'd placed Millie's envelope.

Rose stirred but didn't wake.

Keeping as quiet as possible and praying for just ten more minutes of naptime, Julia slipped the key from the envelope, a very spy-like feeling tingling over her skin. Maybe that was a mother-y skill too—sneaking.

The key clicked into the keyhole, and the box lid popped free as if it had been opened often. How many times had Millie opened this precious secret?

Julia bit down on her bottom lip and raised the lid with a little trepidation. A typed letter with some sort of official emblem waited on top of other papers. She took it from the box and read:

Dear Mrs. Sterling,

This is to confirm that you received the telegram I sent to you regretfully informing you that your son, First Lieutenant Lucas Randolph, has been

reported missing in action as a result of an air operation last night. I am
sorry that I can give no further details. Should additional information
become available you will be notified.

The term missing in action is used only when the person's whereabouts or
the status of an individual is not immediately known.

Please accept my sincerest sympathy. Lt. Randolph was a dedicated pilot
and informant, faithful to his duties and comrades. I hope that new
information will provide news that he is safe.

Again, I wish to convey to you the sympathies of all of us who served
alongside him and understood the value of his particular work, something
many will never know.

Some general's name followed with a signature. Julia reread the note.

So Lucas had gone missing in action. A plane shot down? A mission exposed? Had he been captured and placed into one of those awful prison camps Julia had learned about in high school history class?

Aunt Millie's loss, her hints of otherworldliness, began to make sense.

Someone added a handwritten note to the bottom of the letter in a style she'd seen before. Ah, yes. Emmeline Sterling, the mysterious benefactress. She was Lucas's mother? Had Lucas's German father married an Englishwoman?

Amelia,

I was informed Lucas's plane went down over northern France. He has not
been recovered or located yet, nor has his kit been found. Do not lose heart.
How many times has one of you been in such circumstances only to come
out of it in the end?

What did that mean? Aunt Amelia was a pianist, not a combat pilot.

Our people will keep looking for him until they find him.

Our people?

I've enclosed his most recent letter to you and hope his words will give you strength. His thoughts were always of you and Rosalyn. Hold fast to courage and hope, as I attempt to do, and do not blame yourself for quitting the field to protect Rosalyn.

Lucas would have wanted you to do nothing less. You, my dear, were his everything, and as long as you are safe, no matter where he is now, know you have made the right choice. You have kept his heart safe by living your life.

Yours,

Emmeline

What did this mean? Yes, Amelia had quit her concerts and returned to Appalachia to protect her and Lucas's child from the consequences of his spy-job, but why did Emmeline refer to Amelia as 'quitting the field'? Was it a reference to ending her public musical career?

The corner of a black-and-white photo peeked from beneath another envelope. Julia slipped it from its place, and her vision blurred with a sudden swell of tears. A much younger Amelia, her smile bigger than any Julia could remember seeing on her aunt's face, stood beside Lucas, who held a round-faced baby in his arms. It was the only photo Julia had ever seen of the three of them together. Why had Aunt Millie kept it locked away from the world?

Julia smoothed her fingers over the faces. How many times had her aunt unlocked this box to remove this photo and stare at those faces? She turned the photo over, searching for a date, but found two words instead. *My family.*

Julia knew the pulse and pull of the word *family.* She'd never have made it through the rape without their support—not to mention their love her entire life. Her gaze drifted to the carrier where Rose began shifting in her sleep, a sign that Julia's quiet time was coming to an end. Her body responded to Rose's noises for an upcoming feeding.

Now, as a mother, Julia understood even more why Millie would upend her world to keep her daughter safe. Love inspired courage like nothing else could.

Even Julia's own minute way of stepping into her life as a single mother—as Henry had said—took courage.

A copy of sheet music surfaced next in the pile of papers, but unlike the others she and Henry had found, this one had a note written in the margin. She blinked away another rush of tears. She knew this handwriting too. Lucas.

Dearest,

I located the first special music you ever composed and thought you'd enjoy seeing it once again as a reminder of how far we've come. Of course, at the time, it held no romantic notions. Your mind had not turned in that direction yet, though mine had from the first moment I heard you play. But this is the music that changed our lives from spectators in the war effort to participants.

I blame you for being too brilliant to settle for a life of mere observation and too clever to create a simple code, easy to uncover.

Why not use the music you love and for which I love you?

My clever darling, how I miss you.

Julia read the last four sentences again. Spectators to participants? Code? Julia placed the papers back down, realization sinking deeper with each blink of her eyes. Amelia had been involved in espionage too...through the music.

As if in answer to Julia's unvoiced question, a little book came next in the box—something like a passport-looking pamphlet. Inside was a photo of a young Aunt Millie, only her aunt had glasses and a very different hairstyle. No one would have recognized the beautiful pianist with such a disguise if they hadn't known those eyes for years. The information in the booklet gave a false name and nationality. *French.*

Yes, Aunt Amelia had been a spy.

Julia's breath whooshed out as she rocked back in her desk chair. How had an Appalachian girl become a world-famous pianist-turned-spy then recluse?

A smacking noise followed by a frustrated grunt shook the carrier with Rose's discontent. Julia picked up the box from the desk and moved to her couch, rescued her daughter from breaking into a full-on starving cry, and settled back onto the couch to feed Rose and reread the new information in the box.

As she shifted through the box with her free hand, metal chinked against metal. Her fingers brushed through myriad objects until landing on a vintage emerald ring in an Edwardian setting, the rectangular gem surrounded by tiny diamonds.

A wedding ring?

Julia passed her thumb over the stone and then set the ring back in the box, only to see a small envelope with her name written in Aunt Millie's hand. She pinned a corner of the envelope underneath her leg for pressure, then wedged her finger beneath its flap and broke the seal. A card fell out.

Julia,

If you are reading this then you know more about my past than anyone in our family. You've seen life within a life, the truest and happiest part of my story. Now that I am gone, feel free to share this story if you wish, but I am glad you were the first to know.

I kept my secret at first to protect my family, then I suppose I thought I'd keep their memories to myself. After Rosalyn's death, I spent years nurturing my distance from the world and hiding within the past, too afraid to love again, too terrified to open my heart. But you entered my world and reminded me of the importance of love and relationships and the risk we take to feel connected...the need to feel connected. I'd forgotten. I'd allowed fear to steal my courage, and my world became a fortress instead of a haven.

If I could repeat those years of love and loss, I would. Even with the heartache, I would—because I lived a full life loving and being loved by an amazing man.

Don't get lost in the details of my little secret. Instead, learn from it. I grieved long and hard and perhaps too privately, but we grieve greatly because we love greatly. Yet our grief sprouts hope's wings. We go on and we wait and remember.

Cradle time with a careful hand. We are only given a small number of hours and days with those we treasure. Life is hard and terrifying at times, but as the scriptures say, love is the greatest of all.

Love well and fiercely and with abandon so that when the pain comes, you have the comfort of knowing you lived.

Amelia

∞ ∞ ∞

Henry brought his hired Sedan to a stop at the bakery directly beside Julia's car, stumbled out of the car in his hurry to get inside, and nearly fell on top of his violin case in the process. He was an idiot...but for all the right reasons. Little Rose's entrance into the world had changed things, but the texts over the past week only proved his goal. He was ready to bypass the whole girlfriend phase and go directly to fiancé.

"Slow down, Henry," he murmured as he pushed open the door. "She's just become a mum. She needs—"

"Henry!"

As if from his daydreams, Julia rushed down the hallway toward him with Rose in her arms and a smile more vibrant than he'd seen on her lighting her face.

His future looked beautiful in pale blue.

Dead air followed Julia's greeting as Henry applied the sight to memory, but her puzzled expression forced his thoughts into words. "Hello."

Brilliant, old chap. Smooth.

"You'll never believe what I've found." She grabbed his hand with her free one and pulled him down the hall and up the stairs, Rose's eyes attempting to take in the wild shift of scenes from her perch at Julia's shoulder.

His heart nearly exploded out of his chest. How could he have missed a tiny human he'd only just come to know?

"I opened the box." Julia's shoulders rose with the wrinkle-nosed grin she tossed over her shoulder. The casual knee-length dress she wore hung loose against her body but displayed her post-baby curves. *Oh, this was new.*

Henry pulled his attention back to her face. "You did?"

"I did." She squealed. "And I can't wait to share it with you. It doesn't answer all of our questions, but a few blanks have been filled in at least."

She tugged him through the door of her apartment and into a light-filled room and the scent of peaches. A small red sofa sat in the middle of the room with a matching chair and ottoman to its right, just in front of a window-seat. A round dining table stood behind the couch and led through a doorway into a kitchenette. To the back left a half-open door revealed the end of a bed. A mismatched coffee table with intricate carvings waited atop a decorative rug covering hardwoods, and various paintings and portraits covered the walls, bringing the room together in an eclectic way. It felt quaint and comfortable and warm.

"Let me get the box so you can see." She moved to the desk against the wall and attempted to navigate the box while holding Rose at the same time.

He rushed to her side. "Allow me to help."

"Thank you. I'm just so excited." Instead of giving him the box, she placed Rose into his arms as if it were the most natural thing to do. Rose's bright eyes found his and tightened the connection he already felt with the little one.

"Go, go sit on the couch."

He followed the direction Julia waved and turned Rose so her head rested in the crook of his arm. Her little fingers shot out, gripping at his shirt until she captured a handful. "I'm happy to see you too, duck," he whispered. "I think you've grown."

"Okay, so..." Julia stopped in her walk toward the couch, papers in both hands, and her expression softened. "It's good to see you, by the way."

The way she looked at him sparked a triumphant fanfare of the classic *Superman* theme through his mind. He had the sudden urge to stand and place both hands on his hips like the bold, daring hero she inspired in him, but refrained from launching himself off the couch. He'd always been more the Clark Kent-ish sort.

Could a beautiful heroine ever fall for a Clark Kent? He hoped so in *this* story. "Are you back to stay?"

She nodded and moved a few steps closer. "I need to learn how to do this on my own."

He looked down at Rose. "I'll be happy to help in any way, while I'm here."

Her smile fell, and she shook her head as if to remove whatever thought dampened her joy. She took her place beside him. Shoulder-to-shoulder. "We have almost three weeks left, right?"

"Indeed, we do."

She drew in a deep breath, studying his face. "Then let's not waste any time."

Perhaps Clark Kent could get the girl after all. "Let's not."

She turned back to the papers on her lap and began showing him all she'd uncovered, one piece at a time. "And this was her wedding ring, I think." She held up the piece of jewelry. "Isn't it beautiful? Classy and elegant, just like her."

"Lucas must have known her well."

"It seems there was a deep bond between them, doesn't it? I mean, she wasn't an old woman at all when she came back to the States, yet she never sought another romance."

"Was he ever found?"

She shifted through the papers and tilted a letter for him to view. "This letter from Emmeline is the most recent thing in this box except for her obituary. She died twenty years ago, just two weeks after the date on this letter and, at that time, they still hadn't found anything, but Emmeline's obituary gives us some answers to the questions we had about Lucas's history."

She pulled out an aged newspaper clipping. "Like we thought, Emmeline married a Sweitzer, but it appears she kept her maiden name."

"Uncommon for the time."

"Sounds like she was pretty uncommon all around. From the other bits of information I've found, she was Lucas and Millie's contact when they'd gathered intel. Evidently, she was high up in British Intelligence, but her husband's citizenship status was questioned when war broke out, and he was sent back to Germany." She raised a finger and brow. "That's when Lucas used his connection to his father to gain access into Germany, which somehow allowed him to navigate between the two countries."

"An excellent position for a spy."

"Exactly." She stacked the papers back together. "And when he found Aunt Millie, they made the perfect team. She knew music better than him and had the fame, and they fell in love."

"Through music." Henry pulled the wiggling Rose onto his shoulder, closer to Julia.

"Through music," Julia whispered, her gaze staying in his, silencing his doubts on whether someone like her would ever be interested in someone like him. Light from the window played over golden hair his fingers tingled to touch.

"I wonder if anything has been recovered in the past twenty years?"

"I don't know." Julia ran a finger down Rose's cheek and looked back at him. "Maybe when I come to England for Wes and Eisley's engagement party, we could find out."

"You're coming? For certain?"

Her gaze found his again, answering more with her eyes than her words, saying what he wanted to hear. "I've always wanted to see England."

He couldn't tame his grin. "I'll show you as much as I can."

"I'd like that."

"And perhaps you can contact the War Office to find out if there is anything else to learn about your aunt or Lucas." Rose began to wiggle in his arms.

"That's a great idea." She leaned into the couch and reached for Rose, who'd begun to make a frustrated sniffing noise like a balloon releasing bursts of air. "Listen to that. It's her warning huff."

"Her warning huff?"

"That she's hungry."

The words then the implication clinked into place. His cheeks heated, and he shot to his feet. "Yes, of course. Excuse me."

"Henry?"

He turned at the sweet way she said his name. "Yes, dove?"

Her teeth skimmed over her bottom lip with her grin, her shoulders scrunching. "May I make dinner for you tomorrow night?"

Again, the question took longer to process than it ought. Was she... "A...date type of dinner?"

She narrowed her eyes with a tilt of her head, moving a 'huffing' Rose to her shoulder. "If you'd like it to be a date type of dinner."

"I'm hoping for that general date-like direction."

Her smile bloomed. "Oh, I think a date is long overdue, don't you?"

Chapter Twenty-Four

*O*f course!

Julia finally gets to have a date with Henry Wright, and her daughter doesn't sleep the *entire* night. In fact, her little sweetheart seemed dead set on stealing Julia's rest with a gusto that probably woke Wes, Henry, and Clark Summers in the shoe shop next door. She attempted to calm her little one by every means she knew, but even after a thorough Google search and a phone call to Granny Lewis, nothing worked. And, of course, after her adorable little leech finished eating again for the twentieth time in twelve hours—or so it seemed—she snuggled close and fell asleep just in time for the bakery downstairs to open for business.

Well, at least *one* of them would get some sleep before her date this evening.

A crash in the dining room below woke Rose not an hour after she'd finally gotten into a good sleep. Julia groaned. The last thing she wanted to do was fall asleep during dinner with Mr. Wright. The thought gave her a much-needed snicker.

After several diaper mishaps and Rose refusing to sleep, Julia decided to use the time to go to the grocery store for dinner ingredients. Not a good idea for a half-awake human.

Had she pick up salted butter instead of unsalted? Yes. Had she forgotten to brush her hair? As a matter of fact, yes—and had conveniently forgotten a jacket for the blistering, late March afternoon.

Oh, and another new mother note: Nursing pads aren't as thick as they ought to be.

She winced at the memory of what had become of her blouse in the middle of the produce section. Not pretty. Or comfortable. After spending over an hour driving around Pleasant Gap so Rose would take at least *one* nap, Julia pulled into the bakery parking in the back and prayed for a little time to prepare for this momentous occasion.

Surely God realized how big a deal this date was, right?

"Do you need help?"

The rich timbre of the British accent stopped Julia mid-grab, hand hovering over the Italian bread. Please, Lord, no. He'd seen her give *birth*—well practically. Couldn't she look non-pregnant pretty for him to make up the difference, especially on a first date night?

She nearly whimpered, and tried to hide her bare face and puffy eyes behind one of the grocery bags, but a hint of a purple cat pajama sleeve caught her attention. Yep. She was in her pjs. How did that even happen?

Charming.

"Are you all right?"

"Umm...yes." She kept one of the bags up like a little bandit handkerchief and looked at her daughter, who yawned and then began the hungry huff. "Would you mind grabbing her from her car seat for me while I take in these bags?"

Because that would give her time to run into the apartment and grab a jacket, or something, to cover her shirt stains. Maybe even change? Unlikely.

"Of course."

She didn't wait for him but covered her blouse with a much heavier bag and scurried off toward her apartment, closing herself in the pantry with the groceries. No sooner had she crossed the threshold than the bottom of the bag in her right hand broke. Flour hit the ground and exploded in a cloud of white, shocking her backwards into the pantry shelf, which knocked her canister of elbow pasta over so that the uncooked shells rained down on top of her already-disheveled and now-powdery hair.

She almost sobbed. In fact, her nose began to tingle with the hint of an incoming cry-fest.

Footfalls sounded from the kitchen. "Julia?"

She caught her gasp with her palms and took stock of her appearance in the back of the frying pan she had hanging against the wall. White puffs hovered around her and highlighted her face and hair...oh, and her hair! The high ponytail she'd quickly made before getting groceries had sunk to one side, leaving a poof of hair on the other that seemed to have become a little bowl for elbow pasta.

"Julia?" Henry's voice came from the other side of the door.

"Umm...I'm just putting groceries away."

"What if you allow me to do that for you so you can take care of Rose?"

The pantry doorknob turned but she caught it between both of her hands. "No, no, no. Don't come in."

A pause followed as she tried to pick pasta from her hair. "Please tell me what's wrong, dove."

The entreaty and sweet concern in his voice broke something in her. Everything hit at once, weighing her down in some weird sort of emotional hurricane she couldn't stop. She'd failed at motherhood. Failed at trying to plan a date-night. Even failed to get dressed like an adult, for goodness' sake. How on earth could she ever consider dating, if she couldn't...She looked down at her feet, and tears swam into her vision. Couldn't even wear matching slippers?

She was such a date-failure.

"Julia?" The doorknob turned again, and this time, she didn't catch it in time. He stood in the doorway, staring at her in all her flour-covered glory as Rose huffed in the background.

"The bag broke and the flour spilled out everywhere," she managed to say before catching her sob in her hands and squeezing her eyes closed. "Then the noodles..."

Complete silence surrounded them.

Oh no. He'd walked away. And why not? Her tear streaks probably made her look like the Jack Nicholson version of the Joker. She peered through her fingers, bracing herself for an empty doorway, but strong arms and the warmth of Henry-vanilla wrapped themselves around her. *Oh, how sweet.* Which only caused her to sob even more, right into his wonderfully comfortable shoulder.

Rose's huffs had turned into little bursts of discontent from the other room. Now Julia was failing her baby, too. She wept harder into his shoulder. "Rose...she didn't sleep at all last night. Then I wore pajamas to the grocery and...and..." She sniffled. "I bought salted butter for a flourless torte. Why would I do that?"

"Because you're tired." His soft voice smoothed over her as comforting as his arms around her. "You don't have to make dinner for me tonight. You need to rest."

She pushed back from him, shaking her head, tears scratching her throat. "But I *want* to make you dinner." She wiped at her face, her bottom lip quivering with another need to cry. "Don't you want me to make you dinner?"

He opened his mouth to answer, closed it, and started again. "Of course I do, but we can reschedule."

She returned her cheek to his shoulder, and he brushed a hand through her hair, knocking some of the pasta onto the floor with the movement. She cringed and burrowed deeper into him. Maybe she was dreaming, and she'd wake up from a full night's sleep with an excellent makeup-free skin tone and effortless, flour-free hair.

Rose's cries grew in desperation, and Julia's body responded to the plea. She pushed back from him. All she needed to top off this day was another milk leakage—this time on Henry's shirt. Stellar girlfriend material, for sure.

Nobody warned her about things like this. She folded her arms across her chest to shield any...surprises.

"I have an idea." He cradled her shoulders with his palms. "You feed Rose, then I'll take her while you rest and cook dinner. When you're ready, come collect us?"

Julia dried her eyes with the backs of her fingers, examining him. He didn't look at her like she resembled the Ghost of Christmas Past. "You...You'd do that?"

"I'll do much more if you need me to."

A small smile drifted upward at his words. She pushed her hair back from her face with a sniffle, determined to let him see the happiness he'd brought her—until bits of pasta scattered to the floor. Her smile plummeted into a cringe. "I'm sorry." She looked away from him. "I know I'm a disaster."

Without hesitation, he pulled her back into his arms and kissed her head, her folded arms pinned between them. With gentle guidance he led her out of the pantry and toward the screaming baby in the next room.

"I'll be in my room when you're ready." He headed for the apartment door then paused. "And, dove?"

"Yes?"

"I want to be a part of your life. Crying babies, salted butter, flour, and all."

∞ ∞ ∞

A shower, a half-hour nap, and some 'prettying' up later, Julia felt alive again. She even had time to get her dinner dishes cooking in the oven, all the while listening for Rose's cries from somewhere in the building. A nap and shower had never made her feel like Wonder Woman before. She even tried on one of her favorite floral belted dresses and, low and behold, it fit. A little snug post-baby, but not too bad.

Salad made. Casserole cooking. Dessert cooling in the refrigerator. Now, time to collect her date.

She released her hair from its clips and let it fall loose around her shoulders. For the first time in a long time, even after her crying fit in the pantry, she felt like herself—but a new self, ready for a new journey.

And she wanted Henry to be a part of this journey with her.

With a quick check on the casserole, Julia left the apartment and scanned the sitting room between the two residences. Empty. She walked through the area and raised her hand to knock on Wes and Henry's apartment door, but the quiet strains of the piano downstairs paused her. Only the treble side of the instrument sounded, but the music pulled her toward the first floor.

The sight as she peered into the music room stole every doubt about Henry Wright from her mind. Henry sat on the piano bench, his right hand playing a simple tune while he cradled Rose in the crook of his left arm. He hummed along with the music, adding in a few words. She'd never heard the melody before. Celtic, perhaps? About a cat?

She slid a step closer without catching his attention and noticed Rose's bright eyes staring with rapt wonder up into Henry's face. Julia pressed her fist to her chest, tears blurring her vision. She'd never seen anything so beautiful in her life. He was wonderful.

She drew in a breath and took another step into the room, but his attention was so focused on her daughter, he didn't notice Julia's approach. At that moment, with Rose cradled in Henry's arm, Julia gave her heart to him without one reservation.

Be brave, Julia. Let him know how you feel.

Without making a sound, she slid beside him onto the piano bench. His fingers paused on the keys. Her breath stilled. Then he continued the melody and song as he scooted over to give her more room.

She pinched her hands together in her lap and, with a sigh of sweet resignation, leaned her head against his shoulder. Everything clicked into place. Her eyes closed, and her heart nestled into the acceptance of this belonging.

She loved him.

Rose began making smacking noises with her lips, a definite sign that their privacy was coming to a speedy close, even with the charm of the pianist. He brought the piece to a close, but Julia waited, breathing in his warm vanilla scent and the new freedom in embracing her feelings. "What was the song?"

His shoulder shifted slightly at her question but not enough to change her position against him. "One my grandmother used to sing." His deep voice percolated over her skin, a tender invitation filled with such affection that she slid a little closer just to be near him.

She lifted her cheek from his shoulder and met his gaze. His eyes held hers, their faces mere inches apart, and any hint of fear at his proximity dissipated in his gentle expression. Fear was easier to fight with love as your weapon.

"A sweet song?"

His lips quirked slightly. "About a cat getting lost in a rainstorm and finally being found."

Julia chuckled. "Unexpected."

"That's only one of many unexpected songs my granny used to sing." His gaze dropped to her lips then came back to her eyes.

With a tremor of uncertainty, she raised her palm and smoothed her fingers over his cheek. "Thank you."

One of his brows rose. "For what?"

"You are the sweetest"—she shook her head, words failing to match the emotions pressing in on her chest— "gentlest of men, and I am grateful to know you."

His gaze searched hers as if he were gauging her response to his approach. Every inch of her skin stood on edge, waiting for him to bridge the inches between them, wondering what music might play within her when his lips met hers. Fear's undercurrent tugged ever so slightly at her thoughts, but desire pierced in against it, vying for a chance to see if his kiss was as sweet as the man.

Just as Julia started closing her eyes, Rose's smacking noises took a frustrated and huffy turn. Henry's smile crooked. He looked at her through lowered lashes and she almost split the distance between their mouths just to abate her curiosity, but...Rose needed her.

The kiss would have to wait.

But not for too long, if she had anything to say about it.

∞ ∞ ∞

"You composed your first song when you were seven?" Julia leaned her chin on her palm as they sat near each other at the little table in her apartment. "What instruments were you playing by then?"

"Piano. And the violin too—but poorly. I didn't take up the guitar until I was ten."

"Oh, only ten." She rolled her eyes, enjoying the new intimacy of dinner together and the return of the comradery she'd missed with him since Rose's birth. "What a slacker."

He grinned and leaned back in his chair. "Says the woman who mastered several of Beethoven's piano sonatas by the time she was..." He squinted to the ceiling attempting to remember. "Nine, was it?"

"Well, he was my favorite."

"His work is excellent." He took the last bite of the casserole on his plate. "Much like your cooking."

She placed her palms on the table and stood, keeping her voice low so as not to wake Rose, who was sleeping in the next room. "If you think *that's* good, just wait until you try dessert." He began to rise but she waved him to remain seated. "No, no, let me serve you. *I* must serve the dark chocolate torte. It's just *that* good."

"Very well." He placed his napkin back on his lap. "Far be it from me to steal your joy."

"And it's topped with homemade raspberry syrup from my granny's house." She took their plates from the table and placed them on the kitchen counter along with the dirty salad plates. The vintage apple clock over the stove read nine thirty.

She had, at the most, another hour with Henry before Rose woke. Dessert and then...a kiss? But how was she going to get it?

She took the torte from the refrigerator, rounded the corner, and placed the dessert on the table. Henry's ready smile greeted her as she looked up from arranging two slices on small cream-colored plates. He'd wanted to kiss her several times before. They'd almost kissed twice, in fact.

"This looks fantastic." Henry pushed his fork into the torte.

"It's my favorite, but then I do have a weakness for chocolate."

His gaze shot to hers, his lashes long, smile tipped in the way that quickened her pulse. "Your kryptonite, is it?"

Holy moly! That kissing idea sounded better and better all the time.

Better than dark chocolate torte.

She shot up from the table. "Let me get the...um.... raspberry syrup for the top." A strange junior-high laugh slipped from her lips, and she walked backward toward the pantry. "It's the perfect combo. Raspberries and kisses." She gasped. "I mean, chocolate. Raspberries and chocolate." She thumbed over her shoulder toward the pantry door. "I'll be right back."

Clearly, the last thing on her mind was chocolate. Or raspberry syrup. She sighed and scanned the pantry. How exactly did someone create a perfect kissing moment?

Oh right, the raspberry syrup was stocked on the top shelf—too high for her to reach without a stepstool.

But the perfect height for...a very dashing and helpful Brit right around the corner...

And close quarters tended to encourage romantic-like thoughts, right?

She cast her gaze heavenward. *Is it wrong to pray for a kiss, Lord? If anybody deserves a great kiss, Lord, it's Henry.*

With a deep breath for strength, she peered around the pantry door into the little dining area. "Um...Henry, would you mind helping me for a second?"

"Not at all." He placed his napkin on the table and walked toward the pantry.

The compact pantry. The one that would closet them close together within a mixture of spice smells and vanilla. Oh yes, indeed!

"What may I do for you?"

Kiss me? She cleared her throat, working up to the request, and gestured toward the top shelf. "I can't reach the raspberry syrup up there."

"You wish me to fetch it for you?"

Fetch it? That sounded much nicer and strangely familiar. "Yes, please. Would you mind grabbing...or...um...fetching the syrup, up there in the long-neck bottles?"

With ease he stood on tiptoe and took the syrup from the shelf, then turned to give it to her, but still wasn't close enough for her to initiate a kiss. She frowned and swallowed. *Henry, will you kiss me?* It was so easy to say in her head.

"Um...perhaps you could...fetch..." She scanned the shelves, pausing on a box on the top next to the remaining bottles of raspberry syrup. What had she put in it? "That box, there."

He tilted his head, his narrowed gaze searching hers as he reached for the box, then brought it to her, the top slipping off to reveal Christmas ornaments.

His brows rose. Her face flushed with warmth. "Ah, that's where I put those. I'd wondered." *Sort of. Not.* She winced. There had to be an easier way to go about this.

He stepped a little closer, box still in his arms. "Christmas ornaments in March?"

"Yea...um...obviously not what I thought they were." She forced a chuckle. "I guess you can put those back, if you don't mind."

As he turned, she searched the pantry for something else—something closer to her. And then she saw a perfect item on the shelf above her right shoulder. "Henry?"

He stepped toward her, his expression unreadable except for the slight slant of those lips. "Yes, Julia?"

His voiced zoomed low, raspy, casting a tingle spell down her neck. She took another look at the pitcher, then shrugged a shoulder, offering him a wobbly smile. "Fetch me that pitcher?"

His eyes widened for a second, and then his lips twisted a little in the way she knew showed his pleasure. He'd caught *The Princess Bride* reference. Without breaking eye contact, he reached over her head, took the pitcher, and brought it down between them. He stayed close. Inches away.

"As you wish."

Her grin bloomed Hollywood happy-ending wide, pressing into her cheeks. *Her cue.* With the slightest hesitation, she breached the small space between them and took his face in her hands. His hint of afternoon scruff tickled her palms, deepening the intimacy of her touch. Her throat went dry, a warning from the past, but she refused to retreat.

Not this time.

Henry stared at her, unmoving, a question in his eyes, before he closed them, almost as if he waited for her to finish what she'd started. The smile on those tempting lips encouraged her forward.

A remnant of fear gripped her breath, but she kept her focus on his face. This was the man who'd bantered with her in Aunt Millie's house, who'd quietly offered to help her dad even though it wasn't his preference, who'd carried her down a hillside when she'd gone into labor...the man who'd written a song to strengthen her courage. *Her Henry.* The song he'd written her began a soft melody in her mind, combatting the panicked whispers with a crescendo of hope. Strength.

Studying him, memorizing the crest of his smile and the way his long eyelashes lay against his cheeks, she closed the gap from his lips to hers. He didn't reach for her, but his lips received hers with a welcoming caress. She paused, pulling back just enough to feel his smile spread against her mouth, and then she kissed him again. Longer this time. Easier and sweeter.

One of his hands slipped up to cradle her face. Her arms wound around his neck, palms moving to his hair. Every kiss lingered a little longer, exploring more, giving more, sharing the pleasure of a met expectation—no, beyond expectations.

He kissed like he played music: intricately, passionately, with his entire focus.

And she swooned from the toes up as a grateful recipient of that intense concentration.

He pulled away first, his gaze roaming her face as he tucked a strand of her hair behind her ear. "I prefer this sort of dessert, dove. It's the perfect pinnacle of a lovely evening with a beautiful woman."

She leaned forward, rubbing her nose against his in a playful attempt to stay closer to those tasty lips. "It's the best kind of dessert, you know? Delicious, lingering, and not one calorie. In fact, it may even burn a few."

His soft caress on her face stopped with his fingers on her chin. "I'm happy to indulge in a taste test whenever you wish."

She rewarded his sweetness with another kiss.

"I think you already know this, but I want to tell you that I don't take your affections lightly." He placed the pitcher back on the shelf, so both of his hands could settle around her waist. "I'm not one to trifle with your heart."

"I know." She placed her palm against his chest, committing this moment to memory. "Neither am I."

"And I haven't a great deal of experience with romantic relationships."

"Despite the appearance my circumstances give as a single mom, neither do I."

He brought his lips down for another brief kiss, keeping his eyes closed even when he drew back, as if soaking in the sensations. Oh, how she could identify with him. Her body had never felt so alive with glorious sensations, and her lips wanted to thank him once again for the experience.

"I would imagine you've had more than me." He raised a brow as his fingers trailed down her cheek. "I can count the number of girlfriends I've had on three fingers."

"I can't understand why. You're one of the kindest people I've ever met."

"That's nice of you to say, but relationships require actually *talking* to women. If it weren't for the unique way in which we've been placed together, I don't know as I would have had the opportunity of benefiting from your special attention."

"I've never been so thankful for cupcakes in all my life." She grinned and gave the front of his shirt a playful tug. "And I have a sneaking suspicion we had a few budding matchmakers in our midst."

"I think you're right."

"And I wouldn't be so sure about my romantic experience either if I were you. The only guy who ever made a lasting positive impression on me was Daniel Crane."

His brow rose. "Should I be jealous?"

She laughed and kissed his smile. "Third grade. He left a note on my desk that read, '"Will you be my girlfriend? Check yes or no.'"

His nose slid over hers. "And you said yes."

"I had to," she whispered, eyes fluttering closed. "His penmanship for a third grader was too beautiful to ignore."

"I feel a need to practice my penmanship."

Oh, how his voice melted over her in a wonderful frisson. She could get lost in his touch, his tenderness, much too easily. But she shouldn't. There were things she needed to clarify before dark chocolate kisses and sweet words annihilated her common sense. "Henry, you need to know, before we move forward with this, that I...I won't go into a relationship half-heartedly. I mean, I'm a mom now, and I would look at a relationship with the mindset of forever, not just a few casual dates. And...and I think I already know the answer to this, but...but I want to make sure, because I'm...I'm ready to move forward...with you."

Henry's hands cupped her cheeks and he held her gaze, looking at her as if she were treasured more than anything else in his whole world. "Julia, I've been dreaming of forever with you since we first met."

And she swooned from the kneecaps upward.

"For someone who is more comfortable with music than words, you're doing a fabulous job with them." She breathed out a sigh before braiding his fingers through hers and walking back out into the kitchen.

"You inspire me." He paused and gestured back toward the pantry. "Didn't you want a pitcher?"

She shook her head and slipped her arm around his waist, leaning in to kiss his cheek. "Nope. I just wanted you."

"Oh really?" He pulled her close. "Now *that* is music to my ears."

Chapter Twenty-Five

nd with that first kiss, everything changed, yet in a strange way stayed the same. The friendship they'd developed over the past five weeks smoothed into a deeper relationship with the wonderful bonuses of kisses, hand holding, and hugs.

Julia grinned. And Henry was an excellent hugger.

The morning after their pantry kisses, she came down the stairs to find a note for her on the communication board. When she opened the simple card, a laugh burst out.

Will you be my girlfriend? Please check one.

Two boxes with the words *yes* and *no* followed.

He must have left the note early in the morning, because by the time she'd finally gotten herself and Rose together, Wes and Henry had already left for the day. Her fingers skimmed over the edges of the card. Two months ago, she couldn't see romance in her future at all, and now? Now she couldn't envision her future without Henry. She reached for the pen hanging from a string and thumbtack on the board and with a most decided circle—in purple ink, no less—she gave her answer as her phone buzzed to life with a message.

Have time for lunch today? It's a teacher workday. Soph, Rachel, and I are all free. Adorable newborns welcome. Chops? Lucy's?

Julia looked down at Rose, snug in the baby wrap Julia wore as she navigated some light baking in the kitchen to try to get back into some sort of routine. Lunch with her sisters would be a wonderful break in her usual routine of staying around the apartment and trying out new recipes.

Chops sounds great. I could go for a juicy burger right now.

After breakfast, filling out some college forms, and getting herself and Rose ready for the day, she'd changed Rose's outfit three times in as many hours due to various leaks in several directions—she successfully made it to Chops on time.

Success took on a whole new meaning with a newborn thrown into the mix.

New mom note: Double or triple the amount of time it takes to get anywhere. And always pack extra...everything.

"Oh my goodness, she's on time." Eisley stood from one of the booths located in the middle of the rustic burger and steak joint, coming forward with her arms wide.

"And she looks fabulous," Sophie added. "The shoes are adorable. Stylish yet practical. Very smart for a mama."

Julia scanned her five-year-old jeans, loose lavender blouse, and simple ballet shoes. Oh, Sophie had reached far and wide for that compliment.

"It's all about the clothes, isn't it?" Rachel squeezed her eyes closed and shook her head.

Sophie's palms raised with her usual dramatic flair. "It's *always* about the clothes." The youngest Jenkins's serious expression failed to disguise the mirth in her eyes.

Rachel glanced up with a *what do we do with her?* Look, then unleashed her infrequent smile. "Hungry?"

Julia laughed. "Starving."

"Then you should probably hand over that baby so your hands are free to hold the menu." Rachel motioned a *gimme* wave with her hands. "And I get first dibs because I didn't care about your punctuality or your clothes."

"Hey." Sophie's porcelain brow puckered. "Her ability to look fabulous this soon after having a baby deserves kudos."

Julia laughed, handing a wide-awake Rose to Rachel and taking a seat across from Eisley and Sophie, with Rachel sitting to her right. "I'm not going to lie. It took me an hour just to get myself ready." She raised a finger. "And that wasn't including my shower and hair drying. Seriously, Eisley, how on earth did you do it? I can't imagine going back to work with a baby—and you had two other kids to orchestrate along with a baby."

"Well, you sort it out as you go. I'm glad you have this time to adjust, Jules. Working was super tough on my heart"—she pressed a palm to her chest— "but I think the kids are okay."

"Oh, it's clear you've spent plenty of time with them outside of work," Rachel said, giving Rose a kiss on her cheek, "from all the weirdness."

"Hey." Eisley shot Rachel a mock-glare that dissolved into a smile. "Weirdness runs throughout our family. No one's safe and it can't be blamed solely on me. Have you met our dad?"

The sisters murmured agreement.

Once the server came for their orders, Sophie turned her wide hazel eyes on Julia, her grin mischievous enough to usher images of pixies and fairy dust. "So, what's going on with you and Henry?"

"Good grief, Sophie. The server hasn't even brought the cheese sticks yet, and you're already talking about the main course." Rachel shrugged an apology to Julia.

"Oh no, no." Sophie rubbed her palms together and leaned forward. "More like dessert and I *love* having dessert first."

"Whoa." Julia's palms came up and she laughed. "Here I thought you wanted to see Rose and me or have some girl time, but really you just wanted to pry into my love life?"

"She said love!" At Sophie's squeak heads peeked out from behind other booths scattered across the restaurant.

"Of course we want to pry in your love life." Eisley shrugged. "We're your sisters."

"Take away her caffeine, Eisley," Rachel said.

Eisley gave Sophie a motherly look and slid the tea glass to the center of the table. "No more caffeine for you right now." She turned her grin back to Julia. "And boy talk is totally part of girl time."

Julia's face flushed with a pleasant warmth, the kind of pleasure shared with people who loved her. "Well, I think we're dating."

"You think?" Rachel peered around Rose's head.

"Wait, wait." Eisley placed her tea glass down with a clink. "Look at her face, girls. Julia, have you kissed him?"

Julia's face flamed hotter and she took a quick drink of her tea to bide some time.

"Whoa, Jules. If *Henry* kissed you then this is serious." Eisley's palm flew up like a stop sign. "I mean, really serious. From what Wes says about him, he's been cautious about getting involved with anyone since some pretty hurtful things happened. He must like you a whole lot."

"Well, actually *I* kissed him." Julia shrugged, handing Rachel a cloth to wipe Rose's drooling mouth.

"I am *so* proud of you right now. I knew it would happen." Sophie squealed again, garnering a few more curious looks from other patrons, so she leaned in, her grin peaking into double dimples. "I knew it would happen."

"I don't know about all this." Rachel chimed in with her usual skepticism, a protective streak that ran deep. "I trust Wes, but Julia, you've been through a lot, and I want you to be careful. How is he with Rose? That's a big test for any guy who might come into your life."

A sudden rush of excitement mixed with a little bit of loving defense for her tenderhearted boyfriend. "He's great with her—so gentle and kind and such a natural. You'd think he'd always been around babies. He wrote a piano composition for me, to help with my anxiety, and he's so funny. You can't really see his humor until you get to know him better, but it's wonderful, really, and he's curious to learn about everything but especially about me and Rose. I just love talking with him...or even sitting and listening to music together without talking at all. We fit in this weird way of just knowing already. I can't really explain it, but I think he's one of the best men I've ever known. He's genuinely...good." She offered a light laugh at the wonderful declaration. "I know that may sound strange, but it's true. I've never met a man with such a kind heart. There's this rightness and calm he brings when we're together and I find I'm a better person from knowing him. He's—" She stopped. All three of her sisters stared at her as if she'd lost her mind. "What?"

"I think that may be the most I've ever heard you say at one time," Rachel answered first, her dark eyes narrowed with suspicion.

"And with such animation and joy." Sophie's shoulders scrunched into what could only be an internal squeal of delight. "You're glowing."

Julia touched her cheeks, unable to curb her smile. "I am?"

"It's the glow of love." Sophie beckoned toward Rachel for a chance to hold Rose. "Two kind people and a sweet little baby. It's so perfect. We definitely have to celebrate with chocolate."

"It's true," Eisley added. "Even Wes was blown away at how well the two of you matched from the beginning. It seems Henry thinks as well of you as you do of him."

Julia bit her bottom lip, a smile breaking through regardless. "He does?" Though she knew already because Henry didn't hide things at all. He spoke or displayed them. She *felt* loved because of the way he cared for her.

"Let me just say that I've been pretty skeptical about this whole 'meet and fall in love within a few months' thing, but the two of you are starting to make me wonder." Rachel shook her head, looking between Eisley and Julia and reluctantly giving Rose over to Sophie. "It seems real and right, and a whole lot of scary."

"It *is* real and right." Eisley wiggled her engagement ring. "It may not be like this for everyone, but sometimes God just works things out to have two right people together at the right time, and they're both ready for each other."

"I think it's wonderful," Sophie added as she cooed over Rose.

"So do I." Julia's admittance settled over her, a sweet confirmation of her choice. Her gaze landed on Rose. For both of them. *Though the future did hold a little bit of scary.*

"Well, I don't know what we're going to do with two Brits in the family." Rachel nodded her thanks toward the waitress as she sat the appetizer on the table, the scent bringing a growl from Julia's stomach. "One of us is going to have to find a good old country boy to keep the family balanced."

"You go for the country boy, Rach." Sophie's eyebrows shimmied a little dance. "I'm definitely hoping the third time's a charm on the Brit for *this* sister."

∞ ∞ ∞

Henry rushed through the back door of the bakery after his workday on set. He couldn't wait to see Julia and ensure that all of those stellar good night kisses from the night before hadn't been a part of some dream.

Noise from the bakery alerted him to a busy dinner crowd, and his stomach growled at the scent of some savory dish Amy served as a special. If Julia wasn't available, he'd sit for dinner in the bakery and finish composing the final piece for Wes's movie.

He turned from the hallway to the stairs and stopped at the communication board, searching to see if Julia had noticed his card from this morning. In answer, he found the card in the same place as he'd left it, except with Julia's name crossed out on the front and his name written in its place.

A single purple mark on the inside of the card signified the only change. A pleasant one, to be sure. He attempted to curb his grin, failed, and, looking around as if someone might be spying him, tucked the card into his jacket pocket and started up the stairs.

He'd barely gotten his key in the apartment door when—

"Hello there, Mr. Wright."

He turned to see Julia standing in her doorway. He straightened, taking in the lovely view she presented in her jeans and simple, lavender button-up blouse with decorative sleeves that belled out at the wrists. Jeans suited her quite well.

"Miss Jenkins?"

She took a step toward him. "Have you had dinner?"

He placed his violin case inside the doorway of his apartment. "No. In fact, I was just contemplating the idea of visiting the bakery before Amy closed for the evening."

She gestured with her head toward her apartment. "Well, you could join Rose and me, if you want."

Every day for the rest of my life. "I'd love to."

He slipped into her apartment, and as she closed the door behind him, she leaned over and greeted him with a gentle kiss. "Since we've made it official now."

"Complete with a checked box, even."

"Exactly."

"How did my penmanship compare to Daniel Crane's?"

A little snort-laugh escaped her nose, but she tried to cover it with a poor attempt at a serious expression. "Pretty impressive. Enough to tempt me, obviously."

"Aha. I see the stakes were high."

She linked her arm through his and led him into her sitting area, where Rose swung in her baby swing, hands reaching up for some dangling objects above her. "Hello, duck." He knelt before her, his movements garnering her attention. She stared, her little mouth opening and closing as if she wished to communicate with him. "Very posh seat you have."

"And one she enjoys too. Eisley gave it to me at lunch. Said it made all the difference for Pete when he had trouble sleeping."

He'd heard bits of crying throughout the night. "Is it much harder than you imagined?" He stood and followed her to the little table already set for two.

Ah, she'd hoped he'd come. Very promising, indeed.

"Sometimes, like yesterday." Her nose wrinkled with a grimace. "But then I adjust my expectations, eat too much dark chocolate, and look into that sweet little face and know it's all worth it."

With a sudden turn, he tugged her back toward him and kissed her, reveling in the freedom of the motion and his beautiful recipient's response. He pulled back an inch, keeping her close, studying her face.

"Kissing doesn't make you...fearful?"

"It did at first, but I focused on the melody of the piano piece you wrote me until the fear went away and only—" She looked away, color rising into her cheeks. "Only...um...pleasure remained."

"Kissing you is most definitely pleasurable." He brushed his fingers along her cheek. "And I'm happy to hear it's not uncomfortable for you, because I wish to continue the practice for a long time."

"And often, I hope."

"Most certainly." Which is exactly what he proceeded to do.

∞ ∞ ∞

And the routine began. The three of them would spend mornings together, then separate for the middle of the day so that Julia could run errands, care for Rose, and even help in the bakery a little while Henry completed his work for the movie and checked emails for his projects in England. They'd come back together for dinner each night, sometimes venturing out to a local restaurant and sometimes dining in at Julia's apartment.

Henry wasn't certain whether Julia recognized it yet or not, but they were well-suited for one another. Their relationship settled into his world like a lost piece of his life he'd waited to uncover, deepened by the friendship they'd developed before the first kiss.

"You compose for movies *and* commercials? For some reason, I only thought it was only movies." Julia walked beside him along the narrow path through the forest—a level path with only a few inclines, giving Julia an easy reentry into hiking since delivering Rose.

"And television, if possible. Anything that will pay well." He carried Rose in the infant sling, snuggled close to his heart, and occasionally she'd tilt her little head in such a way as to look up at him and nearly derail him from the path. What a marvelous invention, but how would he ever part with either of them? He pushed the thought away and focused on the present. "In fact, there's a company back home called Visionary Media that's keen to find a permanent composer for their company."

"And you like that idea? Being with one company?"

He nodded, holding back a branch for her to pass. "It will still allow me to dabble in larger movies if I wish, but more importantly, it provides stability in both time and finances."

"Thank you." She ducked beneath the branch, turning her head to keep the conversation going. The path broadened enough that they could walk side-by-side, and without hesitation, Julia threaded her arm through his. He grinned down at the adorable vision she made with her hair back in a ponytail, a ballcap in place, and a T-shirt that read *Life is better with music.*

Oh, she was perfect.

"But you've done all these movies in the past. Would sticking with one company feel like settling?"

"I hope so."

She stopped walking and looked up at him. "You do?"

"I love music." He gestured toward her T-shirt and started walking again. "It's a part of my life and my heart, but my deeper dream, my 'heart dream' as you call it, has always been to..."

"Go ahead."

"As sentimental and old-fashioned as it may sound in this world where everyone is striving for their definition of success, I've always wanted to have a family. And, of course, I love music and always will, but I can't think of anything more pleasing than the idea of having a close-knit family like yours."

She stopped again, studying him with those fathomless eyes. "That's one of the sweetest things I've ever heard."

"Probably not something you should tell your father, though, eh? More items to stack against me."

"I think Dad would probably agree with your definition of success, Henry. He may not voice it"—she chuckled and squeezed his arm close to her— "but he'd agree with what's most important in life."

"My family hasn't known the closeness nor the liberality of love displayed in yours. I think they need to understand there are new and better ways to interact with one another. To develop true friendships among us as family."

"You even see that with my dad and brothers?" She challenged him with a raised brow, her expression wrestling to maintain its mock seriousness.

"They try hard to hide their softer sides, but it comes through in unguarded moments. I've seen it. I believe it's one of the reasons I'm only slightly terrified of your father."

Her grin bloomed again.

The trees up ahead began to thin out, promising a view.

"You seem to be close to your brother. I mean, from the way you've talked about him."

"Yes. Of everyone, except my late grandparents, Matthew has been my closest family relation, but I would say I'm closer to Wes and his family than even him. Friendships weren't encouraged in our home, you see. Competition, perhaps, especially where my younger brother was concerned, but not real relationships. There was a great deal of distance and silence and expectations that no one could meet. My father attempted, as best he could, to be a gentle influence, but my mother wouldn't have it."

"You must take after your father then."

"I like to think so. He was a good man, though easily overrun. I suppose that's why he stayed at work so often."

"My mom is quiet, but she's not afraid to speak her mind when necessary. Dad may be the louder one, but she's just as tough. Sometimes tougher, I think. Heart strength."

"Strength definitely runs through your veins."

She lowered her face with a smile, then looked up at him. "Strength comes in all shapes and sizes—including the quiet, gentle, fiercely loyal sort."

"Thank you." The incline up the last stretch of the path slowed their pace. "I would like to show my family a better way." He glanced down at her, holding her gaze. "A more beautiful way."

Her expression turned thoughtful. "Were Matthew and his wife close?"

He drew in a deep breath, contemplating the question. "They were...kind to one another."

"You say that as if it's a bad thing."

"Not at all." He focused on the path ahead as he searched for the right words. "I suppose it was an unconventional sort of marriage from the beginning. They'd been childhood friends, and Matthew would probably say it never really bloomed into deep romance, just a quiet comradery. They knew each other and the expectations, so marriage blended into the next step."

She shook her head. "I've never heard of a relationship quite like that."

Henry grinned. "Matthew isn't as shy as I am. His occupation as a history professor stretched him more than mine did or does even now despite my moderate success, but neither one of us has the sort of personality that attracts the fairer sex." He waved a hand to her, inspiring her smile. "He enjoys quiet and predictability, so the prospect of stable familiarity worked for him, and particularly for Mother."

"Your mother liked Matthew's wife?"

"Marianne was extremely—compliant. No contradictions, no scandals. No real conversations at all, in fact, but that was Marianne's way until the end. She was a gentle whisper in all of our lives, without...without..."

"A voice?"

Not the word he was going for but apt nonetheless. "I would say she rarely made her voice distinct. She was content to be completely agreeable, which, for me, seemed somewhat disagreeable, if you understand?"

"Yes, I think I do." She pushed back a final branch. "Healthy relationships are about sharing thoughts and ideas, growing from differences, and strengthening similarities. Conversation and healthy debates. I may not have a loud voice, but I want to be heard and find someone who will hear me."

"Yes, I feel the same way. Good conversation requires two voices, doesn't it? Not merely listening to oneself."

She stepped forward onto a rocky ledge that opened the world to a vast horizon of mountains and sky. "It also can make for some excellent harmony in life instead of a solo."

She nudged him with her shoulder, and he leaned over to press a kiss to her cheek. "Indeed. Perfect harmony."

She placed her head against his shoulder and stared out at the view, her chuckle vibrating against him. "As wonderful as you are, I don't think either one of us will be perfect."

"Quite true." He grinned. "Imperfect harmony, then."

Chapter Twenty-Six

*S*he'd inherited a treasure.

Julia sifted through another box of clothes she'd brought from Aunt Millie's, her fingers slipping over carefully beaded evening gowns, swing dresses, and adorable belted dresses Julia would have purchased herself—if she'd ever found ones she adored as much as these.

And they fit her.

She'd just slid into a silky evening gown of a shimmery pale blue when a knock sounded at her apartment door. She glanced at the clock. Three already? With a little spin in her dress, its material slipping over her like water, almost magical, she took one last look in the mirror. Oh, what would Millie have looked like wearing this on stage? Dazzling? Charming? She shook her head as she checked on Rose in her swing on her way to the door. What would it feel like to be admired in such a way? Enchanting? She was certain she'd never enchanted anyone.

Henry waited at the threshold, flowers in his hands, but the look on his face trumped the beauty of the bouquet. His smile faded into an O and his marbled gaze roamed over her as if she were the most mesmerizing thing he'd ever seen.

Her heart fluttered up into her throat as warmth gathered in her face.

Henry looked utterly...enchanted. Her grin pierced her cheeks as she opened the door wider for him to enter. He always gave her his attention and care, complimenting her and showing such tender and specific regard, but this...this was new.

"I...I..." He thrust the flowers forward, continuing to stare at her with wide eyes. "For you."

"Thank you, Henry." She took the flowers and turned, feeling the cool air from in the hallway brush against her barren back. The warmth in her cheeks skyrocketed to boiling. Oh, she'd forgotten about that part of the dress. Maybe Henry wouldn't notice the low cut.

She spun around, and he jerked his gaze back to her face, his brows high.

"Um...I'm trying to figure out what to wear to an engagement party at a place as fancy as the Harrison's estate house."

"Don't wear that one."

A sound like wounded animal slipped from behind her pout before she could catch it. Hadn't he liked it? His expression seemed to suggest he did.

"Not that you don't look amazing." He came forward and placed his palm against her bare shoulder, his touch sending all sorts of delightful zings through her. "You're beyond dazzling." His gaze begged for her understanding. "But I don't think I should be able to have a coherent conversation with a single person in the room if you wore this gown for long."

She squeezed his hand. "You like it!"

"I like *you* in it. Very much. Too much, actually." The look he gave her through those long lashes didn't appear anything like the timid Henry she'd met on that first day. In fact, the way his gaze darkened somehow sneaked in and stole her breath. "It's inspiring some rather unruly thoughts, dove."

Those unruly thoughts transferred directly from his head to hers, and she vaulted at him, linking her arms over his shoulders and finding his lips with hers. They'd kissed plenty of times in their few weeks of being 'girlfriend' and 'boyfriend', as the paper-note box labeled them, but this one took a more passionate turn. His warm hands smoothed over her back, nearly puddling her to the floor. Her fingers pushed into his hair, drawing him closer, urging him to stay right where he was.

A rush of fear twinged in her chest as the kiss lingered and intensified, but she played his tune for her in her mind, stilling the thoughts, embracing his touch.

"This...this material is..." His words tumbled between them on broken air. "It...isn't helping my unruly thoughts at all, I'm afraid."

"I think I like your unruly thoughts a little, Henry." She reclaimed his mouth, and he groaned, tugging her more securely against him.

One of his palms slid up her bare back to her neck, leaving delicious tingles in its wake. She wanted his attention, his kisses, his touch. He loved her. The right way. And she craved his nearness in every way. More and more. The music in her head switched to Chopin—his powerful *Etude in C Major*—heightening the power in their kiss.

She pulled him close, intensifying the kiss, and he seemed to take the hint because his lips took a delightful detour to her ear. Oh heavens! She clung to the front of his shirt, requesting just a little more for a little longer.

Suddenly, Eisley's stories of her struggles to keep her relationship with Wes pure until marriage flooded back into her mind. Julia hadn't fully comprehended the battle, but here, with this gentle man unfurling his well-tended passion on her, she was tempted to explore a physical closeness she'd never imagined desiring. Especially after all that had happened to her.

Love made a difference. Henry's way of caring for her healed her heart, and all she wanted was give back to him, to bathe in his affection.

The word *bathe* brought up all sorts of pictures in her head, so she pulled back at the same time he did.

"I can't—"

"I'm sorry—"

He stepped back and ran a hand through his hair. "You first."

"I think I understand your intimate ideas now." She lowered her gaze and fanned her hand in front of her face. "I really like kissing you, Henry."

Such a beautiful smile spread across his face that she almost rewarded him with another kiss, which probably wasn't the best idea, especially since her body was still humming so vibrantly from his touch that she hadn't quite gathered her thoughts.

"I can assure you, dove, the feeling is mutual." He nodded, clearing his throat. "Extremely mutual."

How could she not love him? He made it so easy from one thoughtful act and gentle smile to the next. Sure, it helped that he kissed with as much purpose as he played the piano, but even apart from his quite swoon-worthy lips, he loved so well.

"I...I know you're not that much older than me, but I still can't understand why you're not taken already."

His brow crinkled. "Pardon?"

"I mean, you're all these wonderful things rolled up in a single man, and it just seems logical that you're a prime candidate for some wonderful woman to snatch up."

"You don't have to snatch. I'm readily giving my heart to you."

She chuckled. "And I'm not planning to let go of you, but...I'm just glad I'm the one, because I've never known anyone as kind and talented and funny and handsome as you, and I guess that's why I'm so surprised you're not—"

He slid a step closer to her. "You think me handsome?"

The rascally turn of his grin nearly distracted her from answering. "Of...of course I think you're handsome. Why is that so surprising?"

He shoved his hands into his pockets and continued to study her. "I've had many adjectives ascribed to me in the past, but neither funny nor handsome has been one of them."

Her brow creased, and she pressed a finger into his chest. "Well, you should have heard it by now, and I'm sorry you haven't, because it's true. And...and you've helped me see that when we're viewed through the right eyes, then we can have a whole new perspective about ourselves."

He traced a finger down her cheek. "I like your perspective, and you're right, it's easy to allow the wrong people to define us if we're uncertain of who we are or who we should be in the first place. You and your family have helped me gain a better view, a clearer one."

"We have?"

"I've spent my life allowing others to measure me, direct me, and I've never defined myself by God's assertion of who I am. You and your family have helped me see that I am more than I thought I was." He returned his hand to his pocket, the memory of his touch leaving tingles across the skin of her cheek. "Being quiet, introverted, somewhat obsessive about music, and quite...um...put off by social interaction on a grander scale is not necessarily a liability. God can still use me as I am, but also, He can make me brave enough to become better. I can change and grow as I gain confidence in who He says I am and can be."

She blinked up at him, a little stunned by his declaration. "My crazy, loud family taught you that?"

"Well, if your father doesn't instill bravery through intimidation, I don't know who would."

Her laugh erupted again, spilling the sweetness of their connection afresh through her. How was she supposed to just allow him to disappear back to England in nine days? "A true statement born from real life experience."

"Indeed. I'm thankful for your family, father and all." His smile softened. "Why don't you finish enjoying your lovely discovery"—he gestured toward her gown— "while I take Rose for a little trip to the piano room until either she needs you or you're finished?"

Julia raised on tiptoe and kissed his cheek. "I think I love you, Henry Wright."

She froze as soon as her heels touched the floor. Had she announced that out loud or only in her head? Henry's gaze fixed on hers, intense and searching.

Oh, what did she do now? An apology didn't seem right. In fact, it would be a lie. She wasn't really sorry. She almost laughed. No, she wasn't sorry at all.

He gathered her fingers into his before returning his gaze to hers. "I know I love you, Julia Jenkins."

His grin broadened as he stood a little straighter. Had her confession done that? She reached for the chain around her neck, a shiver of delight almost emerging in a giggle.

"And because I love you, I'm going to take my unruly thoughts to the music room and leave you to your discoveries." He slipped over to Rose and took her into his arms, cradling her against his shoulder. "I feel quite certain Rose will enjoy a sound lashing of Liszt."

Great with kids. Sweet. Romantic. Loves music. Great kisser.

Yep, he was a keeper. Julia sighed as the door closed behind him. The tune from *South Pacific* surged into her thoughts. *I'm in love with a wonderful guy.*

∞ ∞ ∞

Henry met Julia's gaze from across the table at the Jenkinses Sunday lunch, and his thoughts spun back through countless memories from the previous week. From movie night watching the classic *Amadeus*—which *no one* he knew wanted to watch with him—to Julia in the Blue Fairy gown and the most epic kiss of his entire existence, to playing four-hands piano pieces to Rose after the bakery closed for the night. How did a heart hold so much at once? It was like all of his favorite Bach compositions played through him at the same time until he was bound to explode from sheer joy.

Julia and Rose helped him see what family could look like one day—his family.

And God had brought them to him? Beethoven's *Ode to Joy* burst through the Bach in blaring fullness.

And Julia loved him. He'd replayed that moment a thousand times.

"It's a shame you gotta leave in a few days, Henry," Nate announced from the head of the table. "I got a roof to shingle and could use a good helper."

"Don't trust him, Henry." Eisley's pronouncement cut through the cacophony of children's chatter at the other end of the table. "He's only asking so he can smack your thighs afterward."

Henry opened his mouth to respond, but the thigh-slapping talk stole his response.

"Ain't nothin' wrong with a man lookin' for some good help."

"Shingling a roof really does a job on your thighs, Henry," Greg added, passing a plate of meatloaf Henry's way. "I could barely walk for three days."

"It's 'cause you're too busy playing with animals instead of helpin' your old man." Nate gestured for the beans sitting in front of Henry then winked as the bowl made it into his hands. "My young'uns ruin all the fun by tellin' you my secrets, Henry. I was lookin' forward to seein' if you could squall as good as you fiddle."

Henry's gaze slid to Wes for interpretation. Wes leaned in. "I suppose he means if he slaps your sore thigh, you'll cry out."

217

At the mental image of the Jenkins patriarch slapping sore thighs for the fun of it, Henry lost control of his laugh. Nate was a singular sort whose unique personality had somehow wormed its way into Henry's affections. A diamond in the rough, so to speak.

"I hate to have an excuse for it, Nate."

"Sure you do." He exaggerated his eye roll and took a bite of his meatloaf and beans.

"So, Dad." The mischievous glimmer in Eisley's eyes caught Henry's attention. "Why on earth did you place Henry and Julia across the table from each other. They're dating. They should be able to sit next to each other."

"I told your mama." He waved his fork toward Kay, who raised a humored brow to her husband. "The two of them are around each other enough as it is. The last thing we need is them being all lovey dovey at the table and making me sick enough to ruin this fine meatloaf here."

"I completely agree, Nate." Wes shot Henry a wink as he raised a bite of potatoes to his mouth. "This way we'll only have to ignore their adoring stares at each other across the table."

Julia's smile kept growing as they shared the open enjoyment of their relationship with those gathered around the table. Awkward, yes? But it fit what he'd come to expect from this massive, loud, and loving family.

And somehow, he knew he belonged now. Even to the patriarch.

"Oh, good grief. I see it happening right before my eyes." Nate groaned and placed his head in his hands as if to block the vision.

"Perhaps I can help distract you, Nate."

All eyes turned to Henry, and he sat up a little taller, adjusting to the sudden attention. "Julia mentioned you enjoy the music of *Indiana Jones* and *Superman*. Well, I've composed a four-hands piano piece in your honor—similar feel to those two compositions."

Nate's dark brows crashed together. "A four hands what?"

"It's a piece of music that requires four hands to play."

Nate's brow shot to his hairline.

"A duet, Dad. A piano duet." Julia sent Henry a half-hidden grin. "Henry and I will play it for you."

"You wrote a duet in honor of me?" Nate stared so hard at Henry that Henry thought the man had finished talking—until he finally filled the long silence. "Why on earth would you do that?"

Henry's smile unfurled. He'd made an impression on Nate Jenkins. "Big emotions and big personalities are best described through music, Nate. Superman? Indiana Jones? I think you deserve your own musical theme."

"Oh dear," Kay murmured. "There'll be no living with him now."

∞ ∞ ∞

Nate sat beside his wife in the large den as Henry and Julia took their places at the piano. Julia looked beautiful—happier, Nate thought, than even before...

He pushed the thought of what had happened to his daughter nine months ago from his mind. Her face lit when she looked at Henry, and the boy's expression didn't hide one bit of his care for Nate's girl. Not one.

If Nate were a good daddy he'd take Henry in with a full heart. He might not have chosen Henry for Julia, but—he sighed—he'd have chosen the wrong sort. God knew better.

In the middle of the music—the type that made a man feel like he needed to journey on an adventure—the melody changed to something almost...sweet. Julia played that part. High notes. Gentle-like, pulling from a bluegrass feel. She turned toward him and winked. "It's what we all know is way down deep on the inside, Dad."

He cleared his throat and nodded but his eyes burned anyway. Daggone it. Between the thoughts of God's hand on Julia's life in this way and the music her sweet-talkin' boyfriend composed *in honor of Nate*, Nate was about ready to run from the room and cry like a baby. He'd better go chop down a tree instead. Get the energy out.

If he could make it through the duet.

"He's real good for her, Nate," Kay whispered, her head almost touching his shoulder as she moved closer.

The lump in his throat grew three sizes, so he only nodded.

"He's one of the kindest men I've ever seen, and that's one of the things we've always wanted for our kids. That they'd find someone who shows them kindness and God's love. Henry does that for her."

His teeth clenched so hard they started to hurt his jaw. Then he made the mistake of looking over at Kay, who had baby Rose resting in her arms.

"And we need to prepare ourselves for...for that," Kay whispered down at the sleeping baby, and Nate wanted to rip his own eyes out.

That meanin' Julia and Rose might choose a home across a very large ocean.

The music grew again, bringing back the sound of the brave adventurer, and he studied the profiles of the two in front of him, his arm lowering to Kay's shoulders. He couldn't imagine life without her by his side. Growing up, he hadn't known the type of closeness her family had. His home had been filled with unpredictable affection and harsh words, but she'd breezed in like cool change on a hot day. She'd shown him what love looked like. Taught him how to be brave, even when faced with the troubles of life.

How to be brave.

He looked back at Julia and firmed his chin. Even when letting go.

Chapter Twenty-Seven

ulia kept close to Henry as they navigated the foot-traffic at Charlotte-Douglas International Airport. Wes had offered to bring him, but Julia wanted to soak up every second with Henry—even if it meant pushing through the crowds of a busy airport teeming with passengers and pilots and flight attendants rushing to and fro between terminals. She would take whatever minutes with Henry she could get. She'd never loved a man like this and certainly didn't have any experience with being separated from one, but already a quiet ache gnawed through the magic of their comradery.

Were they to become one of those couples who grappled then failed with the challenges of long-distance relationships? Surely not. But maybe...She pressed her palm against Rose's head, as if to stop her doubts from transferring to her daughter as she lay cocooned against Julia in the baby wrap.

Henry looked down at her, and she saw the same hesitation reflected in his eyes.

For some reason, this separation also felt a little like a test. A proof to her own heart, in a way, that this was more than a passing romance.

"Three months isn't so long, is it?" He cleared his throat and paused before the SECURITY sign, staring at the long lines making their steady way through.

"Not so long," she whispered. "I've heard England is beautiful in June."

His gaze swung to hers. Held. "It is. Absolutely. I can't wait to show you."

She smiled and looked over at the lines, working up the courage to say good-bye when all she wanted to do was beg him to stay.

"We'll sort out a calling schedule straight away."

"My current sleeping pattern will probably fit right in with the time change." She grinned, blinking away unwanted tears.

Without warning, he took her face between his palms and kissed her, in the middle of the airport. She braided her fingers through his hand to keep him there. He pulled back only far enough that his forehead rested against hers.

"Leaving has never been so difficult in all my life."

She bit her bottom lip to keep it from trembling. "I know."

"And, to be completely honest, three months sounds like a lifetime."

She reached up to brush his hair back from his brow, his gaze too sorrowful to hold for long. "It will be good to see if what we have is real enough to withstand time and distance, you know?"

"You have doubts?" His gaze searched hers, all uncertainty gone. "Because I don't. Someone like you"—his attention dropped to Rose— "*both* of you, only enters a person's life once. I won't miss my chance."

She pressed her head against his once more, closing her eyes, filling her lungs with his warmth and vanilla scent. "I just don't like the idea of this distance. I've gotten so used to being near you. To hearing your music next door. To having the longest conversations I've ever had with anyone." A heated tear trailed down her cheek. "I'll miss *you*."

"Julia."

At the whispered sound of her name, she raised her eyes. "My heart will still be in the very same place. You need not doubt my constancy."

"Doubt *you*?" She returned her palm to his cheek, her words scraping over her throat. "How could I ever doubt you? But distance and the expectations of our regular lives can change what our situation looks like right now."

"Of course they can. But, dove, life is all about adapting to situations, and our hearts must choose to hold fast or to let go."

She nodded, drawing strength from the certainty in his voice, the assurance of who she knew he was. "I...I choose you."

His grin crooked and he pressed his lips to hers for a brief kiss. "I choose us, and...and in June, we'll sort out how distance won't be a long-term issue. We'll find a way. What do you say about that?"

"Sounds like music to my ears."

∞ ∞ ∞

Henry wasn't certain what he'd expected upon his return to England, but nothing had changed. Heathrow kept its crowded, busy hum. The railway station pulsed with the bustle of the daily workings of a city, and his brother Matthew, who'd collected him from the railway station, still needed a haircut.

And yet everything looked different.

He'd never noticed how many couples walked on the streets of Matlock or the number of prams in the town park. Matlock wasn't large, but its old buildings gave off the feel of a welcome, quaint place. Julia would like his town.

An ache resurrected in his chest—the same feeling he'd experienced all the way across the Atlantic. The farther the plane took him from Pleasant Gap, the deeper the longing. How were they going to make this work? And in the fastest way possible?

Matthew turned the car away from Matlock and toward the country. On their journey home, a large house set off the road caught Henry's attention. Crandall House. He'd never really paid much attention to the large country cottage on the edge of town, but now, with the for-sale sign still perched in the front yard... "Stop here, Matthew," he whispered then gathered volume. "Here. Just for a moment."

Matthew pulled the car to the side of the road, and Henry jumped out. "What are you doing?"

He ignored his brother and continued toward the house, entering the front garden through an unlatched gate. Crandall House rose ahead of him, an impressive structure of limestone and history. Two levels. Fantastic grounds, from what he could tell. A massive circular drive well-suited for numerous cars. Easy access to town and the motorway.

He peered around to the right. A link, long and framed by windows, connected the large main house to a smaller building of matching color and style. Was it a living area too?

That could be perfect.

A greenhouse roof peeked above a walled back garden, and an excellent view of the rolling countryside spread out from the back of the house with a prospect not *too* different from the rolling hills around Pleasant Gap.

"What in heaven's name are you doing?" Matthew called from the end of the drive, his dark hair and jacket flapping in the morning breeze.

"Thinking." Henry started walking to his brother. "Crandall House has been for sale for well over four months, hasn't it?"

Matthew looked to the house, then Henry. "I suppose so."

"And it's not sold in that time."

"Clearly," his brother responded in his usual droll fashion. "It has two living areas separated by a link. How many families do you think are seeking such a place?"

"Precisely, Matthew." Henry patted his brother on the shoulder. "Precisely."

∞ ∞ ∞

Julia finished her last email to one of her professors proposing a six-week directive study for May to mid-June, right before leaving for England. If she wanted to graduate by December, she'd need one more credit than she'd planned for the fall semester, and she was already doubling up on classes to finish up. Dr. Peterson had always been the approachable sort, so maybe Julia had a chance at an intensive Summer 1 opportunity before she traveled to England. It would help her get her feet wet with managing her continued work with the bakery, taking care of Rose, *and* initiating her own baby steps back into the academic world.

And it was an excellent distraction from missing Henry.

She'd dressed Rose in one of her cutest outfits, all frilly and girly, complete with a hairbow that kept falling off the hairless beauty. Well, her daughter had a little hair—enough to attempt a hairbow, but not much else.

She situated herself on the couch and propped her laptop on a nearby table as she pulled Rose into her lap. Seven o'clock. He should call any minute.

Every evening at seven for the past four nights. She'd never been so thankful for technology in all her life.

The computer signaled an incoming call, so Julia leaned forward and pressed a button, and Henry's face filled the screen. "Hello, dove."

She nearly sighed every time he greeted her that way. Was her grin as ridiculously large as his? Oh man, she was in so much trouble...in the best possible way. Forever. "Hey, my sweet friend." She hadn't quite figured out a term of endearment for him yet. She liked his name. "Have you had a nice day?"

"Better now, of course." He sent a little wave to Rose, who gave wide-eyed focus to the screen. "Hello, duck. I like your hairbow."

Julia adjusted the crooked bow for the tenth time. "We had to dress up for a special occasion, Henry."

"A special occasion?" His eyes took her in. "Are you wearing one of those frocks of your aunt's again?"

She glanced down at the pink shirt dress styled with white polka dots that she'd donned for his benefit—and a little of hers. She adored the vintage piece, even if she ended up changing out of it within the first ten minutes because of baby spit up...or worse.

"Do you like it?"

His smile took a new turn, the same kind she'd learned to interpret as...well...unruly. "It suits you very well." He cleared his throat and raised a brow. "What's the special occasion?"

Julia scrunched her shoulders to contain a little squeal. "I have a surprise for you." She shifted closer to the screen, bringing Rose with her. "Watch this."

With a few quick kisses at the juncture of Rose's rounded cheeks and neck, her little darling made a gurgling sound, then...

"She's smiling." His voice pooled with pleasant surprise.

Julia turned Rose so he could get an even better view. "I know!"

"And is that a dimple?"

"In her chin. Isn't it the cutest ever?"

"It's as if she has a little personality in there."

"Right?" Julia kissed her again and the gurgled smile repeated. "You're happy to see Henry too, aren't you, Rosie?"

"The two of you are the best part of my day."

Julia swallowed through the tightening in her throat. This was the way things had to be for now, and crying wouldn't change it. "Well, it's more like night-time, isn't it? Midnight?"

He squinted and shifted his eyes to the bottom right of his computer screen where, she imaged, the time flashed. "It's still early. I have a few hours of work in me yet."

Rose turned her head at the sound of his voice, searching the room. "Oh, Henry. I think she's trying to find you. Look. When you talk, she turns in your direction."

"That's it." He pressed a fist to his chest as if hit. "I'm searching for flights right now."

She laughed. "As much as I would *love* to see you, don't you have an important interview tomorrow?"

His gaze found hers through the screen. "It's becoming less and less important by the day."

"That's not true. It's your dream job. You have to try." She steeled her reserve and moved Rose closer so the baby had a better view. "Besides, it's only ten weeks and two days until we see you."

"She's smiling at me without the kisses. Look." He sighed. "I miss you both so much. Nothing is the same in my life now. You're everywhere and I can't even reach you."

"I never imagined it could be this hard when you find that special person, you know? I mean, I've been on trips with Aunt Millie when I didn't see my family for weeks, but this?" Julia waved a hand between them. "This is much harder."

"American Airlines has a flight first thing in the morning."

"Henry." She shook her head, welcoming his levity. "Do you think your dreams aren't as important to me as mine are to you?"

He stared at her, assessing, and sighed. "Touché."

"Truth." She adjusted Rose's hairbow again. "Music helps, though, doesn't it? I hear you in music now, like you're nearby. Every violin. I played the song you wrote for me last night...all the way through." She ran a finger down Rose's cheek. "It sounds better as a duet."

"Delta has one that leaves at 6:00a.m. That's an hour earlier than American Airlines."

She laughed and watched how his eyes lit even through the screen. He'd probably have leaned over and kissed her if he'd been nearby. A small kiss. Just enough to share his care, but not enough to garner much attention. "We have an agreement. You can get your dream job, and I'm going to finish school. Then we'll figure out the logistics."

He frowned but didn't argue, though it looked like he wanted to. Bad idea. It wouldn't take a great deal of arguing for her to help him order his airline ticket. They'd best change topics before she found him in her doorway tomorrow morning. "I contacted the National Archives earlier today via email to see if they know anything more about Lucas's death."

"Excellent. No news yet, I'd say."

"No. I have a feeling it will take them a while to respond, and I'm not even sure this is the right person. I've contacted three so far and been redirected every time."

"The mystery continues." He wiggled his brows. "And did you see about the directed study course?"

Why did it surprise her when he remembered little things she'd said? "Only a few minutes ago, so I probably won't hear anything for a couple of days."

"But it's a start, isn't it? Dreams and plans and all that."

"Right. A start for the end of my degree."

"And the beginning of a heart dream?"

She nodded, a fresh wave of warmth rippling through her chest at the sound of his voice. Almost near enough that, if she closed her eyes, she could pretend he sat beside her on the couch as he had almost every night for nearly a month.

At least she could see him. The subtle smile he gave to indicate his joy. The way his eyes lit with interest. How his infrequent laugh transformed his features.

Yes, at least she could see all those things.

"I took the liberty of mailing you a book yesterday, priority."

"A book?"

He looked away, a crinkle forming on his brow. "Yes, well, I thought perhaps you'd appreciate...well..." A slight hint of red darkened his cheeks. Was he embarrassed? Oh, how she wanted to reach through the screen and hug him.

"You see, I…I found a devotional for couples in the bookstore and thought, maybe, you and I could—"

"I love that idea."

His gaze moved back to hers. "I hoped you would. They're not long sections. A page or so each. But I…I want that to be something we share along with music, if you're willing. I've never done anything like it before, so I'm not certain how it will work—"

"I think we can figure it out. Our way."

He nodded, his gaze shifting between her and Rose. "Yes, we can. We will."

"Three months, Henry. That's all."

"Ten weeks and two days," he corrected, tagging on a gentle smile that somehow made the distance shrink and expand all at once.

∞ ∞ ∞

"Henry!" Tall and lean, Andrew Crawford walked down the hall of Visionary Studios, his swagger as relaxed as the smile on his face. "Back from the wilds of Appalachia, are we?"

Henry offered his hand as the two met in the hallway, Andrew a good four inches taller and a great deal more comfortable within the bounds of his father's growing company than Henry felt. His confidence even exuded into the grip in his handshake. "Only within the last few days, actually."

"It looks like you handled it all well." Andrew patted Henry's shoulder as he shook his hand, then turned so they both continued their walk side-by-side down the hall. "Did you happen to find your one true love like our poor friend Wesley, or did they let you leave with your heart intact?"

Henry hesitated, Andrew's usual teasing hitting a bit too close to the truth.

"Oh dear." Andrew stopped, leaning so close Henry shifted back a step. "You did! Good lord, Henry. You too?" He raked a hand through his hair. "I mean to steer clear of America altogether if that's the way of it." His pale blue eyes searched Henry up and down. "I can see it all over you. Seriously?"

The tension slipped from Henry's shoulders into a chuckle. "Oh yes."

"Fancy that." Andrew started walking again, this time at a slower pace. "Two out of the three of us attached to an American. Who would have thought it five years ago when we were finishing up university and setting out into the wide world?" A laugh shot out of him. "Appalachian Americans, at that."

"It was certainly unexpected, but I..." Henry lowered his voice, trusting in the years of friendship he shared with Andrew. "I mean to marry her, Drew. She's the best thing that's ever happened to me."

Drew paused, studying Henry again as if for the first time. "I'm happy for you, for sure. It's been a long time coming, and that's a fact, but Appalachian?"

"Still human, I assure you."

Andrew settled his hands in his pockets and chuckled. "But I'm glad. I am. You deserve a good turn, Henry, if anyone does. And I mean to keep things on the upward spin for you." They continued toward a door at the end of the hallway. "It's taken me months to convince Dad to hire a composer in residence. We needed one about a year ago—it would have saved loads—but you know how he is."

Andrew winked and held his spot in front of the door. "Why walk into change when you can crawl at the pace of a tortoise, right? That's my dad." He placed his hand on the door knob and sent Henry another reassuring smile. "He's got a list of applicants, but you're the one. I know it. I wrote this very position with you in mind. Dad knows you're the right one too. He just doesn't remember it. Yet. But I feel certain you'll jar his memory."

He pushed open the door and led Henry into a room where three men in suits sat at one end of a long table. The board of Visionary Studios. The people with the power to change his life...for the good or the bad. With a deep breath, Henry stepped forward. He wanted this. For himself and his future.

And for Julia.

Chapter Twenty-Eight

"Julia, I think we can discontinue our regular appointments." Karen sat back in the chair, her dark hair pulled back in a bun, her smile confirming Julia's own assessment. She could, with God's help, move on. "You and Rose seem to be in a very good place, and you're stepping back into your life and plans with a healthy mindset."

"It's nice to get back to planning the future instead of fighting the past, you know?" Julia rocked the carrier on the floor with her foot while Rose slept. "Even if my future looks different. I'm not afraid of how the past will affect it anymore."

"I think your future sounds exciting and romantic. And a trip to Derbyshire? You'll love it."

"I'm sure I will." Julia lowered her attention back to Rose. Each day she grew closer to seeing him, her daughter by their sides.

"I think you mentioned Henry is good with Rose?"

Without warning a rush of tears blurred Julia's vision. She looked away. Stupid post-baby hormones. "He's wonderful with her. Gentle and kind." Julia looked up. "He plays music for her. It's really sweet. *He's* sweet."

"I can see how much you care about him."

"I do."

Silence enfolded them, tugging Julia's thoughts into confessions. "Is it weird to be this connected to someone I've only know a few months? I mean, I was a somewhat-mature, independent person before I met him, and now I can't imagine life without him. I look forward to talking with him every evening. I make plans with him in mind."

Karen laughed. "Just because you want him here doesn't mean you've lost independence. It means your heart is ready for you to transition into a future with someone instead of alone. Besides, you could move ahead on your own if you wanted, couldn't you?"

Julia stared at her, ensuring she believed her own answer. "I could. but I don't want to." Memories resurrected her smile as she relaxed back in her chair, accepting her choice without reservation. "I want to share it all with him. It's not just about the romance and the tenderness. It's...well, I just really like him. We fit. We can talk for hours and still have more to say. I'm not worried whether I'm ridiculous or not, or how I look. I...I don't think I've ever been more *me* than when I'm with him."

Karen's brows took a steady climb northward. "Wow. That is pretty special, Julia. People live lifetimes without finding what you've found."

The sweetness of Karen's confession warmed Julia from head to foot. "It's worth all of this crazy distance and missing him, because I'd rather know he's somewhere in the world loving me, even if it's not in Pleasant Gap right now, than not have his love at all."

A shadow passed over Karen's expression, then she leaned forward again, the intensity of her gaze straightening Julia's spine in preparation for Karen's next comment. A challenge. Something unexpected. "Have you ever considered leaving Pleasant Gap? You're financially independent. You've sold the bakery. You'll finish your degree soon. I mean, you're in a perfect position for an adventure."

Heat drained from Julia's face, and she stopped rocking Rose's carrier. "An adventure? What do you mean?"

"You have big dreams and it sounds as if you have someone to share those dreams with. Maybe getting away from Pleasant Gap for a while would be a good thing for you. New places. New people."

"Are you saying move to England?"

"I'm not specifying a place, but it's definitely worth considering." Karen grinned. "If you and Henry end up making a long-term commitment to each other, it's a possibility for you, isn't it?"

"Well, I think he'll probably move here. So Rose can be near my family."

"Sounds to me like you're taking good care of Rose all by yourself."

Julia sat up a little straighter. "I wouldn't want Rose to miss experiencing the loving atmosphere I grew up in, though. My family is crazy sometimes, but they've been a wonderful example to me."

"You do have an exceptionally close family." Karen braided her fingers in front of her, allowing the silence to settle into the discussion. "There's a lot of love. Big enough to reach England, I think." She tilted her head, her attention searching, asking questions Julia didn't want to contemplate. "Are you afraid to leave?"

Julia's stomach clenched in a fight-or-flight response. Leave? Actually move away? "Why would I leave? Everything I love is here."

"The things you love most will always be with you, Julia." She sat up, palms raised. "I'm not trying to force any decision. But if you and Henry are making future plans—"

"We are."

"It's not a bad idea to consider possibilities. If he can't leave England for some reason—a job or family demands—maybe it's a prime opportunity for you to spread those wings of yours. You could probably open a bed-and-breakfast just about anywhere in the world. I doubt you could find another Henry."

Julia reached for the chain around her neck, ignoring the sudden pulse of curiosity. "We'll sort that out when we have to, but for now we're just trying to make it to June."

"Of course. I know you have a good head on your shoulders. And he *has* to if he was smart enough to fall for you." Karen patted Julia's knee. "But don't forget how strong you are. Your family and faith have given you so much to share with the world. Who knows what you might discover if you stretch your horizon."

∞ ∞ ∞

"Henry, what has gotten into you?"

Henry looked up from his plate as his mother bustled into the dining room, her dark eyes narrowed into warning slits. What did she know? Surely she couldn't know he'd removed his grandmother's sapphire ring from the safety deposit box to have on hand for Julia. After all, Father left it to him. Had she learned about his job interview at Visionary Studios? She'd never liked the Crawfords and having one of her sons work for their company wouldn't bode well.

"Mother, it's ten in the morning." Elliott slapped his newspaper against the table and pressed his fingers into his forehead. "Do you really need to start the day with such a tone?"

His mother ignored her youngest son's question and fixed all of her annoyance in Henry's general direction, complete with flaring nostrils. "I don't know what happened to you in America, but you'll not go back. Ever. Again."

Henry kept quiet, which generally proved the best course of action when his mother began spouting that kind of rubbish. As his father used to say, "Answering rubbish with reason is like feeding rubies to goats. A waste of rubies and the goats never appreciate the value."

"Well, explain yourself."

"I'm not certain what I need to explain." Henry looked to Elliott, who'd gone back to his newspaper as if their mother's voice didn't carry through the house like a clanging cymbal.

"How can you feign such ignorance?" Her pitch broke. "Clarice Montague phoned me to tell me how delighted she was that you offered to join the church orchestra." His mother folded her arms across her chest, one dark brow raised in accusation. "The church orchestra!"

Henry laughed. Of all the things to send his mum round the bend, she chose *this* one?

"This is no laughing matter. As you well know, Henry, I've not attended St. Mark's in six months. Not since they brought on that new pastor who preaches the most atrocious things. We agreed to attend Blackburn Hills instead."

"*You* decided to attend Blackburn Hills, Mother. I enjoy St. Mark's and its new pastor."

She collapsed into a chair. "The man talks about bringing street people into the church. The actual sanctuary! Possibly sitting near us." She tapped the table. "And he prays in the most sacrilegious way—"

"He prays as if he knows to whom he speaks." His mother's eyes widened at his rare contradiction. Good. Perhaps he'd made an impression.

"You realize the Gettys are in the orchestra at St. Mark's?"

Or not. Henry closed his eyes and sent up a silent prayer for strength. There were only a handful of people in Derbyshire whom his mother had *not* ostracized at some point in recent history due to some perceived offense or other. "Yes."

"Their grandfather nearly destroyed my father's business. You know that! And you would play with *them* in front of the entire church?"

"I would. The children are not the parents or grandparents."

"Amen to that," Elliott added from behind his newspaper.

Mother placed both of her palms on the table and pressed forward. "Does my reputation, my opinion matter so little to you? Is that how the likes of Andrew Crawford and Wesley Harrison influence you against me?"

"Mother, it's church, not the Rose Ball."

"You stay out of this," she snapped at Elliott. "It's not as though you even remember what a church looks like on the inside, as little as you frequent one."

"Old." Elliott turned a page in his paper but kept his face conveniently hidden. "Stained glass, as a rule."

"Henry, you are not the sort to put yourself out in front of people like this." She stood over him, studying him. "Are you unwell? Has someone forced you to do this?"

"I am quite capable of making my own decisions, Mother, and have been doing so for years." Henry placed his serviette down and turned toward her. "And I've decided that I have talents I can share with the church."

"No one in our family has ever played in the church orchestra. No one."

"We can start with me." He pushed away from the table, ready to end any further tirade with a great deal of distance. All the way, in fact, to Crandall House for a furniture delivery. His family heirlooms from his grandparents had been in hiding too long. Besides, moving sounded better and better with each passing second.

"Who is she?" His mother tapped the table again. "This girl. The one you met in America. She's put you up to this, hasn't she?"

He stared over at his mother, searching for some hint of logic to combat her lack thereof. "You think my girlfriend from America somehow put me up to playing in the church orchestra?"

"She's your girlfriend, is she?"

"Julia." He stood. "Her name is Julia."

He walked past his mother toward the door, her voice following him. "Your father would be appalled at you. Sitting beside the Gettys! They're Irish, you know. Irish."

"I doubt Father would be offended, Mother, since his grandparents were Irish."

"And now you're dating an American? One with a child? Weren't the last two mistakes enough to last a lifetime, Henry? The town is still mumbling about the scandal you brought on our names, and here you are on the brink of another. I will not have it."

"Wait until they all learn he's purchased Crandall House," Elliott added, taking a sip of his coffee as if his announcement hadn't just ruined Henry's life for the foreseeable future. How had Elliott found out? Matthew would never have told him.

"You've done what?"

Henry shot his younger brother a glare before turning back to his mother. "You know I've been meaning to buy my own place near town for some time."

"Clearly you're not ready for such a decision." She patted her hair—as if it could possibly move from its dark, manicured, wave around her face—and took a seat at the table. "It's on the wrong side of town and much too antiquated for you. A place like that will not complement your rising fame at all."

"I believe this conversation is finished."

His mother stepped in front of his exit. "You must end the contract at once."

"I own the house, Mother. I have for three weeks." And he would have moved sooner if some simple renovations hadn't been necessary before occupancy.

"Shocking, I know," Elliott placed down the paper and raised a dark brow. "Henry didn't spend three months deliberating over a decision."

"How did you know?"

Elliott picked a grape off the fruit plate in the center of the table and tossed it in his mouth. "Miriam Clarkson, the realtor who listed Crandall House."

"The Clarkson you're dating?"

"On again, off again. You understand." A strawberry made its way into his brother's mouth. "She said you made a deposit the day after you returned from the States. Impulsive." Elliott toasted Henry with a second strawberry. "Very unlike you, brother. Nice to see there's a bit of a rebel beneath the prefect. What's next? An elopement?" He offered a mock shudder.

"Don't encourage him, Elliott." Mother waved him away. "This is a catastrophe. Why on earth would you purchase Crandall House? You are a single male. That house can easily hold an entire fam—" Her gaze zeroed in on him, and she blocked another attempted escape. "Haven't you learned anything from your past? This only proves that you are not capable of making romantic decisions on your own. She's only after your money. Just like the last one. Why else would a woman want you?"

Elliott winced in Henry's periphery.

The accusation hit an old wound, almost buckling him into silence, but a memory confronted the past head-on—Julia's smile when she'd told him she loved him. The way she asked his opinion, his thoughts. As though he was someone worth giving her heart to regardless of the ocean between them. And God thought he was worth even more than the admiration in Julia's eyes. He loved Henry enough to redeem him. Yes, Henry was worth much more than he'd ever believed.

"I have no plans to—"

"We'll finish the conversation later." His mother looked down at her watch. "Lauren Townsend is here for brunch. And I shouldn't need to remind you that I still have control over your allowance, Henry. Until the day I die."

She rushed from the room, slamming the door behind her, the much too overwhelming scent of her perfume floating in her wake.

Henry shoved his hands into his pockets and rocked back on his heels, praying for patience and strength.

"You have bad luck, don't you, Henry?" Elliott stood and stretched out his back.

"With no help from you." Henry shook his head. "How is it that you can do all of the things she hates, yet she thinks you're perfect?"

"Because, my dear brother, I never get caught." He tossed a grape in the air and caught it in his mouth. "Cheers."

∞ ∞ ∞

Henry brought the small orchestra to a moment of suspended silence as the final strains of the violins faded away. The red light to the right turned to green, and the entire orchestra relaxed. Another recording finished.

"Excellent work, everyone. Two more and we're done for the day."

His phone vibrated to life in the breast pocket of his jacket. He tugged it free and saw Julia's name alight on the screen. But it must be...He checked the time on his watch. It had to be shortly before five o'clock in the morning in Virginia. What was wrong?

"Let's take a ten-minute break everyone." Henry raised his palm to the group. "Thank you."

He rushed to the door of the recording studio and pressed the video chat button as he rounded the corner, out of hearing distance of the orchestra. Julia's face came into view, her eyes tired and a bit puffy, and her hair in some sort of lopsided bun on her head. "Julia? Are you all right?"

"Yes, just a bit stuffy." She rubbed a tissue against her red nose. "But...but I wanted to share something that couldn't wait until tonight. Do you have a few minutes?"

"It's not even five in the morning there."

She nodded, the red rim around her eyes making them look even bluer. "Time is irrelevant when you have a newborn with a cold."

"Did she not sleep again?"

"Barely." Julia rubbed at her nose again. "Poor thing. She can't hardly breathe without elevating her head, so I've been holding her most of the night. I actually fell asleep sitting up on the couch. I mean, all the way up. It was crazy."

"I'm so sorry, dove. Can't you ask your mother for help so you can get a few winks?"

She shook her head. "I have to learn to do this on my own, Henry."

"There's nothing wrong with asking for help, especially since it sounds as if you've taken Rose's cold."

"I know, but I have to try."

"Julia, promise me that if this continues for another night or two, you'll ask your mother or sisters to help. There's nothing wrong with asking for help when you need it."

She stared at him through the screen and sniffled, blinking those large, child-like eyes. "I promise."

"You're very brave, but you're not invincible, especially when you have a sick baby."

"Oh Henry, it's been insane." She brushed back loose strands of hair, shaking her head, her words becoming increasingly hyponasal. "Her sleep schedule is only part of it. The amount of snot and poop?" She shuddered. "So much snot and poop."

Richard, a cellist, paused as he passed Henry in the hall, watching him with a horrified expression.

Henry offered him a tight smile.

Julia kept talking, oblivious in her sleep-deprived state to her somewhat delirious conversation. "I can't imagine having to get up and go to work like this. Can you imagine?" She looked down at her shirt. "I don't think I've changed my clothes for two days."

"And you don't think it's time to phone your mother?"

She tugged at the collar of her T-shirt, staring at it. "Maybe so. It's pretty sad that, for the past two days, my life has consisted of crawling in and out of bed in between bouts of baby diaper-and clothes-changes and eating a copious amount of chocolate that I can't even taste."

Henry caught sight of the orchestra reconvening in the recording room, only missing their director. "I'm sorry to cut this short, but didn't you say you had something in particular you needed to share?"

She blinked as if his question triggered some sort of thought. "Oh, yes. I was awake with Rose and checked my email just now, and guess what?"

He grinned at her adorable confusion. "What?"

"The archivist from Glasgow finally emailed me back. He says he has information that I'd find interesting regarding Lucas and Millie." She wiped her nose again. "And would be happy to put me in contact with an archivist in London who could share the information with me when I arrive in June."

"That *is* excellent news."

"What if they know what happened to Lucas?"

"That would be a good ending to our little mystery, wouldn't it, dove?"

She grinned, the light in her eyes unleashing her pleasure. Even with the red nose and the unruly hair, she was the most beautiful woman in the world.

"I love you, Henry."

"And I love you, dove."

On his way back into the studio, he paused at the recording booth threshold and leaned over to his assistant at the desk. "Becky, would you have time to do a bit of research on florists in Pleasant Gap, Virginia for me?"

Her blond head took on the slow tilt of someone examining a confusing piece of orchestration. "Pleasant Gap...Virginia? In the United States?"

He patted the doorframe, his grin broadening. "Yes, please. There's a special someone there who could use a beautiful bouquet today."

Chapter Twenty-Nine

*J*ulia sat at her desk finishing the final project for her course—a business plan for starting her own bed-and-breakfast. Her mom, who'd helped her start the bakery, had given her some pointers for the B&B, and she'd sent the proposal to Henry too, just too share it with him. He'd come back with a few minor suggestions and a great many encouraging comments, as usual. She grinned and looked over at the newest bouquet he'd sent. Roses. To celebrate Rose's three-month birthday. The flowers were only now beginning to bend with age, a few petals falling onto the desk top, but their pink hues clung to their initial vibrancy.

She rested her chin on her palm and looked out the window as afternoon light bathed the room in a quiet beauty. Just over three months ago she'd held her little Rose for the first time, and now, her life had finally begun to pulse with a rhythm. Motherhood, school, baking, occasionally substituting for the pianist at church—*and* managing a long-distance relationship.

A sweet internal glow pulled a sigh. Life waited in a glorious limbo of unfinished dreams on the verge of completion. So many possibilities, she'd never anticipated a year ago. So many almost-but-not-yet wishes on the brink of coming true.

A year ago, she thought she'd never recover from the tragedy that altered her world, but somehow God made the healing all the sweeter by creating new dreams—better ones—while still allowing her to keep some of the old ones. She touched one of the fallen petals, rubbing the soft silk between her fingers. *Oh Lord, You have shown Your faithfulness to me. Your massive love pouring over all my wounds. Help me to trust You with the almost-but-not-yet. Keep me brave in You.*

"Hey, hey." Eisley pushed open the door with Rose in her arms and an entourage of her three kids following behind. "How's the project writing going?"

Julia turned from her laptop and took a jump-hug from Pete, their resident Spiderman. In fact, he wore the full Spiderman costume this afternoon because today was Saturday—and the rule in her sister's home was school clothes on school days, church clothes on church day, but dress yourself on Saturdays. "Rose spit up *all* over Mama," the five-year-old announced as he drew back from the hug. "She smelled like throw-up."

Julia cringed and looked up at her sister. "I'm sorry, Eis."

Eisley laughed and waved away Julia's concern. "Gracious sakes, Julia, it's not like I haven't smelled like throw-up before. It's practically a perfume brand for the first three years of life."

Julia turned her head to her right shoulder and took a whiff of her shirt, then cringed. How had she failed to notice that?

"I guess I should try to get a sitter at least once a week now, so I can get used to reentry into the big, wide world of real life."

Eisley placed Rose into Julia's arms, and the baby immediately started smacking her rosebud lips. "I don't think it gets more real than what you're living right now, sis." Eisley turned and swept Emily up in her arms. "But Sophie's off from her school job for the summer. She'd loved to earn some extra money."

"That's a great idea."

"And I bet she'd be happy to watch Rose for you during your night classes in the fall too. She's saving up for some big European summer vacation or something." Eisley shook her head. "You know Sophie."

"Everyone knows Sophie, Eisley."

Eisley's palm went to her chest like a pledge. "Truer words."

Julia swept Eisley's kids a smile. "Are you guys excited about traveling to England in two weeks?"

Nathan, ever the dutiful eldest, was quick to answer first. "Wes is taking us to see real castles."

"With dragons in them," Pete added.

"They don't have dragons *in* them, Pete." Nathan looked up at her as if having such a brother was one of the biggest difficulties of his seven-year-old life. "Wes said they had dragon carvings *on* them."

"I see dwagons too," Emily called out, wiggling down from her mom's side to join her brothers beside Julia. "Dwagons." She contorted her toddler face into an expression Julia imagined only Emily thought looked very dragon-ish. "Dwagons scawy."

"The joys of two older brothers." Eisley sat down on the couch. "My little princess will fight the dragons and probably the prince too."

Julia joined her sister on the couch as her nephews tugged the box of toys she kept for their visits from beneath the coffee table and proceeded to pour them onto the floor.

Once Julia was situated and covered for Rose's feeding, she turned to her sister. "How are you doing with handling all the preparation for traveling and the engagement party?"

Eisley rested her head back against the couch but turned to face Julia. "I can't wait to see Wes again. And though I'm not the fancy party type, the Harrisons sure know how to make a girl feel like a queen. Just wait until you see their house, Julia. It's like something from *Pride and Prejudice*. Pemberley for sure."

"Still planning a December wedding?"

"If I could have one sooner, I would." She winked. "But this will work out better for the kids' break in their school year and maybe abate some of the rumors about why we're getting married so fast."

Julia looked up from adjusting her blouse. "What?"

Eisley released a soft chuckle. "Yeah, evidently the only reason movie star Christopher Wesley Harrison would rush into a marriage with Appalachian single mom, Eisley Barrett, is because she's having his baby."

Julia froze, allowing the words to sink in, and then paused a little longer. "Wait. Are you serious? That's crazy."

"Right? And it's not like I could even *be* pregnant with his baby—not that I'm going to share that bit of info on social media—but the big wide world can't seem to wrap its mind around us. I mean, why would he go for someone like me?" She laughed. "Sometimes I wonder the same thing, but you won't hear a single complaint from me."

Julia leaned her head back and closed her eyes, allowing the question to sink deep and lodge near her heart. She'd asked herself that question about Henry, too. Asked God. And over the past few months, she'd grown into an understanding. "Because he's a very smart man, that's why. And God knew something in you and in your life matched what his heart needed most of all, so that apart you're okay, but together you're remarkable."

The sound of her nephews and niece playing with the toys filled the silence, but Eisley didn't respond. Julia opened her eyes and found her sister staring at her. "That was beautiful, Julia. And...something I need to remember."

"Me too."

"You? You need to remember that too?"

Julia's vision blurred with a pool of unexpected tears. "Yeah, because I'm bringing a whole lot into this relationship that most guys aren't looking for. A tragic backstory, as Sophie says, and an instant family. Henry is..." Julia closed her eyes, and a tear squeezed between her lids. "He's wonderful. So kind that I sometimes wonder if he's real. But then he'll do or say something completely awkward to remind me that he is." She grinned and another tear escaped. "But over the past few months, as we've gotten to know each other through phone calls and text messages, I've fallen in love with him even more. Even the awkward parts."

"I can see how God used his gentleness to help heal your heart."

Julia nodded and wiped away a tear. "He cares so effortlessly, like he's been waiting to shower someone with affection for years and I'm the recipient."

"It's pretty crazy when it's so right, isn't it? Even on those days when it feels all wrong because they live halfway across the world." Oh yes, Eisley understood better than anyone else in her life. "But when it's right, there's a sense that you can *rest* in that love. You don't have to pretend or work up the feelings. It's a friendship. I think that's why God uses the romantic relationship between a man and a woman as an example of His love for His church. There's not just a commitment, but a true fellowship between the two, so your heart can rest in that love."

"That's exactly it." Julia laughed. "I've been wondering if something was wrong because it seemed so right—so peaceful—with him. Not the struggle to perform or *be* someone I'm not, but just to rest." She sighed and laid her head against the couch again. "I am resting in Henry's love for me. What a wonderful idea."

"But just because you're comfortable with him"—Eisley's voice took a mischievous turn, garnering Julia's attention— "doesn't mean you can't knock him off his feet once in a while." She paused and scrunched her nose. "I don't mean literally, though with my clumsy track record I wouldn't be surprised if that's in Wes's future. I mean at the engagement party."

"What are you plotting?"

Eisley sat up, her eyes twinkling with enough stardust to light the room. "What are you going to wear? It's a fancy party, so you really can have a princess moment."

Julia shook her head as she pulled a sleepy Rose up on her shoulder to burp. "I don't want a princess moment, Eisley."

"Of course you do!" Her eyes rounded, displaying more of their golden hues. "Those gowns from Millie. The silver one or the blue one...or there's that dark burgundy one with the intricate sleeve designs."

Warmth filled Julia's face at the memory of Henry's response to the blue dress—a wonderful, tingling sort of warmth that spread down her back to where his hands had smoothed against her skin. Oh mercy!

"You'll look amazing in any of them, Julia," Eisley continued, her hands moving with more drama as she continued to speak. "I can see it now. You'll walk in and the whole room will stop to admire you."

"That sounds terrifying."

She stood and gestured for Julia to follow. "Let's go look at those dresses. You're going to love it. As grown-ups, we rarely have a chance to dress up, so it's kind of like prom for adults."

Julia groaned as she stood, careful to keep Rose comfortable and asleep. "I hated prom."

"But Henry will be there, Julia." Eisley tossed a look over her shoulder as she walked into Julia's room. "And you'll want to look lovely for him, I know."

"You're going to keep using him as an incentive, aren't you?"

"I can dig deep for motivation if I need to."

"Did you mean to say manipulation?" Julia murmured with a grin as she entered Rose's room to place her in her crib.

"I heard that."

∞ ∞ ∞

If Julia could navigate an airport with a three-month-old, carry-on, and suitcase while bringing up the end of Eisley's entourage, after two hours of sleep and only one cup of coffee, she could do just about anything. She'd never been up and down so many escalators in her life. Thankfully, Rose traveled like a little dream. She nestled close within her sling, her eyes staring up at the passing lights and watching Julia as if to make certain her world was still okay.

"It's all right, little one. It's just a busy place."

Her daughter showered Julia with a toothless grin followed by a sweet gurgly noise.

"I know someone who is going to be so excited to see you." She cooed down at Rose, the nervousness she'd quelled while collecting her bags and keeping up with Eisley returning with full force. Why was she nervous? It was Henry. *Her* Henry. She talked to him every day. Sometimes twice.

"Did you see the clouds out the window, Aunt Julia?" Pete bounced just ahead of her with Nathan in front of him, and Eisley led the way with Emily in tow.

"I did. Pretty amazing."

"Yep." He gave an emphatic nod. "We were super high."

"Like Superman instead of Spiderman today, huh?"

He stopped and looked up at her, his auburn brows colliding. "Spiderman can't fly, Aunt Julia. He shoots webs like this." He demonstrated the proper imaginary way to shoot webs. "Then he swings from one building to another building and then he does this..." Pete dropped the rolling bag he was supposed to be pulling and crouched on the ground as if he'd landed liked Spiderman.

Julia chuckled as a few onlookers enjoyed Pete's expressiveness so early in the morning. Others didn't quite appreciate the energy level. "Spiderman is pretty cool."

He took a few more steps and stopped again. "Spiderman saved a train filled with a million people, like on the train we just rode."

"Well, I think we rode more of a subway, but Spiderman could totally save one of those too." Julia noted the increasing gap between Eisley and herself and maneuvered her bags so she could get down to her nephew's level. "Pete, I love chatting with you about Spiderman, but you'd better catch up with Nathan before your mama threatens to take away your web blaster again."

The boy's blue eyes popped wide at that possibility. He ran with quick steps, dodging between suitcases and around passenger carts to close the gap between himself and his brother just as Eisley turned to check that the boys were following before she stepped out of the baggage claim area.

Julia pushed loose pieces of hair from her face with her one free hand and chuckled at Pete's antics. She'd imagined seeing Henry again many times. Usually, the daydream involved her wearing a cute outfit that cinched at her newly defined waist, some cute heels to highlight her legs, and her hair flowing around her like some slo-mo runway performance.

After a quick change in the bathroom post baby diaper lap disaster, Julia's cute outfit looked more like her Saturday morning leggings and relaxed-fit shirt, and rather than soft curls gracing her shoulders, she'd secured her hair in a braid to prevent Rose from pulling it for the fiftieth time.

Real life 101.

Oh well, she'd make it up tomorrow night at the engagement party. Her lips slipped into a hidden smile. Maybe a princess moment for her prince wasn't so bad.

Their little Jenkins posse moved with a crowd of other passengers into a large lobby area with people waiting in every direction. Glass walls three stories high covered one side of the massive room.

"There's Wes," Nathan called, rushing forward through the crowd with Pete closing in behind.

Julia turned in his direction, increasing her pace, and found Henry standing next to his friend. In the flesh. Green polo. Jeans. His gaze fastening on hers and drowning out everyone else. She stumbled a little, and he jerked forward as if he could possible catch her at this distance. Oh my goodness, she loved that man.

"Aunt Julia, Henry's here too!" Pete shouted for the whole world to hear. Henry's grin broadened at the boy's enthusiasm, a laugh dancing to life in his eyes.

"Yes he is, Pete."

Eisley's crew nearly attacked Wes, whose laugh rang out through the open room.

Henry stepped forward, his palm against her waist, mouth against her ear. "It's very good to see you. Very good."

He pressed a kiss to her cheek, his gaze promising more once they had some privacy. The part of her hear that had felt out of place for three months suddenly filled with vanilla and Henry. His hand on her back. His breath against her cheek. Heavens! Two things video chat couldn't provide: touch and smell.

She closed her eyes and rested her cheek against his. Yep, she belonged right here. "You too."

He stepped back to look at her again then cleared his throat and diverted his attention to Rose. "And you, duck." He pressed a kiss to her head. She blinked up at him and rewarded him with another toothless grin.

His palm slammed against his chest. "It's even better in person." He looked back at Rose who grabbed his finger with gusto. "Aren't you a beauty?" Once he'd regained his finger and wiped the baby drool from it with an ever-ready cloth Julia kept in her diaper bag, he moved his gaze to hers. "My two beauties," he whispered for her ears only.

"Good to have everyone here," Wes announced, taking Eisley's bags from her as Henry followed suit with Julia. "Henry, do you have your people?"

He swept Julia and Rose a tender look. "I do."

"Then let's get on to my parents' house because they are over the moon to meet everyone."

As they moved forward, Rose began to squirm and whimper.

"I think she wants to get out and see what's going on." Julia maneuvered the sling and drew Rose up into her arms.

"She's gotten so big."

He looked completely gobsmacked, as he'd say, while Julia managed to get the squirming little bundle up on her shoulder. "I have an idea." She stepped up to him and pressed Rose into his arms. "I think you should carry this bundle for a little while."

"But your bags..." His objection held little conviction as he fit Rose snuggly between his shoulder and chin.

Julia nearly melted at the sight. Her daughter had great taste. Snuggles with Henry Wright sounded absolutely marvelous.

"My bags have wheels. If you desperately want to be chivalrous, I'll let you load them into the back of your car, but for now, I think you'll benefit more from snuggles than suitcases."

They walked on at a slower pace as Henry kept looking down at Rose and then grinning over at Julia.

"I love how normal it feels to see you." She shook her head. "Well, I mean, it's much nicer in person, but we can just pick up from the conversation we had last night. Like we just saw each other."

"We did. Through video-chats."

"True." She leaned closer to him. "But I'll take in-person Henry over video-chat Henry any day."

His smile quirked and his gaze dropped to her lips as if he might sneak a taste. Her grin must have enlarged to Disney-sized proportions, because he proceeded to do just that. A quick one, but enough to let her know he was as happy as she was that a screen no longer separated them.

They exchanged a few bits of light information until they made it to his car, where Henry buckled Rose into a borrowed car seat from his brother Matthew. As soon as he took his place on the driver's side of the vehicle and closed out the noise from around them, he sat back and looked over at her. Neither spoke. They just stared at each other in silence. Rose made unhappy noises from the back seat, protesting another captivity.

And then a boyish grin unfurled on Henry's face—a look like Christmas and birthdays and so many other wonderful things in between. "You're really here." He took her face in his hands, placed a gentle kiss against her lips, and stared into her eyes. "Yes, you are."

"I am."

He brought his lips to hers again, a little longer, and pulled back, his gaze roaming her face, his thumb brushing a soft flutter against her cheek. Three months of separation dissipated into nothing, like a foggy dream, and everything settled into clarity. He sighed and started the car, his boyish grin returning as he shifted the car into gear. "Yes, you are."

Chapter Thirty

The world spread in patches of lush green as far as the eye could see, but Henry rarely took his attention from the two beauties next to him. Julia held his hand, and Rose snuggled close against him in the sling as he guided Julia's steps up one rock after another. Hiking didn't appear to agree with the little one. She became fussier and increasingly more vocal, moving against him, huffing and mewling as if she might break out into a cry.

Julia had asked to go on a walk with him—one of his favorites: Stanage Edge. No, it wasn't the same as her Blue Ridge, but once they made it up the back path and onto the rocky ledge overlooking the view, Henry believed the vista would prove almost as breathtaking. Rose may not be as impressed.

"I think Rose is still recovering from the flight." Julia pushed up the next set of rocks with ease, her curves more pronounced than last time he'd seen her now that her waistline had gone down even more post-baby. "Eisley said some babies have a bad response to travel. Although, Rose did great throughout the flight. Slept better on the plane than she does at home."

"Then you got some sleep too?"

"A little. Planes aren't super comfortable, especially when you have a chatty five-year-old Spiderman at your side."

Henry chuckled and steadied her as she slipped on one of the rocks. "Who doesn't want to be a hero?"

"I think Pete's trajectory is on that path for sure."

Rose released another sound of discontent, followed by a rotten sounding cough. "Do you think she's comfortable in this?"

Julia leaned over and brushed back a bit of Rose's hair. "She's not had any trouble in the past."

"Do you think I'm carrying her the wrong way?"

Julia examined the sling. "No, I just think she's an unhappy camper right now."

"There's only a little further to go. Do you want to continue?" He held out his hand.

She took it, grinning, her face flushed from the activity. "I sure do. How about you?"

"Of course." He gave her hand a squeeze as they maneuvered up a few more rocks. "Perhaps later in the week, we can go to Winnats Pass for a hike, near Castleton. It's rather beautiful. And I must take you to Bakewell on market day. You'll love it. And the Lake District is only a few hours away. Maybe Wednesday? It would remind you of home."

"Wherever you want to go is fine with me. I'm just happy to be here with you."

Henry stood a little taller and drew in a deep breath. He felt fairly certain he could leap tall buildings with a single bound.

She laughed and shook her head.

"What is it?"

He helped her up the next rock, and she leaned into him. "I just love that you're so excited."

"Of course I am. I'm introducing you to my home like you did for me."

"I don't think I was quite as thrilled about it as you are."

He paused in the climb and tugged her closer. "You don't understand. Your world in Pleasant Gap is already bright and wonderful on its own. But here? You and Rose bring something bright and wonderful into *my* world. Just having you here makes everything better." He squeezed her hand.

Her smile stilled, her gaze searching his. "I'm happy to learn more about you by exploring your world, Henry."

"Come on, then. I've brought you up the back way to save the best for last." He took both of her hands. "Do you trust me?"

Her lips crooked. "Yes."

"Then close your eyes and hold on."

He tugged her up onto the last rock then led her out onto a rocky ledge overhanging an extensive view of Derbyshire Dales that stretched all the way to South Yorkshire on the cusp of the horizon. Daylight slipped through gray clouds and shone like a gentle spotlight on various points in the distance.

"Okay. Now."

He kept his gaze on her face as she took her first look. "Oh Henry, it's beautiful."

"Not too bad for jolly ole England, is it?"

247

"Not at all."

"What do you think, duck?" He glanced down at Rose and froze. She looked back up at him with a pair of glossy, watery eyes and her round cheeks shone bright red. "Julia, I...I think something's wrong."

Julia followed his gaze, stepping to his side as they both moved away from the ledge to pull Rose free from the sling. Rose's body tensed and she released a shocked cry. Julia pulled the baby into her arms, patting her back and rocking her.

"What...what do you think is wrong?"

Henry placed his palm on Rose's head and studied her face again. "I think she has a fever. Feel."

Julia complied and her gaze met his. "She's burning up. What...what's wrong with her?"

"Come, let's get back to the car."

"Henry, she's really warm. This isn't normal." Julia didn't budge, so he gently directed her toward the descent. "We're in a different country. I can't even take her to her regular doctor. What if it's something they won't fix because I'm American?"

"The doctors will treat her. It's their job, American or not." He kept urging her forward as Rose's cries intensified. "Julia, I've tended to my brother's children before, and babies can develop fevers rather quickly over a great many things. Perhaps she was becoming ill even on the plane. You said she slept a lot."

Julia stumbled, and he caught her again, steadying her against himself until she found her balance. "She...she had a runny nose a few days before the trip, but it didn't seem like anything serious." Her eye filled with tears. "What have I done to her?"

"You didn't cause this, dove." His pulse pounded like a drum solo in his head, but he refused to allow Julia to see his concern. "And she's breathing fine, it seems, judging from her crying. That's a good thing."

Julia nodded, even though her bottom lip gave a tiny quake that pinched at his heart. "What if...what if she's having an allergic reaction to something? We're in a new place."

He studied Rose's red face, but apart from the blotches around her eyes from crying, he didn't see anything like the rash his nephew Connor developed from his peanut allergy. "I don't think that's it, dove. Matthew's son, Connor, has a peanut allergy, and he swells and makes horrible breathing noises. Rose isn't showing any of those signs."

She nodded, following close to him as they continued their descent. When they reached the car, he held the back door open for her to get inside with Rose. "She's going to be fine, Julia."

Rose's screams contradicted the calm in his statement. Her cries took a greater intensity as Julia buckled her into the car seat. *Something was definitely wrong.*

He rushed to his side of the car, gave it a start, and prayed he spoke the truth. His mind raced through myriad examples he'd experienced with Matthew's children, Connor and Mary. What could it be? She was breathing. No rash. No vomiting.

Rose immediately contradicted his last observation by proceeding to do just that, a projectile that even reached Julia's shirt.

They didn't talk in the car, nor would they have heard each other very well over Rose's cries. At one point little Rose sobbed so hard she made pitiful hiccupping noises, and when he caught sight in his mirror of Julia crying too, her eyes closed and mouth moving in what he supposed must be silent prayer, he pressed the accelerator harder.

Just as he turned off the motorway and veered toward the hospital, the car grew unexpectedly quiet. The sniffles quieted little by little.

"She's...she's stopped crying?" Henry caught Julia's gaze in the mirror.

She tugged Rose from the car seat and placed her against her shoulder. "And she's awake." Julia shot her attention back to Henry. "What's going on?"

Henry turned into the hospital's Accident and Emergency car park. "Perhaps she doesn't like hospital any better than anyone else."

Julia graced him with a weary smile and rubbed the baby's back. "Sounds like something a strong-willed girl would do." She sighed. "I think we're in trouble, Henry."

He almost smiled at the way Julia included him in their future story but turned his focus instead on parking the car and assisting his girls from the vehicle. "Allow me to hold her so you can collect your things." He leaned in and took the quiet, sniffling Rose, but as he backed up he stopped. Cold swept through his body. A dark stain, brownish red, marked Julia's shoulder where Rose had rested her head.

"What?" Julia searched his face. "What is it?" She followed his gaze and gasped. "Henry, is that...is that blood?"

He turned Rose's head gently to the side. The same reddish-brown stain oozed from her left ear, smearing down the side of her cheek. His gaze locked with Julia's.

"Let's go."

∞ ∞ ∞

Julia stepped into the Accident and Emergency waiting room with Rose fast asleep in her arms. People still crowded the room, the same as when they'd arrived, but Julia's heart wasn't on the verge of breaking now. No, thank the good Lord. The answer to Rose's problem had been an easy one.

She scanned the room and found Henry pacing back and forth by a nearby window, his hair in erratic confusion—probably from running him hand through it so many times. An overwhelming tenderness swelled through her at the thought of him gently reassuring her as he helped her down the rocky cliffside, of racing toward the hospital without a single complaint.

He looked her way then, his gaze almost passing her by before recognition dawned. Julia met him halfway across the room. "She's okay. Everything is going to be okay."

His body sagged with a sigh, like he'd been holding his breath for the hour they'd been with the doctor, then he pulled them into his arms. Julia rested her forehead against his shoulder, breathing in his comfort and scent. She'd always called her familiar world of Pleasant Gap 'home', but now...now she was beginning to think that home had a whole lot to do with Henry Wright. Something about this feeling, this moment, vied for a place in her heart. "Thank you for taking such good care of us."

"Of course." He nudged her toward the hospital doors and snatched up her diaper bag as if he'd always carried one. Pale pink worked for him. "What did the doctor say?"

"He thinks she had an ear infection before we left Pleasant Gap, but then the flight..." She shrugged and looked up at him as they stepped into the gray afternoon. "Do you know what the eustachian tube is?"

Henry's brows rose.

She grinned. "I only know because Sophie is a speech therapist and has tried to impart every ounce of knowledge she's learned in grad school to the rest of the family."

"I feel certain she lectures with a great deal of animation."

"Like none other." Oh, it felt so good to laugh.

"The eustachian tube is the tube that drains fluid from the ears to the throat so that your ears stay clear of fluid for hearing." He took her arm and gently guided her across the parking lot as she talked. "Well, it also equalizes the pressure outside the body with the pressure inside the body. When we fly our body is constantly trying to equalize the pressure changes."

"And her body didn't?"

"The doctor seems to think that was part of the problem. Evidently, she already had some swelling and fluid in there that I didn't know about, so the pressure was kind of the final straw."

He nodded, opening the back door of the car so she could place Rose into the car seat. "And the blood?"

"Her ear drum ruptured, which then released the pressure inside of her ear."

"And caused her pain to disappear instantly."

"Right." Julia pressed a kiss to the head of her sleeping little one and squeezed back another round of tears. Grateful ones. "The eardrum heals on its own, apparently, and shouldn't cause more trouble, but now we know what to look for."

"That's good news, isn't it?"

She gently closed the door and rose on tiptoe to give him a kiss. "It is."

He cupped her shoulder with his palm and bestowed one of his crooked grins on her—the kind where his eyes lit with pleasure *she* somehow brought into his life. His words from the hike came back to her with renewed curiosity. *You and Rose bring something bright and wonderful into my world.* "I'm so sorry things turned out this way, Henry."

"Why are you apologizing? We received good news about Rose."

But it ruined their lovely afternoon.

"Based on how I thought our little angel was suffering from something much worse than an ear infection, I'd say our afternoon has taken a splendid turn." He brushed a thumb over her cheek. "You must be exhausted."

Our little angel? He'd been hired for his new job—his dream job. Would he really be willing to leave it all for a small-town life in Pleasant Gap? "I'm hungrier than I am sleepy right now."

With a little flourish, he opened the passenger-side car door and grinned. "That's something I can fix."

She exaggerated her sigh and allowed her words to sink deeper than the playful lilt she gave to them. "My hero."

∞ ∞ ∞

Daniel and Eleanor Harrison, Wes's parents, welcomed Julia into their extravagant home as if she'd always belonged, and their raven-haired daughter,

Cate, gave off all the right "sister" vibes, so that Julia felt as if she'd known her for years. After a good night's sleep and a low-key day hanging around the Harrison's expansive manor house with Henry, Julia didn't feel so bad leaving a happy Rose with the babysitter Cate had hired to watch her toddling son, Simon.

How long had it been since Julia had had an adult night out?

A long time.

And she was pretty sure she'd never had one that involved a manor house with the golden hues of sunset bathing the gilded dining-room-turned-ballroom in an amber halo. People dressed in ensembles straight out of costume dramas stood at black-tablecloth-covered tables enjoying drinks and hors d'oeuvres. Oh dear. She couldn't even imagine how her dad would handle something like this.

Eisley and Wes stood at the far corner of the room as guests entered from the grand hallway leading into the house. Well, at least that was an added bonus of already being a guest in the house. One could slip into the room without being noticed.

Her sister wore an elegant purple gown reminiscent of something from the fifties with its draped back and shimmering satin while Wes had his movie-ready handsomeness on full display in a black suit. Julia grinned. What fun God must have had planning a romance for the two of them. So opposite, yet so complimentary.

She searched for her own handsome yet less-flashy hero but didn't see him among the tables and guests. He'd mentioned something about a recording session in the early afternoon that might put him a little behind, so Julia kept near the wall, watching the magic of the room. Chandeliers with glittering crystals hung down like something from a Disney movie and sparkled their lights against the glossy wooden floor. Not too far from Wes and Eisley sat a string quartet, adding classical favorites to the noise of cutlery and chatter.

Mr. and Mrs. Harrison stood next to Wes and Eisley, joining in greeting the guests, the older couple classy in their refined kindness. Eisley had been right. Wes's parents offered welcome as if Julia was a part of their family. Perhaps there were a few more similarities between England and Appalachia than Julia originally thought.

"Hiding back in the corner?" Eisley walked toward Julia, brow raised in a perfect 'big sister' look.

"And near the music."

"Of course near the music." Her sister laughed and looked around the room. "Can you even believe this? It's like a movie set."

"All the more reason to stay in the corner." Julia took inventory of the space again and sighed. "But it's amazing. I can't imagine what it's like to *live* here every day."

"I know." Eisley followed her gaze, then turned her attention on Julia. "And I'm marrying into this family. Who would ever have dreamed it?"

"God." The declaration nestled within her, sweet and hopeful. How often had she underestimate the bigness of God's dreams for her life? For her family's lives? And here was proof she dreamed too small. Too inside-the-box for an outside-the-box God.

If anyone could get Henry to work in America, it would be God.

"So true." Eisley sighed, her smile filled with all kinds of daydreams.

"But Eisley, if *this* is your engagement party"—Julia waved toward the room— "what on earth is the wedding going to look like?"

Eisley's eyes popped wide. "Oh, no, no, no." She waved her hands as if wiping away the thought from the air. "All of *this* is for Wes and his family, so they can have something special for his family and famous friends. The wedding is going to be back home in Pleasant Gap, and Cate is going to use her magical wedding planner skills to make it beautiful." Eisley wiggled her brows, her lips tipping. "Then Wes is going to sweep me away for a two-week honeymoon of my dreams before we return to the real world of Pleasant Gap and a traveling-movie-star life."

"I wonder what Cate will think of Pleasant Gap."

Eisley's laugh lilted into the room. "She can't wait to visit, especially after all I've told her about it." She blinked her gaze back to Julia. "And I suppose Cate's babysitter was willing to take Rose for a few hours while she watches little Simon."

Julia nodded, fingering the simple chain around her neck. "She has my cell number and will text me if something gets tricky, but her babysitter, Laura, was wonderful."

"You can bet Cate's going to make sure she has the best."

"She's great. So down to earth and friendly. She kind of reminds me of Rachel."

"Except Cate is less intimidating than our lovely sister Rachel. Oh, just wait until you spend more time with her. Cate fits right in with us, Julia." Her sister nodded to a passing guest, completely oblivious that the lady was a famous actress from a recent blockbuster. This was crazy. What kind of scene had her family been dropped into?

Eisley waved a hand at Julia's gown. "I'm so glad I talked you into wearing that dress. You look amazing. Henry won't be able to take his eyes off you."

Julia's teeth skimmed across her bottom lip as her smile spread so wide it pierced into her cheeks.

"Oh, good grief, Julia, you are such a lost cause."

As she watched her sister navigate the room back to Wes, Julia grinned. Lost cause? "Funny, I don't feel lost at all." Julia whispered, returning to her alcove of observation and taking in the magnificence of the evening. Lights flickered brighter as evening shadows darkened outside the floor-to-ceiling windows and the music turned from classical to jazz, sending her searching the room for her reticent hero.

Wes took Eisley by the hand and led her to the middle of the room for a dance. Although the idea of her sister dancing—and staying upright without harming anyone in the process—spun Julia's grin into a chuckle, Julia began to believe some little fairy godmother worked her magic over the evening.

"It seems a shame to have a lovely lady hidden in the shadows of the room."

Julia spun around and came face to face with a man near her age who looked incredibly familiar. Eyes she recognized and a smile...well, a smile that looked a little too rehearsed. Too interested.

She slid a step back and offered a small smile. "I'm not a dancer."

"What a shame." His gaze shimmied down her body and back, leaving a chill over her skin.

She suddenly wished she'd worn a much different gown. With an added cape.

"I don't think we've met, because I would remember meeting you."

Her throat tightened as he moved back into her space. She brushed a strand of hair from her face and stiffened her spine, refusing to succumb to the rush of fear clawing her words, her breath. "I'm new here."

"Of course you are." He held out his hand. "Elliott Wright."

Elliott Wright...Henry's brother! Just the knowledge that her defenses responded quite logically gave her a little comfort. "You're Henry's younger brother. He's told me about you."

He lowered his hand but raised a dark brow with his smile. "Well now, that's ominous. What if you take the time to abate my curiosity about your knowledge of me while we dance? You must be Henry's American...friend?" His gaze suggested he knew exactly who she was. Her breath tightened. She wasn't fond of people who didn't say what they meant.

"Surely, if you're my brother's friend, we can be as well?" He held out his hand to her again, beckoning her to the dancefloor.

Dance. The idea of his hands on her waist or his breath near her neck sent ice over her skin. But being a jealous brother didn't make Elliott threatening, did it? No, jealous wasn't exactly the sense his dark eyes gave. Julia glanced over her shoulder in search of Henry, but he was nowhere to be found. With a reluctant turn, she swallowed through her dry throat and took his hand. "Of course."

He drew her forward, keeping them on the edge of the crowd, his body relaxed, his hold comfortable. Julia breathed in and out. *He's not a threat. Be kind.*

"It's a shame my brother left so lovely a prize without escort. He should be ashamed."

Julia kept her posture rigid to maintain her distance from Elliott without impacting the rhythm in the dance. "He's on his way, I'm sure."

"As you are American and actually looking for my brother, I can only assume you are his newest interest?" His attention traveled over her again. "Funny, he doesn't tend toward the exquisite. That's more my category."

His underlying insult toward Henry discolored the compliment. "Has all of your family come to the party, Elliott? I haven't had a chance yet to meet your mother or brother Matthew."

His hazel gaze swept from her face to her hair to her neck. "I wouldn't wish to ruin your evening with an introduction to Mother. She isn't too keen on you."

"What do you mean?"

Elliott's hold changed, tugging Julia closer. A splice of tension coiled in her stomach.

"Let's just say that Henry's previous choices haven't garnered him the best reputation, and the fact that you're American and already a mother hasn't helped your cause." His palm slid up her back to meet her bare skin. His grin slid crooked as if he knew exactly what he was doing. "But I'd be happy to put in a good word for you, if you like. Mother listens to me. I'm her favorite."

Air trembled through Julia's lips, but she leveled him with a stare. "Your hold is too intimate for our acquaintance, Mr. Wright."

Her shift in addressing him with more distance only proved to broaden his smile and bring him closer. "Are you hinting that you'd like to become more intimately acquainted?"

"I am not."

His expression fell into a mock pout. "You say that with such certainty, yet you hardly know me."

"Actions speak clearly enough, Mr. Wright, and yours are not encouraging a good first impression. Besides, my heart and intentions are already securely fastened on someone else."

"You mean we can't be friends?" His lips hinted at a hidden smile. Teasing. Mocking.

"Not with someone who would clearly hit on his brother's girlfriend. No."

He loosened his grip on her, his grin fading from his countenance. "Such faithfulness." His laugh held no humor. "My brother is a peculiar recluse who would rather spend time pouring over music notes than wooing the heart of a lady. What can you possibly see in him that I can't provide for you—and more besides?"

"He's a true gentleman in heart and behavior." Julia's pulse beat in her ears, but she continued. "Can you make the same claim?"

Elliott stopped dancing altogether and took a step back from her. "I see you're the perfect match for my pious brother and his lofty ideals."

"I've always preferred the high road." She raised her chin and pushed on a smile. "The view is a lot better."

"Is everything alright?"

Julia turned at the welcome voice. Henry stood by her side and slid a palm to her waist, shifting so his shoulder somehow created a barrier between her and Elliott. She drew in his strength, his presence, nestling against him. Henry's attention locked with his brother's, brow low, lips tight—an expression she'd never seen on his face before. He'd come to her rescue, his stance clearly setting boundaries. *Off limits.* She snuggled up even closer to Henry's side. Yep, this protective instinct gig worked for her.

"We're fine, thank you." She linked her fingers through Henry's, giving his hand a squeeze to punctuate her words. "I believe your brother and I have come to an understanding."

If any person could glare with a smile pasted on their face, Elliott was the one. "Indeed." He offered a stiff bow. "Good evening."

As soon as Henry's arms came around her, she shivered against him, pressing into his warmth and strength. She'd faced Elliott. She'd stood up for herself. She closed her eyes and lowered her head to Henry's shoulder as they swayed to the music in some makeshift display of a dance.

"Did he hurt you?" Henry whispered against her ear, his palm pushing back her hair so he could see her face. Those eyes, so filled with concern, found hers.

"No. I don't think he had any intention of hurting me."

He tugged her close and sighed into her hair. "Forgive my tardiness. I was later than expected leaving the recording studio and then traffic stalled." He growled. "I should have been here."

"You're here now." She looked up at him. "I stood up to him on my own, but I'm really glad you're here now."

Chapter Thirty-One

enry couldn't shake the memory of Julia's face when he'd arrived at the engagement party to find her in Elliott's arms. He'd rushed through the crowd, pushing his way closer, but Elliott had released his hold on her by the time Henry's path opened, a look of utter shock on his younger brother's face.

When he'd taken Julia in his arms for a dance and she'd trembled against him, a fire had rushed through him with such force that he'd nearly chased Elliott from the room and taken out years of frustration on him. Oh, if he'd only left the studio a few minutes earlier! He would have missed the backed-up traffic from an automobile accident and Julia would never have had to deal with his delinquent brother.

But a glimmer of pride joined his annoyance. She'd stood her ground. Called Elliott out. Refused to bend beneath the fear he knew she felt. He tugged her closer, hoping she knew how proud he was of her. How brave she was.

It wasn't until Julia had gone upstairs to feed Rose that he found Elliott near the drinks, wine in hand. Henry walked up beside him and folded his arms across his chest, surveying the crowd so as not to draw attention.

"Ah, brother, have you come to intimidate me?"

The nonchalance in Elliott's voice flipped a switch inside Henry. He gripped his arms with his hands to keep from taking a fist to his brother's sardonic grin. "I want you to leave Julia alone."

"Is that a command?"

Henry kept his gaze forward, his breaths coming in increasingly short spurts. "It's a warning."

"A warning?" Elliott turned, brow raised. "This is a first. You must be serious about your little American mum."

"You have not tested me to my breaking point, Elliott, though you have tried many times." Henry worked to keep his voice calm. "But I can assure you, I will not warn you again."

"Really?"

Henry shifted his body, the few extra inches he had giving him an advantage he lacked otherwise against his brother's typical bravado and captured Elliott's full attention. "Try me and see."

A flicker of fear waved over Elliott's features, and he shifted back a step, producing a false grin. "You've never had this much trouble sharing your things before, brother."

"Do not trifle with me. I've warned you. I shall not be so generous in the future."

Under his brother's watchful eyes, Henry met Wes and Eisley and soon after, Julia. The evening continued without another hitch. Elliott never resurfaced, though Matthew made a brief appearance, taking time to meet Julia and don his "party face". But Henry knew his older brother hated the larger crowds with a vengeance. He'd learned to cope, as Henry had done, but he kept his visits short.

Henry took pleasure in introducing Julia to some of his colleagues in the movie industry and sharing the time with her. She fit so well into this world. Yes, she looked the part of a beauty, but more than that, she exuded a gentleness and kindness into every conversation. Nothing in his life looked the same with her influence around it.

Yes, he'd moved away from the family home at just the right time.

And once the installers finished with the kitchen in the main part of Henry's new house, he'd take Julia to see it. His gift to her dream. To their future.

They spent the next day touring Matlock, and Julia fell in love with it, just as he thought she would, delighting in the quaint shops and old buildings. As they sat in a quiet corner of a restaurant in Bakewell, sharing a famous Bakewell tart, Henry held a fussy little Rose so that Julia had a chance to eat the strawberry-filled pastry. Her eyes lit as the flavors of almonds, strawberries, and a zing of lemon blended for the signature taste of Bakewell Henry knew so well. "Oooh, this is delicious."

"I imagine you could replicate it." He rubbed a palm methodically over Rose's back as she huffed against his shoulder, fighting sleep.

Julia's eyes glittered in the dim lighting. "Ideas, ideas."

"Perhaps add a dollop of ice cream."

"Or some dark chocolate syrup."

Henry tilted his head with his smile. "Or both."

She pointed her spoon at him, a hint of her father coming out in her grin. "Now you're talkin'."

A chuckle came forth as he watched her enjoy another bite. "I have a rehearsal tomorrow morning, but could we meet for lunch before your appointment at the historical department?"

Her smile faded. "The appointment's been changed."

"What?"

"Laurence Porter, the military archivist who has information on Lucas, has been on a research trip, but his flight was canceled due to inclement weather. He won't be able to meet with me until Monday morning."

"But...but you fly out Monday afternoon."

Her gaze held his, sharing in the hesitancy of having an ocean between them again. Yes, he'd been awarded the job of his dreams, a perfect place for him. He loved it. The comradery he was building among the players, working with Andrew, weaving music to capture stories...but what was all that without her?

Would the company allow him to work remotely? Would she be willing to shift her entire life to England? Surely seeing the house would help! "Should I change my recording time for the commercial? I can if you wish me to join you."

"No, no." She shook her head. "I can just go straight to the airport after the meeting with Mr. Porter."

He paused on the thought, the ache of their separation doubling the sting in his chest. How was it that they only had a few days left together? Parting again would be even more difficult than the first time. "I'll meet you there. At the airport. To see you off."

"Okay." Her whispered response spoke volumes. Neither wanted to face the distance. And for how long? When would his new job allow a holiday? He'd not thought to ask these questions before, but now...now the answers meant the next opportunity to see Julia and Rose.

Rose's noises softened into a hum against his shoulder, her tired little body winning out over her frustration.

"Elliott mentioned something at the party, Henry, and I need to know what he meant."

"I wouldn't put stock in anything Elliott has to say."

"For some reason, this seemed to ring true. It was about your mother."

"Go on."

"Elliott seems to think your mother isn't very happy about the two of us."

"She's upset because she didn't think of it, you see. She's been keen to keep her hands in her children's business for years, but she knows nothing about you and can't discover anything from her gossip network." He shifted Rose to his other shoulder, and her breathing deepened. "Since my past has already set a shady precedent, she's nervous about how you'll impact the conversations of the town in reference to the Wright family."

Julia took another bite of the tart, keeping her gaze from his.

"It may be a rocky start, Julia, but she'll come around. Who wouldn't once they know you?"

Her smile spread but didn't light her eyes. "Family is important, Henry."

Her convictions on the matter pitched deeper than his, at least for his birth family. "Of course, but family can be determined as much by choice as by birth, and I choose you and Rose."

"You shouldn't have to make a choice, ever."

"No, but my family is very different than yours. Yours is healthy and cohesive with love and acceptance binding everyone together. There's unity and care mine has never known. But I'm willing..." He searched her gaze. "I'm hoping to start the right way, with you." He gestured to Rose with his chin. "With us."

"'Us' sounds pretty nice to me."

"I have a certain fondness for it." He grinned. "So, would dinner tomorrow work for you?"

She straightened her shoulders as if readying for a battle. But she wouldn't fight alone. He'd make sure of it.

"Dinner it is."

∞   ∞   ∞

Breakfast with the Harrisons and Cate proved a delight. The warmth among them reminded her of home, except the Harrisons added a hint of refinement to the family teasing. Cate's continued presence, with her ready wit and kindness, only strengthened their growing friendship. The fact that she was a single mom eased the conversation and understanding even more.

Once everyone dispersed to their various places for the day, Julia asked Jacobs, the butler, to drive her and Rose into town. Henry had given her a quick tour of Matlock, to ensure they saw as much as possible of Derbyshire during her visit, but she'd longed to stroll the streets and get a better *feel* of the place Henry loved so much.

Today she had time to absorb the place instead of skim over it.

Limestone buildings of varying heights and designs hugged cobblestone streets, narrowing the lanes punctuated by streetlamps. There was a quaint Victorian feel to the place, but not dark and gloomy like she'd seen in movies, despite the gray sky hinting at a rainy afternoon. Light and warmth reflected off the pale limestone, and people bustled to and fro, going about their business and injecting energy and life into the town.

And the names! She'd not noticed them when she'd toured with Henry.

Queens Head Inn. Market Hall. Olde English Hotel. Holt Terrace. It was simply delightful—like entering a storybook. She breathed in the scents of open air and fried foods, a dusting of floral fragrance and the damp ground of a morning rain. Dreams lingered in the breeze, waiting for her to catch them.

An Old-World air drifted through the streets, charming her senses with a gentle nudge of rightness. She'd always preferred old-fashioned. Vintage. A little yesteryear.

She perused a few bakeries and nearly screamed when she saw a fresh slab of meat hanging in a shop window. The experience only added to the sense of old-timey pouring over the town's atmosphere.

On she walked to the end of the main street, Causeway Lane, nearing the hill from which Riber Castle peered down, its dark stone walls setting it apart from the lighter shades of Matlock, until she came to a vast park framed by the street on one side and a river on the other. Rows of colorful flowers circled a central fountain then spread out to add cheer to the brick sidewalks leading to various attractions throughout the park. Tennis courts. A gazebo. A World War I memorial. Boating. Children's laughter rang from a nearby carousel and play area, so Julia's feet naturally turned in that direction.

Hall Leys Park. No wonder Henry spoke so highly of the place. It radiated welcome.

As she closed in on the children's area, she spotted a familiar figure sitting on a park bench near the swings. Was that Henry? Did he come to the park to enjoy a break from recording?

As she neared, the slightly fuller face and darker hair of the man revealed, not Henry, but Matthew, the eldest Wright brother. She'd met him briefly at the engagement party, and he'd seemed nice enough. A little unusual in his delivery, but nothing like Elliott. There was definitely more of Henry in Matthew's personality.

She stepped closer. He seemed oblivious to her approach, his attention focused on the newspaper he held.

She cleared her throat.

No response. But it had to be him. He and Henry had the same profile. And ears.

"Matthew?"

His dark head came up, and he blinked her into view. He didn't say anything. No greeting. No smile.

Maybe she had the wrong person. But, in her defense, he'd responded to the name. "I...I don't know if you remember me. I'm Julia."

"Julia? From the historical society?"

"Um...No."

His eyes narrowed. "Are you one of Elliott's girls? Because I don't give handouts no matter what he's told you—"

"No, I'm definitely *not* one of Elliott's girls." How many girls did Elliott have? "I'm with Henry. His girlfriend?"

Matthew's expression blanked then, almost like ice melting, his countenance cleared into a small smile. "Yes. Yes. The American."

"Yes. The American." She looked out over the park, searching for any little children that might look like Wrights. "Rose and I wanted to take a tour of Matlock while we were here. It's a lovely town."

"Is it?" He took in their surroundings as if only now aware of the laughter, chatter, landscape, and color encompassing them. "I suppose it has its charm, in its own way."

Silence grew between them until Matthew returned to his paper. What a unique guy. She watched him and almost grinned, patting Rose, who rested in the sling against her chest, so she could *do* something in the awkward stillness. She sat next to him on the bench. "You have two children, don't you?"

He looked up as if he were almost surprised to see her still around but didn't appear annoyed at her intrusion. "Yes."

"Are your children with you today?"

"Of course." He nodded. "I don't come to the park alone. There's really no use for it."

He returned to the paper, leaving Julia once more in silence so she surveyed the playground. A dark-haired girl, probably five or six years old, sat alone on a swing, barely moving. Her little lips pouted, and her gaze stayed riveted to the ground. What a lonely picture she presented. Someone needed to give her a push.

Matthew didn't seem to notice.

A few other children played nearby, but none resembled any of the Wrights. Then a little boy on the slide caught her attention. His dark hair shone in the same shade as Matthew's, but in a mass of curls that tangled in all directions. He seemed as oblivious to the people around him as his dad, waiting for children to take their turns on the slide, but never looking at them or attempting to communicate. Instead, he performed a routine of ladder, slide, one, two, three skips at the end, then starting all over again. The entire sequence looked almost...rehearsed in some strange way.

Odd. But Sophie would know what was different about him. Kids, learning, and communication were her life.

Her attention drifted back to the little girl on the swing. "Is that Mary?"

Matthew looked up again, almost startled, and then followed her gaze. "Yes."

She breathed out a sigh. This conversation was going to require some work. "Is she all right?"

He glanced at his daughter then peered over his glasses at Julia with pale eyes. "I suppose so. Why do you ask?"

"I just thought she looked sad."

"Does she?" He lowered his paper to his lap and turned back to study his daughter, his brow puckering like Henry's when focused. "How can you tell?"

"Well, she's all alone and not even swinging, really."

"I rather like being alone."

"I don't think she does."

He turned back to his daughter. "Really?"

"And is the little boy on the slide Connor?"

Matthew shifted his body a full ninety degrees on the bench so that their knees almost touched. "How did you guess?"

"They look like you."

"Do they?"

Could he really be so unaware? "Yes—their hair and eyes. I haven't seen them smile"—or you— "but I imagine they'd have even more similarities then."

He looked at her as if she were the biggest curiosity in the park. Had no one taken time to draw his attention to these simple things about his children? To help him connect with them?

She gestured toward his son. "Connor must really like the slide."

"Yes. Over and over again. I'm afraid he gets his pleasure in routine from his father." He grinned at his own little joke, and a sudden surge of compassion drew her closer to this little family within Henry's larger one. How much they needed someone to offer a little kindness and guidance.

Is this what Henry had meant about wanting things to be different for the family he chose—the one they'd hopefully create together? An example of something better for his mother and brothers to see? She sighed back against the bench, rubbing a palm down Rose's back. Julia had taken so much for granted.

Mary pressed her palm against her stomach, her frown growing. Julia checked the time. Eleven thirty.

"I wonder, Matthew, if Mary is hungry?"

His gaze swung from his newspaper to her again. "She's made no mention of it."

"When was breakfast?"

"Half past eight, as always. I'm quite a good cook."

She tempered her smile at his little boast. "And they've not had a snack since?"

"No, why?"

"Kids usually need to eat a little more often than adults." Someone needed to take him in hand and teach him...relationship skills. "Because they're growing."

"And here I thought I'd made improvements by at least getting them out of the house, as my nanny suggested. I suppose I'm meant to bring food along, too?"

Julia reached into the diaper bag, in the area with a freezer pack, and pulled out two string cheese sticks she kept on hand for herself, handing them over to him. He groaned. "I do wish Mrs. Langston had written these sorts of things down more carefully."

"Mrs. Langston?"

"The nanny."

"Oh." Julia caught Mary's attention and gestured for her to come closer. The little girl gave a wary look around then left the swing. "Is this her day off?"

"Day off? Good heavens, no. She's having surgery and won't be with us for five days." His shoulders bent beneath the weight of the declaration. "This is the first time I've had the children on my own. I'd hoped Mrs. Langston would recognize that fact and leave explicit instructions."

Very explicit. "What a great opportunity to have time to play with them."

He looked at her as if she'd gone crazy. "Play with them? Do you mean like Henry does? All down on the floor and growling?"

Oh, she could almost envision Henry giving his time to Matthew's children, especially after she'd watched him play with Eisley's three.

Mary came to her father's knee, her dark hair in unruly curls and her socks mismatched. Matthew gave her the cheese sticks almost absently. The faintest hint of a smile upturned the pout, and her dark eyes sparkled up at her dad with pure adoration. Too bad Matthew didn't seem to notice before she ran back toward the swings.

"There are lots of ways to play with them besides rough-housing. Simple board games? Or perhaps painting or drawing or playing music. I bet you could look up ideas online and try a few."

"What an idea!" Instead of returning to his paper, he stared out at his children, almost as if seeing them in a new light. A little encouragement, just a little, could go such a long way in this family.

Julia glanced down at the clock on her phone and gathered up her things, turning back to Matthew. "Would you happen to know where Henry's studio in Matlock is? I thought Rose and I could visit him before lunch."

"Visionary, isn't it? On Bakewell Street."

"Yes.

"I've never been." Quiet came again as Matthew stared over at his children while Mary opened the cheese packet for her brother, who'd stopped his routine long enough for a snack.

"Would you mind pointing me in the right direction?"

He spun back around. "Where?"

"To the recording studio. I'd like to see where Henry works."

"Why?"

Was he truly this unaware of how to build those connections with his own brother? "Because I care about him, and I'd like to show how much I care by seeing what he does and where he works."

"And you think he'd like that?"

She laughed. "From what I know of Henry, yes. I do think he'd like it."

Matthew's brow puckered. "You don't suppose he'd feel it's intrusive?"

"No, because he knows I want to share his world the same way he wants to share mine. It's the way relationships work."

He studied her for the longest time, almost to the point of the silence growing uncomfortable, then he clapped his hands together. "Of course. Yes." He proceeded to give extremely detailed directions, including the color of one of the new street signs at the corner where Julia should turn left.

"Thank you, Matthew. I'm so glad we had the opportunity to meet again."

Matthew paused to study her again and nodded, a smile lighting his entire face so that he looked almost handsome. "Yes. Thank you for the parenting help. I can see why Henry needs you in his life. Only imagine how much more efficient he'll be."

Julia couldn't stop her laugh from erupting from its hold. Not exactly the compliment she'd expected, but from what she'd heard of Henry's mother, an unusual compliment from a member of the Wright family was better than none at all.

Chapter Thirty-Two

*H*enry's mother behaved herself quite well for the first part of dinner. He hadn't expected friendliness—and would have been disappointed if he had—but at least she remained civil, even though her patience waned as the evening progressed.

Why? He wasn't certain.

Julia presented as she always did—kind, generous, and drawing out conversation in an easy manner yet Henry noted the exact moment some internal switch flipped inside his mother despite his girlfriend's impeccable behavior. He'd placed himself as a barrier between his mother and Julia at the table, in the event things turned sour. Rose rested against his shoulder, her little head bobbing back and forth as she looked around. At some point, she turned toward his mother and offered one of her most adorable smiles—the sort that dimpled her chin.

The strained lines on his mother's face softened, and her usual lofty air relaxed into an expression so gentle that she looked ten years younger. Rose seemed to sense the shift and reached her chubby little fingers in the direction of his mother's outstretched hand. Just as quickly, pain seared his mother's features and she pulled her hand away as if she'd been burned then pushed away from her plate.

"Let's do away with these pleasantries, shall we? I know my son, and he's easily persuaded by needy women. What is it that you really want, Miss Jenkins?"

Henry turned from his mother to Julia.

"I'm sorry. Excuse me?" Julia lowered her fork to the table, her gaze shifting from his mother to Henry.

"Mother, what is wrong with you?"

His mother placed her serviette on the table and narrowed her pale eyes at Julia, refusing to look in Henry's direction. "What is it that you really want? Money? Security?" She gestured toward Rose without turning the baby's way. "A father for your child."

"I can assure you, Mrs. Wright, that I am financially independent. And though I know Henry would make a remarkable father for Rose, that's not why I love him."

"Love him." She released a humorless laugh. "You barely know one another. What do either of you know of love?" She waved away Julia's words. "No, what is the real reason? Because I can assure you, if you pursue this fling with him into matrimony, he'll receive none of his inheritance from this estate."

"Mother, that's enough." Henry stood. "Julia, I think our dinner has come to an end."

"I don't care about that sort of thing." Julia rose, but placed her palms on the table, facing his mother with fire in her eyes.

"Please, don't minimize my intelligence by playacting such naivete. Look at this house! This property. Don't expect me to believe you have no design on affixing yourself to him to gain a part of this."

"There may have been other girls in his life who refused to see the man he really is but I'm not one of them. You can keep your money and your house. I'm on ly interested in the man, so I'm not—"

"And what of his reputation? Do you care nothing for it?"

"I have no idea—"

"He's nearly ruined this family twice from want of propriety. An American single mother who has *never* been married will do nothing for our family's good name. You'll only succeed in adding to—"

"We're finished here." Henry took Julia's arm and guided her toward the door. "We're leaving."

"If you truly care about him and his family, you'll return to your country and leave him alone to maintain some sort of dignity."

Henry placed Rose in Julia's arms before facing his mother full on. "If this"—he gestured toward her— "is a picture of my inheritance and the cost of my reputation's salvation then I don't want it. Any of it. When you're ready to apologize to Julia and accept her presence in my life, I will be happy to speak with you. But until then, we have nothing more to discuss."

Henry placed his hand on Julia's lower back and escorted her from the dining room and toward the front of the house, indicating to the butler to have the car brought around.

"Has she been like that your whole life?" Julia's breathless question slowed his pace.

"She became worse after father died." He tucked his arm around her waist but kept his eyes forward, refusing to allow his frustration at his mother to surface more than it already had. "I'm so sorry you bore the brunt of her anger. I'd hoped for better. We'll keep our distance from her in the future."

267

"But she's your mother, Henry. You can't stop seeing your *mother*."

He paused at the front of the hou*se*, waiting for the car. His family's three-story brick colonial, two centuries old, rose behind them. His past. *Not* his future. "We have nothing to discuss if she plans to behave in such an unforgivable way."

"I...I can't understand this. I mean, to make such blatant accusations? Unfounded charges?"

"You understand better now why I've found myself at home with the Harrison family more than my own, and why I wish for a very different start to ours."

Julia looked over her shoulder. "But something...something felt so wrong about what happened back there, Henry. I could almost *feel* your mother's pain. She's so...so broken."

The car came into view from the garage. "There were many things wrong with it."

"She...she looked so hurt, at one point. Lonely, even. She lashed out like some wounded, desperate animal."

Air left Henry's lungs and he turned Julia toward him, hands on her shoulders. "You're looking for ways to understand her when her behavior was inexcusable and accusatory?"

"People always have reasons for acting the way they do. Something in her is wounded and lost."

He took her face in his hands and kissed her. "I love you."

She looked up at him, her expression pleading, sorrowful. "I never want to be the reason you don't see your mother."

He shook his head, running his fingers through her hair. "Give her time. She won't stay angry for long. *I'm* the son she calls when she needs something." He squeezed Julia's free hand. "She's a difficult woman but if anyone can touch her heart, it's you."

"But what if...your inheritance...and her—"

He placed a finger to her lips. "I choose you. There's no question. Her inheritance threat means nothing to me. I'm self-sufficient and have been for years, though she's failed to take note. She needs to feel powerful and in control, so she uses money as a threat. It works with Elliott, but not me." His lips relaxed into a smile. "No, Julia, I choose you and Rose as my family. If Mother wants to come along, then so be it, but she'll not dictate my heart."

The car stopped in front of them and he guided her down the stairs to the passenger side. "Now, we certainly need something to take our minds off this evening. What about a surprise?"

"A surprise?" Julia looked up from fastening Rose into the car seat.

Henry drew in a deep breath. He'd never done anything as spontaneous as buying a house for a woman he'd only known a few months, but nothing had ever felt so right. *And* he'd never met anyone like Julia before. "Tomorrow is our last full day together for a while, so I'd like to end well." He paused and opened the car door for her, drawing in a breath and sending a quick prayer heavenward. "What if I collect you for lunch tomorrow after church, then take you to see *my* home."

Julia straightened and turned, staring at him. "Your...your home?" She gestured toward Wright Hall. "But I thought you lived here."

He couldn't stop his grin. "Not anymore." And after this evening, he was even happier to speak those words. "New job, new future." He touched her cheek. "New home. I have no intention of going back to where I was before you. Only forward. With you."

∞ ∞ ∞

Julia, for once, couldn't blame her sleeplessness on Rose. She couldn't get Henry's family from her mind, especially his mother. Yes, she'd said hurtful things, but something about her manner broke Julia's heart, like a drowning victim fighting against the person trying to save them.

After all the activities of the past week, Julia's emotions frayed at the seams. She almost fell asleep during the church service, but not because it was uninteresting. In fact, the quaint congregation, with its mixed worship service and ready smiles, welcomed her and Rose with the warmth of genuine faith. Some of the hymns sounded a little different than the ones she'd grown up singing, but she knew the praise songs, and from her vantage point in the pew, she could see Henry playing his violin with the small orchestra.

Matthew sat in the far corner, his expression pensive, but Julia didn't see either of the other Wright family members. She closed her eyes and prayed for Henry's family. For the wounds so evident in their brokenness. For the loneliness. And for God to bring people into their lives to inspire healing of those shattered relationships.

When Henry sat next to her before the sermon began and relaxed his arm over the back of the pew behind her, claiming his spot for his whole church to see, another surge of belonging settled over her with the warmth of the cresting sun in Grieg's *Morning Mood.*

Though he kept his focus on the preacher, that boyish grin slid into place and she knew—he felt it too. The rightness. Their little family.

After surviving the swarm of well-wishers wanting to meet Henry's girlfriend following the service, then sharing a quiet lunch at a pub in town, Henry drove them a short distance away from Matlock. Riber Castle still stood sentry in the distance when the car turned off the main road and proceeded up a knoll where two stone pillars welcomed them into a tree-lined lane.

They continued up the lane until a roof came into view above the trees and...she saw it. Julia peered out the passenger window, tilting her neck to see a sharp-pitched roof rising above the trees.

This was Henry's house?

She'd expected some small stone cottage or a little white house.

But this? A three-story structure of limestone and windows and a double-doored entry?

Yet despite its size, the surrounding trees and the ivy climbing the walls gave it a cottage-feel. "This...this is your home?"

He nodded and pulled the car to a stop at the front doors. "Do you like it?"

She exited the car with slow steps, her gaze trailing every inch of the house as if Henry had pulled it straight from one of her daydreams. So many windows! She shuffled forward and then turned to glance behind her for Henry, and her breath caught at the view. Green hills rolled into the distance until they met a smattering of rooftops that marked the edge of Matlock with the distant hills beyond.

She stared at Henry across the top of the car, pulling her bottom lip up and into a smile. "It's amazing."

His eyes lit, and he pinched his grin into place as if he could barely contain his joy. "Let's take a look inside, shall we?"

She nodded, fairly giddy, and took Rose from the back seat. "It's so big, Henry."

"It is. Much more than a bachelor needs, so perhaps I should change that status." He wiggled a brow and led her to the ornate oak front doors.

Julia immediately envisioned Christmas wreathes on display. She grinned over at him and took his hand as he led her through the front doors into an airy room filled with sunlight. Stairs rose in front of them and a smaller room opened to the right. A library?

"And I haven't the furniture to fill it, so the front room may seem a little bare. That's where I could use advice, you understand."

They stepped into the large, front space. Everything about the room welcomed her forward, from the hardwood floors to the chair-rail molding to the stone fireplace with floor-to-ceiling windows on either side that nearly filled an entire wall. All it needed was a touch up or two of paint. Some cozy chairs. A rug here. A wall-hanging there. The room opened through double French doors into another sizeable space with a brick fireplace. The same floor-to-ceiling-windows occupied two walls in this room, facing more to the east.

Her breath stalled. A breakfast room. She could almost see the tables dotting the shiny floor, each decorated with fresh flowers and ready to invite someone to share a cup of tea. Henry continued the tour from one room to the next. A sitting room. The large library with built-in floor-to-ceiling bookshelves just waiting for their volumes.

On they went, each new discovery almost like a glimpse into a magical land of dreams and wishes. Downstairs boasted two large bedrooms with en-suite bathrooms and doors that led out into a walled garden. Upstairs were four more large bedrooms with the same welcoming windows, and Henry hinted at two more rooms on the top-most level of the house, along with some storage space. Julia's imagination burst with possibilities.

It was as if someone had reached inside her heart and tugged out all the little dreams she'd envisioned for her own bed and breakfast. The thought latched and held. Her footsteps faltered as she followed Henry to the back of the downstairs into an enormous kitchen.

"And I knew you'd like this spot. All newly renovated."

She placed her hand on the doorframe and took in the white cabinets and stainless-steel appliances. And industrial-sized refrigerator. Double ovens. Massive stovetop. Sunlight drew her attention to the right where a door opened into a glassed-in walkway.

"That leads to a detached apartment. Where I keep house, at the moment. It's perfect for privacy from the main house. Three bedrooms, a small office, and a cozy living area." He gestured toward the walkway.

She looked over at him and pieced everything together. He'd bought this house...for her. He planned for *her* to join him in England. Her fingers tightened on the doorframe and her stomach roiled. "Henry, I...I can't move to England."

He stared at her, suspended in a smile, and his expression slowly melted.

"I love your house. It's beautiful and perfect in so many ways." Her throat closed with emotion. "And...if I gave you the impression that I wanted to move here..." She waved around her then searched his face, begging him to understand. "England is lovely, and you are..." She couldn't get the words out and pressed her palm to her chest. "I want to be with you, please know that, but I...I have my family and my home."

Though home—as well as her plans and future—was sort of in limbo.

His eyes searched hers, unreadable—which frightened her, because she'd grown to know him so well.

"I...I'm sorry, Henry. I'm just not ready for something like that."

He looked down and closed his eyes, leaning back against the wall. "It's my fault." He shook his head. "I made assumptions and allowed my hopes to run wild. It was clumsy of me. With the new job and the opportunities I have here, I thought...I...we—"

"You have great opportunities here, and I'm so excited for you. It's your dream job and this house—" She gave the kitchen another appreciative glance. "It's exactly what I would wish for if I could choose."

"I moved too quickly. Too thoughtlessly."

"Please." She stepped forward, touching his arm and bringing his gaze back to hers. "I made assumptions too, you know? I thought for sure you'd come back to Pleasant Gap with me."

His expression bowed beneath his disappointment and nearly broke her heart when he placed his palm over Rose's head at her shoulder. "Visionary will consider a distant position, but not for at least two years."

"Two years?"

"Perhaps even three."

She closed her eyes, her heart at war. A gnawing clawed against this conversation, against the certain distance they'd experience for much longer than three months. She pressed a palm to her stomach. "Do you think we're reading this all wrong? Have we been moving too fast if these red flags are showing up now?"

"Do you truly doubt us?"

"I don't want to."

"Then don't." He sighed, his brow pinched. "Sometimes circumstances happen because the world is a broken place or...because God is shaping us, as clay, and we must move and be reshaped with his guidance. Not every problem is an indicator of wrong choice, Julia."

"But two years? Maybe three? What will we do with that?"

He opened his mouth to answer but nothing emerged. An agonizing second passed, then, as if he'd set his mind on his answer, he touched her cheek. "We wait. It's not going to be easy, especially when I feel as though a part of me is absent when we're separated, but I would rather have your heart, even at a distance, than not have your heart all."

She'd wounded him. The creases of pain were etched at the edges of his eyes and the downturned corners of his mouth. And still, her chest battled with some unnamed collision of choices, of desires.

"Do you think you can wait with me?"

She searched his face, her emotions and her heart grasping for another answer. Three years? But when she looked at him, she couldn't imagine being with anyone else. How could any future man match the gentleness and love of Henry Wright? The words clogged her throat, snagging her breath. She couldn't give him what he truly wanted, could she? Leave everything? Enter the world of Matlock and his mother's hostility? Move away from her family?

Yet, Henry would be here. Waiting. Loving. Tears blurred his face from view. "Of course I'll wait with you."

"Then, dove, we'll wait."

∞ ∞ ∞

Julia pressed her face into her hands and stared out the window of the Harrison's home into a moonless night. She should be nestled in that ginormous bed to prepare for a long day of flying, but questions wrestled within her, stealing sleep, twisting up her stomach in a nauseous tangle. She leaned her head against the window sill, tugging a pillow from the window seat and pressing it into her chest.

Why this way, Lord?

A deep quiet answered her, bringing more unrest than calm. She was going home. That was the right choice.

Then why did leaving this way feel so wrong? She squeezed the pillow close. The alternative flittered through her thoughts like an escaped bird. What if she moved to England?

She shook her head and pressed her face into the pillow. No, that couldn't be the answer. *There is no fear in love. Perfect love casts out fear.* The verse breathed through her, but instead of calming the worries, it ignited her defenses.

No, Lord. That request is too big. Too hard. I...I can't.

"I was up and saw your light."

Julia turned toward the whisper in the doorway. Cate peeked in.

"Is everything all right?"

Julia sighed and swiped her fingers beneath her eyes to remove any residual tears. "Henry bought me a house."

Cate stumbled forward, her long dark hair loose from its usual ponytail. "He did what?"

"I know. And it's perfect, except for one thing." She ran a hand through her hair and leaned her head back against the window frame again. "It's just outside of Matlock."

Cate lowered to sit on the edge of the bed, her palm in the air. "Wait, I'm still stuck on the idea that Henry bought you a house." She blinked. "Henry Wright?"

"The very one."

Cate started chuckling then caught her laugh in her hand. "I have to say that feels a bit out of character for him. Were you in need of a house?"

"Actually, yes, but I hadn't planned on it being thousands of miles away from Pleasant Gap. A place for a bed-and-breakfast one day."

"Oh, those do really well here. And Matlock is a lovely tourist town."

"So I've heard." But Cate's enthusiasm wasn't helping the knot in Julia's stomach.

"But that's Henry for you, isn't it? When he cares, he cares big. All in. Extravagant, some would say." Cate chuckled again. "Almost reckless, if you think about it. Poor man. He must really like you. Buying a house without consulting you."

"I hurt him, you know? I mean, he just expected me to move to England."

"And that's not what you want?"

"I want to be with Henry, but moving to England?" Julia pulled her knees up, wrapping her arms around them. Why did everyone assume she'd *want* this. "It's too radical. Too much." She waved toward the crib. "I have Rose to think about."

"Babies are incredibly adaptable, you know. Much more than adults."

"You're not helping, Cate."

"I can't deny that I'd enjoy having you nearby, Julia. I'm surrounded by Wes and his friends on every side. Having a woman in the mix would even up the conversations a bit."

"I'll video-chat with you."

Cate shook her head. "Not the same." Her brow rose in challenge. "Is it?"

No, not at all. Spending the past week with Henry doubled the distance going home brought. "This isn't home."

"Ah." Cate rocked back, hands on the knees of her red pajama pants. "I've always heard that home is where the heart is. So I suppose the question you must ask is, where is your heart?"

Julia scowled at her new friend. "I think you need to go back to bed."

Cate caught her laugh again and stood, slipping toward the door. "What are you so afraid of?"

"Good night, Cate," Julia reiterated, shooting a mock-glare in her direction.

"Good night, Julia."

The door snipped closed and Julia returned her attention to the star-studded view out the window. *Dear Lord, please help Henry find a way to move to America.* Her heart pulsed against the prayer. What about his wonderful job? The part he played in taking care of his mother? His house? Her throat tightened, and tears burned her eyes, but the prayer she should pray refused a voice. What was she so afraid of?

She didn't have an answer.

Chapter Thirty-Three

"Dr. Porter is available to see you now, Ms. Jenkins."

"Ms. Jenkins."

Julia sat up in the chair, coming full-awake, and gave her head a little shake to orient herself. National Archives. London. And an archivist with a tendency toward tardiness, evidently. An hour tardy, as a matter of fact.

Well, at least she'd gotten in a little nap before the flight home.

The receptionist raised a brow, her face otherwise expressionless. "Dr. Porter is available to see you now."

Julia stood, placing a protective palm on Rose's back in the wrap at Julia's chest. "Thank you."

She followed the receptionist down a hallway with offices on either side and stopped in front of one of the last offices on the left.

A small man with Einstein-like white hair stood with a flourish from behind a paper-covered desk. "Ah, Ms. Jenkins. Do forgive my tardiness, if you will." He gestured toward a chair. "I arrived from my research in Cairo yesterday afternoon to a great many unfinished things and am still behind. I appreciate your patience."

He had kind eyes, and Rose had been exceptionally well behaved, so Julia immediately forgave him.

"I'm sorry, Dr. Porter, I don't have a lot time. My flight back home leaves a little before three, and I want to make sure I have plenty of time to get through the airport, especially with a little one." She patted the sling that held Rose.

Dr. Porter's bushy eyebrows shook with his widening eyes. "Oh yes. Of course." He paused, seemingly lost in his stare at a sleeping Rose, then blinked back to the present. "Yes. Well, you've brought sufficient documentation to prove you have legal right to receive any information we have related to Amelia Rippey?"

"Yes." Julia reached into her bag and withdrew the folder she'd prepared. "All the documentation you requested should be inside."

He flipped through the papers, leaning close and holding the corner of his glasses to carefully examine them. Each one. Rose stirred slightly, and Julia prayed her little girl stayed content a little longer.

"Good. Good." He nodded, placing the pages back in the folder. "Everything seems to be in order." His eyes lit with his smile. "Finally, we can settle accounts for the famous Amelia Rippey."

"Famous? You mean Aunt Millie as a pianist?"

"Aunt Millie? There is no Aunt Millie here." He raised a finger and turned in his chair to retrieve a cardboard box from a shelf behind him, his eyes almost glowing. "Only Amelia Rippey, aka Evelyn, the Night Bird."

"Excuse me?"

"Your aunt is known among military historians and archivists because of her excellent skills and ingenuity. She was a smart woman. The historians before me even spoke of her—behind closed doors, you understand." He nodded. "Do you know her story?"

Julia couldn't help but smile at the man—a much-needed smile after the events of the day before. "I only know a little."

He rocked back in his chair, his grin growing. "Ah, well, it's my job to know, isn't it?" He chuckled. "I researched her before I left for Cairo in preparation for your arrival and am delighted to bring her story to light for you." He patted the box. "Your aunt fell into the spy world quite unexpectedly, especially since America hadn't yet joined the war."

Her gaze dropped to the box in his hands. Were there more letters in the box? Photos of Aunt Millie as Evelyn, the Night Bird?

"Lucas Randolph had been in espionage for only a few months when British Intelligence paired him with her on the stage, as a cover. You see, music traveled more freely where little else could." He tapped the box again. "Amelia was not too keen to become involved at first, reticent for change and all that, but after learning of the atrocities of the war, she realized the benefit—the long-term goal—was worth the risk. She became a force to be reckoned with. I'd even venture an estimation that she became a better spy than her husband." Dr. Porter leaned across the desk, his eyes taking on an intense glimmer. "In fact, had it not been for your aunt, Ms. Jenkins, the musical code wouldn't have been created. She was the mastermind behind it."

"Aunt Millie created the secret code?" Julia's smile unfurled with an extra dose of pride. *Her* Aunt Millie. Musician, mother, recluse...spy.

"Indeed. Once she put her heart into the effort, her energies and expertise became invaluable." He raised a brow with his grin. "Though, I do believe Randolph had a bit to do with her decision. She'd have given up anything for their safety." He gazed off into the distance. "And she did, didn't she?"

"Do you mean to protect Rosalyn?"

"The baby? Yes." He adjusted his wire-rimmed glasses. "When she discovered she was expecting their first child at the same time as Randolph was uncovered as a spy, they decided Amelia should disappear."

Julia relaxed back into the chair with a sigh. She and Henry had guessed right. "And where better to go than the obscure and unknown world of Appalachia?"

"Exactly. Who would look for her in a place so remote, it's almost mythical?" He rolled his chair nearer. "Which brings me to the reason we were never able to contact your aunt before her death regarding the discovery of her husband."

Julia's breath caught, and comprehension dawned. "Appalachia." She whispered, sitting back to attention. "Even *you* didn't know where she'd disappeared to?"

"As I said, she was a highly skilled spy and, after Randolph's disappearance, the safety of their child became top priority. You see, at the time, there were many who would have used whatever means necessary to find Lucas." One of his shaggy brows rose. "Anything, you understand. He knew valuable information regarding the war effort, so when his body wasn't recovered, both sides assumed he was in hiding, and the only way to winkle him out of hiding—"

"Was to use his family."

"Precisely."

Which explains why Aunt Millie protected her story for so long.

"Your aunt kept her contact in London, but Mrs. Sterling was the only person who knew where Amelia was, so when Mrs. Sterling passed—an excellent spy in her own right—we had no way of notifying Amelia when we finally located Randolph's remains."

Julia soaked in the news, leaning closer, waiting for the ending of this seventy-year-old story. "You found...him?"

Dr. Porter's expression softened. "Only ten years ago, among a tangle of forest and overgrowth in France, but yes. It is always an honor to finally discover one of our missing fallen."

She didn't understand why, but tears welled in her eyes. How could she grieve for a man she'd never known? Or maybe it was a mixture of joy and sorrow. The fact that her aunt and Lucas had lost each other for so long and now...now *someone* who cared knew the end of their story.

Julia's gaze dropped to the box. "Did you find anything with him?"

"Yes. As you can imagine, many of his belongings were ruined from time and the elements, but a few things remained intact." He offered the box to Julia. "Somehow, because of their location inside the downed plane or by an act of God."

Despite a warning grunt from Rose, Julia slid the box's lid back for a peek. She managed to glimpse a pair of gloves, a broken watch, and something that looked like a ring before Rose began a full-on cry.

"I see you need to care for your little one instead of investigating at present, but when you have time, I think you'll find the letter most rewarding."

Julia's attention shot to his. A letter. From Lucas!

As if reading her mind, he continued. "It's the letter most of our men have on them to give their next of kin should the worst occur. I find them the most potent because they realize the value of last words and lost time."

Julia held his gaze, the gravity of this gift sinking deep. Rose's cry grew louder, so Julia placed the lid back on the box and stood. "Thank you, Dr. Porter."

"It was a pleasure to meet you, Ms. Jenkins. I'm happy these have finally found their home."

$$\infty \quad \infty \quad \infty$$

Henry attempted to make headway through the crowd, but a blockade of people hampered every step. Julia had texted him that she was running behind because of her visit to the National Archives, but he was determined to see her off, one way or another.

He'd stayed awake through the night, berating himself on his impulsive decision to purchase a house when Julia had no intention of joining him in England. Yes, his heart had been in the right place, but clearly, good intentions weren't good enough to fix this problem. How had he been such a fool?

He caught sight of her at the security line, searching the crowds on tiptoe, and his body flooded with relief. He hadn't missed her.

Her beautiful gaze lit when she found him, her smile drawing him forward like the opening strains of a favorite sonata.

"I'm sorry I almost missed you," he breathed out once he'd reached her.

"I was late getting here anyway." She glanced up at the departure screen. "I'm afraid we don't have a lot of time."

"We'll make the time."

Her gaze shot to his, questions darkening those sapphire hues.

Had he ruined it all? He touched her shoulder, drawing her gaze back to his, memorizing this moment and the senses surrounding it. They'd work through the distance, he was sure of it. Why, then, did he feel like he was going to lose her?

"Forgive me, once again."

"Henry." She closed in, shaking her head, watching his face. "It was the sweetest of gestures."

"I hate that we're parting on such a strained note." His fingers, of their own accord, slipped a strand of her golden hair between them.

"Me too. I feel so torn." Her attention, those piercing eyes, found his again, almost pleading. "Your place is here right now. I'm sure of that. With this job and your family." She sighed, her gaze faltering. "Mine...mine isn't. How do we fix this?"

He tugged her close and placed a kiss to Rose's head. "My place is here." He cupped her cheek. "Right here. With you, wherever that may be."

Tears filled her eyes, but she pressed them closed, hiding her thoughts from him. She was wrestling with something, but he didn't know how to help her. What was going on inside her heart? *Don't close me out, dove.*

"Julia," he whispered.

She leaned her forehead against his, saying nothing. Holding the moment in a suspension he couldn't push into motion. What was she thinking? What did she need from him?

"I have to go." The declaration seemed to rip from her, broken. "I'm sorry, Henry." She rocked on tiptoe and placed a kiss to his lips, gaze holding his. "We'll find a way, right?"

The fear in her voice shook him, and for the first time, he felt as if she were slipping to a place he couldn't reach. "Of course we will."

She stepped back into the line with Rose's little face peeking out from the sling. He watched them until they made it to the far side of security and turned to find him across the rows of people. A sea of noise and motion and words unsaid separated them, and he almost jumped the barrier to wrap her in his arms and reassure her.

With a little wave and a sad smile, she was gone.

Julia stared out the plane window, brushing back tears and grappling for a steady heart, but nothing took the ache away. How could her heart keep telling her to leave everything she'd known for a whole new world of unknown? Emotions weren't trustworthy. No. She had to be sensible. And moving didn't make any sense at all. Even after finishing school in December, she'd have plenty of reasons to stay near Pleasant Gap.

Why, then, did her stomach tangle through a nausea storm of "what ifs"? *No, Lord. I'm not brave enough. I'm not strong enough to listen to my heart.*

Rose stared up at her almost as if answering Julia's unvoiced fear. *But God is.*

She smiled down at her sweet little girl, who immediately rewarded her with a toothless grin. Rose deserved a chance to enjoy the wonderful family Julia had known, right? A crazy decision like moving to England for the love of a lifetime would alter Rose's future forever.

I hold the future.

Julia closed her eyes against the reminder, the ache in her chest swelling into a painful knot. But if she let go...then what?

"Henry loves you, you know that?" She touched Rose's little nose, and her daughter's smile bloomed again. "He loves really well, doesn't he? Enough to...make up for a whole family of love? Enough to upend our lives and risk everything?"

Her question shuddered out on a whisper. The white box sat beside her on an empty seat, beckoning her to abate her curiosity—or at the very least distract her thoughts. She raised the lid and skimmed her fingers over the brown leather gloves, worn and weary from use and misuse. The cracked glass face of the pocket watch revealed a foggy view of hours stuck in time. Eleven twenty-two. Had that been Lucas's last moment? Last breath?

Her fingers smoothed over the glass face, then touched a golden chain stuck among some papers. She swallowed the growing emotions and tugged the chain loose to find it had been threaded through a wedding band. A sound like a whimper escaped her. How long had it been since anyone touched this? Saw this precious symbol of a short-lived marriage and a long-loved romance? An inscription on the inside of the ring caught in the overhead lamplight. *Today and forever. Yours.*

Rose cooed, grasping for the chain, and Julia pushed away a tear. "Everybody wants a love like that, don't they, little one?"

A photo peeked from beneath the gloves. Julia slid it into view and almost started crying again. It was the same photo she'd found in Millie's box of the three of them—Lucas, Millie, and their daughter. Lucas held a smiling Rosalyn in one arm, the other secured around his wife in a comfortable and intimate hold. Lucas and Rosalyn both looked toward the camera, but not Millie. Her attention focused solely on the pair beside her, showcasing a smile more brilliant than Julia ever remembered seeing on her aunt's face.

Julia slipped her finger over the words on the wedding band as she surveyed the photo, her breath shaking out another sigh. They'd had such little time together but shared a remarkable love.

Julia pulled another photo from the box—a portrait of Millie, laughing. Julia could almost imagine Lucas staring at his bride, missing her, praying for her, rekindling the memory of her laugh to go along with the photo.

She swallowed another round of tears as she drew an envelope from the bottom of the box. Frayed, a little soiled, but surprisingly intact, just as Dr. Porter had said, the beautiful penmanship on the front held one name. *Amelia.*

Julia's fingers paused, taking in the bittersweet moment like an intruder. Rose gave another contented coo for encouragement, playing with the musical duck Henry had bought her.

With a deep breath, Julia slipped open the sticky envelope and drew out a single page stained here and there with dampness and yellowed from time.

My darling,

If you are reading my letter, I have left this world behind for a different one, and my only regret is not having the opportunity to hold you again or to kiss the sweet cheek of our beautiful Rosalyn. We knew when we chose this path, or rather when it chose us, that sacrifices would be made, but none has been more grievous to me than distance. I have loved you from across oceans and through countless nights as I've never loved anyone.

Our hearts have always been entwined in such a divine way that when I close my eyes, I can almost hear your breath near me and feel your warmth against me. I close my eyes often to breech the miles, to dream of you.

I have loved you a lifetime in these years.

You are the strongest, most courageous person I've ever known, and you will be strong now—even now—my love. God knows the years you have yet to grace this world, but until we meet again, live, my darling. Live with risk and hope and courage enough for two, for I will be with you through this unbreakable love and the smile of our little girl. You have made my life worth every sacrifice, and I would do it all again to have benefited from basking in the affections of such a woman.

Know my last thoughts were of you and our little girl. Know my heart's final beat drummed with love for you. Know the last word on my lips was your name.

I am sorry you must bear the dark days of grief, yet time is but a flicker in eternity and then we will be together again, my love. My only love.

Finally, there will be no distance. Only joy.

Today and forever yours,

Lucas

Julia's fingers tightened around the paper. An ache squeezed between her ribs. Did Henry feel like this about the distance? Did he hurt like this? She pressed a palm against her mouth to catch her sob, but it sneaked out anyway.

"Are you okay, ma'am?"

Julia looked up into the face of a middle-aged flight attendant.

"Y-ye-yes..." The word jumped out of her like sob. She wiped her face, reaching for the side of the sweater she wore in lieu of tissues.

The flight attendant came to the rescue with an entire box.

"Thank y-you." Julia sniffled and pulled out four, dabbing eyes that refused to stop leaking.

"Is there something I can do for you, ma'am? To give you some relief?"

Julia wiped at her face again, another ugly sob wracking her shoulders and shaking Rose into a grin. Poor thing. She didn't know her mama was ugly crying in the middle of a plane. Julia raised her face to the woman. "Could you make a life-altering decision for me so I don't have to?"

The flight attendant offered a sad smile. "I'm sorry, sweetheart. Life-altering decisions are above my pay-grade. But in my experience, most people know the answer already...they just don't like it."

Chapter Thirty-Four

"You can't be serious." Andrew stood on one side of Henry, Wes on the other, neither currently helpful. "You've wanted this job for years. I had it specifically designed for your skill-set, Henry."

Henry paused folding another shirt to place in his suitcase, the weight of the decision slowing his actions. Drew had worked so hard. Henry pushed through the disappointment and guilt by reaching for another shirt. "I do appreciate your going to battle for me on this, Drew, and I'll work until you find a replacement, but I...I have to leave."

"You just purchased a house. What of that?"

"I'll list it when I get back from the States. With the updates I've made, I'm certain someone will want it."

"Perhaps you should take a little time. She only left yesterday," Wes offered. "This is your dream job, a once-in-a-lifetime opportunity you've worked for years to accomplish. Surely she understands that."

"I watched my father work his dream job for twenty-five years"—Henry placed another shirt into his suitcase more quickly now, more certain— "and live in a loveless marriage filled with animosity and coldness. I saw how his job became less of a joy and more of an escape. What if home can become my joy *and* escape? I could perform any job with that sort of home."

"I'd prefer both, if I had the choice." Andrew picked up one of the trinkets on Henry's shelf and studied it. "That is, *if* I ever marry, but the two of you aren't making it appealing. Moving about the world, giving up perfectly good jobs, buying a house one day and selling it the next? No, not appealing at all."

"You're not your father." Wes placed his palm on Henry's shoulder. "You're stronger than he was, and Julia most certainly is not your mother."

Henry nodded. "I'm strong enough to realize that if my heart is where it needs to be, any job I find will suffice."

"You don't think Julia will come around, do you?" Wes nudged a hope Henry kindled but couldn't hang onto.

"I'm not sure. But what I do know is, whether she does or not, I want to be with her. She and Rose are worth this sacrifice. Last night, as I prayed and begged for understanding, I realized that I don't want a day to go by where Rose doesn't know I'm there for her. I don't want two or three years to pass and the only way she remembers me is as a face on a screen. I don't want Julia becoming so acquainted with doing things without me that she doesn't hope I'll show up to help. I want to be with them, and that has to be enough for me."

"You're up to your knees in it, aren't you?" Andrew grimaced in a strange expression of half curiosity and half disgust. "I'm not certain whether to think you're mad or the most honorable bloke I've ever known."

"Or a little of both," Wes added.

"Certainly not." Henry shot his friend a weak smile and added another shirt to his bag.

"I know what it's like to make this choice, Henry. You know I do." Wes's words softened, garnering Henry's attention. "But what sort of job will you find in Pleasant Gap? Have you thought about this practically? Considered options?"

"I'll find a way. Teach music. Give lessons. Learn to bake."

"Learn to bake?" Andrew looked positively horrified. "Is that what love makes you do? Bake?"

Henry lips tipped at the memory of Julia in the kitchen at midnight, baking to relax enough to sleep. Learning to bake didn't sound bad at all.

"If you do learn to bake, Henry, would you practice a chocolate trifle for me?" Andrew relaxed his shoulder against Henry's dresser. "That alone may be worth your move to the States."

He almost grinned. "I'll only be gone a few days, so I can secure things with Julia then begin planning, but I'll see you right. I won't leave Visionary until you have a replacement."

"I don't doubt your word, Henry. Your clarity of mind, perhaps, but not your word."

"Are you certain about this?"

Henry pressed his suitcase closed and met Wes's gaze, relinquishing one dream to hold to another. "I am."

Wes drew in a deep breath. "All right then, I'll see you off."

∞ ∞ ∞

"So, Henry's mother wasn't welcoming."

"At all." Julia moved around her mother's kitchen, sorting through ingredients for chocolate chip cookies. Oh, how she needed to bake—to stir flour and sugar, knead dough and roll cookies—to help her process the crazy going on inside her chest. "But there was this one moment when she looked at Rose that I felt her anger held more...grief than anything else. Almost loneliness. It made me wonder if she'd ever had a daughter-figure in her life, you know?"

"Didn't Matthew have a wife?" Mama sat on a bar stool in her kitchen finishing up the whipped topping for her famous strawberry pie.

"Yes, but it seems that Marianne's passiveness made her less of an active presence in Mrs. Wright's life."

"And Matthew needs some motherly guidance, it seems?"

"Oh dear, yes. Poor guy." Julia poured the dry ingredients into a large mixing bowl. "I don't think anyone's given him practical ways to be involved in his kids' lives. And it's not because he doesn't want to be. It just seems like he doesn't get it."

"And Henry's job? The one at...at...?"

"Visionary Studios. It's perfect for him. You should have seen him in the studio, Mom." Julia paused her hand against the refrigerator door. He'd been amazing directing the small orchestra. Energized. Creative. "He breathed the music and communicated what he wanted to the orchestra in a way that took the sound to a whole new level."

"And he bought you a house?"

Julia paused on her way back to the counter, eggs and butter in hand. "Why do I feel like you're trying to lead me somewhere?"

Mama gestured toward the barstools in the center of the kitchen then took two plates from the cabinet and placed a slice of fresh strawberry pie on each one. Oh, she was even softening the blow with food. This was going to be bad.

"You're not here to make a decision, honey. You already know the right one."

Julia placed the ingredients on the counter and slid onto the barstool. "What...what do you mean?"

"Why do you think you've struggled so much with coming back? Why all the grief and unrest inside?"

"Because I had to leave Henry, of course, and for a long time."

Mama handed her a fork, brow raised like an accusing finger. "No, because you were running from the *right* decision into the *safe* decision."

"Mama, I—"

"Take a bite of that pie and listen a minute." Mama gestured toward the pie with her fork, the slightest grin upturning one corner of her mouth. "It's good pie to go along with my good advice."

Julia sent her a mock glare as she shoveled in a forkful. *Mmm, would she ever be able to replicate this recipe?*

"You're a smart woman and I *know* you've seen God's hand guiding you in a very clear direction. Don't let fear steal the biggest dream of your heart. God has given you the opportunity to start over. To be with a man who loves you. To live the adventure of true love that so few have the opportunity to live. To start your own bed-and-breakfast."

The strawberries congealed in her mouth. "But it's so far away from you. From all of you."

"There is nothing here you love that you'll lose by going to England, but there are things in England you'll lose by staying here. Precious, God-given things, Julia. Open your eyes and see the possibilities." Her mama added a dollop of whipped cream on top of Julia's pie.

"His family doesn't even like me."

"Oh hush." Mama's fork raised to attention again. "From all you've said, I think they *need* you."

"Need me?"

"What if God raised you up in this close, loving family so you'd have the courage, strength, and patience to take the love you know to another place, to show a better way?"

"I can do that?"

"It sounds like you already have." Mama tilted her head, studying Julia with those familiar pale-blue eyes. "Do you love him?"

Julia's gaze never wavered. "I do, Mama. He's one of the best men I've ever known."

"And do you think he loves you?"

"I know he does. He shows it in every way." Her lips softened into a smile. "In the most beautiful ways."

Mama placed down her fork and leaned forward, eyes brimming. "Your granny used to say, 'Those with the greatest potential to fly need the biggest shove from the nest.' God has something amazing planned for you, Rose, and Henry. You may not be moving to England tomorrow, but today starts the plans for tomorrow. You already know the right choice."

Julia's eyes warmed with tears. "It sounds like you want me to leave."

"Girl, I love you more than anything in this world. This family God's given you...like it or not, we're your family forever. Our love goes wherever you do, no matter how far." She cupped Julia's cheek. "But what kind of mama would I be if I didn't strengthen your wings when I knew you were meant to fly?"

Julia sniffled and stared down at her partially eaten strawberry pie. Her heart pulsed in time with her mama's challenge. Yes, she knew the right choice. And the idea twisted every emotion into a battle between fear and faith. A weighing of two different futures. Two different loves.

Suddenly she stood on the precipice, as if her entire past had been a dream and now she had to choose whether to leap out into the unknown or remain in the dream. Every Sunday school lesson, every sermon on faith swirled to life in her head, nudging her closer to the edge, to trust in the God who loved her enough to hold her future in His hands.

Did she truly believe what she'd prayed her whole life? Did she trust that *all* things worked together for her good and God's glory? That the past wounds and wins, filtered through a loving Father's hands, led her here?

She drew in a deep breath and released her fears. There was no mistake. This was the right choice. And yet... Was the right choice supposed to be so terrifying?

"I...I don't know if I'm brave enough."

"You're not." Mama's smile turned as sweet as mountain honey. "You never will be. But the God who's written the story of your life is brave enough for you, so you don't have to carry the courage all by yourself. His love casts out the fear, so you can walk in the adventure He's called you to walk."

She stared at her mother sitting in the same kitchen Julia had grown up loving, eating her famous strawberry pie like she'd done hundreds of times...With a deep breath, her heart skirted to the edge of all she'd known and leapt. The tears came in a hurry, but there was also...peace. An overwhelming and beautiful peace. She'd released the fight to the One who held her future. *I'll go, Lord. Give me your courage.*

Her mama smiled, almost as if she could see inside Julia to the choice she'd made. "Don't let that pie go to waste, now. It's one of my best batches."

"Every batch is your best, Mama." Julia sniffled and pressed the fork in for another taste. Julia looked up at her, gaze burning. "You'll have to call me a lot."

"Of course I will." Mama sat back and picked up her fork. "We can even use that Face-talk thing."

Julia laughed and wiped at her eyes. "You mean Facetime?"

"Right." Her mama took a bite of the pie. "Whatever it's called. And just maybe, I'll finally get your daddy to take me on a big trip somewhere. I've always wanted to see England."

As if he'd heard his name called, her daddy barreled through the door, fresh from a job site if the sawdust, sweat, and dirt gave any indication. He scanned the counter and his grin spread. "Strawberry pie sounds like just the thing for this hardworking man." His attention lifted to the two women, then froze, his gaze locked on Julia's face, his smile taking a downward turn. "What happened?" He rushed forward, his brow darkening into a thundercloud. "Where is he?" He scanned the room. "I'm gonna kill him."

Julia stood from the stool and walked over to her dirty, stinky dad. "Henry hasn't done anything wrong. In fact, he's been absolutely wonderful."

He shifted his attention between them again. "Did somebody die?"

"No, honey," Mama answered, shaking her head. "We've just been celebrating Julia's big decision."

"Have we?" He pushed a hand through his hair, gaze narrowed. "I have a feeling I ain't gonna like it."

Julia stood taller and, for the first time in two days, her smile brimmed free and certain. "I've decided that I'm moving to England after I finish school in December."

His eyes widened, and he looked back at her mother for interpretation. "England?"

"Yes. To be with Henry."

His brow puckered. "But that's plumb across the world."

"I know, Daddy." Julia sighed. "But it's where I'm supposed to be. With Henry."

"What'd I tell you?" He raised a finger to his wife, eyes narrowed. "I said these fancy boys would steal my girls away, and that's exactly what they've done. Good for nothin', music-lovin', pretty talkin'—"

Julia wrapped her arms around her dad's shoulders and pressed a kiss to his cheek, stopping his tirade. "I love you, Daddy."

"I don't like this at all, and I ain't afraid to say so." His grumble lost some of its fight.

"No matter where I am, I love you." She gave him another peck and backed toward the door. "And now I need to go. I've gotta call Henry. He needs to know, and I left my phone back at the apartment."

"Leave Rosie here, since she's napping, and come on back after you've talked to your fella." Mama waved her back toward the stool. "But wait, would you take this extra strawberry pie to Amy on your way." Mama stepped to the refrigerator. "I baked it for the party she's having tonight."

"Of course." Julia breathed deeply of the peace. She even giggled. "Oh my goodness, I feel so much better."

"Why is it then that I feel worse?" Dad grumbled, but not without the hint of a smile...and maybe a glistening eye or two.

She grabbed him in another hug, pressing her face close to his ear. "I'll teach Rose how to play American football. I promise."

His thick arms wrapped around her. "That's my girl."

She clung to his deep love, shown even in his little protective diatribe. "Thanks for raising me to be strong enough to dream big, and brave enough to trust God with those dreams."

He grunted something unintelligible, then stepped back, wiping at his eyes and keeping his head down. "Well, now. I'd better go wash this dirt off." He cleared his throat and gestured toward the plates. "But I expect some celebration pie when I get back, you hear? After all, I'm the one who taught Twinkle Toes how to use a hammer."

"We hear you loud and clear, honey." Mama grinned at Julia as Daddy disappeared down the hallway. "You might not need Facetime to hear your daddy talkin' from across the ocean, Julia. We'll just have him open a window and yell for you."

Julia's smile slipped into a much-needed laugh.

"I heard that!" Daddy called.

∞ ∞ ∞

Julia pulled up in front of the bakery to dash in with the pie and grab her phone before heading back to her parents' house. Her vintage floral belted dress swayed around her in the warm June air, the scent of rain chasing away some of the afternoon heat and promising a damp evening. She loved the smell of rain. Balancing the pie in one hand, she closed the car door with a hip bump, then hunted for her apartment key as she approached the bakery entrance.

She'd thought about her conversation with her mother on the fifteen-minute drive to town, and all the signposts God had used to point her in the direction of England and Henry suddenly blazed clear. Selling the bakery had freed her from that responsibility. Her aunt's inheritance gave her financial independence. A final semester of school? The house Henry bought? His job? The way she'd interacted with Matthew and his kids, even Henry's mother? When seen through the lens of the right decision, God's fingerprints appeared *everywhere*.

Oh, she couldn't wait to tell Henry. She reached for the bakery door. He was going to be so—

"Allow me to assist you."

Her forward momentum came to a grinding halt.

She knew that voice...and nearly dropped the pie on the sidewalk as she spun around to find the source. Henry walked down the sidewalk toward her, his hair rumpled and waving in different directions, just as she liked best. A few tousles of the wind only improved the view.

His approach, his gaze, held her in suspension. No smile, only a look of riveting intensity, refusing to let go of her.

"You...you're here?"

"Yes." He reached for the pie, his gaze searching hers, asking questions she actually knew the answers to now. "I...I had to see you. We need to talk."

"I was getting ready to call you."

He sent her a look over his shoulder as he placed the pie down on one of the café-style tables outside the bakery. "Were you?"

She failed to subdue her smile. "Like you said, we need to talk."

. He stepped back to her, clearing his throat. "I've...I've quit my job."

The newfound smile slipped right off her face. "What?"

"I don't want to wait three years to start a life with you." He took one of her hands in his. "Distance? Time? I have a choice about whether those things separate us, and I won't let them." Tears glistened in his eyes, cementing her decision even more. "I'll work at Visionary until they find a replacement, but my plan is to be here no later than October."

Henry Wright was *definitely* worth the leap. "No, Henry. I can't let you do that."

He ran a hand through his hair, upsetting it even more "I must. You and Rose, well, you're my family, you see?"

"Your family?" she whispered, braiding one hand through his, bringing him closer.

"Or that's what I'd like us to be." His words trailed into a whisper, gaze searching hers. "I feel this...lostness without you near, Julia, and we don't have to live that way."

She stepped within the frame of his arms and relinquished her past. "You're not the one who's been lost. *I* am." Her admittance loosened the rest of her confession, bringing freedom with it. "Too lost and afraid to leap into the unknown. From the moment I stepped into your world, I knew down deep I was supposed to be there with you, but that...that truth seemed too scary, too...big for me."

His brow crinkled with adorable confusion. "What...what are you saying?"

She swallowed through the mixture of emotions gathering in her throat. "We're your family." Her palm came to rest against his chest, over his heart as new tears stung her eyes. Oh, how she loved this man. "And families need to dream together on the same continent, don't you think?"

He tilted his head, still uncertain.

"Besides, you said it yourself. Your gorgeous house is much too big for a bachelor, so you probably need a family and a budding bed-and-breakfast owner to fill it, right?"

His jaw unhinged and those beautiful eyes of his widened as comprehension woke in his expression. "You...Rose...England?"

"If...if the offer's still available, that is." Her teeth skimmed over her bottom lip to contain her smile. What do you give the man you love? His dream. "We wouldn't be able to move until after I graduate, but, if—"

Air, carrying a strange cross between a sob and a laugh, burst out of him. He cradled her face in his hands and pulled her against him, his lips finding hers without hesitation. She laughed against his lips, her hands slipping around his waist to tug him close, basking in the ability to offer him some tiny piece of the joy he'd given her.

"Are you certain?" His raw voice raked the question out on a whisper. "You'll...you'll marry me?" He blinked and stumbled through a nervous laugh. "I...I mean, will you marry me?"

She gave a one-shoulder shrug. "That's how *I've* always envisioned a family."

Another sob-laugh burst out of him, and he tugged her back against him, caressing away any remaining doubts with a sweet lip-on-lip celebration. Her palms spread up his back, his taste, his touch the only ones she wanted to remember for the rest of her life.

His lips spread into a smile against hers, which then turned into a chuckle. He shook his head and stared at her, searching her face as if he didn't quite believe she'd said what she had. "You're going to move to England? Marry me?" He rested his forehead against hers. "I...I don't have words."

"When words are not enough..." She raised a brow. "Music?"

He grinned that pressed smile she loved so much, the one holding laughter behind his eyes. "There is no instrument in the world to do justice to the music in my heart, dove." He brushed a hand through her hair, the look in his eyes stamped on her memory forever. "I'll take care of you and Rose with my whole heart. As long as you'll keep me."

"Oh, I'm definitely keeping you." She framed his face with her hands and settled her lips rather wonderfully against his in a lingering fermata-moment. His arms encapsulated her, a gentle circle of protection, love, and friendship—a promise for their future. This was home. "Today and forever. Yours."

Acknowledgements

What a journey! Without a doubt, this has been one of the most difficult books I've ever written, so maybe that's why I love it all the more. There's a sweetness and joy to Henry and Julia's story that I hope encourages people to see the bigness of God's love and the truth that His dreams for us are always more amazing than ours could ever be for ourselves.

As always, I am not a lone ranger in the development of this story. There's an entire village of people from encouragers to editors who helped bring Henry and Julia's story to the printed page.

First and foremost, I'd like to thank editors Marisa Deshaies and Katie Donovan for your amazing work on this story and your love for me. Your patience and kindness mean so much—and it's just a bonus that you guys fell in love with Henry and Julia too. Katie, I'm so thankful your musical wisdom is boundless.

Rachel McMillan, thank you for being the first person who fell in love with Henry and championed his heroism. He is extremely thankful for your faith in him, as am I.

Not only do you create beautiful books, Roseanna White, but you designed a cover that fit this story perfectly. Thank you so much.

To my AMAZING street team who pray for, celebrate, and brainstorm these stories to life. I am grateful that each one of you choose to spend some of your time in my little world and make my imaginary friends your own.

To my parents, who have always dreamed big for me—I hope I've captured on these pages a small portion of the love you've shown me.

Thank you, Dwight, Ben, Aaron, Lydia, Samuel, and Phoebe for filling my life with music and love. Words fail to express how thankful I am to have each of you in my life. Thank you for loving your wife/mom enough to encourage her to follow her dreams.

And to the Maker of music and Creator of dreams—thank you, God, for the gift of story—and the miracle of forgiveness. Your love gives us wings so we can dream *your* dreams for our lives.

A Note from the Author

So many times, we think of 'bravery' as only being reserved for those who do great feats or sacrifices, but sometimes what appears 'small' may require a great deal of courage. Outside of writing, I work in a profession with children who have special needs, and I see bravery happen every day—in them and in their parents.

Courage happens all around us—from the single mom who chooses to dream for her kids even though the cash-flow isn't great, to the unemployed husband who is going in for another job interview.

Living life in a broken world is *hard*.

But thankfully, we are not left alone in our brokenness. God, in His mercy, is *with us* in our struggles, and through His strength we can be brave.

Julia and Henry both show courage in different ways throughout the book—some big ways and some small. Love helps make them braver.

If God has called us into the deep waters of life in some way, He is faithful to hold us, strengthen us, and give us all we need to complete the calling He's placed on our hearts. He has a strong love—the strongest of all.

Thank you for reading Henry and Julia's story. May the Lord strengthen your heart to answer the calling He has on your life.

So do not fear, for I am with you; do not be dismayed, for I am your God. I will strengthen you and help you; I will uphold you with my righteous right hand.

          –   Isaiah 41:10

ALSO BY PEPPER D BASHAM

Historical Romance
The Penned in Time Series
The Thorn Bearer
The Thorn Keeper
The Thorn Healer

Historical Romance Novella
Façade

Contemporary Romance
The Mitchell's Crossroads Series
A Twist of Faith
Charming the Troublemaker
A Pleasant Gap Romance
Just the Way You Are

Contemporary Romance Novella
Second Impressions
Jane by the Book

About the Author

Pepper Basham is an award-winning author who writes romance peppered with grace and humor with a southern Appalachian flair. Her books have garnered recognition in the Grace Awards, Inspys, and the ACFW Carol Awards, with *The Thorn Healer* selected as a 2018 finalist in the RT awards. Both her contemporary and historical romance novels consistently receive high ratings from Romantic Times, with *Just the Way You Are* as a Top Pick. Most recently she's introduced readers to Bath, UK through her novellas, Second Impressions and Jane by the Book, and taken readers into the exciting world of WW2 espionage in her novella, *Façade.* The second novel in The Pleasant Gap series, *When You Look at Me,* arrives in October and her contribution to Barbour's wonderful My Heart Belongs series hits the shelves in January 2019 with *My Heart Belongs in the Blue Ridge.* Her books are seasoned with her Appalachian heritage and love for family. She currently resides in the lovely mountains of Asheville, NC where she is the mom of five great kids, a speech-pathologist to about fifty more, and a lover of chocolate, jazz, hats, and Jesus.

You can get to know Pepper on her website, www.pepperdbasham.com, on Facebook, Instagram, or over at her group blog, The Writer's Alley.

Made in the USA
Columbia, SC
30 January 2024

31178189R00178